Report upon the Forest of the Punjab and the Western Himalaya

SALZWASSER VERLAG

Hugh F. C. Cleghom

Report upon the Forest of the Punjab and the Western Himalaya

Reprint of the original, first published in 1864.

1st Edition 2022 | ISBN: 978-3-75259-466-9

Verlag (Publisher): Salzwasser Verlag GmbH, Zeilweg 44, 60439 Frankfurt, Deutschland
Vertretungsberechtigt (Authorized to represent): E. Roepke, Zeilweg 44, 60439 Frankfurt, Deutschland
Druck (Print): Books on Demand GmbH, In de Tarpen 42, 22848 Norderstedt, Deutschland

REPORT

UPON THE

FORESTS OF THE PUNJAB

AND THE

WESTERN HIMALAYA.

ROORKEE

MDCCCLXIV.

PREFACE.

In November 1861, the writer of this Report was directed by the Governor General in Council to proceed from Madras to the Punjab, and after receiving instructions from His Honor the Lieut.-Governor, to examine the forests in the Western Himalaya, with a view to obtain reliable information regarding the timber resources of that Province, and to institute a systematic plan of Conservancy and Management.

The exploration of the forests on the different rivers, occupied the summer months of 1862 and 1863, while the winter months were devoted to the inspection of timber depots, brushwood tracts of the plains, and the preliminary arrangements necessary for the formation of a Department.

As respects the natural forests of the Terai, at the base of the Cis-Sutlej Himalaya, in Oudh, Rohilcund, and Dehra Doon, the Reports of Wallich, Royle, and other observers are most valuable; but the only published accounts* of the Trans-Sutlej forests are to be found in the occasional allusions of Thomson, Madden, Moorcroft, Edgeworth, and Jacquemont, which though very interesting, do not furnish any approximate data as to area of forest, kinds of timber available, or means of transport. It therefore became my duty to

* In the Journal of the Agricultural and Horticultural Society of India (1854), is an excellent account of the physical aspect of the Punjab, its agriculture and botany, by Dr. Jameson, Supdt. of the Botanical Garden, Saharunpore. This, however, does not relate to the intramontane forest tracts from which the supply of railway sleepers must be mainly expected.

explore the great rivers, and their tributaries in succession, from east to west, beginning with the Pabur, Tonse, and Giri, which flow into the Jumna, and proceeding west as far as the Khyber Pass.

In 1851, the Most Noble the Marquis of Dalhousie appointed Captain Longden, H.M. 10th Foot, to explore the forests of Bussahir and Chamba. This duty he performed with fidelity and judgment, and his report, though brief, was highly useful. He recommended the establishment of an Agency on the Chenab, and from the depot near Sealkot, the principal Public Works of the Punjab have been supplied with timber during the last twelve years. He also executed good forest charts of Mandi, Sukhet, and Kullu, which are procurable at the office of the Surveyor-General of India.

Since Major Longden's deputation, the forests of the Western Himalaya have been subjected to greatly increased demands in connection with the progress of Railway enterprise, and of advancing civilization. During my inspection, I found that the rudest system of converting and launching logs prevailed, and that the enhanced value of timber had led to an indiscriminate felling of the finest trees, threatening speedily to exhaust the deodar forests, and to deprive the State of those supplies which are essential to the construction of Public Works. The demand is certain to continue, while the sources of supply are limited, and the physical difficulties of transport from the Himalayan forests being very great, systematic and skilled management are imperatively called for.

In January of this year, Dr. J. L. Stewart was appointed Officiating Conservator of Forests, Punjab, and the timber operations upon four of the great rivers are now under the supervision of a forest officer, in accordance with the views expressed in this Report.

My object in the following pages has been, in accordance with my instructions, to describe the forests of the Western Himalaya, where the most valuable timber is found; to enumerate all economic plants* observed during my journeys; and to record the various district rules and tenures, affecting the introduction of Forest Conservancy; so as to present a connected statement of the condition of the wooded tracts of the Punjab and adjacent countries.

A sketch map is given, indicating approximately the position and extent of the deodar tracts, so far as ascertained. It will be observed how small is the area within British territory yielding this valuable timber, compared with the tracts of leased forest in Chamba, Bussahir, and Gurhwal. The course of the rivers, canals, and railways is shown on the map, and the chief wood depots at Rupar, Madhopur, Sealkote, Jelam, and Hushtnugur. The forests of Kashmir are not entered except two, circumstances having prevented me from exploring the main tributaries of the Jelam.

Lists of useful trees and shrubs found in the valleys of the different rivers, have been introduced with the vernacular names carefully ascertained, and their economic uses noted upon the spot; these will it is hoped prove useful.† In compiling the Sutlej and Kangra lists, much assistance was derived from Dr. Jameson's Catalogue of Plants in the Saharunpore Gardens, 1855. The Pushto Catalogue, page 222, had the advantage of revision by the Rev. I. Löwenthal, shortly before his death; and some facts connected with the vegetation of British Lahul, page 151, a district at the head waters of the Chenab, of which little is on record, are entered partly on the authority of the Rev. H. A. Jaeschke, of the Moravian Institution, at Kyelang. I collected seeds and plants largely—the former were distributed at once to various Public Gardens, and the latter will be submitted to the custodier of the Royal

* To aid me in correcting and enlarging these lists, which are of course imperfect, I earnestly request the assistance of all who may have an opportunity of obtaining such information, that I may render them as complete as possible.

† I may advert to the occurrence of the asafœtida plant in Pangi, and the localities given for *daphne* and *desmodium* (as yielding material for making paper in district jails).

Herbarium at Kew, where they can be most advantageously compared and identified. All available books and documents relating to the Kohistan of the Punjab have been consulted, and endeavour has been made to select from them every important fact bearing upon the history or condition of the forests. Works of reference are given under the heading of the different rivers, which are treated of in separate sections.

While this passes through the press, Dr. Brandis is preparing a valuation Survey Report on the Bussahir Forests, which contains exact information regarding their resources. The tract in the Sutlej valley producing deodar, lies between 77° 59′ and 78° 31′ East Longitude, and 31° 23½′ and 31° 40′ North Latitude.

The fuel supply of the plains, available to the railway, has been reported on at length by Dr. Stewart; this is at present chiefly drawn from extensive tracts of low and scattered tree-jungle, which form belts at a little distance from the rivers. One remaining source of supply, likely to become of great importance, has not been entered upon in detail, viz., the plantations on the Western Jumna, Baree Doab, and Inundation Canals. Dr. Stewart proposes to visit these in succession, and will report fully upon them.

In conclusion, I desire to express my acknowledgment of the cordial assistance and co-operation afforded to me by all the Civil Officers of the Punjab.

H. C.

Roorkee, *28th October*, 1864.

CONTENTS.

LIST OF MAPS AND ILLUSTRATIONS.

NOTES

ON THE

VEGETATION OF THE VALLEYS OF THE GIRI, PABUR, AND TONSE RIVERS.

UPON 31st March, 1862, I quitted Simla, accompanied by Captain Houchen, Superintendent of Hill Roads, our object being in accordance with instructions received from His Honor the Lieutenant Governor of the Punjab, to explore the valleys of the Giri, Pabur, and Tonse Rivers, tributaries of the Jumna. The route lay in the first instance by Fagû, and up the valley of the Giri to Kotkai, where there is a great consumption of wood and charcoal in connection with the iron smelting, for which that locality is famous. On our way, we passed in two days fifty mules, and nearly a hundred coolies laden with iron (a mule carries two and a half maunds, and a coolie twenty seers), proceeding *viâ* Simla to the plains.

Deodar (*cedrus deodara*) is scarce in this thanna, but there are eight small forests of chil *(pinus longifolia)*, and kail *(p. excelsa)*, on Government land, and also a clump of cypress *(cupressus torulosa)*, close to the ruined palace. The neighbourhood appears to have been Kotkai.

much more wooded formerly than it is at present; the increase of the iron manufacture supports this opinion, and the innumerable stumps of trees render it certain. The forest revenue is almost *nil*, while the destruction of wood is great, and the preparation of the charcoal in open pits is attended with much waste.

Iron smelting.

The iron is smelted in April and May, after the snow melts, and again in September, October, and November, after the rains cease. During June, July, and August, the manufacture is prevented by the falling of heavy rains. It seems superfluous to give an account of the process, which has been described by others. I may mention, however, that the rude implements employed are not unlike those figured by Col. Yule, in his "Note on the Iron of the Kasia Hills," in Jour. As. Soc. Beng. xi. 857. The aggregate amount exported from Kotkai and Shil, is said to be two thousand maunds per annum.

Charcoal making.

Pits are dug about six feet in diameter at the top, and three feet at the bottom; these are filled with fresh pine wood, heaped up to three feet above the level of the ground. Fire is applied when the first layer of wood is put in, and continues to burn while the rest is being added. A few spades' full of loose soil are thrown upon the top after the pile has been blazing for sometime; thus, a very large proportion of wood is consumed without being charred, and the charcoal produced is inferior. Efforts were made to instruct the people in this matter, but continued example would be necessary to amend the practice.

Woods used for Charcoal.

The wood chiefly used for charcoal is "kail," but the alder "kunch" *(alnus nepalensis)*, which fringes the tributary streams is also employed for this purpose. There are no hard woods available.

The zemindars are in the habit of trimming the young pine trees to an injurious extent, to provide litter for their cattle; often leaving nothing but the leading shoot with a tuft of leaves at the top. We strictly enjoined the people not to head-lop, or otherwise mutilate the trees. Excessive pruning.

In travelling from Fagû, and again in crossing the Shunkun-ridge to reach the valley of the Pabur, the course of the Giri was distinctly seen from its source, where the stream emerges from a wooded chasm; but, in looking along its banks, we could not see any large forest, or learn that deodar or other timber had ever been floated down. The Giri is the most western tributary of the Jumna, which it joins in the Dún, a little below the confluence of the Tonse. In the state of Sirmúr, there may be some sál timber available near the river, but probably little, the valley is barren, and the district officers do not know of any forest. Giri River.

The valley is low, warm, fertile, and dotted with scattered cottages; the mountain slopes are bare. The principal trees observed in addition to the pines mentioned, were *melia sempervirens*, *rhus acuminata*, *ficus*, *putranjiva roxburghii*, *populus ciliata*, *salix*, *alnus*, *pyrus*, *cerasus puddum*, *xanthoxylon hostile*, and *cotoneaster microphylla*, carpeting the rocks. Valley of Giri.

The crops are wheat, barley, several millets, til *(sesamum orientale)*, tobacco, opium poppy, and various pulses *(vicia* and *phaseolus)*. Agricultural produce.

We ascended the Giri, passing through a kail forest, and crossed the Shunkun ridge to Shil, elevation 7,500 feet, where iron smelting has long been practised. Here the tools used in making the Hindostan and Thibet road, were manufactured under Capt. D. Briggs' superintendence; and, in connection with this work, Iron smelting at Shil.

a deodar forest was purchased by Government in 1854. This contains many promising young trees, and should be occasionally inspected by the local authorities. Lord William Hay, late Superintendent of Hill States, frequently visited Kotkai and Shil, and attempted to initiate conservancy rules for the charcoal burning, levying a small rate according to the girth of the trees felled. Charcoal makers should cut only in such places as are assigned to them in Government forests, and a small payment should be required for the privilege, as is the custom under the native chiefs. All the existing wood will be required for the successful working of the iron mines.

Pabur River.

We descended to the level of the Pabur near Ruru, and traced it to some miles above Shergaon,* intending to cross the Changsil range to the Tonse, but the passes not being open, we returned, following the river down to the junction. The main stream emerging from the Burenda Pass, called by the natives "Bûren ghati," is narrow and rocky, presenting a series of small rapids above Shergaon, which renders the transport of timber impracticable. The declivity of the Pabur between its confluence with the Sipun and Shergaon is 254 feet per mile (Gerard i. p. 232). A few miles lower down floating operations would be extremely difficult. The river after receiving the waters of the Andriti, rising near Shatûl, the Pej, and the Mutriti streams, is more suitable for transporting timber; and, with assistance, logs could be sent down during the rains. A few bamboos or long bullies would be required for pushing off the timbers. There are no falls from Ruru to Raeenghur, but two miles below the fort, large boulders obstruct the bed of the river, and this unfavourable condition exists *passim*

* At Ruru it is about a mile; at Shergaon it is half a mile broad.

down to the junction with the Tonse. In several places, a considerable amount of blasting is required to allow the passage of timber, and from the precipitous banks and frequent landslips, it is likely that rocks would occasionally fill up the bed of the stream. The distance from Raeenghur to the confluence, is about twenty-six miles; the average fall of the river is about sixty feet per mile.

Valley of Pabur.

The valley of the Pabur from Raeenghur to Shergaon is wider and more verdant than any other I have seen in the Himalayas, but it is not abundantly wooded. The forests are few, and are chiefly situated on the Changsil range, 2,500 to 3,000 feet above the river bed (left bank). Between Ruru and Shergaon, an extensive forest is seen, occupying two crests behind the ruined fort of Batowli, and three or four miles from the river; it consists chiefly of kail and rai, (*abies Smithiana*) with small clumps of deodar and oak. The kelu (deodar) trees appear to be few and ought to be preserved. On the Pej stream, a considerable forest of moderate sized deodars is seen, three or four miles from the river, which is here difficult for floating. Higher up, towards the Burenda pass* there is a little deodar, but it cannot be made available. In 1861, Mr E. L. Brandreth, Acting Commissioner, Umballa Division, marched down the whole way from the source of the Pabur, through Choara to Raeenghur, and saw no deodar. At a lower part of its course, there is a fine forest of chil, extending more or less for several miles above its junction with the Tonse, where the river is encumbered with boulders.

Timber and fruit trees.

Elms and horse chestnuts, walnuts and mulberries, occur near villages. Many of the trees are mutilated from the tender branches and young shoots being

* *Vide*—Capt. Alexander Gerard and John Gerard's Journey to the Boorenda Pass, vol. i. 1840, also "Jacquemont voyage dans l'Inde." tom. 2 p. 481.

periodically cut off, to be stored as winter fodder for cattle. The dried twigs are lodged in the fork of the denuded trees, and secured with grass ropes; whence, when pasture is scarce, a bundle is taken as required. *Rhus acuminata,* "kakkar," is frequent on the river bank below Raeenghur, many trees were seen which would yield planks 6 to 8 feet long by 2 to 2½ feet broad. Apricots, peaches, and plums abound in this beautiful glen. The Himalayan alder *(alnus nepalensis)*, is a very large and straight tree, fringing the river banks above the junction of the Tonse. In addition to these, *berberis lycium, prinsepia utilis,* (bekul), and *eleagnus conferta* (gehai), are economic plants, useful in various ways.

Agricultural produce.

Broad river terraces from four hundred yards to a quarter of a mile in width are devoted to rice cultivation, for which this valley is celebrated, and through these the traveller's path lies. In spring, the opium poppy is largely cultivated, but in small patches; at the date of our visit, the plants were several inches above ground; the capsules are small, the lancet for making the incision resembles that used in the plains. Tobacco, sesamum, and vetches, including *ervum hirsutum,* "mussur," are grown in small quantity. In warm situations, barley is sown in March; wheat and several millets are likewise extensively cultivated. There was great abundance of wild mustard (*sinapis*) used for the purpose of obtaining oil. The poppy and tobacco ground is frequently weeded, and is kept clean. Previous to its being ploughed by the men, cattle manure is carried out in kiltas by the women.

Above Shergaon, towards the Burenda pass, the food of the people consists chiefly of buckwheat phapur) *fagopyrum esculentum;* the red amaranth (bhatu), and the smaller millets (chini and koda), *panicum miliacum* and *paspalum scrobiculatum* with mandua, *eleusine coracana.*

The Tonse (tumasa or dark), so called in the map from its being skirted in the upper part with gloomy forests, is larger than the Pabur (*i. e.* clear) river. They unite at Tuni, and fall into the Jumna in the Dún, a little above the confluence of the Giri. I ascended the river for two stages above the junction, and followed its course downwards for twenty miles below the Tuni bridge. Five miles above Onowli, the limit of my observations, the river is from fifty to sixty feet in breadth, and is scarcely fordable, even at this the lowest season. I searched for an easy ford among the broad reaches of the river, but without success. The water was four feet deep, and the current strong; the temperature at 4 p.m. was 42°. The bed of the river is stony, but the boulders are not large, and the absence of sand and soil in the channel is remarkable —the strength of the current washes all down, and leaves the boulders clean. In July, August, and September, the river is in flood, and of such a volume as to float timber of moderate length. At several angles, about two hundred logs in the aggregate, of last year's cutting, were seen stranded, some of them ten feet above the present water mark.

Touse River.

Above junction with Pabur.

The banks further up the river towards Kedarkanta, are densely wooded; that mountain is distinctly seen from Onowli, at no great distance, towering to a great height (12,680 feet). Above the junction of the parent streams Rupin and Supin, the river is unfit for floating purposes.

Below junction with Pabur.

The elevation of the rope bridge *(jhula)* at Tuni is nearly 3,000 feet above the sea. The river bed below the *jhula* is stony and tortuous, but there are no very large boulders, and comparatively few logs appear to have been stranded out of five thousand, which by report were sent down last flood. I followed the Massouri road down to Bandrowli, where the Tonse turns south-west, and receives the Shallu and Suinj streams, considerable feeders, rising in the valleys of the Chôr mountain. It did not appear necessary to proceed further, as the deodar forests do not extend lower, the whole flora is characteristic of the outer Himalaya, and the enlarged river is more suitable for transport.

Valley of Tonse. Above the junction of the Pabur near the villages of Mandrat and Onowli, the valley is of considerable breadth; the path runs along the left bank, from which the mountainous ascent is more gentle than on the right bank. The higher slopes 2,500 to 3,000 feet above the river bed, are everywhere crowned with forests of pine (kail, rai, and deodar). In the hot valley for some miles above the *jhula*, there is a forest of tall straight chil, (called "sulli" in Garhwal), which lies convenient for transport on the lower slopes of the hills.

Timber trees. The deodar is seen feathering the highest ridges, but not within two koss of the river until reaching Naintwar, the junction of the Rupin and Supin, here it grows near the stream, and trees have been lately felled, but the logs were much injured by being hurled over precipices.

There is a large quantity of deodar near Bastil, within a radius of six miles from the jhula, but it is not easily accessible to the river. The possibility of fetching it has been proved, as twelve very fine logs, averaging fifty-five feet in length, were brought down to renew the sangla under the orders of Lord William Hay. The expense of transport, however, was very great, and the river, by reason of its sinuosities, does not admit of floating timber of large size. If the trees were divided into sleeper lengths or short logs (say 18 feet as a *maximum*), they would float more safely, and be carried down at less cost and risk.

SISSOO *(dalbergia sissoo)*, is in considerable quantity, and skirts the river bank below the junction; however, it is generally small and crooked. By diligent search, a considerable number of trees yielding sleeper dimensions may be found. It serves well for this purpose (see Madras Exhib. Reports), and also for the manufacture of railway carriages. Hard woods.

TOON (*cedrela toona*), and KAKKAR (*rhus acuminata*). These valuable trees are found sparingly on the river bank below the rope bridge; the best have been removed.

OLIVE (*olea ferruginea*). This tree distinguished by its leaves, which are rust coloured below, is found abundantly on the bare rocks about Tuni. It is much valued in the district, and is often naturally conserved by the inaccessible position of the trees. The unbranched trunk is rarely more than ten to fifteen feet high. The wood is seldom sound throughout; it is prized for making the "tangili" used by the men who prepare the rope bridges.

Apricot and walnut trees are in great abundance; the price of the fresh walnuts is one rupee per thousand, and of apricot oil one rupee for six seers, but it is not made in large quantity. *Ficus macrophylla* "tirmul," yields an edible fruit. Mulberries are planted in the lower valley, and here the gigantic *bombax* and *rottlera* show the sub-tropical character of the vegetation, the rainfall being moderate. Fruits.

The agricultural produce consists of rice, barley, poppy, and tobacco, with the usual millets, and in one Agricultural produce.

damp spot *coix lachryma* (Job's tears), was found. In one or two places a grassy plateau was seen affording good pasturage.

Conclusions.

The affluents of the Jumna are considered to be more rapid in their course than those of the Western Himalayan rivers, and consequently they afford less facility for timber transport than the tributaries of the Chenab, the Jhelum, or the Indus. It is certain that rafts are impracticable on any of the three rivers noticed above. However, I believe, that under good management, single logs cut to sleeper lengths may be taken down the Tonse from Garhwal. The experiment of working the forests of this province was tried many years ago by Major Young, Superintendent, Dehra Dún; the timber is said to have been much damaged, but the scantling being required for architectural purposes, was too long for transport in a river bed interrupted with rocks. Lately, private enterprize has occupied the field; two European contractors have been at work on the Tonse, and are said to have launched several thousand logs last year, with what success is not known to me.

Deodar wood exists in large quantity in Garhwal, and a variety of other useful timbers, oak, elm, chil, kail, etc. The mountain slopes are very steep, and the river Tonse flows impetuously through a rocky chasm, but during flood it contains sufficient water to carry heavy timber. The rush of the torrent would probably erase any ordinary marks, and confusion would ensue if many were to engage in the trade. Wood-cutters are procurable in the valley of Tonse for five rupees per mensem, and mates for eight. The conservancy of these forests rests with the authorities in Garhwal and Dehra Dún, and in each of these districts a forest officer is located.

The Pabur and Giri rivers flow through the principalities of Bussahir and Sirmur respectively, the supply of deodar is scanty in the upper valleys and the volume of water is too small for floating logs. In the lower part of their course, chil and other woods in small quantity and in short lengths are procurable.

OBSERVATIONS

ON THE

SUPPLY OF FIREWOOD AT HILL STATIONS.

During a late visit to Simla, and the adjoining military sanitaria, the great consumption of fuel engaged my attention, and having had an opportunity of discussing the question with Lord William Hay, Deputy Commissioner, and several of the old residents; I beg to offer a few remarks on the supply of firewood at the hill stations.

Simla Station.

European,	280
Native,	700
	980

It is difficult to calculate the requirements of the Simla community. There are at present 980 houses, and I suppose not fewer than 1,800 fires burning daily at an average throughout the year. Thus the consumption is not less than 900 maunds *per diem*.

The following calculation was made at Lord William

MEMO OF WOOD USED AT SIMLA.

Firewood for Europeans, ...	Mds. 2,01,600
Charcoal for do. mds. 12,600, representing in wood, ...	18,900
Firewood for servants of Europeans, . .	13,240
Firewood for Native Residents, . . .	87,200
Charcoal for do. do., mds. 4,400 representing in wood, ...	6,600
Maunds,	3,27,540

= 900 maunds *per diem*. The tehseeldar estimates that each European house burns daily 2 maunds wood and 6 seers charcoal.

Hay's quarters, in the presence of the tehseeldar and vakeels of the Hill Chiefs.

In the Military Stations, Kussowlie, Dugshai, Sabathu, and Jotogh, the amount and value of the fuel (wood and charcoal), supplied during 1860-61, was, according to the returns of the commissariat officer, maunds 67,669 = Rs. 18,045. Military Sanataria.

	Mds.	Rs.
Kussowlie, ...	18,623	4,966
Dugshai, ...	29,372	7,833
Subathu, . . .	16,163	4,310
Jotogh, ...	3,511	936
	67,669	18,045

This is exclusive of the consumption in the houses of officers, the bakery, brewery, etc., and what the Engineer Department requires.

The amount of fuel used in the Lawrence Asylum, Sonawar, during 1861, was, Lawrence Asylum.

Wood, 8,769 maunds,
Charcoal, 697 do.

The Reverend Principal, an accurate observer, considered this amount equal in the aggregate to six hundred trees of 40 years' growth, and adds (which is important), in regard to the use of stoves: "The economy of fuel by using *close* stoves is one-third, but open stoves save nothing. The economy is effected by regulating the draft by means of a revolving perforated valve in front." The cost is stated to be about twenty rupees, the stove being made by a native artificer at the Asylum. The same stove will suffice for warming contiguous rooms, or an upper story, without any additional expenditure for fuel.

The consumption of wood in the winter months at Sonawar, is nearly double that of the summer months. This is not the case at Simla, which is compara- Season.

tively deserted in winter, nor at the military stations, where a detachment only remains during the cold weather.

Building material.

In addition, much timber is required for building and other purposes. On the road between Simla and Mahasu, the principal forest from which house building materials and charcoal are derived, I passed in three hours, within six miles of Simla,

41 woodmen carrying kelú posts and planks,
18 charcoal burners laden,
6 lime burners laden.

This may be considered an indication of the large requirements of the community.

To meet so great a demand, conservancy is extremely difficult. The main supply of wood is drawn from the forests of the Hill Chiefs, which encircle the sanitarium. A very small portion is obtained from thinnings within the station of Simla, which are sold by auction under the orders of the municipal committee.

Woods used for fuel.

The trees furnishing the supply of fuel at Simla, are chiefly

Quercus incana,	Ban.
Rhododendron arboreum,	Bras or Boorans.
Andromeda ovalifolia,	Ayar.
Pinus excelsa,	Kail.
Cedrus deodara,	Kelú.

with other jungle trees and stout underwood. At Kussowlee and Sonawar, the contractors supply principally "*chir*" (*pinus longifolia*), which grows wild on the adjoining hill sides, and splits easily.

The only forbidden wood is "behul" (*grewia oppositifolia*), which emits an offensive smell in burning. The villagers use as fuel the withered stems of *euphorbia pentagona* and thorny bushes.

The ordinary cost of firewood is three annas per man's load, of say 60lbs. The present contract rate at all the military stations is 300lbs. per rupee. Charcoal usually sells at one rupee per maund, of eighty pounds, the best for kitchen use is obtained from ban (*quercus incana*). The price of fuel does not appear to have increased much during the last ten years, it is, however, brought from greater distances. The cost of house-building timber is *much* increased. Price of wood and charcoal.

There has not been much extension of private planting and from the indifferent success of a few amateurs, the wants of the community are not likely to be supplied from this source to any great extent. The late Rev. Mr. Parker planted and carefully tended about 8,000 trees not more than 400 of which are now thriving on the Sonawar Hill, of these chesnuts and walnuts in shady spots grow best. The late Conductor Mines also planted 20,000 trees near Kotgur of which a small proportion only now remain. The nature of the soil, and the drought for nine months of the year, appear to be great hindrances to successful planting on these hills; pine trees, "*chir*" especially, do not grow well in artificial plantations, there are some shady spots in valleys at an elevation of 4,000 to 5,000 feet, with a northern exposure, and favorably situated as to moisture, where small plantations might be formed of such trees as the willow, mulberry, chesnut, and walnut; but I concur with the opinions recorded by Mr. Edwards, and Mr. Barnes with regard to Simla, and Mr. Batten as to Kumaon, that conservancy is much preferable to planting. Planting.

Plantations of the indigenous pines would not answer. At present, we have no record of the growth of Himalayan conifers, but we know that they in- Slow growth of pines.

crease very slowly.* Mr. Batten states "it is diffi-"cult in a garden, with every means of watering at "hand, to show a good sized *chir* tree after ten years "of care," and the Rev. Mr. Parker furnishes the following approximate rate of growth for this tree, *pinus longifolia.* He writes "I think that trees of "the diameter named below have the ages assigned "to them or nearly so.

Old wood	6	inches	diameter,	20	years.
,,	9	,,	,,	30	,,
,,	12	,,	,,	45	,,
,,	15	,,	,,	55	,,
,,	18	,,	,,	70	,,

I believe that wild *chir* trees grow much better on a hill side, (with a north aspect,) scantily covered with soil, than in any garden, and they make more wood than is indicated above, but under any circumstances they form a precarious source of supply.

Introduction of exotics. Several quick growing species of *acacia* introduced from Australia, are reared for fuel on the Nilgiri Hills, but these plants would not bear the severe frost at Simla. There are some sheltered spots at a lower elevation, as near the Soldiers' garden at Subathu, where the seeds of these naturalized plants might be sown as an experiment. As a general rule, the most rapid indigenous growers of a country are best suited for this purpose.

Conservancy preferred to planting. Instead of forming plantations which would require a costly establishment, and be attended with a doubtful result, I would conserve the pine forest, oak copse, and solid underwood which exist. This has been done earnestly and unceasingly both by Mr. Edwards and Lord William Hay, otherwise the natural forest would long since have disappeared. The great points

* Rec. Home Dept., viii., Forests of Kumaon, Supp. p. 8.

are 1st, to prevent the cutting of young trees; and 2nd, to keep out the herds of village cattle which break the young seedlings and deprive them of shade without which their growth is very slow. I consider this of great importance. Experience has shown in other districts the impossibility of preserving a young forest, when woodcutters, cows, and goats are permitted to enter it. Lord William Hay after 10 years' experience states, that "the usual history of a forest on "the hills is this: The woodcutter enters, fells many "trees and damages many others by the tree falling "down the steep slope, the branches not having been "previously cut off. A heap of chips and *débris* re- "mains which takes fire by accident or otherwise, the "villagers send their cattle for pasturage, and in a "very few years some scattered pines are all that "remain of a once flourishing forest."

Hill Chiefs' Revenue from fuel.

I am assured by the Officiating Commissioner of the Cis-Sutlej States, (Mr. Brandreth), that the Hill Chiefs around Simla are now becoming alive to their own interests in this matter, that they derive considerable revenue from the sale of wood and charcoal, and that they to some little extent regulate the felling and clearing so as to prevent particular spots from being denuded.

FIREWOOD.

Raja of Puttiala,	... ...	Rs. 300	per annum,
Rana of Keonthal,	... ...	" 500	
Rana of Kothie,	... ...	" 200	

realized by a charge of eight annas *per mensem* on each woodcutter, these sums were given by the vakeels, but are certainly under stated.

Charcoal is made by a distinct class of persons who pay six annas per ban tree (*quercus incana.*) I had no means of ascertaining the amount of revenue from this source, or the seignorage paid upon deodar (kelú) trees.

Near Simla, the proximity of a large population has made great ravages on the indigenous forests, particularly on the Southern exposure which is the favorite aspect for house sites, and thinly clothed by nature. Where a high price is offered for corn, milk, potatoes, and vegetables, the forests have necessarily disappeared to some extent, and as cultivation extends, the price of wood will rise. The cost is less important than the fact of wood being procurable.

Use of stoves recommended. I would strongly recommend economy in the use of fuel by employing *close stoves* and improved *kitchen ranges*. This has been done with good effect at the Sonawar Military Asylum, and also I believe at the Wellington Barracks on the Nilgiri hills. The surgeon of the Rifle Brigade, Sabathu, (Dr. Fraser) is of opinion, that, "the introduction of stoves into the military stations would be an improvement." It is probable that it would effect a considerable saving of fuel, whilst the surface of air warmed by the stoves is much more extensive. The simple stoves used at the Lawrence Asylum are worthy of imitation.

Construction of storerooms. It also appears to me that enclosures or storerooms are required for the protection of the store of fuel. In well regulated private houses, I am informed that stacking under cover is found useful, particularly during the rains.

Reserves of deodar. I need scarcely urge that the remaining forests of that valuable tree, the deodar, should be carefully preserved. The natives of the hills venerate the groves surrounding their temples, and religiously conserve them; whilst to the state, the wood is of the greatest importance for house and bridge building.

The chir* *pinus longifolia* yields a useful timber which appears to stand well, when applied to roofing, unsquared, and under cover. This also should not be wasted. Reserves of chir.

Whenever the natural forest belonging to Government becomes thin, seeds of indigenous trees (oak, deodar, &c.,) common to such localities should be sown before the rains. This might be done within the bounds of Simla under the orders of the Municipal Committee and in the Military Cantonments by the Executive Engineer or Commissariat officer. The same course should be strongly urged upon the native chiefs (to whom the forests mainly belong), through the civil authorities. Sowing of acorns, deodar seed, &c.

On the Simla range of hills, peat bogs do not exist so far as I can learn, but a sample of turf fuel from the confines of Tibet having been submitted by Dr. Falconer to Dr. Percy, School of Mines, Jermyn Street, London, it is not impossible that this economic natural fuel may yet be discovered.† Search for peat recommended.

Dr. Falconer's views.‡

"The hill stations have long been suffering from a yearly decrease in the supply of firewood. The nearest patches of woodland have gradually been denuded of trees, so that the supplies have now to be drawn from a distance, with increase of labor and an enhancement of the price. The station of Simla was fixed on a spot originally surrounded with trees, im- Want of wood near Simla.

* *Chil* and *chir* are synonymous terms.

† I have since found good peat in the Mid Himalayas at the Sâch pass, resembling Irish turf in its character, and in the *genera* of producing plants.

‡ Since the foregoing was written, my attention has been attracted amongst voluminous correspondence to an able memorandum by Dr. Falconer, late superintendent, botanical gardens, Calcutta, dated 16th Nov., 1853, of which some extracts are annexed.

mediately below the ridge there were wooded crags and slopes covered with *rhododendron*, *andromeda*, and oak, with many other species, while the ridge and slopes upon which the station stands, abounded in deodar and other *coniferæ* and beyond it the lofty ridge of Mahasú was clothed with magnificent forest, descending on either side, a long way down the slope. The trees adapted for most economical wants were in such abundance in the neighbourhood, that had the natural wealth been husbanded with prudence, it would have yielded a continuous and ample supply, but except within the mere boundaries of the station itself, the trees were cut down for firewood with the most wasteful improvidence, and no adequate attempt was made to replace the felled trees by the growth of young plants.

"The attention of the authorities at Simla was long ago awakened to the impending evil, but the circumstance that the forest tracts surrounding the station belonged to protected hill chieftains, who had the uncontrolled management of their own possessions, deprived them of the power of providing a timeous and suitable remedy.

Failure of planting.

"The same want, arising from like causes, has successively affected the stations of Sabathu, Kussowlee and Dugshai, and to such an extent either now felt or in prospect, as to have called for the interference of Government.

"It would appear that in 1845, 20,000 young trees were planted in the Government district of Kotgurh, but with so little success that after eighteen months only 800 survived,* I am unacquainted with the particulars of that experiment, the kinds which were tried, the exact nature of the ground, or the circumstances

* The site of this experiment was unsuitable, being bare grass land. H. C.

under which they were attempted to be grown, being points of great importance in the case, for species which would grow well among the wooded heights of Hattu above would fail on bare ground at Kotgurh below, but I entirely concur in the opinion expressed by Mr. Edwards, that no good will ever arise from forming plantations on ridges, or hills, or slopes, that are now bare and covered with grass, and with him I believe that such tracts have not probably at any time been clothed with trees, that they have always borne grass or herbaceous vegetation.

"But the same objection will not apply to ridges or slopes that have been bared by indiscriminate felling. However denuded they may be now, suitable measures will restore them to their former wooded condition; for where a tree has once grown, trees may be grown again.

"The remedial measures proposed are, 1st, to rear young plantations throughout the hills on new sites; 2nd, to preserve and renew the forests already existing.

"The Superintendent of the Hill States thinks, that instead of forming new plantations on waste lands or where they have not been before, attention should be restricted to the preservation and renewal of the forests and copses now existing. He argues that it would be impolitic to restrain the zamindars in their efforts at extending their cultivation, on waste land and forest clearances, more especially as plantations formed on such lands would not be available for use under 40 to 100 years.

Mr. Edwards' opinion.

"The Commissioner of the Cis-Sutlej States, on the other hand considers with good reason that the remoteness of the prospect of return, even if above 40 years, is no sufficient argument against new plantations, and that it is the duty of Government to

Mr. Edmonstone's opinion.

provide for the future as well as for present wants; he thinks that the best land, when required should be appropriated for plantations, although at the expense of extended cultivation, and recommends that plantations should be formed everywhere within the bounds of the Simla jurisdiction. The number to be limited only by the means available for adequate supervision.

Dr. Falconer's observations.

"Many years ago I passed through the hill country, in question, and the result of my observation is that in the interior, away from the vicinity of the hill stations, wood is generally so abundant either in belts of forest, copses in the low valleys, or straggling trees, that there is no necessity for forming new plantations except in localities where the returns might *be made available for export on any of the great rivers* to the plains. Supposing that such plantations were formed, of what use would they be? In the majority of cases, the timber would be too remote from any of the hill stations to be available with advantage either for building purposes, or for firewood, and the cost of removal to a navigable channel would be equally against its exportation to the plains. On the slopes of the Chôr mountain between Jubal and Sirmûr, within a few days march of Simla, there are sheets of magnificent forest of primeval and stupendous growth, and equal to the building wants of all the hill stations, but which are at present of no use by reason of their impracticable position, as regards means of removal. It appears to me that the majority of the proposed new plantations would be to some degree in the same predicament. The trees grown upon them would be useful only to the zamindars. But although this in itself would be a very laudable object and deserving of the most favorable consideration by the Government, it has still to be shown, so far as I know, that Government interference is required. In the more elevated situations, the hill people have ample supplies in the pine and oak forests, for all their wants, while in the valleys and on the lower heights where pine logs are not available, it will be found that in suitable localities they plant trees adapted to their wants. In illustration, I may adduce the fact that the tree called "*cedrela serrata*" is very commonly grown in ravines near the villages where pines are not to be had. The tree grows with a long straight cylindrical unbranched trunk, and it is consequently well suited as a substitute for pine logs in their buildings.

Conservancy required rather than planting.

"It would seem to me, therefore, that no general system of planting with an organized establishment is required, for the interior districts, and that besides the protective and penal measures mentioned by Mr. Edwards, nothing more is required of Government than encouragement or reward to the head men of the hill communities, by the remission of revenue or limited grants of land, where any great zeal has been distinctly shown in the growth of trees, or in the well conserved condition of any patch of Government forest within the village boundaries. With Mr. Edwards, I entertain no fear of a deficiency of timber, either for building purposes or for fuel in the interior of the hill districts, if the natural sources of supply now in existence are conserved with moderate care.

Annual fires.

"With regard to the conflagrations which are universally described as being so destructive, according to my observation they are almost in every instance, wilfully caused. The practice is very common in all parts of India, where there are extensive tracts of waste or prairie land used for grazing. At the end of the rains the ripe grass dries up, forming an innutritious fodder upon which the cattle soon fall off, and the most ready remedy is to apply fire, and burn the withered straw in order that the young grass shoots, which spring up immediately after, may be accessible for browzing. Firing the grass jungle is universally practised in the prairie "khadur" lands along the Terai, where bullocks and buffaloes are grazed and wherever brinjarahs take their cattle in the cold weather. The same object leads to it in the hill districts. The paharees will bide their time patiently for wind and weather suited to a favorable spread of the conflagration. In very many instances, the dry withered grass is an evil, for which burning is the only cure. Under these circumstances, it appears to me questionable whether any amount of injunction, or penal enactment will be effective against a practice which is so engrained with the wants and the immemorial usages of the people. The best plan would be, to have the plantations in situations not liable to the risk of fire and the sites best adapted, in other respects for planting would be of that character.

Planting recommended at hill stations.

"But the case is very different as regards the necessity for plantations in the immediate vicinity of Simla, and the other hill stations. The increasing scarcity of timber and fuel has been long felt, and a remedy for the want is urgently required,* the planting measures suggested by Mr. Edmonstone might be applied here with great advantage and effect: as regards Simla it would seem advisable, that all the lands around the station that formerly bore wood and

* This requirement has been indefinitely increased by the wants of the railway for fuel and sleepers. H. C.

are now bared, should be carefully planted. The object is of such importance that for a local and partial case, like this, I would be inclined to agree with the Cis-Sutlej Commissioner in the opinion that although it might interfere with the efforts made by the zamindars to reclaim waste land, in some localities this ought not to be regarded as a serious obstacle. The ridge and slopes of Mahasú, which were formerly covered* with the finest timber, present localities for planting that are hardly surpassed anywhere on the hills, all the finest pines and oaks of the Himalaya would grow well there, and if the zamindars have extended their cultivation upon the bared portions, high up towards the ridge it would seem in every way desirable and expedient to restore the whole of such land to its original wooded condition, giving compensation to the interested parties for the appropriation: a partial application of the ground for this purpose would not be sufficient. In Mr. Secretary Melvill's letter it is stated, that for nurseries a very little land goes a great way, and that many thousand trees can be raised on a single acre. That is true as regards seedlings and young plants only; as trees grow up they require room, good oak timber cannot be grown with a less interval apart than 40 feet being equal to $27\frac{1}{5}$ trees per acre; and for the largest pine trees, 30 feet interval or $48\frac{1}{2}$ to the acre. For this reason, therefore, a large area would be required for the timber forests reserved for Simla.

"The chief difficulty in the way of establishing suitable plantations near that station would appear to be the circumstance, that the adjoining forest lands belong to the hill chiefs (of Keunthal and Koti) while Forests belong to Hill Chiefs.

* Ten years has produced a marvellous charge. The Forest has disappeared and vast terraces of potato cultivation have taken its place. H. C.

those in the Government districts are for the most part remote or unimportant. Mr. Edwards is of opinion, that it would be highly objectionable and improper to exercise a direct interference with these chiefs, in the management and conservation of their forests, which he considers they have a right to dispose of as they think fit. This is a question of general administration which is wholly beside my province in these observations, but I would remark that little faith could be placed in the efficiency or eventual success of any remedial measures, which depended merely on the good will and arrangements of the chiefs. They will no doubt gladly avail themselves of any enhancement in the rates imposed for felling trees, that will increase their own revenue, but I doubt if any amount of persuasion, suggestion or advice on the part of the Simla Superintendent, would induce them to undertake sustained measures for the renewal and protection of their forests, involving expense, which could be relied on. The course resorted to by Mr. Edwards, will doubtless lead to some palliation of the evil; but the results will probably be variable and uncertain.

Planting sites to be acquired.

"In order that any planting operations in the immediate vicinity of Simla or the other hill stations, should prove successful, it would appear to me essential that the Government should acquire, whether by purchase, exchange, or other form of compensation, a proprietary right in, or lease in perpetuity of the lands to be so appropriated, and of the villages adjoining them; without some arrangement of this kind, it is not readily obvious how the plantations could be properly managed.

Kussowlee and Dugshai.

"I am not sufficiently acquainted with the localities of Kussowlee and Dugshai to give my opinion as to the special sites upon which planting ought to be conducted near them. They are at a considerably lower elevation, and the kinds of trees both of the pine and other tribes would require to be different from those grown near Simla. The acquisition of the ground for the plantations by the Government would be as necessary in these cases as at Simla.

Fuel available in Pinjore valley.

" Mr. Edmonstone suggests that much aid might be derived in supplying Kussowlee and Dugshai with fuel from the forest slopes on either side of the lower or Sewalik hills, all along the Pinjore valley, which are covered with low jungle. There is no doubt that any quantity of fuel might be drawn from that quarter and transported from Kalka to Kussowlee Dugshai and Subathu, the question is one merely of expense; the cost of carriage of Sewalik fire-wood would fall heavy and it would be much more advantageous in every respect, that the hill stations had sources of supply nearer their own doors, but Mr. Edmonstone's suggestion relieves any cause of anxiety, about fuel for military hill stations, when the resources in their vicinity have been exhausted. For many years past the beams and heavy timber used in the construction of houses at Mussoorie and Landour have in most cases, been carried up the hill from the valley of Dehra below.

Penal measures not required.

" With regard to the penal measures proposed by the Cis-Sutlej Commissioner for the protection of young and undersized trees; if their operation is to be restricted to the forests close to Simla, and the other hill stations, the urgency of the evil might excuse such heavy penalties, but I do not see how they could be enforced in the interior districts, without a large and expensive establishment, nor having regard to what is stated above, that they are there wanted.

The people require timber of all sizes for various economic uses and they have been for ages in the habit of using bark and shingle * for roofing. A large cedar tree is often cut down merely to furnish a few wide planks for doors, the great mass of the trunk being left to rot: and where the timber cannot, by export be turned to a more profitable account, it is not very obvious why restrictions should be imposed on the free use of it. It would appear to me, that any penal enactments of the kind, applied to the interior, would necessarily be inoperative, and the graduated scale suggested by Mr. Edmonstone would probably prove very difficult of practical application to the forests near the hill stations; as it would not be easy in every case, to determine the age of the trees. The highest fines (20 Rs. for destroying trees of less than five years growth) seem to be unnecessarily severe, and on this account calculated to defeat their object. The general protective measures, mentioned by Mr. Edwards as being now in operation, under the new settlement are apparently sufficient for the districts in the interior."

* This wasteful practice continues in Bussahir, but in Kullu and Kangra, the use of slates for roofing has been introduced, and should be encouraged by the authorities. H. C.

THE SUTLEJ RIVER.

DURING the year 1861, the Punjab Railway Company deputed Mr Strong * to examine and report on the forests of the Bussahir State, with a view to more extended operations for procuring sleepers. On this subject the following observations and suggestions † occur to me after carefully inspecting the resources of the Sutlej valley, from the small station of Kotgurh, beyond Simla, to the village of Kanam, three marches above Chini, where the Indian cedar (*cedrus deodara*), ceases to flourish.

Deodar abundant in Bussahir.

I may premise that in the territories of Mandi and Sukhet, and in the Hill States of Koti, Kamharsen, and Bagi, which overlook the lower Sutlej, all the good deodar trees ("kelú") have of late years been removed from within three miles of the river, but the interior hills of Bussahir are extensively clothed with the finest deodar, particularly on the upper parts of the northern slopes, commencing at Nachar, and terminating near the Hangarang ridge, which forms the northern limit of this beautiful tree; and, indeed, of all arboreous vegetation, except birch and junipers.

Size of trees.

The size of the trees is immense. In the Nachar

* His report forwarded with letter No. 373, of 16th Dec. 1861, from Under Sec. to Govt., Punjab Railway Dept., is attached, Appendix A.

† Submitted to Sec. to Govt., Punjab, D. P. W., in letter dated Camp Jagatsukh, 29th August, 1862.

forest, I measured one 28 feet in circumference, 4 feet from the ground, and several in the same clump were not much less. A remarkable tree in this locality is recorded both by Drs. Thomson and Hoffmeister, as 36 feet in girth, but it divides into two trunks. Many cedars may be seen in travelling along the Hindustan and Tibet road, 20 feet in girth, and 100 to 130 feet in height, but from their position on rocky slopes, I was seldom able to measure them.

Supply sufficient under good management. As above mentioned, there is a very large supply of this valuable timber on the banks of the Upper Sutlej and Baspa rivers, sufficient (if the forests be worked with care and good management,) to admit of 8,000 trees being felled annually, yielding, say 200,000 cub. feet, for the wants of the Railway and Public Works Department, and for the people in the Cis and Trans-Sutlej States, without trenching on the capital of the Bussahir forests.

Want of system. Much of the finest timber, indeed, has been cut away in the more accessible places, and there is a want of system and mechanical appliances in the present mode of conducting operations. Unskilled persons are working for immediate profit, without regard for the young trees, or the future supply of timber.

Waste of wood. The description of waste given by Mr Strong is not exaggerated—in some particulars it may be understated. He justly remarks that there is much need of an improved system of felling, slipping, dressing into logs, etc. I particularly noted the obstruction caused by numerous high stumps, which prevent the logs being sent down from above to the river, and the great quantity of scattered wood and forest debris, accumulated in mounds at the foot of the natural water-courses or rude slides, by which the logs are precipitated into the valley falling with a noise like the boom of a cannon. .

The axemen habitually fell the trees at the height most convenient to themselves, viz., four to six feet from the ground, and cause the tree to fall laterally. If it inclines down the valley, the trunk is broken ; if towards the hill, their lives are endangered. I concur with Mr Strong, that low cutting should be introduced; a regulation being made that the trees be cut within two feet from the ground, and that no tree be felled which is less than nine feet in circumference. Further, the trees should be previously marked, if possible. This would be difficult occasionally, when they are sparsely scattered over precipitous ravines, but it would ensure careful selection of timber and the preservation of young trees, thus benefiting the Rajah as proprietor, and the Railway Company as purchaser. **Mode of felling.**

Unless the forest lies conveniently, so that the logs fall into the water, the contractors select trees of second class dimensions, say nine to ten feet in girth, and after felling, divide the trunk into short lengths for easy water transport. Out of several thousand logs which I saw, very few exceeded twelve feet in length, being cut expressly for conversion into railway sleepers. The contractors assert that the addition of several feet in length increases the cost of moving the log to the river, whilst it diminishes the chance of its reaching the plains. Consequently, the finest trees are divided into three, six, or even eight logs, and a straight trunk fit for the mast of a ship is reduced to ten feet lengths. This mutilation of noble trees is most distressing, when we remember how highly these long logs are prized by the Engineers, and how many public works of this country have been delayed, **Scantling of timber.**

because timber of the required dimensions could not be procured.

Improvement of slides. Little care or judgment is displayed in selecting suitable sites for slipping the timber. Some of the slides or "galls" now in use, might be much improved at little expense by a person of skill and experience; others are wholly irremediable, and should never have been tried. In one place, eighteen logs out of twenty were shivered to pieces; the chuprassie in charge should have desisted on seeing the result of the first two attempts, but the contractor finds that if one log in ten reaches its destination, he is amply repaid, and destruction of timber is not taken into consideration.

Rolling logs over snow. Fine wood is often seen overhanging mural precipices, or in situations whence it cannot be removed without certain injury at the ordinary working season. In such cases, it seems advisable to adopt the American system of rolling the logs, during the winter months, over the *hardened snow*, which covers the country, and fills up the hollows to the depth of many feet.* Mr. J. D. Smithe, Supt. Chenab and Ravi forests, has successfully practised this operation on the banks of the Ravi.

Himalayan rivers. My attention was directed as much to the course of the river as to the condition of the forests. The natural difficulties of timber transport on all the Himalayan rivers, are far greater than are experienced on any of those in Malabar or Burmah, (with the operations on which I am acquainted), where the current is much slower, and the banks are usually muddy.

Character of Sutlej. The Sutlej river,† at the season of my journey,

* Or to form slides such as have been constructed in the Alps to meet similar difficulties.

† The Sutlej is the longest of the Punjab rivers; its rise in the holy lakes of

which was the commencement of the rains, is an impetuous torrent, foaming along its narrow, stony bed, confined within rocky banks, generally bare and precipitous. It preserves the same character from Kotgurh upwards, the valley in Bussahir being very narrow, the river is often not visible from the road, but the noise is always heard, as it rushes over the massy boulders. Occasional recesses occur at the bends of the river, where much timber is stranded, and in the course of 120 miles there are several broad tranquil reaches, where banks of white sand and mud may be seen. The average fall has been computed by various † observers (Gerard, Thomson, and Madden) at 50 feet per mile from Wangtu to Bilaspur, and 60 feet per mile from Kanam to Wangtu. The construction and management of rafts above Bilaspur is quite impracticable, they would certainly go to pieces in descending the rapids, and the raftsmen be lost. **Fall of river.**

I noted four or five places in the river bed between Kotgurh and Kanam, where a large number of logs are detained and damaged, but there are fewer rapids in the Sutlej than in the Ravi, and no great obstructions over which high floods do not carry the timber. A little money may be well spent hereafter in clearing the channel by blasting, but I am not prepared at present to recommend the removal of the obstacles. A good superintendent, after the experience of one or two seasons, would be a better judge of what should be done in this way. **Obstructions to floating.**

In the forests of Pegu and South India, a system of branding and stamping with fine cut dies, not easily **Marking of logs.**

Manasarovara and Ráwan Hrad, has been described by the brothers Strachey. Capt. Herbert in 1819, explored the valley from Rupar to Shipki, the limit of British authority, the levels he laid down are recorded in As. Res., vol. xv.

* The fall is 89 feet per mile from the base of Porgyal to Bilaspur, and the river a furious torrent. *Cunningham's Ladak*, p. 128.

imitated, has been found to answer well. This is suited for hardwood planks, but not for unsquared logs of pine wood; nothing less than a notch three inches deep, is sufficient for deodar timber floated down the impetuous rivers of the Himalaya. All slighter marks are liable to erasure, and even these require deepening or renewal, if the log remains one or two seasons in the river.

Register of marks.

The marks should be approved and registered, both in the Rajah's Cutchery at Rampur, and in the Civil Court at Simla. They should be as dis-similar as possible and each merchant or contractor should be restricted to one symbol or device. At present, a contractor uses several, to distinguish the logs prepared at his different felling places, but this inevitably causes confusion and inconvenience in their passage down the river. The numerous and miscellaneous marks used by the merchants on the Ravi and its tributaries, will illustrate the evils of the present practice.

Forest tenures.

The deodar forests of the Upper Sutlej are the property of the Rajah of Bussahir, with the exception of the ancient groves adjoining the village temples, which are understood to be attached to the edifices, and are religiously preserved. Persons contracting to supply the Railway Company or Public Works Department, arrange with His Highness, and obtain permits to fell trees in certain localities.

Seignorage per tree.

Previous to Mr. Barnes' visit to Bussahir in 1859, a bag of rupees secured a permit for felling a forest tract, containing an indefinite number of trees. The Commissioner * insisted that payment should be made

* "Up to the present year, speculators could come up and cut at their pleasure, floating the timber down the river to Loodiana and Ferozepore, *without paying*

for individual trees, and not for portions of forest. This was a step of progress. The levy of seignorage per tree is carried out in nearly all teak forests, also in the Ravi and Chenab forests, and is found to secure the selection of well grown timber, and to a certain extent a more careful felling of the trees.

The contractor or his subordinate, with a detachment of axemen (who are chiefly from Mandi and Kullû) repair to the forests about the end of April or 1st of May, when some of the passes are open, and the snow is beginning to melt. They are occupied till October or November (six months) in felling trees, dressing them into logs, and rolling them to the river or nearest stream. During this period, they live in temporary wooden huts or in caves. The length of the working season is very uncertain. Operations commenced late this year on account of the unusual amount of snow on all the passes, but it is of great importance to begin early, that advantage may be taken of the first rains, to float down as many logs as possible.

Contractors.

Working season.

Mr. T. Arratoon, the Armenian merchant, is the most enterprising contractor working in these forests. I inspected five of his fellings including several mentioned by Mr Strong, (Nachar, Dippi, etc.,) and regretted that I had not an opportunity of conferring with Mr. Arratoon on the spot. He arrived as I was leaving, and we were on opposite banks, without being aware of the circumstance: this was of less

Mr. T. Arratoon.

anything to the Rajah. I have now placed this department under the Wazeers. A rate of two rupees a tree has been fixed as a fair average price, and a speculator must now present a written application specifying the number of trees he requires. A portion of the money will be realized in advance, and an official deputed to see that only the proper quantity is felled, and that the balance is paid before the timber is brought to the river." 28th Nov. 1859.

consequence, as I had discussed forest matters with him some months previously in Lahore.

Wazir Goshain.

Between Nachar and Wangtu, are a large number of logs prepared by the Wazir of Mandi four years ago, which apparently are abandoned, not being considered worth the expense of removal. These logs, however, could be sent down at no great cost.

Estimate of waste.

The contractors give widely different statements of the proportion of logs which safely reach the plains. One asserts that he only succeeds in securing one-tenth. As no register is kept, there is no basis for calculating the quantity of lost and damaged timber, but judging from what passed under my observation in travelling up and down the valley, from the highest felling in Upper Kunawar to the depôt in the plains, it was evident that a large proportion of valuable timber (more than one-third of the whole), is lost on its passage to the river. Again, a great number of logs launched from the slides in Buṣsahir, do not reach the Rupar depôt in the Loodiana district. I should say, that from one-third to one-fourth of the logs felled in the basin of the Sutlej become available for the construction of public works in the Punjab, within two or three years after they are dressed. In this calculation of loss my views nearly coincide with those contained in Mr. Brandreth's letter to Capt. Sim, Consulting Engineer Jan. 8th, 1862.

Rupar depôt.

I visited this place in January, and again in March; on each occasion there was a stock of several hundred short logs, many of them much shaken and splintered, the fractures specially indicating damage, caused by being hurled over precipices. This waste of timber may be partly obviated as I have stated at page 30. A small proportion of the logs were water-worn by river action: some of them seemed to have been three or four years in the water, and the wood is generally more damaged than that which reaches Sealkôt from the valley of the Chenab river. A gang of thirty sawyers was at work, using both straight and curved saws, in the management of which they are tolerably proficient. Rafting commences about twenty-five miles above Rupar, ten or twelve logs being tied together by grass ropes, passed through the drag holes in the usual manner. The best of the logs belonging to Mr. Arratoon had been sent down to Hari ki ghat, convenient to the Punjab Railway. Rafts of deodar had also been floated down to Loodiana.

Woods procurable. [Pines]. *Cedrus deodara*, Himalayan cedar.

The contractors deal solely in deodar wood "kelú," and will continue to do so as long as this prized timber is procurable within easy distance of the river. A native of Rampur has this season felled a considerable quantity of "chil" (*pinus longifolia*), near Serahan. This wood when old and reddish is well suited for building purposes. The "kail," (*pinus excelsa,*) also is used where deodar is scarce.* Other pines, as per margin, are widely distributed in these territories, but their wood is not in demand.

Pinus longifolia, "chil."

Pinus excelsa, "kail."

Abies smithiana, "rai." *Picea webbiana*, silver fir "tos."

[Oaks]. *Quercus incana* "bán." Common hoary oak. *Q. semicarpifolia*, "karsu." *Q. dilatata* "morhu."

There are three species of oak in the Sutlej valley, which are next in importance to the pines. Vast forests of them occur in various places, as on the east side of Hattu, on the upper track between Muttiana and Nagkanda, in Mandi, Sukhet, etc. The trees are of great size, 80 to 100 feet in height, they prefer dry situations, and are not generally convenient to the river. The logs do not float the first and second years, being in this respect like the black wood of Malabar. Oak wood has been well reported

* In the Kangra Hills, this wood is considered next in excellence to the deodar, and superior to the chil. It is the wood principally used at Marri.

of by General Cautley at Marri; Mr. Smithe, Superintendent of Workshops, Madhopur; and by Dr. Campbell of Darjiling.

When the cart road to Nagkanda is opened out, fine straight logs of oak may be brought into Simla. If approved by the railway officers, this timber might be supplied from the Hill States, and launched below Kotgurh, supported by bamboos, or lashed to pine logs. It may be noted that several species of oak are much used for railway sleepers in North America, and there can be little doubt, from their great density, that two of the Himalayan oaks are among the best timbers we have. In its colour and grain the *mohru* resembles the British oak.

Other hard woods.

There is abundance of yew and olive, and a considerable quantity of box and ash in the valley of the Sutlej. The ash and olive occur near the river, the box and yew prefer the higher slopes, and are generally 2,000 feet or more above the bed of the Sutlej. The ash and yew are much esteemed for jampan poles, tool handles, etc. The former in colour, grain, and toughness resembles the English ash. The box and olive being hard and close grained, might be useful to the Railway company for wedges and trenails.

These are the principal timbers of Bussahir, which from their abundance and varied qualities, are valuable for engineering purposes. There are others, as maple, elm, walnut, plane, and alder trees, which being deficient, either in quantity or quality, require no special notice in this communication.

Conclusion.

I have reviewed the different points of Mr. Strong's report, and would again remark, that there is no lack of good timber, but it is indispensably necessary that

European superintendent required.

a European officer of experience, intelligence and energy, should be appointed to superintend the working of these valuable forests. The Sutlej river, though rapid, can be turned to account for conveyance,* and the Rajah is anxious for improvements. I did not venture to ascertain his views, but from all I heard at Rampur, of the trouble he experiences in realizing a small and uncertain revenue from his forests, there is reason to believe that he would readily agree to lease them on equitable terms, or to a seignorage per tree, as is now paid to the Chamba Rajah for those cut in the Pangi and Ravi valleys. The exportation of timber ought to be a steady source of revenue to His Highness, and of employment to the thinly scattered population of Bussahir. The felling and launching of the logs may be effected by contract, or by day labourers under supervision. To allow contractors of all kinds without capital, experience, or scientific knowledge, to exhaust these deodar forests, as they are now doing, is to sacrifice the interests of the Rajah, and to occasion prospective evil to the Punjab. In a few years, little timber would be procurable, and the remedy too late of application.

Result of the present system.

The systematic working of the forests on the Sutlej and Baspa rivers, seems clearly advisable, and I recommend that operations be conducted on a similar plan to that now adopted on the Chenab under the efficient superintendence of Mr. J. D. Smithe, who gives full wages, requires good work, and is esteemed both by the Rajah of Chamba, and the labouring population.

Duties of superintendent.

It would be the duty of the officer appointed to examine and map out all the forests; to indicate the places annually, where the cutting should take place in rotation; to allow felling only where the logs

* This was first proved by Mr. W. Edwards, C.S., formerly Supdt. Hill States.

could be removed; to select and test the working of timber slips; and to prevent damage of every kind.

Probable out-turn of timber.

The probable out-turn of timber in 1862–1863, on the Sutlej, Ravi, and Chenab rivers, as nearly as can be estimated (supposing average floods) is given in round numbers in the margin. The result of working with energy the Pangi forests on the Chenab is thus seen.

	1862-3.
Sutlej,	150,000
Ravi,	100,000
Chenab,	700,000
	950,000 c. ft.

Under the circumstances detailed, it may seem advisable to His Honor the Lieut.-Governor, to establish a timber agency on the Sutlej, which would render available at Rupar a supply of timber for engineering works, both larger in quantity and finer in quality, to meet the demands of various departments, and which appears to be the best means of arresting the waste now characterising the present system in the valley of the Upper Sutlej.

THE BASPA RIVER.

THIS large feeder of the Sutlej river rises behind the cluster of Raldang peaks, near the boundary of Bussahir and Garhwal; it runs a nearly straight course, of fifty miles, falling in that distance about 8000 feet. A long portion of the valley (with the Burenda and Rupin passes beyond) may be seen from the road between Miru and Chini. I was prevented from examining the glen, my time being limited, and the state of the weather unfavourable; but I can corroborate the observations of Hoffmeister, as to the magnificent cedars which stand near the village of Mebar, nearly opposite Chegaon.* Mr. Arratoon felled trees on the Baspa in 1862. It is practicable for timber operations up to Sangla; above which, Major Madden describes it as a raging torrent, with an average fall of 250 feet per mile; he also states that the face of the steep (left bank) is fringed with many superb old tabular headed cedars (*Jour. As. Soc., Beng.*, xv., p. 109). I learned from Lord Wm. Hay, Mr. Brandreth, Capt. Houchen, and others who have explored the Baspa valley, that there is the prospect of a considerable supply of deodar timber being obtained from this source. **Baspa river.**

* Useful information as to the vegetation of the beautiful valley of this impetuous stream may be found in Hoffmeister's travels, pp. 356 to 367, and in Gerard's Kunawar, p. 17. The climate is intermediate between the dry one of Spiti and the moist one of Gurhwal.

APPENDIX A.

FROM

RICHARD JOHN STRONG, ESQ.,

Inspector of Works,

TO

J. HARRISON, ESQ., C.E.,

Chief Engineer, Punjab Railway,

Lahore, Nov. 2nd, 1861.

SIR,—My previous report informed you that I left Simla on the 5th September, agreeable to instructions received, to inspect and report on the several forests in the Bussahir territory.

Nachar forest.

I arrived at the first deodar forest on the 23rd September, and after minutely inspecting the trees standing, those cut, and the logs in the river, I am happy to say they are the best I have seen. The slide down which the timber is sent to the river is good, but capable of great improvement, which, in my opinion, should be made before the logs now lying on the hill are sent down. The majority of slides in these hills are full of broken timber, at once shewing the careless and rough manner in which the logs are treated after felling.

Wasteful felling.

I also beg to call your attention to the way in

which the trees are cut. They commence cutting about six feet up the tree, it being more convenient to work; standing on the high than on the low ground the stumps are left in, and cause great obstructions, as trees felled at a short distance from the slide cannot be rolled to it, and are sent through rough parts of the forest; and, in many instances, logs of good quality get so fixed between the other trees, that they will not repay the labour of removal, and consequently, are allowed to rot; this besides the damage done to the young trees, and the waste in not cutting at the roots, is a great drawback, and I would respectfully suggest that, if possible, an order should be issued to prevent such useless waste. The finest trees are in this forest, and there is, if properly managed, sufficient timber to supply the Company for some years, with the great advantage of being below fifteen miles of the worst part of the river.

One thousand logs are now lying in the forest ready for sending down, these are nearly all cut through in the lengths required, and can be sent to the river in a short time. There are also in or near the river about five hundred logs, which are being floated according to the state of the water. A large number of trees are prepared for cutting next season, some are at least 200 feet high, and of good girth. Allowance in length is made for the transit down the hill.

I measured a tree after felling 122 feet long, the Size of trees. butt end girth 14 feet 6 inches, and the top 12 feet 4 inches; another standing about 150 feet high, girth at bottom 18 feet 4 inches; these are not exceptions, some I measured 26 feet in girth. The average, taking the whole forest, is not less than 15 feet girth at bottom. The soil is black loam, very rich, and the trees are full of turpentine.

In what condition the logs arrive at Lahore I do not know, but if the slide was improved, the logs floated when the river is high, and ordinary care taken, I see no difficulty in any part of the river from the Bussahir forest to twenty miles below Rampur.

Dippi forest. This forest is quite a contrast to the one at Nachar, the timber here is small, and not of the best quality. There are about one hundred logs ready for sending down.

The slide to the river is nearly perpendicular in two places, and the timber is so shaken in going down, as to be useless before reaching the water, and it would be folly, in my opinion, to make a slide at this place for some years, as the trees are young, and should not be cut. A short distance from the present slide, a good one could easily be made when required. In good forests it will well repay the outlay, and prevent the enormous waste which is going on. The timber here is chiefly kelú, and the average girth at bottom not more than 9 feet. A number of the largest trees are prepared for cutting.

Jhaney forest. This forest is nearly the same as Dippi, if anything, the trees are smaller; the slide is bad, in fact, both forests may be considered alike.

Kilni forest. The trees here are of much better quality and size than those at Dippi or Jhaney, but are not to be compared with those at Nachar, about 1000 logs are lying ready for sending down. The slide is good, and so is the river for some miles from here. A good slide could easily be made. The same remarks about waste apply to all the forests. The numerous slides I have passed over are all full of splintered timber, good only for fire-wood. The timber thus wasted would form slides, if properly managed, that would last during the cutting of the whole forests.

In this forest the trees are very good. There are about 1,600 logs cut ready for delivery. I measured five trees, and found them the following girth at bottom, 26 feet 9 inches, 21 feet 6 inches, 22 feet, 18 feet, and 26 feet 4 inches. These are exceptions to the general forest, but the trees are of good girth and height, principally kelú. The forest is large, and the average height of the trees is not less than 150 feet. Kumnay forest.

The slide is good, and the river is also free from rocks for some miles below, which is a great advantage as the logs slide into the river, the bottom of which is sandy.

The above remarks will nearly apply to this forest, the trees and logs are about the same. The slide is good, also the river in which there are a great number of logs, I should say not less than 1,500, but as they are lying on the sands, this prevented me getting near to them, those at the bottom of the slide are nearly all good, and have met little damage coming down. On the hill some six hundred logs are lying, all of good quality and girth. Sampnee forest.

This march I passed through and examined three forests, and conclude that there are not less than from 3,000 to 3,500 logs of good quality cut, and ready to take advantage of the first rise in the river, this estimate includes those already in the river bed.

Great destruction is done to the young trees as in the other forests.

About 2,000 logs are lying in or near this forest, and about three hundred in the river, of good quality and girth. Baspa forest.

The jemadar informed me that 5,000 trees would be prepared for felling by March next, which I can believe; in fact, in all the forests, I have seen large quantities prepared. The river is good at this place at high water, but at present it is very low. It joins the Sutlej about fifteen miles below.

SUMMARY.

	In the forests.	In or near river.
Nachar, ...	1,000	500
Dippi, ...	100	,,
Kilni, ...	1,000	1,000
Kumnay, ...	1,600	,,
Sampnee, ...	600	1,500
Baspa, ...	2,000	300
Total,	6,300	3,300

The above is as near as possible the quantity of timber in and near the forests, but on my way back through Rampur, I saw large quantities at various points of the river, which the first rise of the water will float.

Allow me again to call your attention to the great waste through not having pròper slides in each forest; the destruction of the young trees also calls for interference.

APPENDIX B.

FROM

THE AGENT TO LIEUT.-GOVERNOR, PUNJAB,
Cis-Sutlej States.

TO

THE SECRETARY TO GOVERNMENT,
Lahore.

25th February, 1863.

I HAVE the honor to forward for the consideration and orders of His Honor the Lieut.-Governor, copy of a letter of 20th February, and its enclosures, from the Superintendent, Hill States, Simla, regarding the Bussahir forests, and to state as follows :—

1st.—That I think the plan agreed upon between Major Lawrence and the Rajah of Bussahir, for the appointment of an officer to the charge of the forests, is calculated to increase the Rajah's revenues, and to preserve the forests, to which reckless contractors have already done great injury.

2nd.—That the appointment should be made at once.

3rd.—That the salary of this official should be charged to the forests.

4th.—That the officer should be required to live in the country.

5th.—That he should be under the orders of the Superintendent, Hill States, and of this office, and

6th.—That he should be selected for discretion and conciliation, as well as for knowledge of forestry.

2.—With reference to Mr Arratoon's claims, it will, I think, be time enough to investigate them when preferred; and I see no necessity for inviting them, or delaying the present arrangement.

(Signed) HERBERT EDWARDES.

FROM

THE SUPERINTENDENT, HILL STATES,

Simla.

To

THE AGENT, LIEUT.-GOVERNOR, PUNJAB,

Cis-Sutlej States.

20th February, 1863.

IN his letter, Nov. 19, 1860, to the address of the Secy. to Govt., Punjab, the late Mr. Barnes remarked on the lamentable waste of timber which had been allowed in the forests of Bussahir, owing to the Government of that State not being aware of the increased and increasing value of wood, and having, in consequence, permitted speculators to cut it just as they pleased. Bussahir forests.

In view to remedy the evil, Mr. Barnes appointed a daroga or forest ranger, and laid down certain rules under which traders should be allowed to cut timber. Rules inoperative.

It seems that for some time these rules were pretty generally adhered to, but on my visiting Bussahir in June 1862, I found them almost entirely in abeyance.

This arose from three causes.

1st.—The weak and vacillating character of the Rajah. Reasons assigned.

2nd.—The remoteness of the sites of the forests, rendering them very inaccessible to the Government officials.

3rd.—The dishonesty of traders who desire to continue the practice of cutting wood where they like without payment.

I found that although the Rajah could not resist the importunity of the traders, and was easily persuaded by the presentation of some small offering, to grant them perwanas to cut wood when and where they liked, he was fully alive to the loss which he ultimately sustained, and he expressed himself very anxious to maintain the rules prescribed by the Commissioner.

I accordingly reiterated the orders issued by that officer, and warned Mr. Arratoon and others that they would be strictly enforced, and that no perwana granted by the Rajah in breach of the rules, would be held valid in my court.

Daroga appointed.

I appointed an intelligent and seemingly trustworthy native of Bussahir to the charge of the forests, and gave him strict orders to allow no wood to be cut, until half its value had been paid for, and none to be floated until paid for in full.

I believe that these measures had some effect, but I received several reports direct from the daroga, to the effect that certain parties had again obtained perwanas from the Rajah, and that he could not restrain them from cutting wood at their own discretion.

European officer required.

Feeling assured that unless a European officer is appointed to the charge of the forests, nothing effectual can be done to put a stop to the waste which has been going on for so many years, I asked the Rajah whether he would agree to such an appointment being made. He at once assented, and expressed the utmost willingness to meet the views of Government as regards the preservation of forests.

I now forward a copy of the Rajah's letter of 11th November, 1862, on this subject, and with reference to his expressed desire that speculators should be prevented from cutting wood at their own pleasure, I would beg to recommend, that, in the event of Government appointing an officer to the charge of the forests, he should be vested with full powers; and that no traders should be allowed to cut wood, without, in the first place, applying to him, and that then the traders should only be allowed to cut in the place pointed out by the officer in charge of the forests.

The Rajah concurs.

I lately asked the Rajah if he was willing to give over the sole control of the forest to any officer whom Government might nominate to the charge, I enclose a copy of his reply, by which you will observe that he is very anxious to do so.

Mr. Arratoon's alledged claim.

I believe Mr. Arratoon considers he has certain claims on the Bussahir forests, which cannot be affected by any arrangements which the Rajah may enter upon with Government. I doubt the validity of any such claims, but I think that the point should be settled, and that he should be called upon to advance any claim which he has to make, in view to its being investigated.

Scale of seignorage.

Mr. Barnes decided on the rates marginally noted, for the sale of deodar timber in the Bussahir forests. These rates were fixed with reference to the inaccessibility of the forests, and the difficulty of transporting the wood to the plains, being one-half the amount realised in the forests in the immediate neighbourhood of Simla.

		Rs.	
Trees	4 feet in circumference,	0	7
"	5 " " "	0	14
"	6 " " "	1	5
"	7 " " "	1	12
"	8 " " "	2	3
"	9 " " "	2	10
"	10 " " "	3	1
"	11 " " "	3	8
"	12 " " "	3	15
"	13 " " "	4	6
"	14 " " "	4	13
"	15 " " "	5	4
"	16 " " "	5	11
"	17 " " "	6	2

Increase of rates.

The Rajah desires to increase these rates slightly, and this, I think, might be permitted, as the wood has become more scarce, and the demand has increased.

R. LAWRENCE.

To

COL. R. LAWRENCE, C.B.,

Superintendent, Hill States.

Rampur, 11*th Nov.*, 1862.

SIR,—I find it impossible to arrange for the preservation of the forests of Bussahir. Mr. Arratoon, and other merchants give me great trouble, they set at defiance the orders which Mr. G. C. Barnes issued, and repeated by you, therefore, I shall be much obliged if Government could assist me in preserving the forests, and by preventing these men from cutting trees at their own pleasure.

(Signed) SHUMSHERE SING,

Rajah of Bussahir and Rampur.

To

COL. R. LAWRENCE, C.B.,

Superintendent, Hill States.

SIR,—In reply to yours of the 6th inst., I beg to inform you, that I am quite willing to give to the British officer whom Government may appoint to look after my forests, the sole control over the forests in the territories of Rampur and Bussahir.

The contractors ought to be prevented cutting wood except on the sites that he may point out for them to cut. I am further glad to perceive in the conclusion of your same letter, that all payments would be made direct to me through your office from time to time.

(Signed) SHUMSHERE SING,

Rajah of Bussahir and Rampur.

Memorandum.

Sir H. Edwardes and Col. Lawrence propose European officer for Bussahir forests.

The views expressed by the Superintendent, Hill States,* supported by the Agent † of the Lieutenant Governor, Cis-Sutlej States, corroborate my opinion that the appointment of an intelligent officer to the charge of the Bussahir forests is indispensably necessary to the saving, utilising, and (as far as possible), restoring these forests. I witnessed their condition at a distance from check and control, and the necessity for prompt measures to protect them was apparent.

Rajah of Bussahir desires this arrangement.

The express wish of His Highness the Rajah of Bussahir, that we should undertake the management of these forests, facilitates action in this matter. The proposal of Sir H. Edwardes and Colonel Lawrence, that an experienced, judicious, and skilled officer should be appointed at once, accords with the opinion expressed in my letter of 29th August 1862.

Seignorage to be 3-8 per tree, as on the Chenab.

The superintendent should be in Bussahir during summer, and at the proposed timber depôt of Rupar during winter. The request of the Rajah to raise slightly the seignorage per tree is reasonable, considering the increased value of wood. A uniform rate would be preferable to the sliding scale, (p. 51,) and a fair seignorage for deodar trees would be Rs. 3-8, considering the difficulties of the river and the establishment required. This sum is paid to the Rajah of Chamba on the Chenab, where the deodar forests are similar in size and situation.

* Letter, 20th February, 1863. † 25th February, 1863.

Payment half yearly.

The Rajah might be paid the full seignorage of trees felled, once every six months, or at the close of the working season, by this arrangement he would be a great gainer.

Salary of establishment to be charged against value of timber.

The salary of the superintendent and of the necessary establishment, should be set against the value of timber issued from the depôt at Rupar, as is done in the agency at Sealkot.

H. CLEGHORN.

23rd March, 1863.

NOTES

ON THE

VEGETATION OF THE SUTLEJ VALLEY.

MUCH reliable information concerning the climate and productions of the Sutlej valley, is contained in Gerard's Kunawar, 1833, with Capt. J. D. Cunningham's Notes in the *Jour. As. Soc., Beng.*, xiii. (1844); in Jacquemont's "Voyage dans l' Inde," 1844; in Thomson's Travels, 1852; Cunningham's Ladak, 1854; and in various papers of Major Madden,* Capt. Hutton,† and Mr. W. Theobald, jun.,‡ in the *Jour. As. Soc., Beng.* **Works of reference on valley of Sutlej.**

The Right Honourable the Governor General of India, the late Lord Dalhousie, planned and commenced during his administration, this imperial line of traffic from Hindostan to Central Asia, from which, even in an unfinished state, great benefits undoubtedly have arisen. **Hindostan and Thibet road.**

The road was commenced in 1850, under the superintendence of Major Kennedy, and afterwards of

* Excursion to the Boorun and Shatool Passes in 1845, vol. xv., p. 79.

† Trip to the Burenda Pass in 1836, vol. vi., p. 901. Geological Report on the Spiti Valley, vol. x., p. 198. Trip through Kunawar, in 1838, viii., 901; ix., 489.

‡ Trip from Simla to the Spiti Valley in 1861, xxxi., 480.

Capt. Briggs; the original idea was, that the road should be available for wheeled carriages through its entire length. This plan has now been abandoned, and a good road for laden mules is in progress to the Chinese boundary. A branch road is being made from Kotgur to Serahan, *via* Rampur, the capital of Bussahir, and the principal resort of traders from the north as well as the south.

Wangtu bridge.

The breadth of the Sutlej at Wangtu is about ninety feet; the height of its bed, as determined by Gerard, 5,200 feet. The remarkable wooden bridge which here spans the river is the finest specimen of the kind I have seen. The square towers on either bank are about fifty years old, and existed before the bridge was destroyed, during the Gurkha invasion (Gerard, p. 37); the beams laid across were renewed in 1859; the falling of the bridge in that year threw back a great part of the traffic into other channels. The permanence of this crossing is of vital consequence to the trade with Central Asia. The pushm * traders and grain merchants, whom we met coming down the valley, inquired earnestly as to the state of "Oangtu," which is the only bridge in Kunawar by which laden sheep and mules can cross.

Rope bridges.

Jhulas or rope bridges exist at Rampur, above Serahan, opposite Miru, and at Poaree, but whether swinging or suspension bridges, they are equally unsuited for the passage of sheep and mules.

The want of bridges is much felt, and it will be necessary to erect other jhulas to facilitate access from village to village, when forest operations are carried out.

Want of Medical aid.

With road extension and forest operations in prospect, the sanction by Government of medical aid is an

* The fine wool which forms the material of our shawls.

important consideration. Throughout Bussahir, the hill villagers gather round the traveller imploring medicine; their faith in the skill of European physicians, and in the efficacy of our drugs is remarkable and embarassing. My professional knowledge was called into play in answering endless applications for medicine.

In Bussahir, the inhabitants suffer from goitre, but **Diseases of Kunawar.** not so much as in the valleys of the Pabur and Tonse; the general impression is, that the disease arises from drinking snow water, but this is erroneous, as the people in the higher valleys do not suffer so much as those in low situations.

There is a very large amount of opthalmic disease; the eyes become inflamed by the reflection from the snow, and are further injured by rubbing with dirty woollen cloths. Rhubarb leaves are used in summer to protect the eyes in crossing the passes. The other prevalent ailments are catarrh and rheumatism.

The peculiar advantages of Chini, in possessing a **Climate of Chini.** dry climate and congenial temperature, are very remarkable. The notes of Dr. Alexander Grant, Physician to the Marquis of Dalhousie, which appeared in the Annals of Medical Science, No. I., 1854, contain the best account of the climate and advantages of this retreat, where the Marquis resided during the hot weather and rains of 1850. A summary of Dr. Grant's observations will be found in the Report of the Sanitary Establishments for European Troops in India, No. I., p. 73. (Calcutta, 1861).

In Kunawar, few villages produce more grain than **Food.** the inhabitants require, and food is annually imported into the district. Grain is brought from Garhwal on the east, and supplies must be carried up from Rampur or Simla by all visitors. The people do not part willingly with their grain, even at eight seers per rupee, the present rate at Chini,* and during my tour provisions were brought from a great distance. This fact must be taken into account in connection with forest operations.

In times of scarcity, the people eat Himalayan chestnuts, *pavia indica*, and apricot kernels; they soak them to remove the bitterness, and grind the whole into flour with the inferior millets, forming large chupatties (bannocks). It is desirable to supply seed, and to encourage the growth of esculents in these valleys, where so great a demand has arisen from the influx of summer visitors, and for this purpose, the Agri-Horticultural Society of the Punjab has granted a liberal supply of vegetable seeds for distribution among the inhabitants.

Agriculture.

Agriculture is capable of little extension, from the precipitous character of the hills, and the small proportion of arable land. All the available ground is laid out in terraces, and cultivation is carried on with great care; the soil is good, and the small fields are enclosed with loose stone dykes. As soon as the snow melts, ploughing commences, and the women are sent out with baskets of manure, which has been carefully collected in the lower part of the houses.

Cultivated fruits.

The fleshy and stone fruits of Kunawar are the grape, apricot, peach, apple, walnut, and mulberry. Sungnam is famous for its apples; Akpa for grapes; and Pangi for walnuts. With the abundance of fruit, the beautiful scenery, the delightful and salubrious climate, and the fact that Chini is on the high road to Central Asia, nature renders it one of the most attractive spots in the Indian Empire. Capt. Houchen, in

* It used to be thirty or forty seers per rupee, *vide* Gerard, 1820.

charge of the Hindostan and Thibet Road, is trying to cultivate the Spanish chestnut and English hop, in the upper valley, with fair prospect of success. Mr. S. Berkeley of Kotgur has, with much skill and labor, introduced a variety of choice fruits, including vines, pears, gooseberries, currants, &c.

The same gentlemen have cultivated many European and American vegetables, which grow well; the potato is found to thrive remarkably, as a first crop. As a second crop, it is not matured in Kunawar, and on this account, the turnip is preferred. The inhabitants of the upper valley do not yet cultivate the potato to any extent, but for some stages from Simla, the increased cultivation of this esculent is very surprising, and the growth of the plants is exceedingly luxuriant.* Vegetables. Potato culture.

From Kanam to Miru ridge, are to be found,—*cedrus deodara, pinus gerardiana, p. excelsa, abies smithiana, picea webbiana, juniperus excelsa, j. squamosa, populus alba, juglans regia, corylus lacera, armeniaca vulgaris, pyrus malus, cerasus puddum, quercus ilex,* and *salix alba.* Upper Kunawar. Principal trees.

The principal articles of produce are,—*triticum vulgare*, wheat; *hordeum cœleste*, and *h. hexastychum*, barley; *panicum*, several species (millets); *fagopyrum esculentum*, buckwheat, the great staple at the head of the valleys; *vitis*, vine; *vicia*, vetch; *pisum*, pea; *faba*, bean; *brassica*, turnip, stored for winter and used dry; *sinapis*, mustard seed, used for lamp oil. Agricultural produce.

From Miru Ridge down to Kotgur, I observed the following trees,—*cedrus deodara, pinus longifolia, p. excelsa, abies smithiana, picea webbiana, pavia indica, juglans regia, alnus nitida, acer, fraxinus, morus, grewia, melia, rhododendron arboreum;* the rhododendron was Lower Kunawar. Principal trees.

* The price in May on the field is 2 rupees per maund of 80 lbs.

last seen between Serahan and Poindah. *Rhus acuminata, r. parviflora, cedrela serrata, cerasus cornuta,* and *olea cuspidata* (*ferruginea* of Royle).

Agricultural produce. The crops are in general the same as in Upper Kunawar. There is less buckwheat, and more barley; the yield is large, and the chief risk is from hailstorms, which occur during harvest (May).

My attention was chiefly directed to the wooded tracts of Bussahir; the following notes upon the Hill States lower down the valley, complete the information I have gathered regarding the timber supply on the banks of the Sutlej.

Kotgur. In the neighbourhood of Kotgur, the deodar existed at one time in considerable quantity, but did not attain a very large size. Mr. Minas felled the best trees, and endeavoured to restore the forests, but the seedlings appear to have died off. There are now only a few scattered clumps. The valley is richly cultivated and dotted with numerous villages. Rice is grown below; barley and red amaranth above.

Bajji, Komharsen. The forests in Bajji, Komharsen, and Kotgur, consist principally of ban oak, with kail, and the smithian and webbian pines. The wooded tracts are situated generally along the higher ridges, at an elevation of 8 or 9000 feet; the mountain streams are small and unfit for timber transport, except the Nowtee Nullah, over which* (in Bajji), lies a fine forest of deodar, the first observed on the left bank in ascending the Sutlej; this forest has been considerably thinned. The late Conductor Minas launched some logs from the Kothi territory, which lies south of this stream.

Suraj. On the Dhol and Jalouri Passes, which belong to the main range dividing the Sutlej from the Beas, there is a great abundance of the kursoo oak and of

* On the north slope of Shalli peak, 9,700 feet.

the smithian and webbian pines, but deodar is scarce. One large stream, the Kurpan, flows from the Dhol towards the Sutlej, which it joins opposite Datnuggur. I crossed this tributary at various points where it passes through chil forest, but could not find that timber to any extent was available. Another large stream, the Arni, takes its rise near the Jalouri, and falls into the Sutlej below the Kamharsen bridge.

Major Longden* explored the province of Mandi, Mandi. and ascertained that the forests of kelu are few; he particularly mentioned some very fine trees near Shikaree, the principal peak of the range, elevation 11,000 feet, but these are so far removed from the rivers, that the timber cannot be launched either into the Sutlej or the Beas. A few deodars exist attached to temples, which the people religiously preserve. The Wazir brought down some deodar logs from the hills above Largi last year, but they were mere bullies, and should not have been cut.

The forests of Suket, situated on the right bank of Suket. the Sutlej, consist chiefly of chil *(pinus longifolia)*. The ban oak and kail *(pinus excelsa)*, occur also in considerable quantity. This district, as well as Mandi, does not command sufficient elevation for the plenteous growth of deodar, but one forest exists under Damuni Peak, the summit of which is 8500 feet. The best of the timber was felled some years ago by the Raja, and was taken four miles down to the river, which is 4000 feet lower than the forest. The principal nullahs in Suket are the Kotlu, the Pangna, and the Bros; the fall of these is great, and the available supply of timber appears to be inconsiderable.

After passing Suket, the Sutlej winds through Course in the outer hills. several small independent states, viz., Mangal, Kailur,

* *Vide* M.S. report (1854) and lithographed map, 1858.

Nalagurh, and Nadaon; and below Bilaspur makes a sharp returning bend round the outer range of hills, before it emerges on the plains at Rupar;* the distance is one hundred miles, and the fall 500 feet, or five feet per mile. In none of these states are forests of deodar, or other valuable trees, except chil, which grows luxuriantly on the northern slopes; in accessible positions this pine has also become scarce, but in the more secluded parts, forests still remain. Sissoo, kakkar, mulberry, and toon are available in small quantity.

Patiala.

The Raja of Patiala keeps up a small establishment for the protection of the trees in his hill possessions. There are scarcely any trees on the outer face; tall grasses and bushes † are the prevailing feature of the lower slopes of the Nalaghur valley, and the approach to Rupar, the head of the proposed Sutlej Canal.

Rupar depôt.

A small wood depôt now exists at Rupar; the enlargement of this, and the systematic issue of wood under regulations, above the point where the water is led off to Patiala, will be a great advantage to the Railway Company, the Canal Officers, the Arsenal at Ferozepore, and the inhabitants of the Jullundur and Umballa divisions.

Lower Sutlej.

A line of levels taken between the Jumna and the Sutlej, by Col. W. E. Baker, will be found in the *Jour. As. Soc., Beng.*, ix., 688. A full account of the lower river from Rupar to Mithenkote, by Col. Mackeson, is contained in the *Jour. As. Soc., Beng.*, vi. 169, and some interesting botanical observations are recorded in the Journals of Travels by Mr. W. Griffith p. 315.

* The bed of the river at Rampur is 3,300 feet; at Bilaspur, 1,500 feet; and at Rupar under 1000 feet above the sea.

† *Adhatoda vasica* and *carissa* are the most common below. *Prinsepia utilis* and *euphorbia pentagona* at 4,000 feet.

PRINCIPAL PLANTS

OF THE

SUTLEJ VALLEY,* WITH NATIVE NAMES AND APPROXIMATE ELEVATION.

TREES.

Hill Name.	Botanical Name.	English.	Elevation.	Remarks.
Kelu,	*Cedrus deodara,*	Deodar or Him. Cedar,	6000-8000.	Properly *dewa-daru,* god-timber, probably identical with the cedar of Lebanon.
Kail,	*Pinus excelsa,*	Lofty pine,	7000-11,000,	
Chîl or Sulla,	*Pinus longifolia,*	Fir, long leaved,	1500-7000,	The resin is used as a dressing for sores.
Neoza,	*Pinus gerardiana,*	Edible pine,	5000-10,500,	Wood not used.
Rai,	*Abies smithiana,*	Him. Spruce,	9000-11,000,	The wood of these is much inferior to the other pines.
Pindrow or Tos,	*Picea webbiana,*	Webbian pine or Silver Fir,	8000-11,000,	
Deodar,	*Cupressus torulosa,*	Cypress,	6000-8000,	Wood useful, but trees scarce, not felled.
Lewar or Shur,	*Juniperus excelsa,*	Pencil Cedar,	9000-12,000,	Yields an excellent, light odoriferous wood.
Pama or Talu,	*Juniperus squamosa,*	Creeping juniper,	12,000-13,000	Used as firewood in crossing the high passes.
Tuna,	*Taxus baccata,*	Yew,	9000-10,500,	Wood used for bows and jampan poles.
Paprung or Shamshad,	*Buxus sempervirens,*	Box,	6000,	Wood used for plugs of rifle bullets, also for wood engraving.
Bán,	*Quercus incana,*	Hoary oak,	5000-8000,	The principal firewood in the hill stations.
Bré,	*Quercus ilex,*	Evergreen oak,	8000,	

* This list is a tolerably complete summary of the useful plants found between Rampur and Sungnam.

Hill Name.	Botanical Name.	English.	Elevation.	Remarks.
Mohru,	*Q. dilatata,*		6000-9000,	Yields an excellent heavy wood.
Kursoo,	*Q. semicarpifolia*	Alpine oak,	9000-12,000,	A magnificent tree, timber much esteemed by the natives.
	Q. floribunda,		9000,	
Paharee Peepul,	*Populus ciliata,*	Poplar,	6000,	Wood soft, coma of seeds, a paper stuff.
	———*alba,*	White poplar,		
Akrot,	*Juglans regia,*	Walnut,	7000-9000,	Wood used for gun stocks and furniture.
Kunch,	*Alnus obtusifolia,*	Alder,	4000-5000,	The charcoal employed in iron smelting.
Knor,	*Pavia indica,*	Him. horse-chestnut,	5000-8000,	Seeds eaten in time of scarcity.
Bras,	*Rhododendron arboreum,*	Rhododendron,	6700-8000,	Flowers made into jelly, subacid.
Bhoj-putra,	*Betula bhoj-putra*	Birch,	10,000-13,000,	Bark used for writing on, and covering umbrellas.
Bankimu,	*Corylus lacera,*	Hazel,	8000,	Wood light, compact.
	Acer lævigatum,	Polished maple,	9000,	The knots are hollowed out, and used as drinking cups.
Kow or Wee,	*Olea ferruginea,*	Olive,*	3500-5000,	Wood used for combs, it is much like box.
Cham Khuruk,	*Carpinus viminea,*	Hornbeam,	5500,	Wood esteemed by carpenters.
Eliyun or Ayar,	*Andromeda ovalifolia,*	Andromeda,	7000,	Wood used for charcoal.
Rous,	*Cotoneaster bacillaris,*	Him. mountain ash,	8000-10,000,	Wood used for walking sticks.
Thurnel,	*Benthamia fragifera,*		6000,	The fruit used as a preserve.
Behul,	*Grewia oppositifolia,*		5000,	The branches are periodically cut in winter time as provender for the cattle.
Dhamnoo,	*Grewia elastica,*		4000,	
Toong,	*Rhus parviflora,*	Sumach,	5000,	Wood hard, yellow.
Kakkar,	*Rhus acuminata,*		5000,	Wood prized for furniture.
Titri,	*Rhus semialata,*			
Tuna,	*Cedrela toona,*	Common toon,	6000,	Much used for furniture.
Kagshi,	*Cornus macrophylla,*	Dogwood,	7000,	Charcoal, employed in the manufacture of gunpowder.
	Fraxinus xanthoxyloides,	Crab ash,	7000,	Makes good walking sticks, hefts, and handles.
Gengaru,	*Cratægus crenulata,*	White thorn,	3000-7000,	Used for staves, &c.

* This resembles closely the European olive.

Hill Name.	Botanical Name.	English.	Elevation.	Remarks.
		FRUITS.*		
Juldaru,	*Armeniaca vulgaris,*	Apricot,	7000-13,000,	The apricot does not ripen above Shalkar (J. D. Cunningham), it occurs up to 13,000. It is a common article of food, and a source of wealth.
Aru,	*Amygdalus persica,*	Peach,		It has little flavor
Jamuna,	*Cerasus cornuta,*	Bird Cherry,	7000-10,000,	Simla.
Paddam,	*Cerasus puddum,*	Cherry,	3000-7000,	
Palu,	*Pyrus malus,*	Apple,		The apples in Kunawar want flavor compared with those in Kashmir.
Mehul,	—— *variolosa,*	Wild pear,	3000-7000,	When rotten, the fruit becomes sweet.
Trummel,	*Ficus macrophylla,*	Wild fig,	5000,	Sold in bazar, Simla, flavor pleasant.
Akrot,	*Juglans regia,*	Walnut,	7000-9000,	This fruit ripens well at Pangi, but not much higher.
	Ribes nubicola, *R. glaciale,* }	Currant,	11,000,	Several varieties occur, but the fruit without flavor.
	R. grossularia,	Gooseberry,†	10,000,	Asrung valley.
Ungoor,	*Vitis vinifera,*	Vine,	7000-9000,	The grape is an uncertain crop, and this year (1862), the excess of rain was particularly unfavourable.
Ré or Neoza,	*Pinus gerardiana,*	Edible pine,	7000-10,000,	The neoza or chilgoza pine, is first seen on the Miru ridge, and above Chini becomes a principal tree of the forest. The seeds are collected and stored for winter use, being a regular article of food—the price asked in spring was two annas per seer.
Fenduk,	*Corylus lacera,*	Hazel,	8000,	The nuts are sold in Simla.
Kaiphul,	*Myrica sapida,*	Box myrtle,	4000-6000,	Fruit used for making sherbet.
Unsri,	*Rubus flavus,*	Bramble,	5000-7000,	Fruit used for preserves.
	Fragaria vesca,	Strawberry,	7000,	Common, but produces a small tasteless fruit.
Toothree,	*Morus parvifolia,*	Mulberry,	4000-7000,	Cultivated, foliage prized for cattle.
		‡ **GRAINS.**		
Kunuk, or Gehun,	*Triticum sativum* (two varieties),	Wheat, (red & white),	13,000, Highest limit, 15,000,	The bearded and awnless wheat occur; *kunuk* denotes the flour, not the grain.

* The *plantain* is last seen below Kotgurh, and the *mango* near Rampur.
† This appears to be identical with *R. Himalense,* Royle, fig. in Jacq., ic. t. 77.
‡ Rice is not observed above 6000 ft.

Hill Name.	Botanical Name.	English.	Elevation.	Remarks.
Ujou,	*Hordeum cæleste,*	Barley,	Highest limit, 15,000,	The beardless variety is most esteemed. Barley ripens in the end of May, several weeks before wheat.
Jou,	——*hexastichon,*	Common barley,		Much cultivated.
China,	*Panicum miliaceum,*	Millet,	6000-9000,	In the middle regions it is one of the chief crops.
Kora or Koda,	*Paspalum scrobiculatum,*			This is an inferior grain, only used by the poorest classes.
Jungeru,	*Pencillaria spicata,*	Spiked millet,	5000,	Confined to the lower valleys.
Ogal,	*Fagopyrum emarginatum,*	Buckwheat,	13,000,	At high elevations, these are cultivated to a great extent.
Paphra,	*Fagopyrum esculentum,*	Buckwheat,	13,000,	
Mundwa,	*Eleusine coracana,*	Ragi,	5000,	Perhaps the most productive of all Indian cereals.
Bathu,	*Amaranthus frumentaceus,*	Amaranth,	7000,	This food plant is cultivated on the Neilgherries.
Jowar,	*Sorghum vulgare,*	Great millet.	6000,	Grown only in the valleys.
Bhatwa,	*Chenopodium*——	Goosefoot,	7000,	Entirely a rain crop, grows to six feet high, seeds considered nourishing.

PULSES.

Hill Name.	Botanical Name.	English.	Elevation.	Remarks.
Masúri,	*Ervum hirsutum,*	Lentil,	5000,	In corn fields.
Mash,	*Phaseolus radiatus,*	Black pea,	6000,	The seeds are both black and green.
Urud,	*Phaseolus max,*	Black gram,	6000,	
Batana,	*Pisum sativum,*	Field pea,	8000-14,000,	Cultivated in Kunawar and Spiti.
Bakla,	*Faba valgaris,*	Common bean,	8000-14,000,	
Bhut,	*Soja hispida,*	Soy bean,	6000,	I also saw one patch of this kind of pulse.

ECONOMIC PLANTS.

Hill Name.	Botanical Name.	English.	Elevation.	Remarks.
Bhang,	*Cannabis indica,*	Indian hemp,	3000-7000,	Yields *churrus* and Himalayan hemp.
Atees,	*Aconitum heterophyllum,*	Atees plant,	8000-13,000,	The roots are much employed as a tonic and febrifuge.

Hill Name.	Botanical Name.	English.	Elevation.	Remarks.
Tilia kac-hang,	*A. napellus*,	Wolfsbane,	10,000-15,000,	The roots are used for destroying wild animals.
Moura bikh,	*A. ferox*,	Poisonous aconite,	10,000-14,000,	
Burmot,	*Thalictrum foliolosum*,	Meadow rue,	5000-8000,	Root used as a febrifuge.
Kurrooa,	*Picrorhiza kurrooa*,	Bitter root,	11,000,	Ditto. Exported to the plains.
Chumresh or Simbur,	*Rhododendron campanulatum*,	Alpine rhododendron	10,000-14,000,	Leaves used as snuff, known as *kasmiri* puttay.
Talsur,	*R. lepidotum*,		10,000-14,000,	Leaves highly stimulant.
Kanta,	*Meconopsis aculeata*,	Prickly poppy,	10,000-12,000,	Flowers blue-purple, showy.
Jeku,	*Daphne papyracea*	Paper shrub,	5000-8000,	Paper prepared from the bark.
Koo,	*Celtis eriocarpa*,	Nettle tree,	6000,	Bark used for making shoes.
Soorch,	*Hippophae salicifolia*,	Buckthorn,	10,000,	Berries form a good preserve mixed with sugar.
Lodh,	*Symplocos paniculata*,	Symplocos,	7000-9000,	Used in dyeing with madder.
Bhekul,	*Prinsepia utilis*,	Prinsepia,	4000-8000,	Used for hedges, yields an oil.
Moorub,	*Desmodium.*		7000,	Bark is used as a paper stuff.
	Rumex acetosa,	Sorrell,	6000-8000,	Widely distributed.
	Oxyria reniformis	Mountain sorrel,	6000-8000,	Used as a native remedy.
Kafi,	*Chaptalia gossypina*,	Shepherd's tinder,	7000-9000,	The tomentum on the under surface of the leaves is employed by the hill people as tinder.
Kusbul,	*Aplotaxis fastuosa*,			
	Tanacetum tenuifolium,	Tansy,	10,000,	Odour pleasant, useful for flavoring puddings.
Karonda,	*Carissa edulis*,		3000-5000,	Fruit made into jelly.
Gehai,	*Eleagnus conferta*,	Oleaster,		Fruit edible, acidulous.
Nepari,	*Delphinium brunonianum*,	Musk plant,	14,000,	Smells powerfully of musk.
Chitra,	*Berberis lycium*,	Berberry,	3000-9000,	The extract "Rasut," is prepared from the root and a yellow dye.
	B. aristata,		6000-10,000,	
	Indigofera pulchella,	Wild indigo,	7000,	Rocky hills, abundant.

Hill Name.	Botanical Name	English.	Elevation.	Remarks.
	Capparis obovata,	Caper,	3000-5000,	Fruit pickled.
Nigala,	*Arundinaria utilis,*	Hill bamboo,	9000,	Used for wicker work, and for lining the roof of houses.
Bichu,	*Urtica heterophylla,*	Neilgherry nettle,	4000-7000,	Yields a valuable fibre.
Puya,	*Bohineria nivea,*	Rheea,	4000-6000,	Furnishes a textile fibre of great value.
Siharu,	*B. salicifolia,*		6000,	Used for making ropes.
Kurroo,	*Gentiana kurroo, Kashmirica, G.*	Him. gentian,	10,000,	Near the eternal snows.
Cherayita,	{ *Ophelia paniculata, O. purpurascens, O. speciosa,* }	Chiretta,	7000-9000,	These annual plants supply the chief portion of the bitter root, exported to the plains.
Piperi.	*Tulipa stellata,*	Tulip,	4000-6000,	Bulbs edible.
	Leontodon taraxacum,	Dandelion,	6000-10,000,	Yields the officinal extract.
Raee,	*Sinapis glauca,*	Mustard,	Up to 11,000,	Much cultivated. Several species of *sinapis* are grown as salads and condiments.
Jira,	*Cuminum cyminum,*	Cumin of Scripture,	7000-9000,	Abundant in pasture, seed, exported to the plains.

NOTE.—An admirable description of the configuration of the hills, and of the botanical features of the valley of the Sutlej, is contained in Thomson's Travels in the Western Himalaya. In determining the native names of the plants of Bussahir, much assistance may be derived from consulting the copious index of Royle's Illustrations of the Botany of the Himalaya, and Jameson's Report of the Botanical Gardens, North West Provinces, 1855.

This list of plants may be found useful by visitors to Kunawar, and by the Engineers of the Hindostan and Thibet road, who have many opportunities of making additions and corrections.

THE BEAS RIVER.

THE Beas* takes its name from a sacred pool at its source, called "Vyas Rikhi," situated in the Rotang pass, at the head of the Kûllû valley, the elevation of which is 13,000 feet above the level of the sea. This river is well known from the writings of Moorcroft (Travels i. 190), Gerard, and A. Cunningham; (*Jour. As. Soc., Beng.*, x. 1.) for seventy-five miles it flows southwards, through the British province of Kûllû, then bends towards Mandi, and debouches from the hills at Mirthal, after a winding westerly course of one hundred and twenty-five miles.

Journey from Lahûl to Kûllû.

In August 1862, Mr. J. D. Smithe, C.E., and I crossed the Rotang Ghat from Lahûl. We separated at Sultanpur, when I travelled along the bank of the river to Larji, noting the forest resources of the valley and the different tributaries which flow into the Beas; the following is an abstract of the information then gathered.

Rotang Pass.

August 27th.—Passing over the Chandra river by the Koksur bridge on the 26th, we crossed the Rotang, and descended to the head of the river Beas, leaving the ruins of Lena Sing's Dharmsalla (elevation 10,500 feet) *en route*. The road is an irregular flight of stone steps, nearly four miles in length. The descent was slippery and very fatiguing. These

* The Beas is considered to be identical with the Hyphasis of Arrian, the Greek name being a corruption of Vipasa, the Sanskrit.

steps interfere very much with the progress of laden animals, and are a serious inconvenience to the traffic along this important line of communication.

Contrast in Scenery.

In crossing the Mid-Himalayan range, the change from the treeless mountains of Lahûl to the well wooded slopes of Kûllû is very striking. In the valley of Chandra, for five or six miles there is not a bush to be seen, but on crossing the Rotang, we at once return to a land of trees. The higher slopes are clothed with birch, alpine oak, and four species of the pine tribe. In the valley below, the tree vegetation consists of deodar, alder, elm, and poplar, besides orchards of fruit trees around the numerous villages.

Scenery of Beas valley.

The scenery of the Beas valley is particularly beautiful, and differs from that of the Sutlej and Chenab. The river terraces are wider and more verdant, and the mountain slopes present fewer scarps and precipitous rocks. The river is fringed with trees, and studded with green islands. There is a good riding path close along the bank, which does not exist upon any other river in the Punjab Himalaya.

Tributaries in Kûllû.

Nine notable tributaries join theBeas in Kûllû, these are—

1. *Sarahi*, unfordable and spanned by a wooden bridge, three miles from Burwa.
2. *Manóli*, a very considerable stream.
3. *Raini*, rises in Spiti, rapid and impracticable for transport.
4. *Phari*, or *Pharini*, spanned by a wooden bridge, 60 feet long.

NOTE—Kûllû proper contains not less than 24,000 sq. miles, and includes the upper valley of the Beas from its source till it enters the native state of Mundi. Its southern limits rest on the river Sutlej. (*Barnes' Settlement Report*).

5. *Doangnu*, a mountain torrent, which rushes over large rocks.

6. *Parbati*, this tributary has a course of fifty miles and is nearly as large as the Beas. Deodar logs have been floated down, and Major Longden made a special inspection of its banks. The hot springs* at Manikarn is much frequented by pilgrims. West of this, near the village of Choji, the Parbati is much obstructed by massive rocks, and logs can only pass when the river is in flood; lower down the bed is clear and the stream increases rapidly in size, as it flows towards the Beas.

7. *Sirbiri*, a considerable feeder, which rises in the mountains of Bara Banghal. There is a small amount of Deodar near the village of Luma five miles from the junction at Sultanpur. Timber can only come down in full flood. Kail and tos are abundant in the valley of the Sirbiri.

8. *Bijoura*, this stream divides Mandi from Kûllû and irrigates several tea plantations.

9. *Goput* or *Gomati*, joining on the left bank is small and ill adapted for transporting timber, which can only come down during a flood, in this respect all the streams in Kûllû are alike.

Deodar forest in Kûllû.

The deodar forests in Kûllû are of limited extent, compared with those of Chamba and Bussahir, and the average size of the trees is smaller (4 to 8 feet) in girth. The tree occurs in various parts of the district, but is nowhere abundant. The only locality where there is a considerable forest, is in the higher part of the valley above Jagatsukh, between Manôli and Burwa, at an elevation of 7000 feet.

Mr. Barnes' valuation.

The late Mr. Barnes, when Deputy Commissoner

* Mr. Smithe noted the temperature at 203°, and in Major Longden's diary it is entered at 201°.

(March 20th, 1851,) stated his opinion that more than five thousand rupees worth per annum could not be supplied from Kûllû. Timber is now rising in value, and during Major Longden's explorations some patches of Deodar were discovered on the Parbati. Mr. Barnes' estimate may therefore be considered as much under the prospective annual return from these forests.

Manôli forest.

This forest extends in a narrow strip four miles in length, for the most part on the right bank of the Beas.* There are patches and groves lower down on both sides at some height above the river, but there are not in the aggregate perhaps ten thousand mature trees in the valley. A considerable quantity of dead and fallen timber is scattered through the forest.

Previous felling.

In 1848, Mr. Ter Arratoon felled some fine trees. Subequently, Wazir Goshain of Mandi and three other native merchants, felled a considerable number; in proof of this several hundred large stumps† remain in the Burwa plain. Few native merchants have applied for permission to fell of late years, it is doubtful whether they found the speculation so remunerative as they expected. Many of the remaining trees are undersized and are not worth five rupees per tree, (the required seignorage,) according to the present market value of timber.

Suitable for conservancy.

The trees in the Manôli forest chiefly grow close to the edge of the river, down which it is practicable

* Major Longden (1852) estimated the number of trees above three feet in girth in the Manoli forest at 4000; the finest clump being on the right bank round the temple (Horma) containing 1500 trees, 8 to 10 feet in girth.

† At Burwa in 1839, there was "a forest of noble cedars," (*A. Cunningham, in Jour. As. Soc.,*) the girth of many of the stumps (1862) was fully eight feet, and on counting the rings, the average age was ascertained to be 70 years The stumps *very frequently* give off perpendicular shoots or horizontal ones which become perpendicular, forming an elbow. This *remarkable fact* of a coniferous tree being reproduced from the stump has also been observed by Dr. Brandis in the Deodar forests, between the Tonse and Jumna.

(though somewhat difficult), to float timber, and under all the circumstances, this tract should be reserved for Government purposes. It possesses *three special* advantanges, being (1) easy of access, (2) convenient for supervision (near the Asst. Commissioner's Head Quarters at Nuggur), and (3) within British territory. The timber could be launched into the Beas without much breakage (always a heavy per centage) owing to the bank of the river at this point being low.

The breadth of the Parbati is about one hundred feet, and the body of the water at the confluence is nearly as large as the Beas. Major Longden inspected the valley in 1852, and found some patches of deodar, chiefly at Jerri and Uchich, (*vide* accompanying sketch map,) these were convenient to the stream, and had been partly felled. This forest, though limited, appeared to him suitable for conservancy, and generally to resemble the Manôli forest. Official correspondence shows that three hundred and fifty deodar logs were made over by Wazir Goshain to the late Mr. Minas on the Parbati, near Jerri; one of these was twenty three feet in length, proving what the forests produced fifteen years ago, and also the capability of the stream for transport. (Estimate of cost, *vide* p. 78).

Parbati forests.

It is of great moment to reserve specially these Government forests on the Beas, which will always be within control, and which (Manôli and Parbati) under good management, will yield a perpetual supply of good timber.

Importance of reserving them.

In the valley of the upper Beas, above Sultanpur, there is abundance of kail (the dhar-chil of Chamba), elm, maple, oak, (two species,) and walnut. On the Parbati, not far from the sacred hot spring of Mani

Useful woods in Kûllu.

Karan, there is a considerable supply of box,* (*buxus sempervirens*) "shamshad;" of the *cupressus torulosa* (twisted cypress,) and of the olive (kahû). A large forest of chil, *pinus longifolia* is found below Karsole on the Parbati.

Tributaries in Suraj. At Larji, the Beas is joined by two large tributaries, the Sainj and the Tirthan. The Sainj is the larger and runs a course of fifty miles; the valley was explored by Major Longden, who found little deodar. The Plach Tahsildar informed me that kail, chil, and deodar in small quantity come down this torrent. I proceeded along the bank of the Tirthan, from Bedath to Larji, and saw a few small deodar logs, but could not learn that the Suraj forests had ever been worked, either on the Tirthan river or on the Kunden stream, which flows into it. There is no deodar forest, but a few clumps occur here and there, generally around temples (deotas). In the higher slopes, there are dense forests of the less valuable pines and of the alpine oak, *quercus semicarpifolia*.

Roads in Kûllû. With the exception of the Rotang pass now under repair, the state of the roads and bridges in Kûllû is very commendable, and presents a great contrast to the condition of the communications in the adjoining Hill states, Chamba, Chota Lahûl, and Bussahir.

Tributaries in Mandi. The Ul, a large tributary of the Beas, rises in the Dhaola Dhar, where it separates Chota and Bara Banghal. It is formed by the combined streams Barlagur and Andalagur. On the former are forests

* The Agricultural and Horticultural Society of India awarded a prize to Captain W. Hay, for bringing to notice the box tree of this valley, which is larger and more abundant than in other parts of the Himalaya (*Jour. A. H. Soc.*, xi. 413. 1859). Two hundred short seasoned logs are now available at the Sultanpur Tahseel. The largest of these are six feet long and twenty two inches in girth.

of birch, alpine oak, tos, and rai; on the latter, the same trees with deodar interspersed. Major Longden mentions the existence of a small forest in Chota Banghal, near the village of Tramar or Tramahar, the site of which appeared suitable for the growth of deodar. At favorable seasons, the Ul river contains a sufficient body of water for timber transport. After running a course of seventy miles and receiving the water of the Utrsal, it falls into the Beas near Mandi. A good view of the course of the Ul is obtained from the Goghur-dhar near Futikal, the watershed between the Ul and the Beas. Iron deposits in this district are worked by the natives to a considerable extent.

The Sukhet river rises in the Sikander Dhar, and, flowing north for thirty miles, discharges its waters into the Beas. There is a small tract of deodar near its source, which is being felled by the Raja (1863). Sukhet.

This British taluqa contains a few kelûs south of Thamser Joth, near the junction of the two main feeders of the Ul, and along both banks of the Andalagur, where the stream is small and obstructed by large boulders. Chota Banghal.

This isolated pergunnah, which is British territory, contains some deodar forests; these were opportunely discovered by Major Longden in 1853, after Wazir Goshain of Mandi had been cutting surreptitiously. So far as I can learn, no felling has since been permitted, and the wooded tracts near the source of the Ravi have partially recovered. The forest is difficult of access to the Ravi on one side, and separated from the Beas by the snowy range on the other. Bara Banghal.

Five large tributaries, rising in the Dhaola Dhar take a southern course; these are fed entirely by rain and melted snow, and are much encumbered in the Tributaries in Kangra valley.

upper parts with huge boulders; they join the Beas in the following order.

1. *Binwa*, runs a course of forty miles, passing Bijnath and falls into the Beas near Tira. Chil and kail timber are brought down this stream in small quantities.

2. *Nigwal* or *Nagawal*, rises further west, and flows parallel to the Binwa through the beautiful pergunnah of Palam, joining the Beas at Sujanpoor-Tira, noted for its manufacture of fire-arms.

3. The *Bangunga* passes under Kangra fort, and winds through the pergunnah of Katôch. This river affords great facilities for transporting useful timbers from the Burgiraon forest. Chil, oak, and bamboos are procurable, but there is no deodar.

4. The *Gaj*, rising near Rihlû, is a large feeder and meets the Beas after a course of sixty miles. Chil, bamboos, &c., are taken down from the Haripûr Talook.

5. The *Chakki*, rises near the Chuari pass, and is the longest of the northern tributaries (seventy miles). In some places, this stream is 2000 feet broad, when in flood. Chil from the banks of the head feeders can be brought down in the freshes, which rise 13 or 14 feet, and occasionally alter the channel.

Tributaries from the South.

The tributaries from the South are two, the Man and the Kunihar, these join the Beas near Nadaon, and during the rains are employed for transporting Chil timber to the plains.

Hoshiarpur Chil forests.

On the second range of hills there are two Chil forests known as Punjal and Lohara, these are supervised by native watchmen, and yield a small annual revenue. The applications for wood are chiefly from merchants of Amritsir who pay 5 Rupees

NOTE.—These chil forests and bamboo jungles should be marked off as Government demains, and worked under a regular system.

seignorage per tree and float the logs down the Beas from Dehra.

In the Sewalik range of hills, there are two Bamboo Jungles, called Bindraban and Karrampure, in 1859 these were placed under conservation by Col. Lake. One is worked while the other is closed for four consecutive years. Printed passes are furnished at the tehseel, stating whether the bamboos are required to go by land or by water. The price of the best description is three rupees per hundred, and eight annas is the charge for cutting them. Bamboo Jungle.

The chief tributaries, and their general capabilities for supplying timber having been noticed, the following table containing most of the trees in Kûllû and Kangra, will show the great variety of useful and ornamental woods which may be procured in these districts.

I.—Statement showing the Forest Revenue in Kangra including Kûllû.

Year.	Forest Income.			Cost of Establishment.		
	R.	A.	P.	R.	A.	P.
1858-59,	4,538	6	9	84	0	0
1859-60,	6,026	0	11	84	0	0
1860-61,	5,276	6	1	1,128	0	0
1861-62,	6,152	2	4	2,280	0	0
1862-63,	7,012	1	1	2,580	0	0

Philip Egerton,
Dy. Commissioner.

Note.—The Forest Establishment at present consists of

1 Moonshee, ...	Rs. 20
4 Head Rangers at Rs. 25, . .	100
1 Ranger, ...	15
1 „	10
11 „	70
Total,	215

215 × 12 = 2580 *per annum.*

The kinds of wood sold, were:—

Chil and oak, .	4,949
Bamboos, . .	69,980
Decayed trees, .	1,674

II.—Statement shewing the Forest Revenue in the District of Hoshiarpur.

Year.	Forest Revenue.			Credited to Government.			Credited to Forest Fund.			Paid to owner of land, and others.			Cost of Establishment.			Miscellaneous Expenditure.		
1858-59,	6166	13	10	5924	3	0	..	..	..	177	10	10	65	0	0	..	..	..
1859-60,	8124	10	8	7504	14	0	..	..	..	331	12	8	288	0	0	..	..	..
1860-61,	5550	7	9	5060	11	7	..	..	..	201	12	2	288	0	0	..	..	..
1861 62,	6586	8	8	438	9	5	5237	1	1	617	11	2	288	0	0	5	..	0
1862-63,	8452	2	6	799	9	8	5864	1	0	738	9	7	348	0	0	701	14	3
Total,	34,880	11	5	19,727	15	8	11,101	2	1	2,067	11	5	1,277	0	0	706	14	3

R. YOUNG, *Dy. Commissioner.*

NOTE.—The Establishment consists of seven forest rangers on salaries from 4 to 5 Rs. = 29 × 12 = 348 Rs. per annum.

The proceeds of 1862-63, were derived from the chil forests and bamboo jungle, in the following proportions :—

Chil,	. .	Rs. 2,242	7	4
Bamboo,	. .	6,209	11	2
		8,452	2	6

In the Kangra district four species of bamboo occur :—

1. *Bans*, the hollow bamboo of the plains. — *Bambusa arundinacea.*
2. *Bur*, solid bamboo of the lower hills, of which spear handles and clubs are usually made. — ——— *stricta.*
3. The *Nirgali*, or small bamboo of the hills, growing at elevations from 5 to 8000 feet. — *Arundinaria utilis.*
4. The *Garroo*, or still smaller hill bamboo, growing at higher elevations, probably up to 12,000 feet. — ——— *falcata.*

III.—Estimate of Felling and Transporting 100 Deodar trees from Kûllû to the Plains.

A native of Sultanpore previously engaged in timber trade estimated the cost of felling 100 deodar trees on the Parbati, and delivering 200 logs at Nadaon, as follows :—

	Rs.
24 Wood-cutters at 4 As., for 8 days, .	50
100 Coolies at 4 As., for 12 days, launching logs,	300
20 Taroos for 5 months, at 5 As., . . .	500
Catching at Nadaon, ...	100
	950
Add for sundry contingencies, ...	150
	1,100

Supposing the average size of the logs to be 35 cubic feet, this would give Rs. 15-11, as the cost of bringing down 100 cub. feet.

USEFUL TREES AND SHRUBS OF KULLU AND KANGRA.

	Hill Name.	Botanical Name.	English Name.	Remarks.
Conifers.	Kelu	*Cedrus deodara,*	Deodar or Him. cedar.	Grows on north slope of Dhaola Dhar, and in Kullu.
	Kail,	*Pinus excelsa,*	Lofty pine.	In Kullu not in Kangra.
	Chil or Chir,	*P. — longifolia,*	Long leaved pine.	Grows luxuriantly on north slopes, timber best at 4-5000 feet.
	Neoza,	*P. — gerardiana,*	Gerard's or edible pine.	A few trees across the Dhaola Dhar, near Ulassa on the Ravi.
	Tôs,	*Picea webbiana,*	Webb's pine or silver fir.	The wood is not much valued, shingles are laid on the roof of houses. The rai is often 100 ft. high, and 5 ft. in diameter.
	Rai,	*Abies smithiana,*	Him. spruce.	
	Deodara,	*Cupressus torulosa,*	Twisted cypress.	At the head of the Parbati (Longden).
	Bramhi or Rakhal,	*Taxus baccata,*	Common yew.	In Kullu, very scarce.
	Leuri or Suri,	*Juniperus excelsa,*	Pencil cedar.	On the crest of Dhaola Dhar and in Lahûl.
Oaks.	Bahn,	*Quercus incana,*	Common Him. oak.	The English residents at Dhurmsala use this timber for beams and rafters.
	Mohrû,	*Q. —— dilatata,*		
	Kharsû,	*Q. —— semicarpifolia,*	Apin o oak,	Seldom grows below 8000 feet, and ascends above the range of pines.
	Baloot,	*Q. —— ilex,*	Evergreen oak.	Very rare, becomes common at Marri and in the Trans-Indus Hills.
	Chinar,	*Platanus orientalis,*	Oriental plane.	Of giant size and great beauty in Chamba.
	Mandal,	*Acer caudatum,*	Maple.	Wood not esteemed by natives.
	Maral,	*Ulmus campestris,*	Small leaved elm.	Many fine trees of the *murali* or *mehun* in the upper parts of Kullu, 30 ft. in girth, wood esteemed, but not the *himburch*.
	Himbureh,	*U. — erosa.*	Large leaved do.	
	Akhrôt,	*Juglans regia,*	Walnut.	Most valuable for the fruit as well as the wood, which from old trees is dark-colored & handsome.

Hill Name.	Botanical Name.	English Name.	Remarks.
Goonh, Knór, or Jooah,	*Pavia indica*,	Indian horse-chestnut.	A pieturesque tree, wood sometimes used for furniture, very abundant in Kullu, at 6 to 8000 ft.
Dimri,	*Cedrela serrata*,	Hill toon.	Recognized by its long racemes of flowers.
Kunch or Koish	*Alnus nepalensis*.	Him. alder.	Bark used in tanning, wood for gunpowder charcoal.
Bhurj or bhoja-putra,	*Betula bhoj putra*,	Paper birch.	Sanscrit name of the delicate bark used as paper, for covering umbrellas and lining hookahs, &c.
Jhanji,	*Corylus colurna*,	Hazel.	A good sized tree, called *sharoli* on the Parbati.
Shamshad,	*Buxus sempervirens*,	Box tree.	Abundant near Manikaran, wood in demand for engraving, and plugs of rifle balls.
Kanoch, or Tum,	*Fraxinus xanthoxyloides*,	Crab ash.	Very small, occasionally jampan poles are made of it.
Sannan,	——— *floribunda*,	Large ash.	This was introduced by Mr. Macleod from Pangi to Dharmsalla. In toughness resembles English ash.
Halêo,	*Cornus macrophylla*,	Dogwood.	
Rirhi,	*Viburnum*,	Elder.	There are several species.
Kurun or Tut,	*Morus parvifolia*,	Mulberry.	Wood highly esteemed.
Karrak,	*Celtis orientalis*,	Nettle tree.	Planted in avenues, Kûllû.
Kahû,	*Olea cuspidata*,	Olive tree.	Valley of Parbati; varies much in the shape of its leaves, and appears to be *O. Europea*.
Ekulbîr,	*Datisca cannabina*,		Root exported to Amritsir as a dye-stuff.
Ringal or Nigala,	*Arundinaria utilis*,	Hill bamboo.	Shepherds' pipes, baskets, and mats are made of it.
Rouns,	*Cotoneaster bacillaris*,	Indian mountain ash.	The *alpenstocks* of travellers are made of this wood.
Eliyun,	*Andromeda ovalifolia*,	Common andromeda.	Leaves injurious to sheep and goats.
Bras,	*Rhododendron arboreum*,	Common rhododendron.	Tree gives posts 6 in. in diameter, wood brown.
	——— *campanulatum*.		
Bré or Kathi,	*Desmodium*,		Bark used for paper-making in the jail at Dharmsalla, the plant is very abundant.

FRUITS AND ESCULENT ROOTS OF KULLU AND KANGRA.

Hill Name.	Botanical Name.	English Name.	Remarks.
Aru,	*Amygdalus persica*,	Peach.	In gardens thrive vigorously and yield fine fruit.
Mundla aru,	——— *var*,	Nectarine.	
Juldaru,	*Armeniaca vulgaris*,	Himalayan apricot,	Fruit a staple produce in Kûllû, and common article of food, they are small and firm-fleshed, so that they dry well.
Aru bokhara,	*Prunus domestica*,	Garden plum,	Several varieties of plum, damson, and greengage are cultivated at Holta plantation. The seeds are freely distributed to all applicants.
Alûcha,	——— *var*,	Himalayan greengage.	

Hill Name.	Botanical Name.	English Name.	Remarks.
Paddam,	*Cerasus puddum,*	Common bird cherry.	Occurs as far as the Indus, a sacred tree among the Hindoos.
Gilas,	——— *var,*	Kashmir cherry.	In gardens.
Aru ballu,	——— *var,*	Kabul cherry	
Jamun,	*Cerasus cornuta,*	Him. bird cherry.	Grows to a large size, wood esteemed.
Seb or Palu,	*Pyrus malus,*	Apple.	The apples want flavour compared with those of Kashmir.
Nas patti,	—— *communis,*	Pear.	
Mehal or Kainth,	—— *variolosa,*	Wild pear.	Yields a valuable wood, brown, hard, fine grained.
Bun-Mehal,	—— *baccata,*	Crab apple,	
Bhee,	*Cydonia vulgaris,*	Quince,	In great abundance at Nuggur, fruit used for preserves.
Mitha-tendû,	*Diospyros tomentosa,*		Two large trees at Jagatsukh bungalow. Fruit edible.
	Eriobotrya japonica.	Loquat.	This Chinese tree gives well developed fruit of good flavor.
	Rubus flavus,	Yellow raspberry.	A very pleasant fruit, Kûlû.
Akhi,	——— *purpurens,*	Him. raspberry.	
	Fragaria vesca,	Strawberry.	Wild strawberries common, but produce little fruit.
	Rheum emodi,	Common rhubarb.	
Chukri,	—— *moorcroftianum,*	Small stalked rhubarb.	The *emodi* is less active as a purgative, and more spongy in texture.
Sural.	*Pueraria tuberosa.*		Tubers exported to the plains.
Darim,	*Punica granatum,*	Pomegranate,	Seeds and rind medicinal.

TREES OF THE LOWER HILLS.

Tun,*	*Cedrela toona,*	Toon tree.	Wood of a red color, esteemed for furniture, very durable.
Champa,	*Michelia champaca,*	Champa tree.	Only known as a cultivated tree.
Sissu, Tali,	*Dalbergia sissu,*	Sissoo tree.	This valuable tree does not thrive so well as in Goojerat and Jhelum.
Sál or Sakhu,†	*Shorea robusta,*	Saul tree.	
Kakur,	*Rhus acuminata.*	Sumach tree,	Both species yield beautiful wood, the native name "*kakur singhi*," is from the long curved excrescences.
Tung,	—— *parviflora.*		
Behera,	*Terminalia belerica,*	Beleric myrobalan tree.	

* The Jaswan Dún was once famous for toon wood, but scarcely a tree is left. I have urged the Zemindars and English settlers to plant it along the banks of water-courses in Kangra Valley.

† There is a small clump of sal trees in the eastern portion of Kangra valley near Sujanpur-Tira; a few also occur near Rajpura in Hoshiarpur, which is the western limit of its growth.

Hill Name.	Botanical Name.	English Name.	Remarks.
Hur,	——*chebula,*	Chebulic myrobalan tree,	Valuable tree, the fruit yields a dye and medicine.
Arjun,	——*glabra,*		Timber used for railway sleepers.
Tendu,	*Diospyros,*	Hill Ebony,	The heart wood is generally small.
Mowah,	*Bassia latifolia,*	Mowah tree,	The seeds yield a fatty oil, and the flower a spirituous liquor.
Tejbul,	*Xanthoxylon hostile,*		The aromatic fruit is used as a condiment.
Dhamûn,	*Grewia elastica,*		Valued for the elasticity of the wood.
Phalsa,	—— *asiatica,*		Yields a pleasant sub-acid fruit.
Behul,	—— *oppositifolia,*		Bark employed for making ropes.
Timbul or Tremul,	*Ficus macrophylla,*	Broad leaved fig,	Fruit edible, sold in the bazars.
Barna,	*Cratœva religiosa,*		
Kunear,	*Cassia fistula,*		Fruit collected for sale.
Kheir,	*Acacia catechu,*	Catechu tree,*	
Sirissa,	——*elata,*	Doon Siriss tree,	Confined to the outer hills, bordering on the plains.
Bér,	*Zizyhus jujuba,*	Bér tree,	Wood used for clogs aud saddle trees.
Jamún,	*Eugenia jambolana,*		A large tree, fruit edible, wood useful.
Kuddum,	*Nauclea cordifolia,*		Wood yellow, decays when exposed to wet.
Kamela,	*Rottlera tinctoria,*		Up to 3000 feet, the dye is sold for 18 rupees per maund.
Nim,	*Azadirachta indica,*	Neem tree,	Planted. Very scarce.
Bél,	*Aegle marmelos,*	Bél tree,	In Kangra valley, fruit collected for medicinal use.
Pahari Erind,	*Jatropha curcas,*	Purging nut,	Along the base of the mountains.
Dhái,	*Grislea tomentosa,*		Flowers employed to dye red.
Khajúr,	*Phœnix sylvestris,*	Wild date,	Bank of Beas above Mandi.
Gundéhra,	*Nerium odorum,*	Oleander,	Root poisonous.
Keor,	*Holarhena antidysenterica,*		Bark an astringent medicine.
Chá,	*Thea viridis,*	Tea plant,	Very extensively cultivated in Kangra valley and Kullu.
Kutchnar,	*Bauhinia variegata,*		
Maloo,	—— *vahlii,*		Leaves used for packing, bark for making rope.
Aonla,	*Emblica officinalis,*		Wood used for framework of wells, fruit preserved as a pickle, bark astringent.

* Major Madden describes the process of manufacturing catechu ("*Kuth,*") in the Turaee, *vide Jour. As. Soc.*, *June* 1848, p. 565. Dr. Hooker also, *vide Him. Journals*, I., p. 52.

At Dharmsalla, there is a station and soldiers' garden, and an *arboretum* belonging to Mr. D. F. Macleod, C. S., well wo thy of a visit, containing many introduced Himalayan trees of great interest. Box, ash, and various conifers as well as many European fruit trees adapted to this hill station; it is perhaps the only collection of indigenous Alpine trees in the Punjab. At Amb, there is an old Mahomedan gard n, containing gigantic specimens of toon, champa, *artocarpus integrifolia, mimusopse lengi, cupressus sempersirens* and *platanus orientalis.* At Holta plantation, there is a large stock of *stillingia sebif ra,* the tallow tree of China, *rhus vernicifera,* the varnish tree of Japan, and other economic plants. Tea culture has flourished even beyond Dr. Jameson's expectations, and has extended beyond Kangra valley into Mandi and Kûllû. The culture seems to be limited only by the amonnt of available land.

The following trees are of frequent occurrence in the Jullundur Doab, in topes and avenues :— Trees of Jullundur Doab.

Acacia arabica, . .	Kikur.	*Morus,* . .	Tut.
—— *sirissa,* . .	Siriss.	*Melia sempervirens,*	Bokhein.
—— *modesta,* . .	Pulahi.	*Cordia latifolia,*	Lessora.
Dalbergia sissoo, . .	Sissoo.	*Salmalia malabarica,*	Simul.
Ehretia loevis, . .	Chumrar or chelah.	*Ficus religiosa,*	Pipul.
		Ficus indica, .	Bur.

The plain of the Jullundur Doab, between the Sutlej and Beas rivers, presents, in the cold weather, a sheet of rich cultivation. Jullundur and Hoshiar-pur are highly ornamented with avenues of trees; but the district generally is scantily wooded. There is no indigenous timber for building purposes. The principal woods used are chil and mango; the former is supplied from certain forests in Hoshiar-pur and Kangra, on application to the tahsildar, and prepayment of seignorage. Bamboos are likewise available in the low hills at three rupees per hundred. Along the slopes of the Dhaôla Dhar, there are considerable forests of chil, ban, elm, horse-chestnut, and walnut. Deodar is brought from the higher hills by the Sutlej and Beas rivers, but the supply is uncertain and very inadequate. Jullundur Doab.

There do not appear to be any special obstacles to the transport of timber on the Beas. The character of the river is very similar to that of the Ravi, but the Upper Beas is certainly more favorable than the Upper Ravi, and the position of the trees at Manôli and on the Parbati, is more convenient than in Barmawar and Bara Bansu. The fall is great, and the logs will require to be guided among the numerous islets which are fringed with alders. These islands arrest the progress of the logs in their passage down the river, but do little injury to them; whereas the rocky masses in the Ravi cause very great damage to Character of Beas. Numerous islands.

wood in its course to the plains. After the month of August much labor is required to move the stranded logs into the water, but, below Bijoura little assistance is needed during floods.

Rafting practicable. At Nadaon, the rafting of timber commences, and as far as Dehra the Beas is well suited for it. Below Dehra* the river divides into several channels, and large rafts cannot easily pass in the cold weather. Below Mirthal these channels re-unite, and rafts proceed without difficulty to the depôt at Hari-ki-ghat, where the Beas joins the Sutlej. The united stream bears the name of Ghara till the confluence with the Chenab.

Fall of river. The whole length of the Beas is 350 miles from its source to its junction with the Sutlej. From Manôli forest to Larji the fall appears to be nearly sixty feet per mile. From Larji to Mandi, a distance of twenty-five miles, the fall is 1000 feet, or forty feet per mile. From Mirthal, a distance of 150 miles, the fall is only 1600 feet, or 10·06 feet per mile. *(Cunningham.)*

Working season. The working season begins earlier, and is more certain than in the Sutlej valley. The Kûllû district is accessible to workmen at all seasons. The river begins to rise in April, and falls towards the end of August, after which large logs are stranded among the islands in the upper portion, or in the shallows below Nadaon. Several hundred logs were lying between Nuggur and Bijoura at the time of my journey. There is an extensive sheet of cultivation in some places between the forests and the river, and care must be taken to

Note by Mr. Smithe. *"I have seen the Beas river for some miles above Dehra, when at its lowest, having gone down on a mussuck raft in the cold weather. Small rafts of three logs each, such as are made on the Chenab, and called 'Jûndas,' can always pass without difficulty, but these would only be used three months of the year, as during nine months much larger rafts can go down, there being ample water for floating them. Rapids and whirlpools are met with as in other rivers, but there are no real difficulties to be overcome."

roll the logs over the fields before sowing or after harvest. Buffaloes could be profitably employed in dragging the logs along certain tracks to the river upon a pair of small wheels, this would save damage to cultivation.

Economic working.

The Kûllû valley being British territory, and the trees growing close to the river, it appears to be a favourable locality for sawing up timber in the forest, by which a great saving of material would be effected.

Railway requirements.

The prospective requirements of the Punjab Railway from the forests of the Beas for 1863 and 1864, are 400,000 cubic feet of timber. The principal deodar forests are those on the Manôli and Parbati streams in Kûllû; these, as already intimated, are of limited extent, and even if all the ripe trees were felled, this large quantity could not be supplied. With diligent search and economic cutting, perhaps one-half as a maximum, may be expected. If creosoted chil *(p. longifolia)* should meet with approval, a large amount may be brought from the Kangra and other hills.

Iron mines.

The spurs of the outer Himalayas contain ferruginous deposits in abundance, and mines are actually worked along the whole range both on the north and south faces, from the Sutlej to the Ravi. The smelting process at Shil and Kot Khai has been alluded to at page 3; and, in connection with the local supply of fuel, the requirements of the iron manufacturers of Kangra and Mandi must be kept in view. Under the Sikh rule, this iron was extensively used for gun barrels, and the importance of these mines induced Sir John Lawrence, K C.B., Chief Commissioner of the Punjab, to appoint (1856) a committee to report upon them. The committee visited twelve mines, and from their report I have abstracted the following information as to the extent of these iron deposits, which is not generally known.

Committee on Iron ores 1856.

The committee consisted of Major Lake, Commissioner of the Trans-Sutlej States; Mr. Marcardieu, Geological Surveyor; Captain Fagan, Artillery; Mr. J. D. Smithe, C.E.; and Mr. J. L. Rickards, C.E. They visited twelve iron mines, two of salt, one of lead, and one of copper.

List of mines.

Name.	Description of Mineral.	Matrix.	Remarks.
In Bir taluqa. Dewal	Magnetic Iron.	Quartz.	Water power abundant, fuel scarce.
Naolitha	Do.	Mica Schist.	Water power abundant, ore plentiful and easily worked, some portions of the valley well clothed with forest.
Dharmani	Do.	Do.	
Khod ki Khad	Do.	Do.	
Mulla	Do.	Do.	
Surmani	Do.	Do.	
Dhewat	Do.	Do.	
Nari			There are furnaces at these places, ore for which is procured from the Dharmani.
Buklay			
Gari			
Manikaran	Do.	Quartz.	Not worked at present.
Gerai	Lead.	Do.	Formerly worked by the Sikhs.
Chall Pujar	Specular Iron.	Do.	Worked on a small scale by the natives.
Dodru	Copper.	Do.	There is a tradition that the mine was worked by the old Rajah of the country.
Futtepur	Magnetic Iron.	Mica Schist.	Worked on a small scale.
Durani	Salt.		Extensively worked.
Kuman	Magnetic Iron.	Mica Schist.	Worked on a small scale.
Guma	Salt.		The Durani and Guma mines together, give a clear income to the Mundi State of Rs. 80,000.
Manuni	Iron.	Decomposed Mica Schist.	Not worked.

Chief seat of manufacture.

"The chief seat of the iron manufacture is at Mandi and Bir in the valley of the Ul. Along the whole of the left bank of that stream iron ore is found in more or less abundance. Dharmani is the centre of a cluster of mines now worked by the natives, and from this point to Naolitha, eight miles above, and to Dewal, six miles below, the mountains are richly charged with ore, and supply many furnaces in the Mandi territory, as well as in the Bir Taluqa. The deposits of iron are more extensive, and that ore is a constituent part of the whole formation."

"In consequence of a slip on the face of the hill, the veins at Dharmani are exposed to a considerable extent, on this account, as well from the circumstance of the schist being particularly soft, the natives chiefly resort to this mine, and carry the ore to villages in the neighbourhood, where no mines have been worked, but where fuel is more abundant."

The Dharmani mine.

The committee in their report further state—

"While the native processes are unsatisfactory in their results, the expenditure of fuel is extravagant. The following details show approximately the number of trees which are annually expended in the manufacture of iron in Bir, by which it will be observed that for the production of one ton of crude iron, some twenty-eight fine trees have to be sacrificed; while, to purify that iron for the market, an expenditure still more considerable must be incurred."

Extravagant expenditure of fuel.

	Maunds.	Tons.
Estimated out turn of iron in Bir, per annum, ...	2,800	100
Charcoal expended for this amount of iron, ...	5,600	200
Weight of wood required for this amount of charcoal, ...	28,000	1,000

Estimate of wood and fuel consumed.

Supposing each tree to give about ten maunds of wood 2,800 trees are annually expended on the manufac- of iron in Bir.

NOTE.—The bark of the chil *(p. longifolia)* is much employed in the smelting of iron ore. Loose pieces may be taken, but the trees must not be decorticated.

Forest conservancy urged by committee.

"If iron were made on an extensive scale by the native process now in vogue, no extent of forest would be sufficient, and, although the banks of the Ul and its tributaries are in some places well clothed with timber, it would soon be expended, if measures were not taken to renew the supply by means of plantations, and a proper forest conservancy. Were this point judiciously attended to, and improved methods of manufacture introduced both for charcoal and iron, the supply of fuel might keep pace with the demand. When the timber in the immediate neighbourhood of the mine was exhausted, it could be brought at no great expense from the higher mountains, and be floated down the various streams which intersect the Taluqa of Bir. It may be noted here that, although at some distance, vast quantities of fuel could be procured from Kûllû, which is a highly wooded country, and contains some large and extensive forests."

European officer required.

Under ordinary circumstances, perhaps, it might be of less consequence to locate an Assistant on the Beas, but, considering the enormous indents for railway sleepers for the next three years at least; the pressing demands for other public works; the great consumption of fuel for iron manufacture; and the prospective want of wood for tea-boxes in Kangra valley, I recommend the immediate nomination of an officer to carry out the necessary operations, (marking trees, launching logs and registering the seigniorage in communication with the revenue authorities of the district. It is impossible to prevent the felling of trees, placed in such a convenient locality as Manôli, without an Assistant Conservator, whose services would be of great value in examining the forest resources of this division and in carrying out strict conservancy management.

The forests of Kûllû are extensive, but the woods

of Kangra and Hoshiarpur are open and sparse. They have all acquired an increased value from the advancing prosperity of the district and the approach of railways. Heavy drains are being made upon them, and the remaining woods must be husbanded and turned to account as much as possible. This can only be effected by the reservation of tracts as Government domains and the marking of mature trees by skilled persons to meet the annual demands.

It may be useful to insert here for ready reference the following paragraphs of the well known report on the settlement of Kangra by the lamented Mr. Barnes, C. S. It will be observed that the views are not always in accordance with the principles of forest conservancy, but considerable progress has since been made, *vide* Mr. E. C. Bayley's rules, amended by Col. Lake (p. 91), and sanctioned by Punjab Government, 25th January, 1859.

Rights of Wastes and Forests.

"Extensive wastes and forests are usually considered the undivided property of Government. But even here there are subordinate tenures which cannot be overlooked. There are certain castes in the Hills, such as "goojurs," and "guddis" who cultivate little, and keep herds of buffaloes, and flocks of sheep and goats. Such classes have a claim upon certain beats of the forest which they regard as their "warisee," subject to the payment of pasturage tolls. The forests of the lower Hills are apportioned out among the guddis or shepherds of the Snowy range, who, in the winter season bring down their flocks to graze. In the same manner, the goojurs with their buffaloes, will take up divisions on a hill side, and carefully respect their mutual boundaries, Not unfrequently, as buffaloes rejoice in different shrubs and grasses from those which sheep and goats affect, a guddi and a goojur will possess a concurrent claim upon a certain tract of forest. Either would instantly resent the intrusion of another of the same tribe, bringing the same class of animals to graze but as their respective herds delight in different esculent matter, the rights of the two are perfectly compatible.

Forests in ancient times.

"In the time of the Rajas, the forests were strictly preserved, for game-keepers (Rakha) were entertained to patrol the bounds and prevent the intrusion of the profane. Once a year, the Raja would order a grand battue. The people were collected as beaters, and match-lockmen were posted on every tree. The Raja himself would have a place prepared at some eligible break. Then would commence the business of the day. The beaters led on by drums and fifes and all sorts of discordant instruments, drove the game towards the shooters, and the forest would resound with a constant succession of shots. The slaughtered victims, chiefly wild pigs, would be collected in heaps, and rare was the battue, when no injury occurred to the beaters.

In present times.

"These preserves are still kept up in the jageer estates of their descendants. But in the Government lands, the people on our accession broke loose, and for the first three years could not be restrained from reckless devastation of the timber. Now again there has been a reaction, and the people have framed laws for mutual observance, with the express object of maintaining the forests. Every one may gather fuel, but he may not cut green wood, and for building purposes, he can fell timber on the issue of an order from the headman of the village."

It is much to be regretted that the just rights of Government to the Forest land were not distinctly declared in the settlement records. An attempt has been made to obtain the best portions by compromise, these should be demarcated as Government reserves.

REVISED RULES FOR THE PRESERVATION OF TIMBER IN THE GOVERNMENT FORESTS OF THE KANGRA DISTRICT.

---

1. No tree of any kind available for building or other purposes of timber to be felled of a less diameter than one foot, except with special permission.

2. No tree of the above description, whatever may be its size, is to be felled for purposes of fuel, except with special permission.

3. No tree, of any size or description whatever, is to be felled within 100 yards on either side of any public road or way, except with special permission.

4. No tree of any kind whatever to be felled without permission.

5. This permission will be granted on application through the Tehseeldar, who will forward it for sanction to the district authority; but for the inferior kinds of trees required *boná fide* for agricultural or domestic purposes, the permission of the headman will suffice.

6. The Tehseeldar will state, in forwarding the application, whether the applicant is entitled or not to cut timber; and if he be entitled, whether the application made is duly proportioned to his wants. All applications should be in a printed form.

7. Proprietors of land, or hereditary cultivators,

are entitled to cut and appropriate whatever timber they may require, for building or agricultural purposes, on paying a fee of four annas; and trees unfit for timber, as fuel, or their leaves as fodder, gratis.

8. The Deputy Commissioner may, if he sees reason, grant timber (on a limited scale) to others for special purposes, not being for sale, either gratis or on favorable terms; and to soldiers in the ranks of our army on the same terms as proprietors of land.

9. Every application shall specifically state the name, caste, father's name, and residence of the applicant; and the number and kind of trees, the object for which, and the forest from which they are required; a printed form of application to be used.

10. Persons buying timber, are required to deposit, on the grant of their application, the full value of the timber to be cut, or to give satisfactory security for the payment of the same, without reference to the quantity the cutter may be able to remove.

11. When an application is sanctioned, the Tehseeldar shall issue an order (specifically worded as the original application) to the Lumberdar of the village within which the forest is situated.

12. This order shall continue in force for four months only from its date. If the wood be not cut and removed within that period, the order shall be of no further validity, and any wood cut and the price of any portion not cut, shall be forfeited to Government.

13. The Lumberdar, to whom the order is addressed, and all village officials in general, shall be responsible that its conditions be duly fulfilled. On receipt of the order the Lumberdar, shall point out to the grantee the limit within which he is entitled to cut.

14. Any person having a grant, who shall cut trees except within the boundaries of the forest specified in the grant, or who shall cut trees of a kind not specified in his grant, or in excess of the number, or for a purpose other than that specified in his grant, shall be liable to a fine not exceeding 100 rupees, and trees so illegally cut shall be forfeited to Government. Half the amount of the fine levied shall invariably be given to informers.

15. Any person cutting a tree within 100 yards of any public road or way, or cutting a tree fit for timber of less diameter than one foot, or any such tree, of any size whatever, for fuel shall be liable to a fine of 10 rupees for each tree so illegally cut, half the fine being payable to informer, provided that the total amount of fine shall not exceed 100 rupees.

16. Any person cutting any tree whatever without permission, to be liable to a penalty of 30 rupees, for each tree so cut, half the fine being payable to informer; provided that the total amount of fine shall not exceed 100 rupees.

17. Any Lumberdar, to whom a grant to cut wood may be directed, failing to point out the forest specified, and its boundaries to grantee, or neglecting to report any breach of the conditions of such grant, to be liable to a fine of 25 rupees.

18. Any Lumberdar, willfully conniving at any breach of these regulations, or himself violating them, to be liable to a fine not exceeding 100 rupees, or in aggravated cases to dismissal from his office.

19. Persons having an ancient right to graze, gather dry wood, or to collect leaves for manure, in any Government forest, are with the undermentioned restrictions, still entitled to these rights.

20. In order to promote the growth of seedlings,

both for timber and fuel, the third part of every Government forest shall be preserved for three consecutive years, or for such periods as the local authorities may determine.

No one shall set fire to grass within the Government forests, and grazing in the preserved portion shall be prohibited altogether, for such period as the local authorities may determine; no trees shall be cut in the preserve for fuel, nor any leaves collected for fodder, at any time of the year.

21. Any person violating these restrictions to be liable to a fine not exceeding 50 rupees.

22. Any person not being permitted to cut wood, who shall on any pretext take a cutting instrument into a Government forest, or any person whatever who shall take a cutting instrument into any portion of a forest preserved under Rule 20, shall forfeit the instrument.

23. Any person refusing to give up such instrument, to be liable to a fine not exceeding 20 rupees.

24. Any person willfully injuring or destroying trees planted on the roads, or for any public purpose, shall be liable to a fine of 20 rupees for each tree, provided that the total amount of fine shall not exceed 100 rupees.

25. The boundaries of each Government forest shall be marked out, either with a ditch or boundary pillars. A sufficiency of land for the requirements of the zemindars for fuel and grazing shall be excluded, and the remainder divided into three lots, two only of which shall be open for grazing and cutting during the year. Twice a year, on the 1st of September and on the 1st of March, the Putwaree should report regarding each forest preserve; whether during the previous six months it has escaped confla-

gration as well as injury from the grazing of cattle, and what is the general state of the forest, and particularly of the young trees in it.

26. Each forest shall be visited by a Government official, of not less rank than a Thannadar, once every three years, and he shall then blaze all trees fit for cutting, sufficient for the average demand of the three following years. No tree shall be cut that has not been blazed, under any pretence.

The receipt from the sale of timber shall be thus divided.

Net Revenue to Govt. per rupee, annas,			5⅓
Forest Conservancy Fund,		,,	6⅔
Perquisites (villager's) viz.,			
Forests,	1 anna,		
Village Community,	1 ,,	,,	4
Putwaree,	½ ,,		
Lumberdar,	1½ ,,		

The keepers of closed forests shall receive during the time the forest is closed, the average amount they would probably have received had the forest remained open.

28. Prizes shall be awarded according to the annexed scale for kelu or deodar planted in localities where they were formerly unknown, and seeds of these trees shall be gratuitously distributed each year to the forest keepers by the Deputy Commissioner.

For the first twenty Deodars raised above 5 feet, ...	Rs. 5	0	0
Ditto 50 ,, ...	,, 10	0	0
Ditto 100 ,, ...	,, 20	0	0

29. Charcoal burners shall be allowed to remove one load per diem of wood and charcoal, on their taking out an annual license at the cost of one

rupee, but this rule only applies to those who sell wood or charcoal in neighbouring towns or markets. Licenses will be granted by the Tehseeldar.

Supplementary Rule for Dharmsalla Forest.

A Chuprassee shall be specially appointed to watch this forest, receiving two rupees batta monthly, in addition to his regular pay from the Conservancy fund.

For every tree cut in this forest by European or native residents, and officials, including those in the Department of Public Works, a fee of four annas shall be paid; for the ban, or common oak, eight annas.

P. S. Melvill,
Officiating Commissioner and Supdt.

JOURNAL

FROM

HOLTA IN KANGRA VALLEY TO CHAMBA BY THE WARU PASS.

THE object of this journey was to ascertain the condition of the forests upon the Ravi, the suitability of the river for timber transport, and to collect every kind of information that might be interesting, regarding the vegetable products of the Chamba state. So far as I know, the only record of a journey across this part of the Dhaola Dhar (white mountain) is contained in a short memorandum by Mr. P. Egerton, C. S. (*vide* Supplement *Punjab Gazette*, 27th November 1861, page 129); the following extracts from my diary may therefore prove useful. Preliminary remarks. Mr P. Egerton's memorandum.

22nd June 1862. I left Holta at 9 A. M., my object being to reach Bara Bansu, at the head of the Warû pass. I kept along the right bank of the Awa stream, following for a mile and a half an old water-course, which leads to the Government Tea plantation, and afterwards a well worn sheep track, rocky, and steep, but practicable for coolies, and which might be opened for mules at no great expense. At present, letters, money, salt from Mandi, and sheep are taken across this pass, which connects a fine pastoral country with the tea district of Kangra.

Trees of lower ascent. The principal trees of the lower ascent are "ban," the common oak, *quercus incana,* "bras," *rhododendron arboreum,* "nuni," *celtis*—, and *ficus cordifolia?* I reached Paprud at half past one o'clock, (four and half hours) where I halted; the weather was threatening, but I found a sheltering rock and space for my camp, with wood and water close to the path. High on the opposite slope are several hundred tos and rai trees of good size. A path from Bandlah joins the Holta track near this place.

Indigenous drugs. An intelligent guddi (shepherd), who had been employed as a tea sorter at Holta, gave me the names of some of the indigenous drugs procurable in this range, which are collected and sent to the plains; "kurroo," the root of *picrorhiza kurrooa,* sold at Rupees 2 per maund; "balchur," *nardostachys jathamansi,* a small hairy root with a smell like valerian; "sirru," *sinapis,* wild mustard; "kashmiri putta" leaves of *rhododendron campanulatum,* which are pulverised and used as snuff; "koot," the root of "*aucklandia veracosta,*" price, rupees 2 per maund; "atees," *aconitum heterophyllum;* "ishtapri," a long root, apparently of "*polygonum bistortum,*" known from Lahore to Peshawur as "anjabur;" "chukri," the root of the small stalked rhubarb, *rheum moorcroftianum* (Royle), yielding a valuable medicine, while the leaf stalks are agreeably acid and cooling; "tror," eaten as a vegetable.

Trees of upper ascent. 23*rd June*. Paprud to Brenda. It had rained heavily all night. I started at 7 A. M., continuing the ascent, and reached Brenda at 10·30 (3½ hours). The kelu *(cedrus deodara)* does not occur in the valley of the Awa; but several ravines are feathered with tos *(picea webbiana)* and rai *(abies smithiana)*. The common rhododendron *(r. arboreum)* grows peculiarly prostrate and flattened from the continued pressure of heavy snow. A number of "munal" pheasants, (*lophophorus impeyanus,*) were seen to-day at the foot of the pass; a small snake was also observed of a brownish colour, and about two feet in length; it fixes on the lips of sheep while they are grazing, and its bite is said occasionally to prove fatal. Three very large flocks of sheep were feeding on the short sweet grass, where the snow had recently melted. The guddis are civil and good humoured men, refusing payment for milk. There is no level camping ground at Brenda, and as there was every indication of heavy rain, the heights above being enveloped in thick clouds, I halted for the night in a large and roomy cave. The guddis arranged a supply of dry grass and absinth upon a ledge of rock, and the keen blast was shut out by a screen of rhododendron twigs stretched across the entrance of the cavern.

Herbaceous vegetation.

The following herbaceous plants in flower were brought to me by the guddis; they may be worthy of note as inhabiting the outer slope of the Western Himalayas at a part of the range which no botanist except Mr. Edgeworth* has examined; *aquilegia vulgaris*, pink columbine; *potentilla atrosanguinea, anemone vitifolia, corydalis*, two species; *euphorbia, sedum rubrum, roscoea purpurea*, a ground orchid with pink flowers; *iris, acanthacea*, (blue); *angelica glauca*, "chûra," (Edgeworth in *Lin. Soc. Trans.*, 1845; p. 53), having a warm aromatic root,† which is given to goats to

* Mr. E.'s collection was communicated to the Herbarium at the Royal Gardens, Kew. The Himalayan plants were described in the 20th volume of the Trans. Lin. Socy. of London.

† Small pieces of this root are mixed with dal and ghee to give a flavor like celery.

increase the flow of milk; "padalli," another umbellifer, the root of which is used for the same purpose. "simbul," an umbellifer, resembling the "jira," (cumin seed), it has an edible bulbous root said to be much relished by bears.

European species.

I found *caltha palustris* very luxuriant in water-courses, identical with the European marsh marigold, and *sibbaldia procumbens*, in high pasture land, another British plant which extends into the rainy Himalaya. Many representatives of European genera, and some genuine British species, flourish here; but continued travelling has prevented me from examining critically the collection of plants made during this excursion, which suffered much from the incessant heavy rain.

24th June. Brenda to Keratogot. I left the cave at 5 A. M. and crossed the pass into Chamba. This day's journey occupied fully seven hours, and was very fatiguing to the porters. The plants observed were, *juniperus excelsa*, *anemone obtusiloba*, *artemisia;* "chermar," very abundant, and a pink flowered *allium*, "lussun."

Excellent pasture.

The path took me up the right bank of the Awa to its main source, over long stretches of dirty compressed snow, on the edge of which there is excellent pasture for sheep and goats, which usually feed on the outer Himalaya until August, when they cross the Ravi and remain for two months longer, returning to the plains in excellent condition in October or November. Two rupees for every hundred head of sheep or goats, are

NOTE.—Under the shadows of the cedar-like deodara pines and long-leaved oaks, the vegetable forms of Europe and the north of Asia are found covering the granitic rocks that form the substrata to the soil of the Indian mountains. They are not (often) the same species, indeed, but they are similar forms: junipers, alpine birches, gentians, parnassias, and prickly species of ribes. (*Humboldt's Cosmos, I., p.* 11).

paid to our Government as pasturage tolls, and one rupee for a like number, is paid for a similar privilege in Chamba.

The rudest of twig jhulas are the usual communications across the Ravi, but good wooden bridges (sanglas) are kept up for the sake of sheep at Oli, Ulasa, and elsewhere. Passage of rivers.

I reached the *Waru* (*i.e.* pointed rock) at 9·30 A. M. (4½ hours from the Brenda cave). The ascent for the last two miles is very steep, often like a winding staircase and is chiefly over rock. The whole crest of the ridge from Waru to Chuari (near the Dalhousie end of the range, a distance of 50 miles) consists of gneiss over clay slate. True roofing slate is found on both sides of the range, and numerous localities, north and south, yield iron sand in abundance, which is collected by the natives and worked into a very superior metal (*vide* Memorandum on the produce of the Himalaya, 1860, p. 46, in Selections from the Public correspondence of the Punjab Administration).

From the Waru, or summit of the pass, there is a splendid view on a clear day; to the south the Holta plantation, the rice fields of Kangra, and the windings of the Beas. On the north side, the view is intercepted by various peaks of the mid-Himalaya, which separate Chamba from Lahul, and from the watershed between the Ravi and the Chandrabagha. The height of these summits is given in the degree sheet, No. 3, of the Topographical Survey, 1860; the Black Cone is marked 19,000 feet, another near the Kukti pass 20,000, and the snowy peak of Mani-mahais, between the Ravi and the Budhil, rises to a height of 18,500 feet. On the west of the pass, the height called "Kalamithi" rises apparently 1,500 feet, and on the east the snowy summit of Chetrund or "Kiri Katu" View from the Waru pass.

about 2,000 feet above the "Waru" cairn; Chetrund is not named in the degree sheet, but its position is marked 14,000 feet.

Alpine plants on the summit.

Round the cairn, on which the guddis deposit flowers, rags, pieces of old iron, and deodar painted red, the ground is covered with short grass, among which a small blue *gentian*, and white *anemone* are conspicuous; still more striking are the bright yellow *caltha palustris*, and the elegant *primula rosea* which with a dwarf *salix* were abundant in spots where the snow had recently melted. Many plants of wild rhubarb, *rheum moorcroftianum*, were found about 600 feet below the Waru, and I dug up the roots with an alpenstock; the species differs from the Asrang plant, the leaf stalks being very short, two to four inches in length, and the cordate leaves covered with a short pubescence. The roots of both species are more spongy, from the excessive rainfall in the outer range, than those found in drier passes of the Mid-Himalayas; the quality of the root continues to improve towards Tibet, where it is found on a northern aspect and in a dry climate.

Dhaola Dhar range.

The morning was beautiful, the temperature at the cairn being 66° Fahr. at 10 A. M. The boiling of water indicated an elevation of about 12,500 feet. Juniper wood, the nearest fuel procurable is distant two-thirds of a mile below the Waru. The southern face of the hill, on which Waru stands, is bare, rocky, and wall-like; in this respect, the whole range presents much uniformity, and I conjecture that the last two miles of all the neighbouring passes will be found difficult. I may particularise the "Kuarsi," behind Dharmsalla, the ascent to which is considerably steeper, and the pass about 1,000 or 1,500 feet higher than the Waru. It passes under the Tural, the highest peak of the Dhaola Dhar range, 16,315 feet. (*Vide* degree sheet, where it is called "Talung"). The northern aspect is green, and has a more gentle slope than that by which I had ascended; but there is no wood on the upper portion of the range. The road *viâ* Manhé which Mr. Egerton travelled eastward of Chetrund, is longer and easier on the north side of the ridge, but is said to be equally steep on the south.

On the Chamba side, fifty yards below the cairn, the descent was over snow, which continued for a mile and a half down a ravine, on the elevated sides of which were gorgeous masses of *rhododendrum campanulatum*, the dwarf *r. lepidotum*, the handsome *corydalis govaniana*, *gagea elegans*, and *cassiope fastigiata*. On both sides of this ravine, and about eight hundred yards below the Waru, the birch *(betula bhojpatra)* is found, and rolls of its bark were being blown over the snow. **Descent to the Ravi.**

The great mass of snow at this season on the north, (in some places twenty feet deep) and the large patches in the ravines on the south, indicate an elevation of about 12,000 feet. The snow was continuous in the valley and adjoining slopes for a distance of at least two miles. The "kurroo," (*picrorhiza kurrooa* of Royle) was growing in the belt of the birch, below which tos and rai appeared in quantity with an occasional deodar, but this tree is becoming more scarce every year; considering the continuous felling in the Ravi valley, this result is not surprising. **Snowbed.**

The village of Gironda on the other side of the Ravi was in view during the descent. About four koss (six miles) from the summit I reached, at 3 P. M., a cave called Keratogot, at the confluence of two streams. Heavy rain fell during the afternoon; as some parts of the path are rocky, narrow, and, during wet weather, very slippery, the coolies did not arrive till 6 P. M. **Gironda.**

There is in summer, a considerable travelling to and fro of guddis who take their flocks to Chamba and Lahul, while part of their families remain in the Kangra valley.

25*th June*. From Keratogot to Agralli. Following the rocky path for three miles down the left bank of the stream called Chunni ka kol, I reached Tanaiter, a village consisting of eight houses, around which there was a considerable extent of wheat and barley cultivation. The head man had a large store of grain in his house, and seemed to prize highly a supply of Mandi salt, some of which is periodically given to the flocks. Two koss further down the stream the villages of Surri and Urni were seen on the opposite bank. The path leading to them travelled by Mr. Egerton, is not so steep as the descent to Tanaiter. The guddis informed me that an active young man leaving Urni at daylight may reach Holta at sunset; the path by which I came is shorter but more steep. The time occupied and the stages of my journey were as follows:

Stages of journey.

Holta to Paprud,	. . . .	4½ hours.
Paprud to Brenda,	. . . .	3½ ,,
Brenda to Keratogot,	. . . .	7½ ,,
Keratogot to Agralli,	. . . .	3½ ,,
	Total . .	19 hours.

In fine weather Holta to Brenda would be an ordinary stage, and next day over the pass. It must be remembered that the wet weather had commenced, and that I travelled during breaks in the rain, resting in caves (kood) in order to keep the tents dry, without which precaution progress by the rugged path would have been difficult. On this the short road, there is no village between Kallain, two miles from Holta, and

Tanaiter in Chamba, consequently travellers must engage coolies for the whole distance and should carry two or three days provisions with them. On the other road by which Mr. Egerton travelled, at about twelve miles from Holta there is a village (Manhé), but neither supplies nor coolies are procurable.

Agralli, standing at an elevation of 8,000 feet, contains eight houses, and is prettily situated, overlooking the confluence of the Chunni ka kol with the Ravi. Here I joined camp with Mr. J. D. Smithe, Superintendent of the Chenab and Ravi forests. **Agralli.**

The opening of a mule path from Holta to Bara Banghal at the head of the Ravi, would be an important measure. This isolated pergunnah is in British territory, and contains a variety of hill produce, which at present finds no outlet. It is reasonable to suppose that if a path was made from the thriving settlement of Holta, a traffic would spring up in wool, hemp, iron, cumin seed, munjit, kussumba, drugs,* boxwood,† daphne fibre, bees wax, &c. These products are at present sparingly conveyed by a difficult and circuitous route, *viâ* Chamba and the Chuari pass to Nurpur. **Advantage of a mule path.**

It is probable, that if rendered accessible, the residents of the Kangra district would avail themselves of the fine climate of the upper Ravi valley, and occasionally resort there, especially such as suffer from chronic bowel complaints, and who find the more humid atmosphere of Dharmsalla unsuitable; we know that the climate of Chini in Kunawar, which is protected from the periodical rains, has proved beneficial to many. At Bara Bansu wood is plentiful, water **Bara Bansu.**

* Rhubarb is very abundant, and was used this season at Madhopur, as a substitute for the Russian variety. It makes an excellent tincture and the powder is efficacious in doses one-third larger than the drug of Apothecary's Hall.

† This is carved into neat boxes for holding ghee, snuff, tinder, &c.

good and abundant, and the soil rich, but there is no extent of level ground.

Climate.

The climate was pleasant during the two days we remained here, the temperature in a hill tent being about 64° Fahr. at noon. A fine mist floated up the valley of the Ravi, while it rained heavily on the mountain tops of the outer range, which appeared to arrest the clouds. So short a stay does not warrant any conclusion, but the shepherds describe the climate as comparatively dry, and the aspect of the country indicated a moderate rainfall.

Proposed sanitarium.

As a sanitarium in this direction has been suggested by Mr. McLeod, and a committee was appointed in 1861, to visit the adjoining tract of Barmawar, who reported favorably except in regard to access, I would suggest that a hut be built for the use of the civil authorities and forest officer, and that the nature of the climate be proved by a self-acting rain guage, before taking further steps. A forest hut would also be useful for preserving tools, office furniture, &c., which are yearly brought up from the plains at a considerable expense. The total cost of building would probably not exceed Rs. 150.

Bara Banghal.

This remote taluqa, Bara Banghal, has occasionally been visited by sportsmen for Ibex shooting; but as little is on record, I requested Mr. J. D. Smithe, who left me at Sultanpur and returned to Bara Banghal, to favor me with a note of his observations, as follows.

"The village of Bara Banghal, near the source of the Ravi, (here called Rawa) is about 8,400 feet above the level of the sea, and from 200 to 300 feet over the river's right bank, which here flows through an exceedingly rocky and precipitous country.

Spur on right bank.

"A large and nicely rounded spur descends with easy slope from the Mid-Himalaya to the north of

Bara Banghal, and is separated from the village by a stream. On this spur, about 1,700 feet above the river, there is a fine grassy plot with a good deal of moderately level ground without trees; two hundred feet lower there is shrubby vegetation, and nearer the river the sides and point are well wooded. From this spot, there is a good view of the snowy range, which is crossed by the Thamser, Gaura, and Makori passes;* the lower slopes are wooded with fine trees overhanging the river, here joined by the Feroza and other streams. The confluents on the right bank at Bara Banghal come from very large glaciers. The Gaussa pass and "black cone" (19,533 feet) are at the head of the western glacier. On the Lahul side this pass leads near the junction of the Chandra and Bhaga rivers.

"At about the same elevation (10,000 feet), on the opposite bank of the Ravi, there is a large spur from the Thamser and Gaura passes, between the Jeralu and Feroza streams; its crest is large, with easy slopes, and the top seen from a little distance appears to be somewhat level. It resembles the plot on the right bank above described, but is rather larger. Immediately below its crest, this spur is clothed with shrubs, and is well wooded over the Ravi and Feroza. It is easier of access than the opposite spur. A path could be made from the pass above Holta with easy gradients by Chunni, Surri, and Urni, to the western Jeralu stream (opposite the village of Kanara) then over Jeralu Joth, passing low down on the spur by a gentle slope; the path would then descend to east Jeralu stream which flows from the Thamser pass and ascend at the same inclination to the grassy spur on the left bank of the river.

Spur on left bank.

* Thamser pass, ... 15,850 feet.
Makori " .. .. 15,485 "

Scenery.

"From this last there is a grand view; to the west the Kailas peak at Mani-Mahés, covered with snow, which is the highest point in this direction; whilst to the north, the Gaussa black cone in the Lahul range, with large glaciers coming from it, the "Nagora" on one side of the cone and the "Lalonee" on the other are objects of which one never tires, each variation of light bringing a new picture before the eye.

"I have not been on these plots of ground, but either of them, seen from a short distance, appears to be well suited for a limited sanitarium during the rainy months. The left bank would be preferable on account of its western aspect and easy approach.

Building materials.

"Materials for building are close at hand; stones on the spot, lime not far distant, and fine timber immediately below the ridge. Water probably is at some distance, but a small stream could be led along either side of the spur without difficulty.

Road to connect the Ul and Ravi valleys.

"A short loop line of road over the Chunni pass above the villages of Chunni and Surri would open out the Ul valley and connect it with the Ravi. This pass is easy and low, and is the high road between Chamba and Mandi, from whence the people of Chamba obtain their supplies of salt. The track is bad at present, but very little labour would make it fit for laden animals."

THE RAVI RIVER.

The Ravi, the smallest and most rapid of the Punjab rivers, rises in the British pergunnah of Bara Banghal, and continues its intramontane course for about 130 miles, debouching from the plains at Shahpur. The average fall of this portion according to General A. Cunningham, the first European who visited its source, is 115 feet per mile.

The Rawa, as it is called in Bara Banghal, is formed of several impetuous streams, issuing from beneath large glaciers, at an elevation of 14,000 feet on the south side of the Mid-Himalaya, and east and west of large spurs, running from the outer range. The fall of this portion is 183 feet per mile; the bed is obstructed with rocks for many miles during its passage through the districts of Bara Banghal and Bara Bansu into Chamba. About forty miles below its source the Ravi proper is joined by two large feeders, the Budhil and the Nai or Duna. **Ravi proper.**

There is not a large supply of deodar timber at the head of the Ravi, either in the territory of the Raja of Chamba, or in the British district of Bara Banghal. The mature trees adjacent to the river have been felled to a great extent, and those remaining are generally immature or high on the banks. The feeding streams flow from the outer range or from the southern aspect **Supply of Deodar.**

of the Mid-Himalaya, and hence the floods come down earlier than in the other Punjab rivers and subside sooner.

Bara Banghal.

The district of Bara Banghal is shut in with high hills on every side, with only a cleft in the rocks as an outlet for the Ravi, it can be easily understood, therefore, why it is a comparatively rainless country. The volume of the river at this part is almost entirely due to the melting of the snows; all the streams which come from the glaciers meet in Bara Banghal and combine to form the Ravi, while the drainage basin of the river is narrow along its whole course, and protected from the heavy rains of the monsoon. The great floods in the lower Ravi, are from the Seul, which flows through a wide open valley, from the Siawa, and from other streams below Chamba, where the high hills recede and the periodical rains fall in abundance.

Budhil river.

This tributary rising in the Lahul range, issues in part from a lake at Mani-Mahés, a mountain much frequented by Hindu pilgrims. At the junction, the stream is about half the volume of the Ravi. Its whole course is forty-five miles, and the fall is 314 feet per mile (Cunningham.) Barmawar, the ancient capital of the Barma family, is beautifully situated over this stream; the carved temples are shaded by lofty deodars. The Rajas of Chamba were wont to preserve carefully the forests fringing the holy Budhil, but felling was commenced here by the present Raja in 1858 to supply the British Government, and when granting permission to carry on forest operations in 1860, the district of Barmawar was specially named by the Raja, as being considered good for the work; the forest within a certain distance from the temples being reserved.

Duna or Nai river.

The Nai rises in the Kalidebi pass in the Mid-

SECTION OF THE TISA NULLAH.

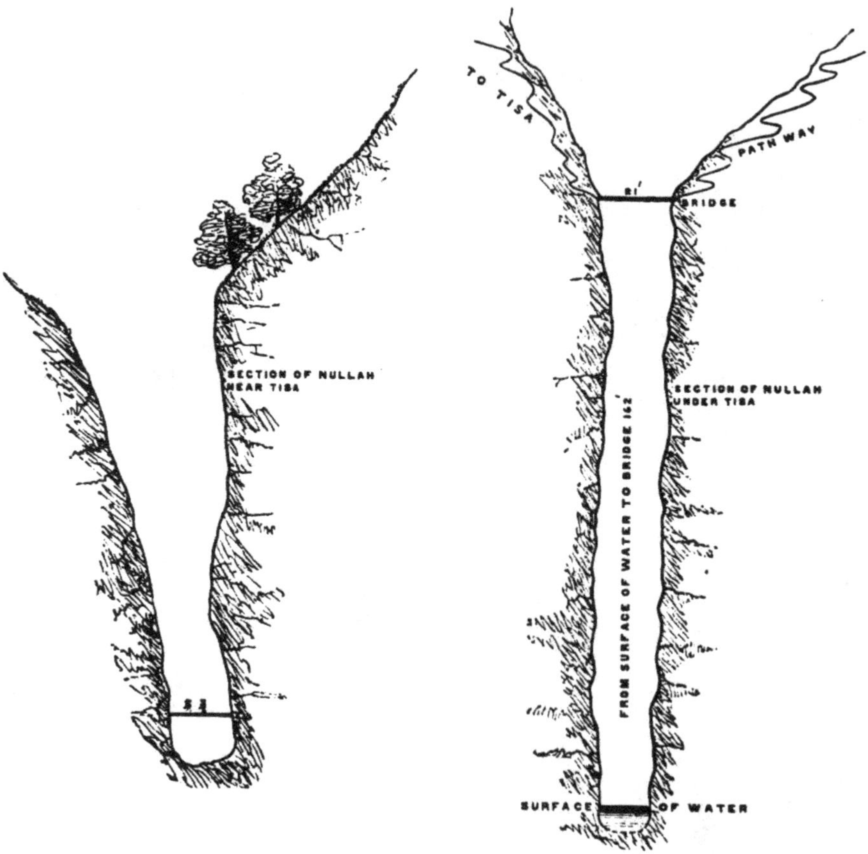

Himalaya. General Cunningham,* crossing from Triloknath, followed the stream from the source to its confluence with the Ravi, a distance of thirty miles. The fall is great, 366 feet per mile, (Cunningham) and timber comes down only in floods. Mahomed Sultan, contractor, felled trees in the deodar forest over the Nai in 1860-61. It is very desirable that this small valley should be examined with a view to forest operations, as a fair portion of the annual supply may be obtained from it. From the high ridge on which *Koti* stands, there is a good view of the course of these two tributaries.

The Seul river, a large feeder from the north, Seul river. drains a considerable basin between Chamba and Badrawar and falls into the Ravi below the capital. It rises in the Mid-Himalaya near the Sach pass, and receives several long tributaries from the adjoining mountains. These are impetuous torrents, generally flowing through rocky chasms 15 to 18 feet wide, and often 80 to 100 feet deep. Clumps of deodar occur at the heads of these streams, seldom visible from the path below, until the traveller approaches the top of the valley. The tributaries of the Seul are very precipitous, and like most feeders of the Himalayan rivers, difficult for timber operations. A section to scale of the Tisa nullah, where the sides are only 20 feet apart, 162 feet above the water, will convey an idea of the narrow gorge through which the timber passes down to the river. The valley of the Seul should be carefully examined. Major Longden reported in 1851, that 5000 logs might be expected annually from the forests of the valley, and so far as Mr. Smithe and I could judge in travelling up the bank of the main stream, we consider the estimate to be correct; but to

* Jour. As. Soc. Beng., x. 107.

procure this quantity much labour will be necessary, and a great amount of supervision required, as the forests are scattered and separated from each other by deep ravines.

Seul valley.

The valley of the Seul is open and highly cultivated, containing much comparatively level ground in old river terraces, high above the present bed of the stream. This fertile tract, called "the garden of Chamba," supplies the capital and Dalhousie with grain, and is worthy of a good road on account of its agricultural produce and the large number of inhabitants. The improvement of the present track would be of value to the Forest Department in proceeding to and from Pangi, and also to travellers from Badrawar, who cross the Seul at Manjeer by mussuck ferry, where the river is broad and the bed sandy.

Siawa river.

The Siawa falls into the Ravi above Bissôli: by this stream deodar has been and may be brought down from the territories of Jummoo. The Maharaja keeps the felling of timber in his own hands, and only sells to merchants when it is in the river. By this wise policy, contractors not having ingress into the forests, the wooded tracts of Jummoo are almost uninjured.

Valley of Ravi. Characteristic vegetation.

On the higher slopes of the upper Ravi the deodar, inferior pines, and birch are conspicuous. In the cultivated valley below, the walnut, *quercus ilex*, *daphne*, mulberry, and alder, are striking objects from Bara Bansu to Bassu. The olive and kakkar *(rhus)* are first observed where the Kuarsi stream joins the Ravi near Walassa. The edible pine *(pinus gerardiana,)* grows in one or two small clusters on a ridge with a

NOTE.—The vegetation of Chamba closely resembles that of the adjoining province of Kullu. *Fothergilla involucrata* appears in this upper part of the Seul valley and in the basin of the Chenab.

northern exposure, near Walassa, but does not generally ripen its fruit; the occurrence of this tree indicates a dry climate. The twisted cypress (*cupressus torulosa*) occurs in a solitary clump at the junction of the Budhil with the Ravi, but is not found further to the west. *Pinus longifolia* was first seen between Guriat and Chatrari, and is abundant between Chamba and Shahpur. The *desmodium* (paper shrub) is exceedingly plentiful in the districts of Chota and Bara Banghal, and in the Ravi valley; the plant having a wider range, and the bark being more easily stripped off, the fibre will be available in the plains at less cost than that of *daphne papyracea.* A large pipul tree and two umbrageous specimens of the oriental plane, "chinar," *platanus orientalis*, are close to the ancient temple at Maila. A few miles from Chamba, there is a fine avenue of hill toon, *cedrela serrata*, and the sissoo occurs in clumps but does not attain a large size.

The town of Chamba occupies a beautiful site near the river, at an elevation of 2,807 feet above the sea;* the number of houses is about a thousand; these are generally one storied, built of wood with shingle roofs; a few of the better class are slated and are ranged round a rectangular open space, covered with grass, like an English village green, where the Persian game *chaugán*, or hockey on horseback, is often played. The population numbers 6,000. The thermometer rose to 90° during the day (July 10th); the vegetation and aspect of the vicinity resembles that of Rampur on the Sutlej. A large wooden bridge or sangla across the Ravi, is being re-built at a point where the river is 165 feet in width, and a new residence for the Raja is in course of construction. Chamba.

* 3,015 feet. A. Cunningham. *Jour. As. Soc. Beng.*, x. 110.

Forster (*Journey*, I., 282,) describes Chamba as "a mart of the first note in this part of the country," 1783. See also *Vigne's Kashmir*, I., 153.

Roads in Chamba.

Except the road to Dalhousie, which is twenty-four miles in length, and passable for horses, the only riding path from the capital leads towards the Seul; therefore, moving about the district is attended with great difficulty. The tracks could scarcely be worse, in many places they are steep zig-zag paths, exceedingly rugged and dangerous, affording an insecure footing, and from a false step there is no recovery. There is every reason to believe that improvements in the communications will take place rapidly. Major Reid, Superintendent, proposes to extend the road up the valley of the Seul, and also to erect four wooden staging huts between Chamba and Bara Bansu, which will be convenient for travellers.

Previous timber transactions in Chamba.

The history of our timber transactions with the Chamba State up to 1854, is fully detailed in a letter of the Chief Commissioner to the Government of India, dated 31st January, 1854, the main facts in which are as follows:*—In 1851, the Wazir of Chamba agreed to supply any amount of wood on six months notice at Shahpur, at 3½ tussoos per rupee. At the same time, Major Longden was appointed agent to receive the timber, to examine the forests of Chamba, and to see the agreement fulfilled.

Wazir fails in his agreement, 1851.

The result of this arrangement, to use Sir John Lawrence's words, was "a lamentable failure. The Chamba authorities not only did not fulfil the agreement, but evaded it altogether; not a timber was felled. We received only what had been cut down in former years, and a large proportion was decayed and

* In 1850, the rate was two and a quarter tussoos for a rupee. A tussoo is equal to nine-tenths of a cubic foot.

worm eaten." The Wazir was pledged to furnish Government with 10,000 logs annually, *i. e.*, 850 *per mensem*, but 320, or little more than one-third the number promised, were delivered at Shahpur, and "this including a very large proportion of inferior timber."

Abolition of Shahpur Agency, 1854.

With the sanction of the Government of India, the Shahpur Agency was abolished in 1854. The annual reports of the Director of Canals and other Engineer Officers shew, that Public Works were often at a stand still from want of wood, and this for a succession of years. The supply appears to have been very inadequate in quantity, and of a worthless description.

Depot at Chun, 1858.

In May 1858, the Chamba authorities excused their shortcomings, stating that the chief difficulties occurred from obstructions in the bed of the river near Chun, about 35 miles above Shahpur. To deprive them of this excuse, the Chief Commissioner directed that the Raja's timber should be taken over above that point. For three years this new arrangement was carried out, but without any improvement in the supply of timber, proving what had been previously a matter of doubt, that the Chamba authorities made no efforts to send down wood from their forests.

Conditions of felling timber, 1860.

The Commissioner of the Trans-Sutlej States (Major Lake) represented the matter on several occasions to the Raja, who consented in December, 1860, to an arrangement whereby the British Government should fell timber in his territory, on the following conditions.

1.—That no wood be cut except that indicated by a servant of the Raja, deputed for the purpose.

2.—That payment be made at the time of felling.

3.—That supplies and workpeople be provided by the Canal Officers.

4.—That the Canal Officers pay for the timber (trees felled) at the market rate.

Ravi forests worked by Government, 1861.

Felling operations commenced in the following working season (1861). It was supposed that this new arrangement would increase the quantity of timber and effect the desired object of procuring a constant supply of sound and useful wood, which was the more necessary now in order to give steady employment to the saw mills, erected at Madhopur in the beginning of the year.

Operations in 1861.

During the first year under the new system, seventy-two gangs of workpeople were employed, receiving payment in cash at rates higher than they were accustomed to, and with which, after personal enquiry, I can state that they were well pleased. The following work was done on the upper Ravi and Budhil rivers.

Deodar logs put into the river,—

Bara Bansu, ...	9,377
Barmawar, ...	2,515
Chenota, ...	1,892
Total logs,	13,784

About half of these logs were upwards of twenty feet in length. From imperfect knowledge of the country and rivers, and from late launching, only about 2,000 logs reached Madhopur during the year.

Operations in 1862.

The Chenab and Ravi Forest Agencies having been united, and placed under Mr. Smithe, C.E., in March

NOTE.—In 1862 timber was felled in Chenota, but so late that little could be launched. The Raja expressed his hearty approval of the manner in which the four conditions were fulfilled, and his disinclination to incur the responsibility attached to him under the old system. The trouble and difficulty of working his forests and sending down the timber, being great, he is anxious to be rid of it.

1862, an assistant to carry out the details of the work became necessary, and Mr. Doering, Assist. Civil Engineer, was appointed to the Ravi.

Deodar logs put into the river,—

Bara Bansu,	9,996
Barmawar,	8,135
Chenota,	117
	18,248

Timber slides.

During 1862, work was conducted in 51 galls (ravines with timber slides) over the Ravi and its tributaries, viz.:—

First class galls,	10
Second class galls,	19
Third class galls,	22
Total,	51

Of these, one was on the right bank, twenty-four on the left bank, and twenty-six in nullahs. On account of the large number of slides in tributary nullahs, the timber cannot come down so speedily as was expected, the floods being dependent on the occurrence of heavy local rains. There is no stronger proof that the work on the Ravi is of a very difficult nature, than the fact that so large a proportion of the slides are of the third class. Great labour is required in many cases to get the timber down. Many of the slides have been improved, and others will require improvement from time to time.

Forest districts.

The forests on the Ravi are divided into four work-

NOTE.—The classification of slides is as follows:—

Under 5 per cent. breakage of logs,	1st class.
„ 15 do. do. do,	2nd „
Above,	3rd „

ing districts, viz., *Danchru*, at the head of the Ravi; *Huli*, a little lower down; *Chenota*, over the Kuarsi, a tributary of the Ravi; *Barmawar*, over the Budhil.

Danchru.

In this district, which is twenty miles in length, rugged and precipitous, there are eight galls, and 1,130 trees were felled in 1862,—

Second class galls, .	2	Trees obtained, .	367
Third class galls, .	6	Ditto, .	763
Total,	8	Total,	1,130

One of these is on the right bank of the river, four on the left bank, and three in nullahs. There remain only about 500 trees fit for felling, and 1,000 undersized; most of these, including the full grown timber, are in third class galls. The Danchru district is not suitable for planting, the ground being rocky and inaccessible, and the river small.

Huli.

The district of Huli is twenty-five miles long, and contains twenty-four galls, from which the following approximate number of trees was obtained during 1862,—

First class galls, .	3	Trees obtained, .	165
Second class galls, .	9	Ditto, .	1,218
Third class galls, .	12	Ditto, .	933
Total,	24	Total,	2,316

About 1,600 full sized trees are available, in second and third class galls. There are also upwards of 4,000 undersized trees, of which 2,400 are in second class, and 1,600 in third class galls, but these are at present too small for felling. Four of the ravines, near the river, are well suited for planting trees, and in two of them there is now much fine young timber.

Felling was carried on in this tract during 1861 and 1862. The district is thirty-five miles in length, but the information regarding its timber resources is defective. All the galls lead into the Kuarsi stream, and this detracts much from the value of the wood; the nullah being rocky, and containing little water, the timber takes a long time to reach the Ravi. Chenota.

In this district which lies over the Budhil stream, timber operations are carried on for a distance of forty miles. There are 19 galls, down which in 1862, the following trees were brought,— Barmawar.

First class galls, .	7	Trees obtained, .	177
Second class galls, .	8	Ditto, .	1,868
Third class galls, .	4	Ditto, .	463
Total, .	19	Total, .	2,508

About 1,800 mature trees remain, and the undersized ones have been estimated at 3,500, many of these are little under the standard size, viz., five haths (8 feet) in girth. The trees are found over the three classes of galls in somewhat the following numbers,—

Class of galls.	Full grown trees.	Undersized.
1	200	500
2	1,150	2,000
3	450	1,000
	1,800	3,500

The deodar appears to thrive exceedingly well in

NOTE.—It must be understood, that the number of deodar trees here given as available and undersized, on the Ravi and its tributaries, are estimates only, as near as could be arrived at in a first season, with works of an important nature in hand, demanding all attention.—J. D. S.

this district, which is favorably situated for plantations. There has been much felling, and trees are no longer plentiful. The large proportion of good galls in Barmawar renders strict conservancy desirable. The stream is a fair one, and is visited by periodical floods which bring down the wood.

Estimate of trees available.

Mr. Smithe estimates the aggregate number of mature deodar trees, available in three districts of the upper Ravi at 3,900, and of undersized trees at 8,500. It being of great importance to test the accuracy of his observations, I requested his successor, Lieut. Chalmers, to inspect the various tributaries carefully, and to prepare a sketch map shewing the number of trees on each stream, which is annexed.

NAMES OF STREAMS ON THE UPPER RAVI, INDICATED ON SKETCH MAP BY LETTERS OF THE ALPHABET.

A.	Ravi.	M.	Harser.
B.	Jeralu.	N.	Duna.
B′.	Danchru.	O.	Rilya ka Kud.
C.	Urni.	P.	Gunch.
D.	Chunni.	Q.	Lil.
E.	Nagaru.	R.	Brai.
F.	Garoh.	S.	Jowli.
G.	Pani Nalla.	T.	Kuarsi.
H.	Huli.	U.	Torla.
I.	Kolo.	V.	Samber.
J.	Kola.	W.	Korki.
K.	Chobia.	X.	Kathor.
L.	Budhil.		

NOTE.—Mr. Smithe's and Lieut. Chalmers' estimates accord sufficiently to prove that in 1864 the felling of deodar trees must be very limited.—H. C.

ESTIMATE OF DEODAR TREES AVAILABLE ON UPPER RAVI.

Galls as numbered on Sketch.	Name of Gall.	Probable number to be felled and put into river, 1863.	Must be passed over snow.	Must be sawn into sleepers where felled.	Remarks.
1	Danchru and Ritta Pani,	...	100	...	Estimate for kols (streams) not visited, but taken on native report, 1,000 trees in addition, making the total number of deodar trees available, 7,550.
2	Sagee and Dung, . .	...	250	...	
3	Kanar Gont, . .	...	150	...	
4	Phalagi, ...	...	...	...	
5	Kotela, ...	...	200	...	
6	Chunni, ...	...	100	40	
7	Kohlee Seleng, . .	...	50	...	
8	Pundbun, ...	...	...	...	
9	Kalasug, ...	...	150	...	
10	Loin and Suroo, . .	...	...	...	
11	Jeralu ki Kol, . .	...	80	...	
12	Kankelee and Passoo, .	...	50	...	
13	Pani Nalla, . . .	...	40	...	
14	Huli, ...	100	40	...	
15	Losun, ...	100	50	...	
16	Lara, ...	100	...	...	
17	Pakoo and Loshur, .	300	}		
18	Duig, Munsal, Banera, .	300	} 200	50	
19	Purlottu and Kurena, .	300	}		
20	Mahoun and Chenota, .	150	...	100	
21	Ulasa and Jolaker, .	...	40	50	
22	Mahoun and Rait, .	100	300	...	
23	Gemashatan, . .	200	...	...	
24	Gemasht to Kukti, .	1,500	...	...	
25	Do. Do. .	200	...	...	
26	Right bank of Budhil, .	50	...	...	
27	Pata, ...	...	50	...	
28	Lunerdi, ...	...	10	...	
29	Kathor, ...	...	...	200	
30	Brai, ...	...	...	200	
31	Jowlee, ...	...	...	100	
32	Lil, ...	...	...	150	
33	Gunch, ...	...	...	100	
34	Rilya ka Kud, . .	...	...	100	
35	Sewar, ...	...	...	200	
		3,400	1,860	1,290	

J. CHALMERS,
Officiating Supdt., Ravi Forests.

Size of tree and average cost of logs.

The trees yield on an average four logs, each containing twenty five cubic feet. The cost of cutting and carriage to the river is about one rupee per log. Mr. Smithe calculates, that after paying five rupees of seignorage per tree to the Raja, and allowing for breakage, losses, and sundry expenses, deodar logs may be eventually landed at Madhopur at four annas per cubic foot, but to me this seems doubtful. There are various obstructions which render this rate problematical. Many new slides must be opened, and until they are in order the breakage is very great; but the chief obstacle to such a rate is the heavy loss from the appropriation of timber by native merchants and others, who live by an illicit trade in wood.

Prospective supply of timber.

The large cities of Amritsir and Lahore being near the Ravi, the demand for timber brought down this river has been very large for many years. The forests in Chamba require rest, and it would be for the interest of the Raja to reduce the felling to an annual average of five thousand trees, including every species of useful timber. The proposed arrangement of a long lease is absolutely necessary for the protection of the forests, which at the present rate of felling, will not yield *mature* trees for more than five years.

Forest revenue of Chamba.

The forest revenue of Chamba has more than doubled (nearly trebled) within ten years, as proved by the payments. The timber agent has dealt faithfully with His Highness, paying seignorage on every tree felled, without causing any expenditure to the Raja, who admits that traders have not dealt with equal honesty, and is

Timber Revenue of the Raja.
1862-63.*

Paid direct to Raja, . .	70,000
For labor in Chamba, .	60,000
	1,30,000

* In 1863-64, money payments in Chamba amounted to about 1,55,000 rupees.

desirous of being relieved of the annoyance connected with endless river disputes.

Superintendent of Chamba.

The recent appointment of a Superintendent of Chamba is calculated to produce beneficial results to the State; the Raja, having found himself unable to control the various traders and contractors, has requested Major Reid to ascertain the extent of the forests in his territories, and to exercise a wholesome supervision over the operations of any person who may be allowed to fell on the Ravi or Chenab rivers. The adoption of our rules as to girth and low cutting is an important step towards conserving the forests.

Waif timber.

The right of collecting waif timber, until 1861, was sold annually to the highest bidder by the Deputy Commissioner, through whose district the river flows. From the careless marking of the numerous timber merchants, this lease has often proved a profitable speculation, large sums being realized; it has given the lessee an opportunity of tampering with marks and appropriating the timber belonging to merchants, and latterly the temptation has proved so strong, that he has meddled with Government timber.

The trouble and annoyance arising from this malpractice, induced the Government Timber Agent to apply for the right of collecting waif timber, which, after some correspondence, was granted in 1860, on payment of rupees 1000, to the district funds of Goordaspore.

Result of collecting waif by Government.

The result of collecting waif by Government, is as follows:—

1861-62.

	R.	A.	P.
To District funds for royalty, ...	1,000	0	0
Receipts above expenditure, ...	944	11	6
Paid to Government,	1,944	11	6

1862–63.

	R.	A.	P.
To District funds for royalty, ...	804	0	0
Receipts above expenditure, ...	6,800	6	10
Paid to Government,	7,604	6	10

Average value of lease.

The average annual rate paid to Government for five previous years, by native contractors for collecting waif timber was under 1000 rupees. It is therefore obvious that the collection should remain with the Government officer, whose duty requires him frequently to inspect the river; this system will aid in protecting our own timber.

Islands in Ravi.

There are several large islands in the bed of the Ravi, on which much timber is stranded on its way down. It is very desirable that the right to waif on these islands should be definitely settled. The main channel varies, and a river law is much wanted. The value of the timber lodging on the islands amounts to several thousand rupees annually, now claimed by the Jummoo authorities, and hitherto, to prevent annoyance, yielded to them; but the passive cession of that to which they have no right,* has made them more unreasonable in their demands. (*Vide* p. 128.)

Advantage of saw-mills.

The advantage of machine-cut timber is well known to every one acquainted with practical working in wood. First, the prime cost of sawing by machinery is one-fourth that of hand labor; and second, the trueness with which the saw works, diminishes the cost of manufacture one-quarter more in carpenters wages. Saw-mills should be placed high up the rivers, where they enter the plains. From thence to the large towns, transport is only paid on what is actually required by the purchaser, waste and refuse is thus left at the highest practicable spot, and reduced to a minimum.

* I am assured that these islands are included in British territory in the original settlement maps.

Saw-mills at Madhopur.

The building and machinery of the saw-mills at Madhopur, situated on an island, at the head of the Baree Doab Canal, appear to be strong and substantial. They are always ready for work whenever timber may be brought. Formerly sawyers had to be collected from amongst the agricultural population, and were procured with difficulty. When the timber stock has been low, both native contractors and the Railway Company have availed themselves of the use of the machinery, and the saw-mills have thus been kept at work, otherwise, from the deficient supply of Government timber they would have remained idle.*

Sissoo plantation.

On the same island in the bed of the river, formed by the soil taken out of the deep diggings for the Canal, is a promising sissoo plantation, consisting of several thousand seedlings, about four years old. The percolation of water keeps the soil and air moist, and the situation is favorable for raising young trees. It is in fact an experimental nursery from which the canal plantations are supplied.

Australian introductions.

Here to a small extent Australian trees have been on trial for two years. Of these, *eucalyptus*† (three species), with *acacia stricta* and *robusta* (from Ootacamund), are in a thriving state, and promise well under the fostering care of Captain Dyas, Director of Canals. *Casuarina torulosa* and *muricata* shew a remarkable growth; the olive and oriental plane are also planted out in the station of Madhopur.

Hydraulic observations.

An accurate register of the fluctuations of the Ravi has been kept at Madhopur for many years. The

* In 1863, Mr. Arratoon and Chevalier de Córtenze, large contractors, have had their timber sawn into sleepers.

† There are twenty-six *eucalyptus* trees planted out, some 16 feet high, (1863,) raised from seed which was received from Sydney. This experimental introduction of Australian trees into the Punjab is most interesting. Of Indian trees there are Toon, Teak, Plane, Neem, Siriss, Jhamún, Mulberry. The Carob, *(ceratonia siliqua)*, from Malta, is also under trial.

guage is read and recorded every morning and afternoon. A guage has this year (1863) been put up on the Chenab at Aknore, by Mr. J. D. Smithe, and will be daily registered by the Pangi Timber Agency establishment there. Similar registers might be kept on all the rivers in the Punjab, at as many points as possible. This is an important subject in connection with the floating down of large quantities of timber. The peculiarities in the rise and fall of the rivers are of great interest to the Hydraulic Engineer, and a knowledge of the variations may in many ways be of value to Government.

ROUTE FROM BARA BANSU TO CHAMBA.

	Miles.
Agralli to Garoh, . . .	8
Garoh to Deole, . . .	8
Deole to Huli, . . .	8
Huli to Seur, . . .	14
Seur to Walass, . . .	16
Walass to Guriat, . . .	10
Guriat to Chatrari, . . .	10
Chatrari to Bassu, . . .	16
Bassu to Maila, . . .	16
Maila to Chamba, . . .	13
Total,	119

ROUTE FROM CHAMBA TO KILAR IN PANGI.

Chamba to Pokri, . . .	9
Pokri to Dahn, . . .	9
Dahn to Kalail, . . .	7
Kalail to Haslund, . . .	12
Haslund to Tissa, . . .	10
Tissa to Byra, . . .	14
Byra to Ulias, . . .	9
Ulias to Wo-an, . . .	9
Wo-an to Shepherd's Camp, . .	6
Shepherd's Camp to Duna, . .	22
Duna to Puntu, . . .	15
Puntu to Kilar, . . .	6
Total,	128

REPORT OF THE RAVI TIMBER AGENT,

1862-63.

---

1. The work performed in the forests on the Ravi in 1862, shews a large increase over that of the previous year, 6,083 trees having been felled, 18,248 logs put into the river, and 9,352 logs marked and left in the forests, making a total of 27,600 logs of timber. Of this number 15,354 were in the Bara Bansu district, at the head of the Ravi proper, and 12,246 in Burmawar. *Trees felled and logs launched, 1862.*

2. Mr. Doering, Asst. Engineer, being new to the work, and unacquainted with the language, was not able to expedite operations at the beginning of the season. The result is evident, only 3,876 logs were secured. The floods in the Ravi in 1862 were unusually early, and not one log had been put into the water when the heavy floods on 1st, 4th, 5th, 6th and 14th July, passed down. Two more days of flood occurred on the 20th and 21st, and only one flood in August. *Floods of 1862.*

3. The seasons 1861-62, have not been favourable for timber operations as regards the river. In 1858, there were 12 floods in August; in 1859, 11; in 1860, 12; in 1861, 9; and in 1862, only 1. Since 1858, there have been no floods in September. The receipts have been 41,360 cubic feet, of which 21,601 have been issued. *Years 1861-62, unfavorable.*

Work done in saw-mills at Madhopur. 4. During the year 294,450 square feet have been cut by the saw-mills, which worked part of 213 days, and remained idle 152 days: the water wheel made 374,043 revolutions; in September, the revolutions were 76,225, cutting 57,832 square feet.

Revenue from waif. 5. The waif (unmarked) timber, yielded a considerable increase. In 1862, 12,410 cubic feet of good useful wood were caught, and Rs. 5,778-8, were realized from sales of firewood.

Timber receipts and expenditure. 6. The following table shews receipts and disbursements on timber in 1862-63.

	RS.	A.	P.
Expenditure in forests including Seignorage, ...	44,067	0	0
Collecting in plains and converting, . .	6,181	0	0
Total Rupees, . .	50,248	0	0
Timber sales, ...	15,058	5	9
Expenditure over receipts, . . .	35,187	10	3

Waif receipts and expenditure. 7. On waif receipts and disbursements were—

Expenditure on collecting, marking, and selling, ...				2,307	6	8
Paid to district treasury for royalty, .				804	0	0
Total Rupees, . .				3,111	6	8
Sales 12,410 cubic feet, at 3 feet per rupee,	4,133	5	4			
Sales of firewood, .	5,778	8	0			
				9,911	13	4
Receipt over expenditure, . .				6,800	6	8

Islands in Ravi. 8. Several islands in the Ravi being claimed by the Jummoo authorities, were abandoned by the

* The deficit on the year's transactions is 28,387 rupees.—H.C.

	7.	8.	9.	10.
Marks in use t Chumba Rajah. No. 2 mark no by him chiefly.	Zungun. 	Kutorah. 	Dal Tulwar 	Panchang. 
Mahomud So and Sheik J.. marks on abov purchased of t -jah.	Panchang. 	Panchang & cho kunti 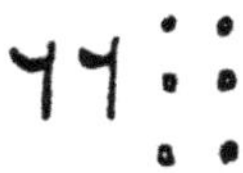		
Do: Do: on. purchased fr Chumba Merchant	Kowāl. 	Topee. 		
Do: Do: on felled by the Chumba, (Ra	Musagin 	Pingin 	Arrie 	Kiwah. 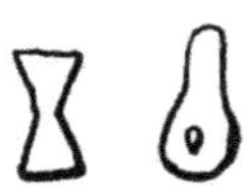
Do: Do: on felled by the tributaries Ravee.				

True Copy.

...re firm. J. D. Smithe, Supdt.

Chenai and Ravee Forests.

Government establishment and the timber on them given up. The marks on about 100 logs cut by our establishment in the Chamba forests, were erased by the inhabitants of Basouli and other places in the Jummoo territory. The timber thus lost to us and the abandoning of waif, may be valued at between 3,000 and 4,000 rupees. The logs stranded on these islands will be collected by the Jummoo authorities until their claim is disproved.

Extensive depredation.

9. The Ravi agency has suffered severely this year by the removal of marks on timber; this is done by the native merchants whenever they have an opportunity, which often occurs, as the timber is brought down by floods and left on the islands and banks along 200 miles of river.

Erasure of timber marks.

10. No amount of supervision will stop this fraud, which is often practised at night and the perpetrators are never discovered. The extent to which it prevails will be understood by stating the quantity and value of timber so appropriated by merchants. From information received, I estimate the logs lost by the agency this year, from erasure of marks at 2,000. As this was chiefly done when the early floods brought down first class wood, I take the contents of each log at 20 cubic feet (not a large average); this gives 40,000 cubic feet, which, selling at 6 annas per cubic foot, represents a value of 15,000 rupees, and nearly all has been appropriated by two or three native merchants.

Remedy proposed.

11. The system of removing marks is carried on to a great extent on the Ravi by the timber merchants, who appear to think little of it and fight each other with their own weapons; but this cannot be done by a government establishment, and were a man placed every half mile along 200 miles of river bank,

such frauds would not be prevented during the night. There is only one effectual remedy, the merchants should purchase their timber from the Government agency as is now done on the Chenab, and the altering of marks would cease.

27,000 logs in transit. 12. None of the logs launched in 1862 have yet been landed, therefore, a large supply may reasonably be looked for whenever the floods come in 1863, as timber to the extent of 27,000 logs is already in the river waiting for the rains and floods to carry it onwards. All the timber received as well as that appropriated by merchants and others was cut in 1861.

Proposed Establishment. 13. An establishment is required to watch, catch, and land the logs as they come down. No establishment, temporary or permanent, has yet been sanctioned for the Ravi, it has hitherto been put on and removed as required. Much remains to be done to bring the work into good order, and to protect our timber as far as possible. When arrangements are matured and matters now in dispute settled, I have no doubt the establishment will admit of reduction. At present, I believe the estimated establishment to be necessary.

Office required. 14. The accounts have hitherto been kept in the Executive Office of the Baree Doab Canal workshops. From the date of my leaving, the two charges will be separated, and an office becomes requisite for the Ravi timber Agent.

Cost of Establishment. 15. The estimate for establishment this year is 10,776 rupees, subject to reductions amounting to 1,312 rupees, which leaves the sum of 9,464 rupees to be sanctioned up to the 30th April, 1864.

30th April, 1863. J. D. Smithe.

Establishment Required for the Ravi Forests.

1 Assistant, - - -	Upper Ravi, - - - -	250
1 Sub-Engineer, - -	Saw-mills, - - - -	256
1 Baboo, - - - -		50
1 Moonshee, - - -		15
2 Chuprassis, - - -		10

Working Establishment.

1 Chuprassi, - - -	Oodeypore, - - - -	5
2 „ - - - -	Seul river, - - - -	10
1 „ - - - -	Chobra, - - - - -	5
1 „ - - - -	Sangpoor, - - - -	5
1 „ - - - -	Kaul, - - - - - -	5
1 Moonshee, - - -	Sindara, - - - - -	12
1 Chuprassi, - - -	„ - - - - - -	5
1 Moonshee, - - -	Basouli, - - - - -	15
2 Chuprassis, - - -	„ - - - - - -	10
1 „ - - - -	Mow, - - - - -	5
1 Moonshee, - - -	Saw-mills, - - - -	10
2 Chuprassis, - - -		10
1 „ - - - -	Bheeri, - - - - -	5
1 „ - - - -	Bussoo, - - - - -	5
1 „ - - - -	Akwank, - - - -	5
1 „ - - - -	Deroh, - - - - -	5
1 Moonshee, - - -	Bara Bansu, - - -	15
9 Chuprassis, - - -	„ - - - - - -	45
1 Moonshee, - - -	Barmawar, - - - -	12
8 Chuprassis, - - -	„ - - - - - -	40
1 Moonshee, - - -	Chenota, - - - - -	12
5 Chuprassis, - - -	„ - - - - - -	25
1 Moonshee, - - -	Head Quarters, Forest Officer, - - - -	15
1 Chuprassi, - - -		5
1 Head Constable, - -		7
4 Policemen, - - -		24
		898 × 12 = 10,776

The Moonshee at Sindara has been discontinued, and some of the Chuprassis being only employed part of the year, there is a reduction of 1,812 rupees.

J. D. Smithe.

NOTE—The *data* obtained from Mr. Smithe's Report, 1862-63, shewn in a tabular form analogous to those of the Pangi Agency, stand as follows:—

	1861-62.	1862-63.	1863-64.
Number of trees felled, - - - -	3,292 logs bought at 2-8 each, 2,402 trees at 5 each,	6,083	5,948
Number of logs marked, - - - -	13,784,	27,600	19,727
Number of logs launched, - - - -	13,784,	18,248	20,250
Number of logs left in forest, - -	None,	9,352	15,192
Number of logs received at Madhopur,	150,	3,876	4,444
Cubic contents of ditto, cubic feet, -	3,491,	41,360	69,799
Average contents, cubic feet, - -	$23\frac{1}{4}$,	$10\frac{1}{2}$	16
Square feet cut by saw-mill, - - -	307,317,	294,450	
Cubic contents of timber (round and sawn) issued, cubic feet,	18,135,	21,601	57,119
Waif timber caught, cubic feet, - -		12,410	16,779
Expenditure, rupees, - - - -		53,359	The other items cannot be filled in till the close of the official year.
Realized by sales, rupees, - - -		24,969	
Excess of expenditure, rupees, - -		28,390	
Cost of establishment, ,, - -		10,776	
Logs lost, } Estimated, cubic feet, -		2,000	
Average contents } Estimated, cubic feet, -		20	

2. A statement of profit and loss cannot be prepared, as the amount of timber on hand and of outstandings is not given.

3. The rates cannot be calculated as to the sum expended in bringing down 100 cubic feet and the money realised on the same quantity. In another year, a fair average may be struck.

4. Mr. Smithe returns $10\frac{1}{2}$ feet as the average cubic contents of logs received, and that of logs lost at 20 cubic feet, the difference is remarkable; the explanation offered is that the largest logs are tampered with, and that the waif being taken along with the logs cut in 1861, reduced the average.

5. It is stated that of the 18,248 logs launched in 1862-63, none were received during the year. The 3,876 logs, therefore, received at the depôt must have belonged to previous years. It is important to ascertain the proportion of logs launched and received during a series of years.

6. The excess of expenditure over income is large, but the receipts are increasing. 70,000 rupees is the estimated income for 1864-65.

THE CHENAB RIVER.

THE Chenab or Chandra Bagha is, next to the Sutlej, the largest and longest of the Punjab rivers. From the junction of the Chandra and Bagha at Tandi, in British Lahul, to Aknûr, where the river debouches upon the plains, its length is about 300 miles. The fall, according to General A. Cunningham, is 34 feet per mile from Tandi to Kishtawar, and 26 feet per mile from Kishtawar to Aknûr. (*Ladak*, p. 119.) Chenab or Chandra Bagha.

I traced the course of the main river (in company with Mr. J. D. Smithe, Superintendent, and his Assistant Mr. J. A. Murray) from Darwas, near the Maharajah's boundary to Tandi, a distance of 100 miles. The confluent rivers were also explored separately for some distance upwards, before we returned by Koksur and the Rotang pass to Kûllû.

In geological and botanical features, the valley of the Chenab closely resembles that of the Sutlej; both rivers rise in arid regions and flow between lofty ranges of mountains, generally rocky and precipitous, but often finely wooded. Valley of Chenab.

The weathered rocks of the high passes are black slate; mica schist gives colour to the water; white sand banks are occasionally seen, and water-worn rocks are observed in various places fifty feet and upwards above the present bed of the Chenab, showing Geology.

that the channel has gradually sunk. Dr. Thomson gives the following description :—" The range parallel to the Chenab on the north, has probably a granitic axis, for boulders of granite were common on the upper part of the ascent on both sides of the pass, though I did not anywhere see that rock *in situ*. On both sides the first rock exposed was a fine grained gneiss, with large crystals of felspar. Lower down, on the north face, I observed mica slate with garnets." (*Travels, p.* 304.)

Botany.

The flora of the pergunnah of Pangi, through which our path lay, agrees in most respects with that of Kunawar. From Darwas to Tilaknath on the Chenab the same gradual change of vegetation takes place which is observed from Taranda to Kanam on the Sutlej, the number of species being smaller in Pangi than in Kunawar.

Character of Chenab.

Above Darwas,* the Chenab is a rapid, noble river, running through a deep rocky channel. From the twig bridge at Kilar, elevation 7,000 feet, the course of the river may be seen both up and down to a considerable distance. On 1st August, it was swollen and muddy, and apparently as large as the Sutlej at Rampur, but much more even in its flow. The bed of the river is not often interrupted by rocks, and the Chenab offers fewer obstacles to timber transport than any of the other Punjab rivers; except in one or two places taroos, (*i. e.*, men supported on mashaks), are not required to disengage logs, until the river reaches Aknûr.

Deodar tract.

The limits of the deodar tract belonging to Chamba in the Chenab valley are from the nullah Sansai, which forms the boundary between Chamba and Jum-

* Of useful plants, the edible pine *pinus gerardiana*, occurs abundantly near Darwas, a large umbelliferous plant, yielding assafœtida, grows north of Kilar, and the pencil cedar (*juniperus excelsa*) in considerable numbers from Tilaknath to Kyelang the Moravian settlement.

moo, up to within two miles of Triloknath, altogether about eighty miles. Above this the elevation is too high, and the *tos*, *kail*, juniper, and willow, are the only indigenous trees. The deodar grows on both banks of the river, but more abundantly on the left, and though the trees are smaller in size than those on the Ravi, the forests are much more extensive and more uniformly composed of *kelu* than any others I have seen in the Kohistan of the Punjab. In many places, the trees grow close to the river, which, as already mentioned, is better suited for timber transport than the Sutlej, Beas, or Ravi.

Much has been written as to the quality of the Chenab timber, which is generally admitted to be somewhat inferior to the Ravi wood. The difference arises from peculiarity of soil and elevation, and perhaps also from the configuration of the valley. The Pangi timber has been very extensively used for various purposes in the Punjab during the last ten years. Quality of Pangi wood.

Captain Dyas, Director of Canals, Punjab, writes, "I tried some experiments upon the timber from the "two rivers. The Chenab wood was perfectly clean "and sound from Pangi; I also obtained some of the "best procurable timber at Umritsir from a Ravi "river merchant, to compare with the Chenab wood. "The results of the experiment follow in the form "given in the Appendix of Paper No. II., Strength "of Materials, published at Roorkee." Captain Dyas' experiment.

MEAN RESULTS.

Description of Timber.	Dimensions.			Breaking Weight.	Do reduced to units of L. B. D. 1ft. 1in. 1in.	Weight in lbs. per cubic foot.
	in.	in.	in.			
Chenab deodar,	18	1½	1½	1,348lbs.	599lbs.	28·62
Ravi deodar,	18	1½	1½	1,821lbs.	808lbs.	35·75

"The constant for transverse strength obtained by experiment at Roorkee for the Chenab timber as shewn in the Appendix above quoted, was 583lbs., which it will be observed agrees very nearly with the constant obtained by the experiments at Madhopur, viz., 599lbs. The weight per cubic foot however in the two sets of experiments varies considerably. At Roorkee, the weight of a cubic foot of Chenab timber was found to be 23·06lbs. at Madhopur it was 28·62lbs. The Superintendent of the Pangi Timber Agency lately informed me that he had found the weight of a cubic foot of the Chenab deodar to be 16 seers or 32lbs. I lay some stress on the subject of weight, because, of the same species of seasoned timber, that which is heavier is also stronger and more durable."

Comparison of Ravi and Chenab forests.

In the valley of the Ravi, the river flows at an elevation of 4 to 5,000 feet, and the trees grow on precipitous crags over the feeders, 2,000 feet above the main stream. In Pangi, the river bed is 7,000 feet high, and the trees are often found close to the Chenab, in narrow gorges and without free circulation of air. At Sanch nullah we observed a large number of trees with unhealthy bark, apparently caused by crowding and excess of moisture; this, however, is a solitary case, and much of the deodar is of the finest quality. Moreover, in the early years of the agency, trees may have been felled at the wrong season, and the wood may have been immature. As the felling has extended up the valley and to a greater elevation, the wood procured is of a better quality.

Deputation of Mr. Prinsep, 1850.

In 1850, Mr. E. Prinsep, C.S., then Assistant Commissioner of Sealkote, visited the Padar and Kishtawar districts to inspect the deodar forests in the Maharajah Golab Singh's territories, and effect arrangements for the supply of materials required for building the Sealkote Cantonment. He ascended the valley of the Chenab from Aknûr to near the Chamba boundary, and part of the valley of the Butna, a large tributary. It is recorded by Colonel Harley Maxwell, then Executive Engineer, "that his labours were attended with the greatest success." Deodar wood was supplied from Padar and Kishtawar, and the Maharaja Golab Sing, consented to forego duties on timber passing through his jurisdiction, but felled within British territory.

Exploration of Major Longden, 1851.

In 1851, Lord Dalhousie proposed that Major Longden should be deputed to examine carefully the whole of the Himalayan range from Chamba eastwards to the north of Simla; this duty that officer fulfilled in 1852-3, and after inspecting the forests of the territories bordering on the Sutlej, Beas, Ravi, and Chenab, recommended the establishment of an agency on the last of these rivers, which was sanctioned in March, 1854, when he was appointed Agent.

Pangi Agency, 1854.

From the statements of the Chamba Raja and his people, and from the recorded opinion of Mr. McLeod, then Commissioner of the Trans-Sutlej states, it is evident that Major Longden, who commenced the Agency and was in charge for two years, possessed remarkable powers of physical endurance, untiring zeal and other qualifications for conducting the difficult duties committed to him. He commenced work in the lower part of the valley near Darwas, and made his head quarters at Kilar, being dependent on the Raja for labor and supplies. Mr. Ter Arratoon had previously felled trees in Pangi, but ceased to do so in 1854.

Successive Agents.

After conducting operations for two years Major Longden was succeeded by Lieut. Peyton in 1856, by Major Thomas in 1859, and by Mr. Smithe as

Superintendent of the Ravi and Chenab forests in 1862. Mr. Murray, who had already served one year in Pangi, being appointed upper Assistant.*

Qualifications of Forest Officer.

The Forest officer should be a man of judgment, energy, tact, and experience, capable of exercising magisterial power, and of settling disputes between employers and employed. The allotment of forest, the testing of slides, the prompt payment of laborers and of His Highness, rest with him. Mr. Smithe has shown himself able to arrange and organize details. He is of a conciliatory bearing, not easily over reached, and well acquainted with native character.

Defects of previous management.

Until the appointment of Major Reid, (1863,) the great defect in forest operations on the part of the Chamba state was want of supervision by an intelligent head. A vakeel now accompanies the agent in his tours, keeping a record of trees felled, which is compared with the weekly return made to that officer by his munshis, any difference being settled in the forest without delay. Not so with the numerous traders, whose work is desultory and without system. In the beginning of the season they ingratiate themselves with the Raja, by presenting a nuzzur; but no record is kept of their work, no vakeel accompanies them, and at the end of the season no one can tell whether 500 or 5,000 trees have been cut. The Raja is now alive to the evil of this reckless system, which would speedily exhaust the largest forests.

Contractor Mahomed Sultan.

The only contractor at work upon the Chenab is Mahomed Sultan, who has conducted operations for three years, and has launched a large amount of timber. His logs are generally smaller than those cut by the Agency. He pays nominally 5 Rs. per

* The duties of upper Assistant are to make preparations (p. 139); to register mates of gangs and receive their security; to pay the workmen, to check the weekly returns of the munshis, and to exercise general supervision in the valley.

tree, but the stumps not being counted, it is probable that the rate is much lower.

Traders should receive every encouragement to **Traders.** purchase timber at the depôts of issue on the plains, but in the deep chasm rivers of the Himalaya competition is impossible, and one party alone can work; divided interests lead only to wrangling and endless disputes.

The forest establishment is sanctioned for seven **Working season.** months, but a month and a half being required for reaching the forests, collecting and hutting laborers, and arranging for supplies, the average length of the working season is not six months. Preparations should be made by the end of April, and the experience of ten years shows that work should cease by the middle of October, when the establishment returns to Sealkote, and the laborers to their homes, before the passes are closed for the winter.

The melting of the snow commences in May and **Season of flood.** the river acquires its largest volume in July and August. The feeders appear to be more swollen in a hot season, than when the rainfall is unusually great, as in 1862. Major Longden reported that a log was received at the depôt 10 or 12 days after launching, but he worked lower in the valley than is now done. Logs launched after the end of August seldom reach Sealkote the same year.

The wood-cutters bring their axes, and sharpen **Tools and Sawing.** them at their own cost. A small store is kept from which tools are supplied, if axes are broken or if laborers come without. The use of the saw is unknown in the valley, and the introduction of trained sawyers, would, at present be very costly if expedient.

From the commencement of the Agency to 1862, **Supply of Food.** the forest employés obtained food from the stores of the Raja at such rates as he pleased to charge, but this arrangement was attended with inconvenience, difficulty, and discontent. To meet the necessities of the work people, (the valley not producing food beyond the wants of its inhabitants) it was resolved in 1862, to import atta, salt, &c., from the adjoining valleys of Padar, Seul, and Kûllû; this system has worked well. The food is sold at cost price, the carriage being debited to the forests.

Hutting.

The coolies arrange for their own housing, and usually occupy temporary sheds formed of the branches and bark of *pinus excelsa*,* or *abies smithiana;* as many as thirty or forty men occupy one shed.

Want of Medical aid.

Epidemics were not known till 1863, when small pox appeared among the workmen; cases of dysentery and accidental injury occur every season. The services of a medical subordinate would be specially valuable. For two years a native doctor, on 40 Rs. per mensem, was very useful in Pangi; the hardships of a forest life were distasteful to him, and no successor has been found. With an increasing number of laborers and the recurrence of serious accidents, medical aid is urgently required.

Average labor.

From Major Longden's enquiries and Mr. Murray's experience of three years, it appears that on an average one man fells during the season twelve trees, converts them into logs, and launches them. The rolling of the logs is the most harassing part of the work, and becomes more difficult as the distance from the river increases.

Rates of payment.

The workpeople have been paid for felling, rolling, and marking logs, at the following rates which are similar to those upon the Ravi.

* One of the duties of the officer is to watch that the deodar and reserved woods are not used for this purpose.

	Haths.				
	5-6½	6½-9.	9-11.	11-15.	Above 15
	Rs.	Rs.	Rs.	Rs.	Rs.
Felling and cutting into logs, ..	12as	1	1-2	1-8	2
Rolling into the river, ...	1-4	1-8	1-14	2-8	3
Marking 100 logs,*	3				

It may be premised that a "hath" is equal to 1½ feet and that no trees are allowed to be felled under 6 haths = 9 feet. Trees of less girth were formerly felled. When the logs are broken, five annas are deducted from the payment; when undersized trees are cut, the mates are fined at the discretion of the Agent.

Advantage of small coin.

Between Chamba and Kilar, a distance of 180 miles, there is not a village where change for a rupee can be procured. The supply of small silver coin to Pangi is a great desideratum, which would facilitate payments, prevent disputes, save the carriage of copper, and please the people of the district.

Working in gangs.

The laborers are collected by mokaddams or mates of gangs, who receive small advances at the beginning of the season, and give security for fulfilling their engagements. The logs are counted, and the work checked weekly in the progress report. At the end of the season all the accounts are adjusted before leaving the forests. The following number of laborers was employed:—

1861, ...	850
1862, ...	1,018
1863, ...	1,897

* The government timber mark on the Ravi and Chenab is a double penticle, with the year of felling.

These were divided into gangs, and distributed over both banks of eighty miles of river.

Galls or slides in Pangi.

In 1861, fifty galls were used on the Chenab, and the following tabular statement shows the number in each district:—

District Darwas,	14	District Shor,	15
,, Kilar,	6	,, Tindi,	7
,, Saneh,	6	,, Lahul,	2
		Total,	50

In 1862, the number was 53; their character and position as follows:—

	Right bank.	Left bank.	In nullah.	Total.
1st class galls, ...	18	10	8	36
2nd ditto, ...	5	6	...	11
3rd ditto, ...	2	4	...	6
		Total,	...	53

This shows the large proportion of first class galls; the per centage of breakage in launching numbers of logs, is of importance, representing a great amount of timber during the season. The average breakage on the Chenab is only 5 per cent., which contrasts favorably with the Ravi, where the largest number of galls is third class. (*i. e.*, above 15 per cent.)

Darwas

In the Darwas district, which is fourteen miles long, there are the following galls:—

First class galls, ...	7
Second do., ...	5
Third do., ...	1
Total, ...	13

Seven of these are on the right bank, five on the left,

and one in a nullah. Upwards of 2,600 trees were felled in 1862. About 2,000 full sized trees remain in three of the first class galls; about 500 in one of the second class, and a few only in the third class, which are now fit for felling. There are 10,000 trees under four haths in girth. Two of the first class galls must be considered exhausted for the present, only immature trees being left in them. This district, is favorable for planting, the galls being open, generally good and close to the river.

The Kilar district* extends for eighteen miles on both banks, and is generally rocky and precipitous. Kilar.

First class galls,	... ...	2
Second do.,	... ...	1
Third do.,	... ...	3
Total,...	... ...	6

Two of the galls are on the right bank and four on the left. 4,000 trees were obtained in the district in 1862; a large number of them from the three third class slides, which had been condemned in previous years, on account of the great breakage in sending down the timber, but by making bunds across at intervals to arrest the velocity of the logs, they are successfully worked and rated as third class. It will be necessary to adopt this system extensively as the trees become exhausted in the more accessible places. Time, labor, money and superintendence, are required, without these timber will not be procurable. About 600 trees are fit for felling in one first class slide; a few only in the second class, and 1,500 mature trees remain in two of the third class galls.

About 10,000 trees have been observed in favora-

* In this district a small bungalow was built by Major Longden, which is considered the head-quarters of the valley.

ble positions for felling, but they are not fit for present use, barely one-third having attained the standard size.

Sanch. This district is thirty miles in length, and contains six galls, all first class; two are on the right bank and four in a nullah. Upwards of 2,000 trees were felled, one gall alone yielding half that number. There are about 5,000 trees under four and a half haths girth, and therefore not ready for use; about 4,000 are fit for felling, but they are in difficult places, where much labor is required to get them into the river. As long as trees can be found in more suitable situations, this district will not be much worked.

Shor. The Shor district extends forty miles, and has 14 galls, seven on the right bank, and seven on the left.

First class galls, ...	8
Second do., ...	4
Third do., ...	2
Total, ...	14

The forests are at a great distance from each other, but the galls are generally good and well situated for launching timber. 4,000 trees were obtained during the season. In two of the first class galls about 1,200 trees were observed fit for felling, and about 500 in a second class gall, but not many in the third class. There is much undersized timber. *

Tindi. The Tindi district is small, and the trees are much scattered.

First class galls, ...	11
Second do., ...	1
Total, ...	12

Six galls are on the right bank, four on the left,

* Major Longden, in 1853, made a small plantation of *cedrus deodara* on the river bank, between Rai and Sanch; it contains about 1000 promising trees, the known age of the plants will afford useful *data* as to rate of growth.

and two in nullahs. One of the nullahs is very rocky. The district yielded 2,000 trees in 1862. About 1,500 trees were observed in two of the first class galls suitable for felling, and 500 in the second class gall.

In Chota Lahul, there are only two galls, both first class; one on the right bank, and one in a nullah. From the first, 100 trees were brought down this season. In the second, 50 pencil cedars *(juniperus excelsa)* were felled, and about 500 remain; they are of no great size, and all the largest are decayed in the centre. Between the forests and the river in this and the Tindi district, a few villages are situated, surrounded by terraced cultivation, which interferes with the launching of logs. **Lahul.**

From the valley of the Seul there are four well known passes, leading into the pergunnah of Pangi, viz., Sach, Chéni, Chara, and Drati. The first of these is closed nearly two months before the others, and remains impassable for a longer period. The second leads direct to the Sach jhula, and is most convenient for entering and leaving the valley. **Passes into Pangi.**

There are two passes from Barmawar into Chota Lahul, the Chobia, and the Kalichu, or Kali Debi,* the latter leading from the source of the Nai to Triloknath. Barmawar is connected with British Lahul by the much frequented Kukti pass, which is considered easier than the other two. By this route large flocks of sheep cross every year to Lahul for pasturage. The forest officers have great opportunity of obtaining useful information, and might enter and return from Pangi by different passes every year, if duty permits. In communication with the Superintendent of Chamba much knowledge of the Mid-Himalaya will thus be acquired. **Passes into Lahul.**

* A. Cunningham, in *Jour. As. Soc. Beng.*, x., 107.

Want of roads.

The only communications in Pangi are narrow rugged tracks, running along either bank according as the mountain slope is favorable. Many parts overhanging the river are almost impassable for a laden man, and between Salgrain and Madgrain especially, the difficulties are such that even dogs and unladen sheep must be carried. This prevents the importation of supplies from Kûllû, and obstructs all trade along the river bank. Ponies occasionally cross the Gurdhar pass from Triloknath to Sach, thus avoiding the river. An excellent riding path extends to the boundary of British Lahul, and if the bad places in the Pangi tracks were improved so as to be passable for mules, the rich valley of Padar would be connected with Kûllû. Pangi would then be accessible earlier in the season, *viâ* the Rotang pass, which is crossed by laden mules, and is in good order.

Bridges.

From Triloknath to Darwas the river is spanned by ten bridges, made of birch or witch-hazel* twigs, at the following places:—

Soorj,	Kotul,
Kilar,	Raie,
Kagul,	Purtie,
Mundlah,	Shor,
Sach,	Tindi.

Three of these on the main track are maintained by the Raja, while seven have been erected for forest purposes. It is now arranged that jhulas and bridges are to be renewed by His Highness, in consideration of the enhanced seignorage paid. If urgently required, the work may be done by the forest officer, and the Raja's account debited. The suspension bridges in Pangi are of witch-hazel twigs, and in Lahul, of birch. A superior sangla with close wattling of wicker-work has been formed (1863) at Kilar, by Mr.

* *Fothergilla involucrata*, witch-hazel.

Murray, and over this laden sheep and goats have crossed the Chenab. There is also a wooden sangla near Triloknath.

The transit of letters was formerly attended with considerable expense, special messengers being engaged for the season to carry the dâk, but on account of the increased timber revenue it has been arranged that letters should be carried free by the Raja's dâk every second day to the forest officers. Dâks.

The following statement of trees felled in Pangi is compiled from records in the Agency office, Sealkote. Ten years statement.

1853, Mr. Arratoon,	5,034
1854, " " to 21st June,	938
1854, Major Longden,	5,477
1855, " "	2,837
1856, Lieut. Peyton,	1,873
1857, (Mutiny),	None.
1858, "	None.
1859, Major Thomas,	5,987
1860, " "	4,872
1861, Mr. Murray,	11,197
1862, " "	12,513
1863, " "	13,000
1862-3, Mahomed Sultan, (estimated),	10,000
Total,	73,728

These were all first class trees, of which, this range can only supply 5000 to 6000 a year. It is obvious that no forest in the world can bear such excessive cutting.

The work in Pangi was superintended by Mr. Murray, with the following establishment, sanctioned for five months. Pangi Forest establishment.

17 Moonshees,	1 Native doctor,
44 Chuprassis,	1 Jemadar,
1 Treasurer,	6 Burkendazis.

The staff of moonshees depends on the number of gangs of workmen; they are stationed in the forests, and their duty is to measure the trees, and keep a return of work done. One of them is located at each end of the valley, to purchase supplies. The chuprassis see the logs properly marked and carefully launched, noting the amount of breakage. The jemadar and burkendazis form the treasure guard.

Weekly return of trees felled and logs launched.

Mr. Murray prepares a weekly return of trees felled from the reports of the moonshees; this is shewn to the Raja's vakeel on Saturday, and any difference is settled at once. A weekly report of logs launched is also kept for comparison with the catching at the Sealkote depôt.

Scantling.

Logs of greater length are brought down the Chenab than by the Sutlej, Beas, or Ravi. The largest proportion of timber has been cut expressly for railway sleepers (12 feet). A considerable number of logs, 18 to 20 feet in length, have been launched; if required longer for particular purposes larger scantling can be procured but at an additional rate, as long timbers are more difficult to move, and more liable to breakage and stranding.

Useful woods.

Besides deodar, which is the principal object of forest operations, the wood of other trees has been sought by different public departments. The following is a table of the varieties brought down:—

			1862.	1863.
Akrot,	*Juglans regia,*	Walunt,	logs 207	25
Sunnu,	*Fraxinus,*	Ash,	„ 253	222
Davidiar,	*Juniperus excelsa,*	Pencil Cedar,	„ 150	..
Munner,	*Acer,*	Maple,	„ 28	33
Jamun,	*Prunus padus,*	Bird Cherry,	„ 23	2
Bhoj,	*Betula Bhoj-putra,*	Birch,	„ 3	57
Moral,	*Ulmus,*	Elm,		128

Previous to 1862, there was little demand. From

the hurried nature of my visit I cannot estimate the number of trees available. The elm attains a large size, and with the maple and bird cherry (*Prunus padus)* is abundant. The ash* is not common, and the walnut is much valued by the villagers for its fruit. The birch and pencil cedar are in large numbers in Lahul, but the logs are small and float past the depôts if the taroos are not vigilant.

Specimens of the various kinds of timber procurable in Pangi and Lahul have been deposited in the Madhopur workshops; another set has been sent to the Punjab Exhibition. **Specimens of wood.**

Two maunds of deodar seed and one of the large ash were collected for sowing in suitable localities. **Seeds.**

Rhubarb roots, cumin seed, and "koot," the root of *aucklandia veracosta,* are largely produced in the valley. The discovery of asafœtida, alluded to in page 134, is interesting, and may be turned to account. **Drugs.**

British Lahul consists chiefly of the mountainous tract, contained within the angle formed by the rivers Chandra and Bagha, but extends 25 miles below their junction at Tandi. This province divides Kûllû from Ladak and Tibet, and resembles the last in character. **British Lahul.**

There are few indigenous trees. That which gives character to the district is *juniperus excelsa,* or pencil cedar, the "shukpa" of Lahul, and "lewar" of Kunawar. It forms small forests, especially on the southern slope of the hills at an elevation of 9 to 12,000 feet. The tree seldom attains 30 feet in height and 6 feet in girth; but Thomson (*Travels, p.* 257) mentions "one perhaps 40 feet high" and **Vegetation of Lahul.**

* There are two species of ash, one is a large tree, occasionally 12 or 15 feet in girth. The small variety (*Fraxinus xanthoxylloides*) is very common, but its stem is only large enough to make handles of tools.

I measured one below the monastery at Kyelang, 13 feet in girth. The bark is red, separating into *laminæ* like birch, and apparently a good material for brown paper. The wood is used for house and bridge building, and is adapted for ornamental cabinet work; it is fragrant, harder, and less odorant than W. Indian cedar; of this tree Jacquemont wrote, (*Voyages, tom.* 2, *p.* 373,) " C' est là qu'on fait avec le bois de *junip. arborea* les seaux, les vases de toute espèce, qui servent à contenir l'eau et le lait en Kunawar, et qui s'exportent en Ladak et à Garou." The ground below the trees is generally rocky, bare, or covered with a strong smelling *artemisia*, large thistles, or various species of rose.*

Kail-pine. The kail, " som-shing," *pinus excelsa*, is the largest tree in Lahul, but is less frequent then the pencil cedar. On the left bank of the Chandra, about three miles above the junction, there is a forest of this tree, and a small patch occurs above Kardang, from which the Moravian mission house was built. These two tracts have been thinned of late years, and measures should be adopted to preserve the scanty arboreous vegetation of Lahul, where traders to Ladak experience so much difficulty in obtaining necessary fuel.

Birch. The birch, " tagpa," *betula*, is usually a crooked and stunted tree, but sometimes exceeds one foot in diameter. The annual bridges over the mountain torrents are made of birch twigs, and the bark is used instead of paper for the draft forest returns.

Willows. Willows, " chung," *salix alba*, are planted round almost every village and along water-courses. The slender branches and leaves serve as food for sheep and goats.

Poplars. There are two species of poplar, *populus balsa-*

* A wild yellow Persian rose, *R. eglanteria*, here finds its eastern limit.—*Flora Indica*, Vol. I., p. 209.

mifera, "yarpa," and *P. nigra*, planted near villages, but in much smaller numbers than the willow.*

Hippophae salicifolia, "tser kar," a stout shrub with spinous branches, is frequent in the valleys. The yellow berries are extremely acid, but when boiled with sugar form an agreeable and wholesome preserve. The natives use the branches for dry hedges and fuel, and they are so valued for this purpose, as to be considered village property. A species of *prunus*, "litsi," ripens in September, with a tolerably sweet fruit, something like the cherry. A gooseberry, "bilitsi," with small woolly sour berries is common, and a black fruited *ribes*, "rasta," resembling in taste the European red currant, is largely eaten by the people. Roses, "sewa," are in great abundance, and are used for fuel and hedges. The yellow rose occurs only near villages, and was perhaps originally planted. English and American vegetable seeds and fruit trees supplied to the missionaries in Lahul, have succeeded well and do not degenerate so much as in the plains or as at Kotgurh. The fruit trees which thrive best are the apple, walnut, and apricot. Vines have died out, the climate being too cold, but the hop is now under trial. Oats, potatoes, and scarlet runners, flourish well. The Lahul villagers have quickly learned to appreciate the value of the potato, and eagerly apply for seed; this is the only instance in which they have been induced to depart from their usual routine of crops. The herbage consists chiefly of *artemisia*, *cuminum*, *chenopodium*, *pedicularis gentiana*, *cirsium*, &c. Fruits.

* It is evident from the above that no timber except pencil cedar and birch can be expected from Lahul. The food resources of the district are important in connection with forest operations. Much botanical information regarding the province has been acquired by the Rev. H. A. Jaeschke, Kyelang, who has explored the district thoroughly and possesses an extensive herbarium.

Spiti.

The adjoining province of Spiti* I did not visit, it is more barren than Lahul, the arboreous vegetation consists of only a few willows and poplars, growing in ravines on the banks of streams.

ROUTE FROM KOKSUR TO DARWAS.

NAMES OF STAGES.	DISTANCE, MILES.	REMARKS.
Koksur,		Below Rotang pass, (13,000,) where snow lies till June. A good new bridge over Chandra.
Sissu,	9	Road easy.
Gondla,	10	Road easy.
Kyelang,	10	Road narrow but safe. Moravian mission station at Kyelang close to the right bank of the river. The road from Kûllû to Le by Bara Lacha pass, *via* Kardang, runs along opposite bank of Bhaga.
Lot,	8	Supplies plentiful, road good and easy.
Jhar or Jaharma,	8	
Tirot,	10	The last village in the province of British Lahul.
Triloknath,	9	A Hindoo temple here, much visited by pilgrims; two miles from Triloknath, cross Chandra Bhaga, by a wooden bridge. Path good and easy.
Madgrain,	9	Cross Bendee and Chandra Bhaga by wooden bridge.
Salgrain,	12	Path very dangerous, impracticable for ponies and sheep, laden coolies must proceed with care.
Tindi,	10	The Drati pass leads to Tindi.
Rowlee,	9	
Tuttialla,	8	
Shor,	6	A frail twig bridge.
Parti,	6	
Raee,	6	
Sanch,	9	Path very bad opposite Cheni pass.
Sidh,	9	
Kilar,	6	Head-quarters of forest officer, opposite Sach pass.
Darwas,	12	A large village near the frontier of Raja of Chamba. Path tolerable.
Marches, .	20	
Total miles,	166	

* It communicates with Lahul by the Kulzum pass, a depression in the Mid-Himalaya. The climate is almost rainless.

On 20th June, 1854, the Chief Commissioner of the Punjab arranged with the Maharaja Golab Sing, that no assistance of any kind should be required from His Highness' officers by the Agent, but at the same time the forest officers were at liberty to employ any Kashmir subjects who might seek employment of their own free will. Agreement with the Maharaja.

The portion of the Chenab which passes through the territories of the Maharaja of Kashmir, about 200 miles long, has not been well explored, and a good description of the channel between Darwas and Aknur would be useful. Major Longden followed the course of the river from Pangi to Sealkote, but left no account of his journey. Brief notices of this tract are found in Thomson's* and Vigne's† Travels. Obstructions are known to exist in the river at Akola and Lori in Padar. A moonshee was sent from Pangi in October, 1862, to inspect this portion of the river, and to observe where the wood was stranded; he counted upwards of 31,000 logs, and reported that in many places there were piles of timber difficult to reach or to count. The great discrepancy between the number of logs launched and received in 1862, rendered me desirous of ascertaining the amount and position of stranded timber. The following table is supplied by Lieut. Chalmers, who, accompanied by Mr Murray, made an adventurous journey down the river bank in November, 1863, after being detained in Pangi by a snow storm, which prevented them from crossing the Sach pass. Chenab in Kashmir.

* P. 305 † Kashmir, I., p. 200.

RETURN OF LOGS FOUND IN CHENAB BETWEEN THE CHAMBA BOUNDARY AND RIASI.

November, 1863.

MARCHES.		1863. SEASONS LOGS.	OLD LOGS.	REMARKS.
FROM	TO			
Nullah Sunsai,	Seul,	2,000		
Seul,	Toli,	2,975		
„ other side of river,		775		Government mark cut out of one log, another altered to that of Maharaja.
Toli,	Jhar,	552		
Jhar,	Pyas,	2,813		
Pyas,	Kishtawar,	5,000	1,200	4 logs partly cut into planks and partly into firewood, reported to Kardar.
Kishtawar,	Junglewar,	546	30	
Junglewar	2nd Junglewar,	1,045	93	
2nd Junglewar,	Ashar,	333	20	
Ashar,	Butote,	230	13	Found 7 planks, said to belong to Soba, cutwal, on one of which was Government mark.
Butote,	Ranbirpore,	238	10	
Ranbirpore	Dhumkund,	7,008	2,398	One log with mark cut out.
Dhumkund,	Ganga,	1,400	200	
Ganga,	Thangur,	13,000	5,000	One log bearing our mark on under side, and Sooltan's above.
Thangur,	Purhund,	325	144	
Purhund,	Labsoora,	362	275	
Labsoora,	Riasi,	212	48	4 Government logs cut up here, part of them still remain.
	Total,	38,814	9,431	15 logs with marks altered or destroyed.

Duties of Lower Assistant.

The Assistant, Lower Sub-division, has the supervision of the Chenab between Riasi and Ramnuggur, a tract 100 miles long, including the district of Bajwat, which is intersected by numerous large streams. The duty consists of catching logs in the floods, clearing numerous islands of stranded timber, controlling the establishment during the summer, and in the winter months selecting, allotting, and invoicing the timber: all this affords ample occupation.

RATES OF LABOR IN THE LOWER SUB-DIVISION CHENAB FORESTS, FOR THE YEAR 1863-64.

From	To	Catching and landing logs, per 100 c. f.	Removing from the water, per 100 logs.	Rolling into the river, per 100 logs.	Despatching, per 100 c. f.	Despatching, per 100 logs.	Rolling to the back of Depôt, per 100 logs.	Cutting numbers, per 100 logs.	Cutting drag-holes, per 100 logs.	Taroos and carpenters, per diem.	Mates of coolies, per diem.	Coolies, per diem.	
		RS.	RS.	RS.	RS.	RS.	RS.	AS.	RS.	AS.	AS.	AS.	
Riasi - - -	Aknur,	0-12	6-4	2-1-4	1-8	...	...	8	1	4	3	2	Kashmir Territory.
Aknur - - -	Kala Chuk,	0-12	...	...	1-0	...	...	8	1	4	3	2	„ „
Kana Chuk -	„ „	0-12	...	...	0-14	...	...	8	1	4	3	2	„ „
Bajwat - -	„ „	1-0	3-2	3-2	0-12	...	...	8	1	4	3	2	British Territory.
Kala Chuk -	Wazirabad,	1-0	4-0	2-0	...	12-0	{ 3-0, 2-8, 2-0 }	10	1	4	3	2	„ „
Wazirabad -	Ramnuggur,	1-0	{ 12-8, 9-6, 6-4 }	{ 12-8, 9-6, 6-4 }	...	...	...	10	1	4	3	2 to 3	„ „
Ramnuggur -		1-0	...	...	...	...	...	10	1	4	3	2 to 3	„ „
Clearing Islands,		1 to 2-8	...	...	...	...	...	...	1	4	3	2 to 3	Throughout lower Sub-Division.

Timber supplied to Public departments.

STATEMENT OF TIMBER SUPPLIED TO DIFFERENT PUBLIC DEPARTMENTS DURING THE LAST THREE YEARS.

Departments.	1861-62.	1862-63.	1863-64. *
Punjab Railway Company,	4,59,744	3,91,890	1,00,517
Exec. Engineer, Amritsir,	...	31,041	...
Executive Engineer, Lahore,	16,622	...	...
Ditto, Lahore and Peshawur Road, 1st Division,	...	...	9,040
Executive Engineer, Lower Canals,	2,665	...	...
Executive Engineer, Mooltan,	...	...	4,526
Ditto, Sealkote,	11,934	4,735	15,617
Harbor works, Kurrachee,	35,180	...	5,642
Boat Bridges (Deputy Commissioners),	14,779	3,893	16,701
Civil works, (Ditto,)	14,419	5,071	5,497
Private Parties,	32,132	1,02,241	95,300
Total cubic feet, ...	5,87,475	5,38,871	2,52,840

Rates for timber of Chenab forests.

The rates for timber issued from the agency, sanctioned in 1862,† are as follows:—

up to	12 feet long		4	c. f.	per Rupee	1.
12	„	20 „	3	c. f.	„	1.
20	„	30 „	2·5	c. f.	„	1.
30	„	40 „	2	c. f.	„	1.
40	„	50 „	1·5	c. f.	„	1.

These rates apply to all purchasers. Above 50 feet timber is not procurable.

Timber supplied to Punjab Railway.

Orders have been issued for affording every assist-

* The column 1863-64 includes six months only.

† These rates are low, so that the purchase of timber at the depôt, and the re sale at stations, &c., is a profitable business.—H. C.

ance to the Punjab Railway Company; and any delay in measuring or removing the wood is reported. The following table shews the quantity of timber supplied to the agent and contractors:—

1859.	1860.	1861.	1862.	1863. [six months.]	Total supplied during 5 calender years.
Cubic feet.	Cubic feet.	Cubic feet.	Cubic feet.	Cubic feet.	Cubic feet.
29,124	1,00,794	3,05,173	5,30,625	1,60,064	11,25,781

The following are some of the principal purposes for which timber is required by the Ordnance Department: shafts and wheels of carriages, platform planks and sleepers, ammunition boxes, helves of tools, musket-stocks, and plugs for Minie rifle balls. For shafts, ash is well suited; for felloes, babul and oak; for spokes, babul; for naves, sissu and elm; for platforms, deodar; for ammunition boxes, elm; for musket-stocks, walnut; and for helves, ash and damun. Ordnance department.

Specimens of the following woods were sent to the Punjab Exhibition by Mr. Murray, and 46 kinds of timber were contributed by the Raja of Chamba. (Official Handbook, p. 225):— Pangi Woods.

Keling,	*Cedrus deodara,*	Baida,	*Salix.*
Chir,	*Pinus excelsa,*	Chun,	*Pyrus.*
Chilgoza,	*P. Gerardiana,*	Piniate,	*Prunus.*
Tôs,	*Abies Webbiana,*	Piake,	
Rai,	*A. Smithiana.*	Jamun,	*Prunus padus.*
Davidiar,	*Juniperus excelsa,*	Kurgh,	*Pyrus.*
Akrôt,	*Juglans regia,*	Kilar,	*Fothergilla involucrata.*
Sunnu,	*Fraxinus,*	Tangi,	*Corylus colurna.*
Sungel,	*F. Xanthoxylloides,*	Kuneloo,	
Munner,	*Acer,*	Bhoj,	*Betula Bhojputra.*
Moral,	*Ulmus,*	Paper,	*Buxus sempervirens.*
Rous.	*Cotoneaster baccilaris,*		

REPORT OF CHENAB TIMBER AGENT.

1862-63.

1. The Secretary to Government of India, Financial Department, in No. 1,513, of 15th April, 1863, requested data to assist in determining whether there has been sufficient return from the Pangi timber agency for the year 1862-63.

2. A comparison with the returns of 1861-62 shews that the establishment employed this year has been smaller whilst the work done will bear comparison with that performed in the previous year under more favorable circumstances.

3. I proceed to shew the work done and the cost of doing it,

Work.	1861 62.	1862-63.	1863-64.*
Number of trees felled,	11,197	12,706	13,230
Logs trimmed and marked,	52,899	58,980	63,216
„ rolled into river,	45,456	66,101	62,650
„ left in forests,	7,443	† 787	9,343
„ arrived at depot,	34,147	29,282	37,626
Arrived in plains, cubic feet,	7,60.550	5,32,865	7,62,583
Average contents of logs in depôt, cubic feet,	22·27	18·19	This cannot be filled in till 30th April, 1864.
Measured and sold, cubic feet,	5,87,475	5,38,871	
Balance in store 30th April, logs,	16,358	19,023	
„ „ in cubic feet,	1,96,120	2,48,138	
Average contents of logs in store 30th April, cubic feet,	11·98	13·04	
Issued to Punjab railway agent,	1,38,858	3,30,849	
„ to railway contractors,	3,20,885	1,63.381	
Total for railway in cubic feet,	4,59,743	4,94,230	

* The column 1863-64 has been added for comparison from data up to December, 1863.—H. C.

† This is the number of trees, estimated at 2861 logs.—H. C.

Expenditure.	1861-62.	1862-63.	1863-64.	
	Rs.			
Establishment bills,	23,412	15,024	21,359	Estimated.
Travelling allowance,	3,656	3,558	3,390	
Contingent bills,	1,972	4,434	1,685	
Labor,	43,664	46,624	83,500	
Purchases,	36,082	41,986	52,000	
Total expenditure for year,	1,08,793	1,11,627	1,61,934	
Sales of timber,	1,31,823	1,45,384	2,25,000	
Outstanding balance on 1st May,	79,470	64.790	Cannot be filled in till 30th April, 1864.	
„ year's transactions,*	„	29.488		
Old debts recovered,	„	44,168	39,571	

4. It will be seen that although the receipts of timber were 2,27,658 cubic feet less than in 1861-62, the sales were only 48,604 cubic feet less, whilst the product of the sales was rupees 13,561 more.

5. The forest establishment crossed the snowy range in April when the work of collecting laborers and storing supplies commenced at once. This was a great addition to the work of the agency, which in previous years had confined its operations to the felling of timber, laborers and food being supplied by the Raja of Chamba on the indent of the agent.

6. In a country so thinly peopled as Pangi, where food is grown sufficient only for home consumption, little assistance could be expected, and the greater proportion of labor and food was procured from Kistawar and Padar, with some from Badrawâr and Kûllû. There being no roads in Pangi, supplies are carried, where practicable, on sheep and goats, otherwise upon men's backs.

7. A large number of men were taken from forest work to carry supplies; and this draw-back will continue until paths are opened out for laden cattle.

8. Although the providing of labor and supplies were duties which had not previously devolved upon the agency, yet 1,509 trees were felled, 12,232 logs were trimmed and marked, and 20,645 logs were launched in excess of similar forest work in 1861. The rolling of the timber into the river is the most difficult and arduous work.

9. The receipts in the plains have been less than was expected; but they depend entirely upon the state of the river, which during 1862 was low, particularly in the higher part where timber operations are carried on. The continued and unusual rains and the cloudy atmosphere prevented the great mass of the snow from melting, whilst the rains were not heavy enough to cause floods in the river.

10. Some slight floods occurred in the lower part of the river in July, before

* The old debts are in course of recovery.—H. C.

any quantity of timber could be prepared. Only 2,806 logs were launched by the first week of July, when the flood came. In August when much timber was in the river the flood failed altogether. A *pansal,* or water gauge, has been put up at Aknur, and we shall in future have a correct register of the variations of the Chenab, of which we are at present ignorant.

11. The small number of logs caught at the lower depôts, Wazirabad and Ramnuggur, proves that the *taroos* were not idle at the upper catching places. A large number usually pass Riasi and Aknur, and are secured below, whereas this year few passed these depôts. The necessity of catching higher up the river must be insisted on; and I believe eventually the establishment at Ramnuggur may be dispensed with, except for a short time each year.

12. The low average of cubic contents is also due to the want of floods in the river. None of the larger logs or butt ends came down. The only timbers that arrived were small and medium sized.

13. Taking the establishment and travelling allowance bills as establishment, and the sales of timber as work done, it will be seen that the cost of establishment was 20 per cent. in 1861, and only 12 per cent. in 1862. The forest work compared in a similar manner shews a still more favorable result.

14. Mr. Lennox, Lower Assistant, estimates that only 250 or 300 logs of this season's preparing arrived in the plains, and that upwards of 29,000 logs caught this year, were launched previous to 1862. This is a low estimate, and I doubt its accuracy, as the logs could only be judged of by their weathered appearance, no distinguishing mark having been used to indicate the particular year's work. Instructions have been issued to mark each year's logs, and future reports will shew what proportion arrives in the plains and the time occupied in transport.

15. Of fancy woods prepared and launched, the ash and walnut will be very useful to the ordnance department; pencil cedar, cherry, &c., will find ready purchasers, many applications having already been made for them.

16. This year the standard size of trees felled was raised from 4½ to 5 haths in girth. I have directed that in future none under 6 haths in girth (or 9 feet) be felled. The result may be a smaller number of trees felled but those larger and more mature. The seignorage on trees paid to the Raja of Chamba, having been raised from 3 Rs. to 4 Rs. per tree, renders this course still more desirable. Other improvements involving extra supervision have been introduced, such as insisting on low cutting of the trees; these measures will aid materially in making up for the extra seignorage, and send more timber into the market without increasing the expenditure.

17. Rules of the Pangi timber agency have been printed and circulated, and a system of measuring, allotting, &c., has been established. This will aid the despatch of business at the depôt, and relieve the office of much work.

18. The establishment herewith submitted for sanction for 1863-64, amounts after making the temporary deductions, to Rs. 17,053. The slight increase is chiefly due to Mr. Lennox's rank as 1st Class Assistant Engineer; in the tabular

statement submitted for 1862-63, a 2nd class Assistant was applied for. A European subordinate will be required to look after the saw-mills to be erected on the Chenab river.

19. In conclusion, I must not omit to notice the services of Mr. Murray, Upper Assistant. For three years he has performed an arduous task in an inhospitable country, subjected to great exposure; the large amount of work done in the forests, extending over an immense extent of ground, is due to his exertions. Mr. Murray is deserving of consideration for the successful manner in which he has carried out the orders of Government.

J. D. SMITHE,
Superintendent.

ESTABLISHMENT REQUIRED FOR THE CHENAB FORESTS.

1 Superintendent,	Office Head Quarters.	500
1st Assistant,		350
2nd ,,		250
Native, ,,		150
1 Supervisor, (dispensed with,)		100
1 Clerk,		70
1 Writer, (5 months,)		40
1 Sheristadar,		30
1 Moonshee,		20
2 Chuprassis,		12
1 Chokedar,		5
1 Chuprassi,		5
WORK ESTABLISHMENT.		
1 Sub-Overseer,	Riasi, left bank,	20
3 Chuprassis,		15
1 Sub-Overseer, (6 months,)	,, right bank,	9
1 Chuprassi,		5
1 Sub-Overseer,	Aknûr,	25
4 Chuprassis,		20
1 Tarroo, (6 months,)		6

* I concur in the above commendation of Mr. Murray, and consider that his local experience for three years renders his services specially valuable.—H. C.

Establishment		Station	Rs.
3 Chuprassis, - - - -	(6 months,)	Kanachuck,	15
1 Sub-Overseer, - - - - - - - -		Bajwat,	20
1 Ditto, - - - - -	(6 months,)		8
4 Chuprassis, - - - - - - - -			20
1 Sub-Overseer, - - - - - - - - -		Chûni Depôt. and river,	25
1 Ditto, - - - - - - - - - - -			10
1 Ditto, - - - - - -	(6 months,)		6
4 Chuprassis, - - - - - - - -			20
1 Sub-Overseer, - - - - - - - - -		Wazirabad,	15
2 Chuprassis, - - - - - - - -			10
3 Chuprassis, - - - - - -	(6 months,)	Ramnuggur,	15

Forest Establishment.

Establishment		Station	Rs.
1 Sub-Overseer, - - - - - - -	Sanctioned for five months.	Triloknath,	25
1 Ditto, - - - - - - - - -			10
4 Chuprassis, - - - - - - -			20
2 Sub-Overseers, - - - - - -		Tindi,	20
8 Chuprassis, - - - - - - -			40
1 Chuprassi, - - - - - - - -		Salgrain,	6
1 Sub-Overseer, - - - - - - -		Shor,	10
3 Chuprassis, - - - - - - -			15
1 Sub-Overseer, - - - - - - -		Parthi,	15
3 Chuprassis, - - - - - - -			15
1 Sub-Overseer, - - - - - - -		Raie,	12
2 Chuprassis, - - - - - - -			10
1 Sub-Overseer, - - - - - - -		Kolab,	10
2 Chuprassis, - - - - - - -			10
1 Sub-Overseer, - - - - - - -		Sanch,	25
1 Ditto, - - - - - - - -			10
6 Chuprassis, - - - - - - -			30
1 Sub-Overseer, - - - - - - -		Kilar,	10
3 Chuprassis, - - - - - - -			15

Establishment	Sanction	Station	Pay
1 Sub-Overseer,	Sanctioned for five months.	Darwas,	15
2 Chuprassis,			10
1 Sub-Overseer,		Forest Head-Quarters.	15
1 Treasurer,			40
1 Native Doctor,			40
1 Jemadar,			7
6 Burkundazes,			30
1 Chuprassi,			5

Rules of the Pangi Timber Agency.

1.—*Situation of depôts.*—The timber depôt will be as near Sealkot as the varying channel of the Chenab permits. Secondary depôts for issue are at Wazirabad and Ramnuggur.

2.—*Indents called for in April.*—During the month of April, each year, notice will be inserted in the *Government Gazette* and Local papers, calling for indents from persons requiring timber. These indents will be received in the Agency office till the end of July following.

3.—*Examination of Indents.*—The Superintendent can reject any indent or part of indent, compliance with which, in full, would preclude compliance with minor requisitions.

4.—*Allotments made.*—As soon as the quantity of timber to be disposed of is known (about September) the allotments will take place, and persons indenting will be informed when, where, and to what extent, their requisitions will be complied with.

5.—*Priority of Supply.*—Indents will be registered and allotments made by the Agency according to the date of receipt of indent. The issue depends upon the arrival of agents.

6.—*Reserve for Public Works.*—A reserve will be left to meet unforeseen wants of Public Works, till the last month of the official year.

7.—*Requisitions for official year.*—Requisitions hold good for the official year, *i. e.*, from 1st May to 30th April. The balance of any indent, unless renewed, will not be carried on to a second year.

8.—*Deputing agents.*—On the receipt of the notification, (4) persons, who are to obtain timber, should despatch agents to receive and remove their allotments. If no intimation be received, that an agent has been despatched within 30 days of date of notification, the allotment will be resumed, and the Superintendent will cancel the indent registered in his office.

9.—*Agents to represent employers.*—Agents should receive full authority to represent their employers, to grant receipts, to take over charge, and to remove the timber from the depôt.

10.—*Measuring, how conducted.*—The agent, on arrival, is to apply to the officer in charge of the depôt, who will direct the measuring by his moonshees, with Government rods of standard length. The agent must be present and remain until the measurements are complete.

11.—*Objections, to whom to be made.*—Objections to quality of timber, mode of measurement, or any other point, to be made on the spot, that they may be enquired into. If not arranged with the assistant in charge of the depôt, an appeal lies to the Superintendent, which should be made at once.

12.—*Receipts given daily.*—Receipts to be given by the agent at the close of each day's work, shewing the depôt number, length, girth, and contents of each log. The granting of these receipts to be considered as receiving charge of the timber, after which all liability shall rest with the purchaser's agent, and any loss arising from floods or other cause, shall be borne by him.

13.—*Removal of timber.*—To prevent inconvenience to other parties from the accumulation of timber, it shall be removed, without delay, as may be required by the Superintendent.

14.—*Cash payments.*—The business of the Timber Agency is conducted on a system of cash payments. In the notice of allotment (4), the approximate value will be stated. A deposit of 25 per cent. must be paid before measuring commences, and the remainder before removal. Indents will not be received from persons indebted to the Agency.

15.—*Inferior timber.*—Inferior descriptions of timber will be sold at the end of the season, in small lots, to suit traders; due notice being issued of time and place of sale. The conditions are cash payments and immediate removal.

16.—*Sales of fire-wood.*—Fire-wood will be sold in lots, at the same time, by private tender or public auction, at the direction of the Superintendent, and according to the state of the market.

J. D. Smithe,
Superintendent.

1st May, 1863.

Memorandum by Dr. Brandis on the foregoing Report.

1. The number of logs left in the forests in 1861, was 9,900
" trimmed and marked in 1862, ... 58,980

Total, ... 68,880

This does not correspond with the following figures:—
Number of logs rolled into the river in 1862, ... 66,101
" left in the forest in 1862, .. 787 trees = 2,361

Total, ... 68,462

2. Logs arrived at depôt in 1861,	.. ..	34,147
" " 1862,	.. ..	29,282
	Total, ...	63,429

From para. 14 it would appear that very few of the logs rolled into the river in 1862 were received during the year under review. It may, therefore, be supposed that, say 60,000 logs, belong to 1859-60-61. Now it is known that in 1859 and 1860 the following timber was felled :—

1859, ...	5,987 trees,	yielding	25,874 logs.
1860, ...	4,872 "	"	20,470 "

No operations were conducted in 1857-58. If, therefore, it could be ascertained how many logs were launched and received at the depôt in 1859 and 1860, the data of the present report would enable us to form an estimate of the annual losses of timber in transit. Major Thomas estimated the losses at 25 per cent.

3. If I understand the figures correctly, the net profit of the department stands as follows, for 1862-63 :—

A. Cash surplus, 1862-63. Receipts			145,384
Less expended, ...			111,627
Difference, ...			Rs. 33,757
B. Add difference of value of timber on hand at the commencement, and close of the year, cubic feet, ...	248,138		
Less, ...	196,120		
Difference cubic feet	52,018, value		Rs. 12,740
		Total	Rs. 46,497
Deduct difference of outstandings at the beginning and close of the year, ...		79,470	
.. ..		64,790	
		Rs. 14,680	14,680
Profit on 30th April 1863 for operations of 1862-63, ..			Rs. 31,817

The valuation of the timber on hand at Rs. 24-8 per 100 cubic feet is based on incomplete data. Rs. 277,207 was the amount actually received on account of timber sales during 1861-62, but it does not appear to what exact quantity of

NOTE.—Sales in 1861,	.. ..	587,475 cubic feet.
1862,	.. ..	588,871 "
Total,	.. .. ..	1126,346
Realized in 1861, Rs.	.. ..	131,823
1862,	.. ..	145,384
Total, Rs.	.. ..	277,207

or Rs. 24-8 per 100 cubic feet.

timber this figure corresponds. If the timber on hand on 30th April, 1861, and the outstandings on the same date had been given, a statement showing the profit of the operations of season 1861-62, might be prepared in a similar manner. The cash surplus of that year was Rs. 23,030.

4. The two last items of 1862 enable us to determine the rate realized for 100 cubic feet, as follows :—

Amount of sales in 1862, ...		145,384
Add outstanding on account of 1862, ...		29,488
	Total Rs.	174,872
Deduct old debts received in 1862, ...	„	44,168
Amount corresponding to timber sold, ...	Rs.	130,704
Cubic feet of timber sold, ...	„	538,871

This gives Rs. 24-4 for 100 cubic feet, a near approximation to the rate obtained under No. 3. To find the expenditure incurred on 100 cubic feet of timber during 1862, it is requisite to know the per centage of losses noted in No. 2.

5. The low cubic contents of the timber forming the balance in hand at the end of each year deserves notice.

The logs received in 1861, measured, ...	22·27	cubic feet.
Those remaining on 30th April 1861, ...	11·98	„
The logs received in 1862, measured, ...	18·19	„
Those on hand at the close of the year, ...	13·04	„

It is evident that in both years the best timbers were picked out and sold, and the smaller timbers left. If these can be disposed of at the same rate as the large logs, there is no harm in this selection, but the accumulation of small logs should be avoided. It is supposed that purchasers are to a certain extent permitted to select their timber.

D. Brandis.

Object of Pangi Agency attained.

From the foregoing review, it will be seen that the Pangi Timber Agency has effected the desired object, in bringing down a larger and better supply of timber than formerly. Previous to its existence, public works were often stopped for want of timber, which was scarce and high-priced. In 1861-62, four and a half lakhs of cubic feet of deodar were issued to the Punjab Railway Company, and 60,000 cubic feet to different officers of the Department of Public Works;

this quantity being twice as much as was brought down the Chenab by all the native traders during the same year, and sold at half the price. In 1862-63, nearly five lakhs of cubic feet were supplied to the Punjab Railway Company; and 40,000 cubic feet to Government officers. Various hard and fancy woods have been procured and something has been done to restore the forests by planting which should be systematically carried out if a long or perpetual lease can be arranged.

The financial result is favorable. The sales of the last two years are given below* :— Financial result.

		1861-62.	1862-63.
Sales of timber, ...	Rs.	1,31,823	1,45,384
Whole expenditure, establishment, labour, &c.	„	1,08,790	1,07,126
	Rs.	23,033	38,258

It is proposed to erect a saw-mill at the head of Bajwât island, and the scheme has received the sanction of the Government of India. Great advantage will result from sawing up the timber as it enters the plains. Saw-mill proposed.

From the commencement of the agency, the chief timber depôt has been near Sealkot. But circumstances have changed. The demand for wood at that station is now small, and Wazirabad is certainly the most convenient locality, the Lahore and Peshawur road affording great facilities for transport. The depôt has accordingly been moved to that place. Removal of depôt to Wazirabad.

The river becomes navigable for rafts at Aknûr, 53 miles above Wazirabad, and down to its junction with the Gara (300 miles) no obstacle to navigation occurs. The demand for boat building materials is increasing. Increase of boat building.

* (Vide *Report of Administration of the Punjab, 1863*, p. 75.)

THE JELAM RIVER.

Jelam river.

The Jelam is the most western of the five great rivers of the Punjab, and takes its name from the town of Jelam. It drains the valley of Kashmir, and flows through the pass of Baramula in the lofty range of Pir Panjal.

Principal tributaries.

The principal tributaries, joining in succession, are :—

1. Jelam proper (Behat).
2. Vesha.
3. Sind.
4. Kishenganga.
5. Kunihar, or Nainsûkh.

Course of the river.

The whole mountain course of the Jelam, (in Kashmir, called Behat,) is, according to General Cunningham, 380 miles, and its fall about 8,000 feet, or 21 feet per mile; but in the plain of Kashmir the fall is only 3 feet per mile. From the hills to its junction with the Chenab below Jhang, the general direction is southwest and the length about 240 miles. The whole length from its source to its confluence with the Chenab is about 620 miles.

Hydaspes of Arrian.

The Jelam is the Hydaspes of Greek historians. Arrian* and Strabo† record that Alexander the Great was supplied by this river with wood from Kashmir, of which he constructed boats.

* Hist. Indica., Chapter XIX.

† "Alexandrum, ait, in sylva montium emodorum multam abietem, pinum, cedrumque, aliasque arbores navibus compingendis idoneas, caedi jussisse atque in Hydaspem, deduxisse, e quibus classis constructa sit." *Strabo*, Lib. XV., p. 480.

There are no records descriptive of the timber resources of the Kashmir valley, but much valuable information is scattered through the Travels of Vigne, Von Hugel, Jacquemont, Thomson, and Moorcroft; the observations of the two last writers are specially valuable.

The province of Kashmir* consists of an extensive plain surrounded on all sides by lofty mountains. It is the upper part of the basin of the Jelam, and is separated from the valley of the Chenab on the south by rugged and often snowy ranges, and from the basin of the Indus on the north by the main axis of the western Himalaya. The mountains on the north are for the most part bare and rugged on their southern face, while those which lie to the south appear from the plain to be magnificently wooded with forests of pines and deciduous-leaved trees, descending almost to their base.† Province of Kashmir.

Kashmir is traversed in its whole length by the river Jelam, which rises at the east end of the valley, and winds from one side of the plain to the other, at one time washing the base of the northern hills, at another receding to a considerable distance from them. The Jelam flows with a tranquil stream, and being navigable throughout the whole of the level country as far up as Islamabad, for boats of considerable burden, is the great highway for the traffic of the country, in which, notwithstanding its being perfectly level, wheel carriages are unknown. At Islamabad the stream is small, but it gradually enlarges by additions from both sides as it descends. Near the town of Srinagar it is from fifty to a hundred yards wide, often very deep, and in few places Jelam navigable.

* The great width of the valley and broad sheets of water, favoring rich cultivation by an abundant population, are characteristic features of Kashmir.

† Thomson's Travels, p. 279.

fordable, even at the driest season. The elevation of the bed is 5300 feet.

Trees of Kashmir.

Jacquemont describes the climate and vegetation of Kashmir as very similar to those of Lombardy. The deodar is abundant, and is extensively employed in the construction of houses, temples,* and bridges. The forests also contain *pinus longifolia* and *excelsa, abies webbiana*, walnut,† maple, poplar, willow, yew, and a species of juniper. The oriental plane, "chunar," (*platanus orientalis,*) is probably found nowhere more abundant or luxuriant than in Kashmir, though it is not indigenous. The absence of oaks, *rhododendron*, *andromeda* and *pinus gerardiana* is remarkable.

Timber trade.

On the accession of Golab Sing, he monopolised the timber trade, and the price of wood is double what it formerly was. The only kind of wood floated down the Jelam is "diar" (*cedrus deodara*); when the snow melts, it is brought down the various streams, collected by Government, and sold at Jelam. It is calculated that the average annual supply is about 2000 logs (exclusive of the British timber from Kaghan,) some of the logs are fifty feet in length.

Groves.

By orders of the Mogul Emperors, a grove of *chunar* and poplar was planted near every Kashmirian village; these were protected by a heavy fine on every tree felled, but the Sikhs destroyed many of them. Ex-

* The Jama Masjid consists in great part of wood, a dome and spire of timber of rude construction, resting partly upon wooden pillars, and partly on side walls. The number of pillars is three hundred and eighty-four; they are formed of an assemblage of square blocks of deodar, about a foot in diameter, laid at right angles to each other, so that each face presents a succession of butts and sides. The same timber is also employed in the construction of bridges over the canals and rivers. These bridges are massive and solid, the piers and platform being almost entirely composed of deodar; upon one of them the Zein-al-kadal, a line of shops, (also built of wood,) the best in the city of Srinagar, is situated.—*Moorcroft*, Vol. II., p. 120.

† The quality of the wood for gun-stocks and furniture is little inferior to that of Britain.

tensive groves of mulberry trees, planes and poplars, elms and willows, still constitute one of the greatest beauties of the country and give an European aspect to the scenery.

Moorcroft and Hugel directed attention to the abundance and excellence of the fruits of Kashmir, and much valuable information is given by Royle in his "Illustrations of the Botany of the Himalaya," and in his Appendix to Vigne's Kashmir.* Those which attain maturity are the apple, pear, quince, peach, apricot, plum, almond, pomegranate, mulberry, walnut, hazelnut, pistachio and melon. The cherry "*gilas*" is indigenous and is cultivated in orchards from which it has been introduced to Pangi, Dharmsalla, &c. The bullace (*Prunus insititia,*) is found nowhere else in a wild state. The vine is extensively cultivated. The recent manufacture of cider by the Maharaja upon a large scale is worthy of notice. Fruits.

Many of the medical plants of Kashmir were collected and delineated by Dr. Honigberger, late physician to the court of Runjit Singh, who tested their properties. His vocabulary of local names† proved useful in identifying the drugs sent to the Punjab Exhibition. Drugs.

An excellent map of Kashmir with part of the adjacent mountains surveyed on the basis of the Great Trig. Survey of India, by Captain T. G. Montgomerie, R. E., has been recently published in the Surveyor General's office, and supplies a want long felt. This map colored to indicate the forest tracts, would be extremely valuable in illustrating the timber resources of the province. Map of Kashmir.

* Captain W. H. Lowther has recorded an interesting account of the natural productions of the valley and the chief gardens of Srinagar in the *Jour. Agri-Hort. Soc. of India,* Vol. VIII. (1853.)

† *See* "Thirty-five Years in the East." By Martin Honigberger.

The instructions of the Lieut. Governor required me to visit the forests of Kaghan along the banks of the Kunihar, the only tributary of the Jelam which I have personally explored. The deodar forests in Kashmir above the confluence of the Kishenganga and Jelam proper, remain to be examined.

FORESTS OF KAGHAN.

THE valley of the Nainsûkh, or *Kunihar*, is about one hundred and twenty miles in length, from the source of the river in the Lalusar lake to its confluence with the Jelam. The general course of the river is south-west. From the junction upwards to Balakôt, the valley is open and of considerable breadth; the lower slopes are naked or sprinkled with chil, (*pinus longifolia,*) while on the northern aspect of the distant summits may be seen with a glass the tall stems of the deodar and webbian pine.

Above Balakôt, the valley becomes contracted and the mountain sides are in many places very precipitous. A path along the bank of the river was made by Col. Jas. Abbott; this has been opened out for laden mules by Lieut. H. Blair, R. E. Places are pointed out along the track where mules and ponies have fallen into the stream.

Maps. The Kaghan valley has not yet been included in the series of the Great Trigonometrical Survey, but is about to be brought within the triangulation; the existing maps are (1) a survey sketch of the river from its source to Garhi Habibulla Khan, by Captain Nightingale, Dept. Public Works, 1853; and (2) a military sketch of part of Kaghan, by Major Lumsden, Deputy Quarter Master General.

In ascending the valley, the first clump of deodar occurs before reaching Kawai, but the trees are of small size. A few miles further, the northern slopes of the mountains, from the village of Páras up to Narâin, are clothed at intervals with fine cedar trees, "*en masse*," usually mingled with "biar," (*pinus excelsa*). Above the village of Narâin, the forest is more sparse, and the trees become stunted as the traveller ascends to the source of the river, where none exist. Felling has taken place chiefly between Páras and Jereíd, and there is much outlying timber left by contractors. The position and extent of the deodar forests, which lay adjacent to the river and its two chief tributaries, are shown in the accompanying copy of Captain Nightingale's survey sketch. **Deodar forest.**

The average dimensions of the mature trees are much smaller than in the forests of Chamba and Bussahir; perhaps 9 to 10 feet in circumference, 4 feet above ground, may be taken as a full average. There are a few specimens of giant growth, but these are exceptional and the size diminishes in the higher part of the valley. **Size of Trees.**

The whole valley is British territory; the Syed and Swati proprietors receive a half share of the former seignorage, which was Rs. 1-8 per tree; the rate has been raised, but they receive 12 annas per tree as before. The present seignorage for deodars is Rs. 5 in Hazara, and Rs. 2 in Kaghan. Major Adams, Deputy Commissioner, consulted me as to raising the rate in Kaghan, as the value of wood in the plains is increasing. I think Rs. 3 a fair average price, **Seignorage per tree.**

considering the size of the trees and the difficulty of transport.

Prospective supply.

After travelling up and down the Kaghan valley, and ascending two high spurs, from which a full view was obtained of the two principal tributaries (Bhunja and Mannur Kus), I am of opinion that as a *maximum*, one-thousand deodar trees per annum may be taken without producing permanent injury to the forests. Capt. Melville, of the G. T. Survey, informs me that on the left bank of the Kishenganga, there is a large extent of deodar forest,* above the junction of the Kurna river, only separated from the Nainsûkh by the Kaghan range, and also in the side valleys from the Kashmir range. These tracts are in the Maharaja's dominions.

Character of the Nainsûkh.

The river at the time of my visit, 25th October, was very low; at Garhi Habibulla Khan the breadth was about 70 feet, and the depth in midstream, 3 to 4 feet. The current during flood is very rapid, and like all hill torrents the depth varies to extremes. With regard to timber transport the appearance of the river up to Jereíd does not indicate any special obstruction to floating logs of moderate length, say 12 to 14 feet, and is more favorable than the upper Ravi. About six miles below Kaghan the river bed is tortuous and blocked up with large boulders, around which the water flows, and as has been observed in other rivers, the best pieces of forest are over the obstructed places. The Syeds state, apparently with truth, that it is only at the highest flood that logs are carried over these rocks and then with considerable damage.

Fall per mile.

The height of Garhi bridge above the sea is 1,800 feet, and of the river bed at Kaghan village 6,600 feet,

* Mr. T. Arratoon confirms this statement.

according to Capt. Nightingale's observations; the distance between the two villages measured on the map is 70 miles, consequently the average fall of the river may be roughly estimated as not less than 65 feet per mile.

First attempt to get timber for boats.

The earliest forest record is an order, 8th March, 1852, by the Board of Administration, to Colonel Abbott, then Deputy Commissioner Hazara, directing him to use his best endeavour to get timber down the Kunihar (*i. e.* Nainsûkh) river to Jelam. In reply, he mentioned the following difficulties, viz., "that Kaghan had no thanna, the glen was under the tyranny of the Syeds, whose oppression he had not been able to bridle. It would be difficult to ensure the payment of the laborers (gujars) employed to fell the trees. All recompence would be divided between the Syeds and Pathans. He recommended an agent being sent to Garhi to purchase the logs, and that he would try to bring the wood cutters down to receive their dues."

Colonel Becher's and Major Adams' experiments.

Colonel Becher made the first experiment in 1855-56; there is no record of the result, but I believe it was not satisfactory. Major Adams made two attempts in 1860 and 1861, which may be considered partially successful. He arranged with malliks for the felling of a thousand trees and the launching of the logs, which were not less than twenty feet in length, while Major Robertson entertained during the flood a gang of taroos to land them at the depôt on the Jelam. 1,800 logs were put into the river, of these 1,500 passed Balakôt, and 900 were landed at Dangalli, the remaining 600 were appropriated as waif timber by the Maharaja of Kashmir, the marks having been obliterated. Including all losses, however, the timber was cheap; and here

I may remark that Major Adams' management of the Hazara forests has been careful, judicious, and progressive.

Contractors.

Several contractors from Rawal Pindi have purchased trees in Kaghan forest, and, from the circumstance of their having lodged money for a second supply, it may be assumed that the speculation was remunerative. However, all report that the operation was attended with much difficulty, and though the logs were reduced to ten and twelve feet, about 300 of them remain stranded between Balakôt and Garhi.

Road and Bridges.

A good mule path has been opened by Lieutenant Blair from the Balakôt thanna through the lower forest, and is now carried as far as Jereíd. There is an iron suspension bridge at Garhi and wooden sangas at Balakôt, Jereíd, Kaghan, and Narain.

Working season.

The best season for felling is the cold weather, when the sap is at rest; probably the end of October, November, and March, would be most convenient, the people not being engaged in the fields during these months. The snow on the Kaghan mountains begins to melt in March, and in April the river acquires considerable volume. To get the timber down the same year it is felled, early launching of the logs is of the first importance. The season of full flood is from the 10th of May to the end of July, with short intervals of comparative quietness.

Protection of timber.

The position of Balakôt thanna at the mouth of the glen, and only a few yards from the river, effectually checks any attempts at carrying on an illicit timber trade, and there is no outlet but by the Nainsûkh. The chief loss and difficulty hitherto has occurred during transport down the Jelam. Great care and vigilance will be required to secure the timber from surreptitious removal.

There appears to be no difficulty in obtaining labour. I saw a hundred Kashmir coolies working cheerfully at the road. If large bodies of workpeople were required it might be necessary to import food, but for the previous experiments willing hands were found in the valley itself. The Syeds were ready and anxious to enter into arrangements for felling timber, and putting it into the river.* On this point Major Adams' opinion is as follows, "liberal payment and considerate treatment will secure the labours of the gujars in Kaghan, through the Syed and Swati maliks, and the more use that is made of the maliks in carrying on forest operations the better." Wood-cutters.

In addition to the deodar, there is much "chil" and "biâr," (*pinus excelsa,*) crab ash, olive, hazel, walnut, maple, and hill toon; the rhododendron is rare. The size of the trees is less than in the valleys to the eastward. The large ash is found on the Thandiâni and Mochpûra ranges, but not in Kaghan. The absence of oaks also, except *quercus ilex*, of which a few trees occur, is very remarkable. Woods procurable.

There is abundance of *rhubarb* near the *Sufa Mallhúk* and in other places. The "safed jira" (cummin seed) is brought down in quantity. The *daphne oleoides*, paper shrub, is in great abundance from a little above Kawai to Kaghan. "Kût"† (*aucklandia costus*) is collected, but they say that owing to intestine war in China, the demand is diminished. Hill products.

There are vines which with little care yield fine, small black grapes; the stems are allowed to climb over trees. Apples of large size and good flavour are abundant. Figs are indigenous, but small; Fruits.

* The rate of payment for felling, dressing, marking, and launching logs is Rs. 2 per tree.

† In passing loads of *Kût*, the aromatic odour is distinctly perceptible.

"amlôk," *diospyros lotus*, grows in abundance; the fruit is purple when ripe, about the size of a pigeon's egg, and is eaten fresh, or dried like prunes. Apricots, peaches, "gawâi," (*eleagnus*,) berberry, mulberry, and pomegranate are found. The edible pine (*pinus gerardiana*) does *not* occur.

Exports. Exports do not appear to be numerous. Large flocks of sheep* are brought down; the flesh of these is highly prized. The valley is famous for ghee, which is quite solid and cuts like cheese; about a dozen mules, laden with this commodity passed us daily. "Urd," (*phaseolus radiatus*,) barley and wheat in small quantity are procurable. Maize or Indian-corn is largely cultivated, its flour constitutes the chief sustenance of the inhabitants. Honey and wax are exported to the plains. A little gold dust is brought across the range through Chilas from the valley of the Indus where gold washing† is carried on to a considerable extent.

Imports. Salt from the Salt range is taken by the return coolies in considerable quantity, and British piece goods, (calico, &c.,) sparingly. The common Peshawur blue cloth is in general use. The winter garments are woollen and home made. A few brass utensils are imported.

Conclusions. 1. A large extent of deodar forest lies in the valley, but the supply of timber will not be great, as the river becomes almost impracticable for floating, six miles below Kaghan village.

2. The trees are smaller than in Chamba and Bussahir, but the quality of wood is excellent.

* Not the *dumba* or ordinary broad tailed sheep of the Afghans. An attempt has been made to cross the indigenous sheep with the English merino, to improve the wool. A truss of merino wool, produced in Hazara, was valued in England at 1*s*. 6*d*. a lb.

† We met two Mussulmans who had been engaged in this pursuit.

3. The best position for a depôt is 20 miles above Dangalli, in the Pindi district. Taroos (*see* p. 134) are useless on the Nainsûkh.

4. A letter from the Punjab Government to the Maharaja of Kashmir requiring respect to be paid to the forest mark would be useful.

5. A small establishment in Kaghan is necessary, say, one jemadar and four chuprasis. The co-operation of the Deputy Commissioner, Rawal Pindi, is essential. The catching and landing of the logs requires much attention; the best system would be proved after one or two trials.*

Experiment in 1863.

The forest operations, for political reasons have *remained under the Deputy Commissioner,* but as a special case, Lieut. Blair, engaged in making a road through the forest, and popular among the Syeds, was requested to repeat the experiment by felling 800 trees, (say 2,400 logs,) and removing the wood left in the forest. Much timber is required at Abbottabad for various works, the surplus will be available for railway purposes. Lieut. Blair superintended the felling in Kaghan whilst Captain Strutt watched the arrival of the logs at Salgrain, and rafted them to Jelam. By the personal superintendence of these two officers the result was successful. The logs have realised a profit, although several offenders were convicted of wood stealing.

Kaghan forests to be reserved.

As there is no great pressure for wood in the N. W. Punjab, the annual felling in Kaghan may be restricted to 800 deodar and a fair proportion of other trees. If a tramway or other public work should hereafter be undertaken, these forests will be of great value.

* A few intelligent chuprasis would be necessary at certain points on the Jelam.

LIST OF PLANTS OBSERVED IN KAGHAN.

Akhrot,	*Juglans regia.*	* Charâi,	*Juniperus excelsa.*
Akukira,	*Viola.*	* Cheta-buta,	*Abelia triflora.*
Amlōk,	*Diospyros lotus.*	Chīl,	*Pinus longifolia.*
* Amulgūch,	*Cerasus puddum.*	Chenjul,	*Urtica pulcherrima.*
Anōch,	*Fraxinus xanthoxyloides.*	Chora,	*Quercus ilex.*
Arbunbūl,	*Hedera.*	Chotial,	*Rheum.*
* Ardâwal,	*Rhododendron arboreum.*	Chumiâri,	*Cerasus puddum.*
* Arkhar,	*Rhus.*	* Dadrū,	*Rhamnus virgatus.*
Ari,	*Armeniaca vulgaris.*	Dâmān,	*Grewia oppositifolia.*
Asmâni,	*Ephedra saxatilis.*	Darūni,	*Punica granatum.*
* Babrang,	*Myrsine africana.*	Diâr, †	*Cedrus deodara.*
Bāchmāl,	*Astragalus.*	* Dodar,	*Pyrus kumaonensis.*
Banafsha,	*Viola.*	Drâwa,	*Cedrela serrata.*
* Bagnū,	*Populus ciliata.*	Drék,	*Melia azedarach.*
Bankhor,	*Pavia Indica.*	Dug-kenti,	*Indigofera.*
Ban-sinjli,	*Cratægus oxyacantha.*	Gamâi,	*Eleagnus.*
Bart,	*Prunus padus.*	* Gūch,	*Coriaria Nepalensis.* *Viburnum fœtens.*
Barphulī,	*Euonymus.*	Guddikum,	*Meconopsis aculeata.*
Batangi,	*Pyrus variolosa.*	Gunger,	*Sageretia.*
Batkar,	*Celtis caucasica.*	Guldāgh, * Gwaldakh,	*Ribes* (2 sp.)
Batula,	*Aplotaxis candicans.*	Gurunda,	*Prinsepia utilis.*
Bān,	*Rhus cotinus.*	* Gwalidar,	*Diospyros* (male plant, *Amlok* being the female.)
Biâr,	*Pinus excelsa.*		
Biliri,	*Clematis grata.*		
Biridi,	*Hederacea.*	Jaing,	*Viscum.*
Bīs, ‡	*Salix.*	Kachan,	*Abies smithiana.*
* Būna,	*Albizzia mollis.* *Edwardsia mollis.*	Kâi,	*Ulmus campestris.*
Burj,	*Betula bhojputra.*	Kalakāt,	*Prunus padus.*
Būtten,	*Euonymus.*	* Kalkut,	*Viburnum cotinifolium.*
Chamkat,	*Desmodium tiliaceum.*	Kanōcha,	*Salvia moorcroftiana.*

† The usual name of the Deodar in Kaghan is *paludar.*
In Dr. Stewart's list "bis" is *Myricaria Germanica.*

Kandar,	*Cornus macrophylla.*	Pîmâr or Pisumar,	*Labiata* (strongly scented.) *Plectranthus rugosus.*
Kalkoli, Kankol,	*Eleagnus.*	Pitni,	*Zizyphus* (fruit edible) *vulgaris.*
Kanji,	*Asplenium.*	Phipni	*Rhamnus virgatus.*
Kantiân,	*Rosa webbiana.*	Pishor,	*Fothergilla involucrata.*
Katli,	*Rumex acetosella.*	Puâri	*Ficus caricoides.*
Kâhû,	*Olea Europea.*	Pukûna,	*Rubus lasiocarpus.*
Kenchirunga,	*Astragalus.*	Ratanjōt,	*Onosma echioides.*
Khangar,	*Pistacia intigerrima.*	Ratankāt,	*Andromeda ovalifolia.*
* Kikri Kurkni,	*Spiroea Lindleyana.*	Rēen,	*Quercus incana.*
Kenti,	*Indigofera.*	Rewan,	*Picea webbiana.*
Kuti-lal,	*Daphne oleoides.*	* Rich-uklu,	*Viburnum cotinifolium.*
Kuwari,	*Ficus caricoides.*	Shîkakul,	*Pastinaca.*
* Lelar,	*Itea nutans.*	Shial or Shila,	*Sarcococca pruniformis.*
Lûni,	*Cotoneaster baccillaris.*	Shrol,	*Alnus nitida.*
* Makhmâl,	*Astragalus spinosus.*	Siki,	*Euonymus.*
Mamaikh,	*Umbellifera.*	Sinjlî,	*Zizyphus flexuosa*, or *Cratægus oxyacantha.*
Maslun,	*Polygonum bistorta.*	Sofaida,	*Populus alba.*
Munjît,	*Rubia cordifolia.*	Sûmb,	*Fraxinus.*
Nasputti	*Pyrus communis.*	Sûmlû,	*Berberis lycium.*
Nîlatari,	*Cuscuta longiflora.*	Tetri,	*Rhus.*
Palar,	*Epimedium elatum.*	Timbur,	*Xanthoxylon hostile.*
Paludar,	*Cedrus deodara in* Kaghan, and *picea webbiana* in Hazara and Murree.	* Tila-pattar,	*Acer sterculiaceum.*
* Pâras,	*Prunus padus.*	Trikhana,	*Acer cultratum.*
Phuliân, Phulwâr,	*Rosa macrophylla.*	Uklu,	*Viburnum fœtens.*
Phût,	*Lonicera.*	Urni,	*Corylus colurna.*

As very few Europeans have visited the upper part of this interesting valley, and most of those as sportsmen only, this attempt at giving a list of the flora may be read with interest. The "reen" oak *(quercus incana)* and *pavia indica* were found in Hazara, and not in *Kaghan;* the *rhododendron arboreum* is very rare. This brief list is very incomplete. Herborisation was under difficulties as snow fell. The striking feature of the flora as compared with that of Hindustan is the want of trees and paucity of forms. The great part of the vegetation consists of European families—*compositæ, cruciferæ,* and *umbelliferæ*; whilst orchids and ferns are almost wanting. Bulbous plants and grasses can only be found during summer.

Names marked with an asterisk are entered upon the authority of Dr. J. L. Stewart, who made a short excursion into the valley of Kaghan in 1861, and placed his list of plants at my disposal.

Rafting of timber.

Light rafting commences about 60 miles above the bridge of boats at Oin, a village on the left bank, where Mr. Arratoon had a depôt when he was engaged in timber trade from Kashmir, and where the materials for boat building are now collected. Dangalli, on the right bank, 35 miles from Jelam, is the site of an ancient town, and appears to be the highest point where large rafts can be formed. Wood is stored here for the requirements of Rawal Pindi, and sawn planks are transported on camels or bullocks.

Saw-mill at Dhulial.

At Dhulial, 11 miles above Jelam, there is a saw-mill of simple construction, formerly used by the officers of the Lahore and Peshawar road; it has not been worked since 1856, but might be put in order for cutting sleepers. The canal which feeds the mill has a tendency to silt up.

Maharaja's tribute.

An annual tribute of 450 deodar logs is paid at Jelam by H. H. the Maharaja of Kashmir. After reserving the timber required for the bridge of boats it has been customary to sell the remainder at the current rates.

Price of deodar.

The native merchants in 1863 sold deodar at $2\frac{1}{2}$ cubic feet per rupee. For the wood brought down from Khagan the following rates were sanctioned by Government, the logs being divided into five classes:—

1st	class,	8 annas,	per cubic foot.
2nd	class,	7 „	
3rd	class,	6 „	
4th	class, sleeper length,	5 „	
5th	class, very short.	4 „	

Other woods procurable.

Besides deodar, chir, (*pinus longifolia*) partal (*p. excelsa*) and anundar, are obtained at Jelam, and the rates per cubic foot have generally been about

4 annas chir, 5 annas anundar, and 6 annas partal. Toon in smaller quantity is procurable; sissoo of fine quality is scarce, but the islands in the river are covered with young trees which promise well. An extension of planting on *belas* is most desirable.* Splendid mulberry trees also grow on the islands, but most of them belong to Kashmir.

The district has been carefully examined by Dr. J. E. T. Aitchison, who gives an enumeration of the plants composing the flora, in the *Jour. As. Soc., Beng.*, 1864. The principal timber trees are †— Flora of Jelam.

Capparis aphylla,	Karil.	*Acacia Arabica,*	Kikur.
Cratæva religiosa,	Barna.	———*modesta,*	Phulai.
Zizyphus jujuba,	Bér.	*Tamarix dioica,*	Lai.
Pistacia integerrima,	Kangar.	*Olea Europea,*	Kahu.

The building of boats is much increased. There are two patterns, one full-decked the other half-decked. Boat building.

* The plan proposed by Mr. Thornton of planting alluvial lands newly thrown up, where they promise to be permanent is excellent. This scheme has been pressed upon local officers by the Financial Commissioner, in his Circular, No. 13, of 1864. The following are from the last Reports:—

The Deputy Commissioner, Jelam, says, "Including the islands of the river, 66 acres of land have had sissoo seed, to the extent of 50 maunds, broadcast over it, in the manner prescribed by Mr. Thornton, in one of his Circulars, when Commissioner of this Division. Great success has attended this in some instances. On the island near Jelam, the young trees of 9 years are 30 to 40 feet high, and average 6 or 8 inches in diameter. There is another grove in an alluvial deposit at Khoora, and a fourth on an island, Suggerpoor. At these four places there cannot be less than 100 acres of this most useful timber. I am yearly thinning out numbers of the trees, training them and fostering their growth, and with every success."

In Gujrat, the Deputy Commissioner reports, "about a lakh of young trees have been produced and planted out during the year, chiefly Sissoo and Sirris, which are best suited to the soil and climate of this district. I have considerably increased the nurseries formed on Bela lands, in the rivers, for the production of Sissoo forests."

† For further information regarding the Jelam district, see the "Camps and Battlefields of Alexander and Porus." By Capt. Abbott, R. A., *Jour. As. Soc.*, 1848. "Diary of a Trip to Pind Dadan Khan and the Salt Range." By A. Fleming, M.D., *Jour. As. Soc.*, 1849. Descriptive Notice of the Jelam District. By L. Bowring, B.C.S., *Jour. As. Soc.*, 1850. Report on the Geological Structure and Mineral Wealth of the Salt Range. By A. Fleming, M.D. *Jour As. Soc.*, 1853. Survey of the Jelam River. By Lieut. Foster, I. N. *Punjab Govt. Reports*, No. VI., 1861.

Sissoo and mulberry are used for knees and bends; the rest of the boat is generally deodar, but for the floor-planking chir is preferred. Lieut. Chalmers informed me that some of the boats were ten years in good order. The best oars are made of the large ash.

Navigation and fuel supply. The navigation commences at Jelam. The river skirts the salt range for a hundred miles, and we may anticipate a greatly increased traffic in salt, cotton, and coal. Jelam and Pind Dadan Khan are well adapted for fuel stations, having high banks; the supply of firewood on the low hills is abundant; we have no data of the yield, and annual inspection is desirable.

FORESTS OF HAZARA.

It seems desirable to give an outline of the progress of forest management in Hazara, which except Kangra and Hoshiarpur, is the only well wooded district of Punjab proper; this summary may prove useful to other districts in which the conservancy of forest tracts and jungles is being initiated.

1855. In the year 1855, draft rules for the conservancy of forests in the hill districts were forwarded by Mr. Temple, Secy. to the Chief Commissioner, and an annual report was called for.

1856. In 1856, Captain Becher, Deputy Commissioner, reported the position and extent of the principal forests in the district, and remarked, "These forests occur at intervals on the higher ranges, extending over a great space, and are often situated where the want of roads and water carriage renders them almost useless." The chiefs and headmen of villages were directed to observe that no wanton destruction took place; the Deputy Commissioner enjoined that young trees should be spared, and intimated that infringement of the forest rules would be punished by a fine not only on the offender but on his village.

Seignorage.

One rupee was charged upon each tree (deodar, biar, and chil): the trees were marked by burkundazes before being felled. Captain Becher considering that the demands were chiefly on the part of Government, and that the forests were widely scattered and often on the frontier, did not think it expedient to entertain an establishment, but recommended conservancy through the chiefs and the people themselves, controlled by the thannadars and their establishments, who reported any destruction observed in their occasional visits.

Rules framed and rangers appointed.

In the same year, the Commissioner, (Sir H. Edwardes,) forwarded a set of rules, which he and Capt. Becher considered well adapted to the circumstances of the district. This code received the sanction of the Chief Commissioner in January, 1857, and with slight modifications is now in force (p. 192). Two rangers were attached to each of the ten police stations:—

RECEIPTS.		EXPENDITURE.		
1856-57.				1857.
	Rs.		Rs.	
Seignorage,* (2 years,)	992	Establishment, ...	867	
1858.				1858.
Seignorage, ...	503	Establishment, ...	837	
Balance of 1857, ...	125			
Rs.	628	Rs.	837	

* Seignorage minus the share paid to Zemindars.

1859. As it appeared doubtful whether the forest conservancy would be self-supporting, a reduction of four rangers was made by Capt. Becher in March, 1859, but in this year a great demand for wood arose for house building at the Murree sanatarium. Ash was found useful for the shafts of gun carriages, bullock carts, and the oars of boats, and timber was required for the lines, mule-sheds, &c., of the regiments stationed at Abbottabad. Under written permits and after pre-payment of fees, 1,422 trees were felled, chiefly deodar, biar, chil, ash, and walnut, and 812 bullies or saplings.

Receipts.		Expenditure.	
	Rs.		Rs.
Seignorage, ...	831	Establishment, ...	614
Waif timber, ...	25		
Fines for breach of rules,	153	Balance, ...	395
Rs.	1,009	Rs.	1,009

The result of this year's operations was satisfactory, and a good beginning was made. The indents were chiefly for wood for public buildings at Murree, Abbottabad, and Haripur, but there was reason to believe that a steady demand for timber would continue, and experience was obtained as to the tracts most requiring supervision.

Transport. Up to this date, the timber was carried on men's heads along rude paths made by contractors; the transport has since been facilitated by the formation of the military road from Murree to Abbottabad *viâ* Dungagulli. Timber is now carried by this road from the forests of the Môchpura range to the Dôr, near

Dhumtour, down which it may be floated, when there is sufficient water; or it is taken on to Abbottabad. Small timber cut in the Barangulli range, can also be floated down the Dôr. The Nainsûkh and Jelam are united at the northern end of that range, the prominent peaks of which marked on the map, are Mian Jani-ki-chowki, Lall Bhai ka Dera, and Dewan Sir. From the Thandiani forests, the new path is now the outlet. Timber is carried down to Nuwashahur, by men, thence the road is practicable for bullocks, camels, or even carts.

In 1860, the result was more favorable; the de- 1860.
mand for timber increased, while wasteful felling and surreptitious cutting were in some measure checked. Further experience led to a re-distribution of the forest rangers. Numerous applications were made to the district officers, and the following trees were felled; a half share of the seignorage being paid to the land-owner, the other half credited to the forest fund:—

Deodar, ...	1,193	Olive, ...	107
Biar, ...	918	Kangar,...	4
Chil, ...	188	Hard wood saplings,	1,133
Walnut, ...	21		3,564

Receipts.		Expenditure.	
	Rs.		Rs.
Balance, ...	398	Establishment, ...	550
From D. P. W., ...	500	Balance, ...	1,781
Seignorage, ...	975		
Fines, ...	343		
Confiscated logs and waif timber, ...	115		
Rs.	2,331	Rs.	2,331

Out of the surplus, a grant of 700 Rs. was sanctioned by Government for improving the forest track to Thandiani; this has been a boon to the sudder station, and has facilitated the carriage of timber. An offshoot into the Turnawai forests is in contemplation.

The police under the new system being relieved of the duty of supervising forests, the appointment of two head rangers (jemadars) on 12 rupees each per mensem was made, and the establishment now consists of—

	Rs.
2 Jemadars, ...	24
9 Rangers, ...	54
Total per mensem, ...	78
Total per annum, ...	936

1861. In 1861, Major Adams reported a considerably increased demand for timber during the year; from the formation of roads in the country where some of the principal forests are situated, supervision is now more easy and effectual, and smuggling more hazardous and less frequent. The number of trees of

Receipts.		Expenditure.	
	Rs.		Rs.
Balance, ...	1,781	Establishment, ...	700
Seignorage, ...	1,820	Grant for roads, ...	700
Fines, ...	185	Marking trees, &c., ...	44
Waif timber, ...	101		1,444
		Balance, ...	2,443
Rs.	3,887	Rs.	3,887

Note.—In the first four months of 1862, the receipts were Rs. 1,346, and in the official year 1862-63, Rs. 5,665: the annual net revenue of the Hazara forests may be considered about Rs. 4,000.

all kinds sold was 5,373; they were chiefly felled in the Môchpura range and in Kaghan.

Visit to Hazara.

This summary shews the progressive steps taken for bringing the forests of Hazara under supervision, and proves that an encouraging commencement has been made. During my visit to the district, I inspected the whole of the Môchpura range, travelling from Murree to Abbottabad along the crest of the mountain: afterwards ascending the Thandiani hill, and descending to Mansera *viâ* Turnawai, I traversed the Pukli valley, and had arranged to accompany Major Adams through the Junawal hills to Darbund and Torbela, on the Indus, but he was prevented from leaving Abbottabad. I had an opportunity of conferring with the Commissioner and Deputy Commissioner as to the district generally, and was accompanied by Lieut. Blair, Executive Engineer, in the ascent of the valley of Kaghan. My conclusions regarding the forests on the Nainsûkh, and the fitness of that river for timber transport are noted in page 178.

Present rules sufficient.

If the Hazara rules are followed carefully, and amended as altered circumstances may indicate, successful conservancy may be expected. If the proposed operations on the Nainsûkh succeed and the forest revenue continues increasing from year to year, it may be advisable to unite the forests of Hazara with those of Murree and the Salt range, forming an extensive charge requiring the supervision of an assistant conservator.*

Forest fund.

At the close of 1861, there was an available balance of Rs. 2,443. I recommend that the forest fund be kept distinct, and that small grants be made

* This was proposed in forest Budget 1864-65. The charge of these scattered forests will afford ample occupation to an active officer, whose head quarters should be part of the year at Murree and part at Jelam.

for restoring exhausted deodar tracts, planting ash and toon, and other similar purposes.

Table of rates. The seignorage of the more valuable trees (p. 195) is lower than in Murree; the market being more distant and the demand less. The land-owners have hitherto received a half share, while in Murree they receive one-eighth. I agree with Major Adams that it is not necessary to increase the amount paid to the land-owners though the rate be increased, as the amount they receive is very liberal.* The only remark which occurs to me is that the elm (*ulmus campestris*) and mulberry (*morus*) may be added to the list of trees paying seignorage: one rupee for elm and eight annas for mulberry, may be sufficient till the demand is ascertained.

Deodar. The deodar is not abundant in Hazara (except in Kaghan) and is becoming scarce. I only observed it on the north side of the Môchpura range,† towards the Jelam, and sparingly on Thandiani. The price has been raised to check consumption. The remaining trees should be allowed to stand for seed, and the timber required obtained from the Nainsûkh at Garhi. Promising clumps of young trees should be protected from cattle by a fence.

Ash. The large ash (*fraxinus*) yields a valuable wood which is much prized in Peshawar, but the tree is not abundant.

Culture of Potatos. Three points connected with forest management were referred to by Major Adams—first, the cultiva-

* From 1st February, 1862, the rates of seignorage were altered, generally much enhanced, but the amount which had previously been paid to the land-holders remained as before with trifling modifications in some instances. The consequence of these changes is that except in the cases of toon, ash, deodar, and biar, the land-holders share is now one-fourth, or double what it is in the Murree Tahseel. Their share of the seignorage on each toon and ash tree is Rs.; on each deodar, and biar tree, 12 annas.

† From the top of Môchpura, above the Dungagulli bungalow, there is a fine panorama of the Kashmir hills, the valleys of the Jelam and Indus, Swat, the whole of Hazara, with the Hindu Kush, bounding the view to the west.

tion of potatoes. The growth of this important esculent is rapidly extending, yields good returns and merits encouragement. Forest land is always preferred, but the finest pieces of forest need not be given up for this purpose. There is abundance of suitable land available without sacrificing any valuable timber. Woods containing deodar, ash, and oak, should always be reserved, whilst clumps of the less valuable trees, as the Smithian and Webbian pines may be sacrificed.

Barking of trees for tanning materials.

The Himalayan oak *(quercus incana)*, chil *(pinus longifolia)*, and small *rhus* (*R. cotinus*), are employed for tanning. The oak when well grown is a valuable tree, rather scarce in some parts; the others are very abundant and of comparatively little use as timber trees. The oak therefore is preserved, unless it be stunted, and the other two are barked by the village mochis free of charge. The bark of the *chil* is picked off without the axe; the *rhus* "*tung*," is cut down entirely but speedily springs up again.

Burning of grass.

The burning of grass by zemindars and herdmen is a third point. It is a matter of great difficulty to frame rules, sufficiently stringent to protect the forests without being in some measure harassing to the people. It seems best to leave it to the officer charged with the conservancy arrangements to deal with each case as it arises, and to allow him a discretion to enforce or relax the penalties attached to the breach of the rule as it stands. The burning of grass within forests which yield deodar, biar, and other valuable wood, or in places whence there might be danger of the fire extending to them, must be strictly prohibited, but I would not interdict it in those tracts which yield *chil* only, unless they are upon the bank of the Jelam or other navigable river.

RULES FOR FOREST CONSERVANCY

IN

HAZARA.

---

1. The forests now existing in Hazara are under the exclusive charge of Government to preserve them from destruction and waste.

For deodar (except in Kaghan) ash and toon special permission is required.

2. Within the hills and forests the land-owners and their cultivators may fell such trees as are actually required for the building of their *own* houses, cattle-sheds, &c., or for the manufacture and repair of *their own* agricultural implements, but intimation must be sent to the nearest thanna. The thannadars send weekly reports to the sudder station, whence they are made over to the Jemadar of rangers, and he sends his subordinates to inspect the localities.

3. When villages with no forests of their own, have hitherto enjoyed the prescriptive right of cutting timber from the hills, or land of other villages, for *their own* use, they will have the same privileges as land-owners and others mentioned in rule 2.

Clearing for cultivation requires permission.

4. No one is permitted to fell trees for the purpose of clearing ground for cultivation without the special permission of the Deputy Commissioner in writing.

Saplings not to be cut.

5. Zemindars, &c., are forbidden to fell young forest trees or saplings of any tree for fuel or *for sale*

or for other purpose than that given in rule 2, and under any circumstances saplings of deodar, biar, ash and toon, are forbidden.

6. Zemindars are forbidden to give or to sell any trees of those kinds which pay seignorage to other people than those included in rules 2 and 3, or to allow trees to be removed without the order of the Deputy Commissioner. Trees not to be sold by Zemindars.

7. Zemindars are permitted to graze cattle and sheep in the forests in question, but are strictly forbidden to set fire or to allow others to set fire to old grass in the *vicinity of forests* in order to get a new crop of grass, as this injures and destroys the trees. No excuse of accident or ignorance will be listened to. Grass in the vicinity of forests not to be burnt.

8. Zemindars, travellers, and others, are forbidden to set fire to trees, (growing or dead,) for the sake of frightening wild beasts or warming themselves in cold weather, or cutting torches out of the trunks of growing trees, by which practice many fine trees have been annually destroyed in these hills. Trees not to be cut for torches or fired for warmth.

9. All persons, not land-owners, or cultivators of land, or those specified in para. 3, as having prescriptive right, (not excepting Government agents or officers of any Department,) who require either saplings or trees for any purpose, must apply to the Deputy Commissioner, who will give them a written order, on pre-payment of a fee for each tree according to the printed scale; half of which will be given to the land-owners, and half will be kept by Government on account of the forest establishment. Application to be made to the Deputy Commissioner.

10. Brushwood being abundant on all the hills in Hazara, and the demand being small, there is no present necessity for imposing any restriction on its use. Brushwood may be cut without restriction.

11. No person is allowed to fell or injure, or let his cattle injure trees or groves planted by Govern- Government plantations not to be injured.

ment on the sides of roads, in cantonments, civil stations, or elsewhere.

Sacred groves not to be injured.

12. No person is allowed to cut or injure the trees in Ziârats or groves held sacred by the people.

Fines inflicted for breach of these rules.

13. Any person or persons, land-owners or others, who shall break any of these rules, or commit any act of injury to the forests or trees thus taken under Government protection, will be fined at the discretion of the civil authorities, to an amount not exceeding one hundred rupees for each offence realizable, if necessary, by sale of personal property or in default of payment, commutable to imprisonment for not more than three months.

Thannadars to carry out these rules.

14. It shall be the duty of the several thannadars within whose circles the forests lie to carry out these rules, for which purpose forest rangers are allowed to them.

RULES FOR THE GUIDANCE OF PURCHASERS.

1.—All applications for timber or fuel must be accompanied by a cash remittance, or the receipt of a Thannadar of Hazara, for the amount, and must be made in writing either to the Deputy Commissioner or Assistant Commissioner at Abbottabad, the Extra Assistant Commissioner at Harripore, or the Tahsildar at Mansera.

2.—The application must specify the name and residence of the applicant, the number and description of trees, the locality in which they are to be cut, and the time required for carrying the timber off the ground. A month will ordinarily be allowed for felling the timber.

3.—If the trees be not felled, and the timber removed within the period fixed, they will be forfeited; but an extension of the period will usually be granted, if written application be made.

4.—An order in Persian for the required number of trees will be given to the applicant—this must be presented to the Jemadar of forest rangers who will have the trees allotted and marked in presence of the bearer of the order—and till they have been so marked no tree can be felled.

5.—Breach of forest rules is punishable by fine or imprisonment.

ABBOTTABAD,
1st *February*, 1862.

ROBERT R. ADAMS,
Deputy Commissioner.

N. B.—One Jemadar of Forest rangers will be found at the Thannah of Nara on Mondays, the other at the Tahsil of Mansera.

HAZARA FORESTS.

Rates of Seignorage on Trees and Fuel.

No.	Description of timber.	Rate per tree. RS.	AS.	P.	Remarks.
1	Toon, *cedrela toona*, - - - - -	6	..	..	
2	Ash, *fraxinus*, - - - - - -	6	..	..	
3	Deodâr, *cedrus deodara*, - - -	5	..	..	In the Kaghan glen, Rs. 2.
4	Biâr, *pinus excelsa*,- - - - - -	3	..	..	
5	Barungi (oak,) *quercus*, - - -	2	..	..	
6	Walnut, *juglans regia*, - - - - -	2	..	..	
7	Kangur, *rhus integerrima*, - - - -	2	..	..	
8	Dhamun, *grewia*, - - - - - -	2	..	..	
9	Drawa, *cedrela serrata*,- - - - -	2	..	..	
10	Chir (fir,) *pinus longifolia*, - - -	1	..	..	
11	Palundar, *picea webbiana*, - - - -	1	..	..	
12	Reen (oak,) *quercus incana*, - - -	..	8	..	
13	Phoola, *acacia modesta*, - - - -	..	8	..	
14	Horse chesnut, *pavia Indica*,- - -	..	8	..	
15	Yew, *taxus baccata*, - - - - -	..	4	..	
16	Olive, *olea Europea*, - - - - -	..	4	..	
17	Sirrus or Sirree, *acacia sirissa*, - -	..	4	..	
18	Amlok, *diospyros lotus*, - - - -	..	4	..	
19	Khyr, *acacia catechu*, - - - - -	..	4	..	
20	Khai, *ulmus campestris*, - - - -	..	4	..	
21	Batkar, *celtis Australis*, - - - -	..	2	..	
22	Bankow, *vitex*, - - - - - -	..	2	..	
23	Luni, *cotoneaster*, - - - - -	..	2	..	
24	Kala kât, *prunus padus*, - - - -	..	2	..	
	All others coming under the general name of "Bankâti."	..	2	..	
	Lime Kilns,	2	..	..	Per kiln of 100 maunds.
	Soorkhi Ditto.	1	8	..	" "

Note.—The ash and toon are priced high, but being scarce, the rate of Rs. 6. per tree may remain, as it is very desirable to preserve the existing trees for seed. If the rates for deodar in Kaghan were raised to Rs 3, it would be nearer the price in other districts. The walnut, hill toon, (drawa,) and Kakkar or Kauger, seem to be undervalued and ought to be Rs. 3. The charge for yew, olive, elm, and bankow, certainly ought not to be less than 8 as.: and as the demand increases it should be raised. The mulberry should be added to the list of seignorage-paying trees, perhaps at the same rate as yew, elm, &c.

THE FORESTS OF THE MURREE HILLS.

THE sanatarium of Murree is situated on the summit of a ridge at the western extremity of the Himalaya, overhanging the plateau of Rawal Pindi, from which it is forty miles distant. Its position is 34° N. latitude, 73′ E. longitude, and its elevation above the sea, level is about 7,300 feet.

Character of the flora. On the southern slope the vegetation presents the ordinary features of the western Himalaya, but in a paucity of forms. In following the upper road to Abbottabad the flora soon resembles that of Kashmir, and contains a greater proportion of European plants than any of the other hill stations.

Dr. Fleming and Bellew's reports. Dr. A. Fleming traversed the range as a geological surveyor, and enumerates the principal trees in the *Procs. Agri-Hort. Soc., Punjab*, p. 56, 1851. His collection of plants is deposited in the Royal Herbarium, at Kew. Dr. A. Gordon recorded, "Notes on the Topography of Murree," in *Jour. As. Soc., Beng.*, xxiii., 461, and an interesting communication from Dr. Bellew, is published in the Report on Sanitary Establishments for European Troops. *Rec. Govt. India*, Calcutta, 1861, No. II., Military Department.

Scenery. The general appearance of the station is very striking; though the back ground is less grand than that of Massuri, Simla, Dharmsalla or Dalhousie, yet the varied positions of more than a hundred residences on different heights and acclivities, many of them hid in forest verdure, others on naked points of rock form a picturesque landscape.

The forests clothing these hills are composed chiefly of the following trees: Four species of pine occur—the deodar or diar, *cedrus deodara,* is found on Mount Môchpura, extending from 7,000 feet to its summit. It grows on the precipitous limestone cliffs, but is not abundant. It is not seen on the Murree range or outer hills towards the Jelam. The "chil," *pinus longifolia,* covers the lower hills from 2,000 up to 6,000 feet. It grows to a large size and yields a valuable timber, which is strong and durable as long as it retains its resin. This tree abounds, particularly on the northern slopes. The "biar," *pinus excelsa,* seldom grows below 6,000 and ranges up to 9,000 feet It resembles the chil, but is of a darker green color, with shorter and finer triangular leaves, having five in a fascicle instead of three, and with a smooth instead of a rough bark. The cones are much longer than those of the chil, and its wood is superior, forming the chief material for house building at Murree.* The "pelundar," *abies smithiana,* is very abundant. It is tall, straight, and handsome, ranging from 7,000 to 10,000 feet. Trees 10 feet in circumference, 3 feet above the ground, and 100 feet high are not uncommon. The wood is white, and though occasionally used for boarding, is not so good for beams, as it rots quickly if exposed to damp. Pines.

There are three species of oak; "rinj" *quercus incana,* never attains a great size. It has a range from 4,000 to 7,000 feet, and frequently forms fine woods Oaks.

* The wood of *pinus excelsa* is little valued at Simla. The difference of quality in the wood is remarkable, and may be attributed to the soil and climate, and consequent development of resin at Murree.

on the northern slopes. "Barungi," *quercus laxiflorâ*, is a magnificent forest tree, seldom seen below 6,000 or above 7,500 feet. The leaves of the young trees are covered with prickles which gradually disappear in the older ones; many of which are 12 feet in girth, and from 80 to 100 feet high. "Barcha," *quercus floribunda*, is not common, its timber is very hard and much valued.

Other trees.

The maple tree, "trekudna," *acer cultratus*, is abundant near Murree, but generally small. On Môchpura there are some very large specimens of plane, *platanus orientalis*. It has been introduced into gardens at Lahore, but does not thrive in the plains. *Rhododendron arboreum* occurs on the plainward slope. Two species of elm, the Himalayan horse chesnut, wild pear, bird-cherry, poplar and willow, are all common.

Area of forest in Murree hills.

Around the limits of the sanatarium for which compensation was paid, the area of forest tract supplying timber and fuel is calculated at 11,000 acres by Capt. Birch, but the whole area "cannot be less than 200 square miles, of which half is cultivated," the other half is available for pasturage and fuel. No reserves have yet been made, but Major Cracroft, Deputy Commissioner well remarks, "when a distinct mountain tract can be found of sufficient extent to be separately demarcated, it will be taken up." This is of great importance for the interests of the general public, and special examination is desirable for this purpose.

Establishment.

The Assistant Commissioner, Murree, has an establishment of 1 jemadar and 12 chuprassis, at a monthly charge of rupees 68, who if restricted to their special duties should be sufficient to supervise the forests around the station.

The annual receipts and expenditure for 1861 and 1862, were as follows :— Forest revenue.

	1860-61.		1861-62.	
		Rs.		Rs.
Receipts,		1,910		2,227
One-eight share to Zemindars,	238	621	278	1,045
Establishment,	383		767	
Total.		1,289		1,182

Any person desiring timber applies to the Assistant Commissioner, who specifies from what forest it should be taken. The applicant is referred to the Tehsildar with orders to collect the fees in advance, after which a chuprassi is deputed to mark the very trees to be cut. A limited time, varying with the number of trees indented for, is allowed for felling; if exceeded, the trees lapse to Government. Applications for timber.

When timber is required for public purposes the allotted fees are paid, but Government gives trees and brushwood freely to the peasantry for building their houses, and for agricultural implements. The number of trees taken by the villagers free of charge in 1861 and 1862 was :— Zemindars' privileges.

	1860-61.	1861-62.
Fir trees,	643	496
Brushwood,	32,483	32,623

There are 112 houses in Murree, and the quantity of fuel used in the bazar may be estimated at nearly the same amount as is used by visitors.* The three largest consumers have given their approximate annual consumption, viz. :— Consumption of fuel.

The Brewery,	33,000	maunds.
Lawrence Asylum,	3,000	,,
Commissariat,	20,000	,,

* The daily consumption is estimated at 250 maunds *per diem*, during the season.

USEFUL TREES AND SHRUBS OF MURREE AND HAZARA.

Hill Name.	Botanical Name.	Remarks.
Akhrôt,	*Juglans regia.*	Occasional.
Amlôk,	*Diospyros lotus.*	Common in the hills and gardens.
Anōch,	*Fraxinus xanthoxyloides.*	
Ardawal,	*Rhododendron arboreum.*	Not common in Hazara.
Ban-kahû,	*Vitex*	Wood useful for housebuilding.
Ban-khor,	*Pavia indica.*	Wood used for making large dishes.
Barat,	*Embelia.*	
Barcha,	*Quercus floribunda.*	
Barungi,†	——— *laxiflora.*	A large tree; wood used for housebuilding.
Batangi,	*Pyrus variolosa.*	Frequent.
Batkar,	*Celtis Australis.*	
Biar,	*Pinus excelsa.*	Second only to deodar; scarce at Murree.
Birmi,	*Taxus baccata.*	Highly esteemed for jampan poles.
Bis,	*Salix.*	Twigs used for basket-work.
Bokhain,	*Melia.*	
Būna,	*Acacia sirissa.*	Common.
Cheta buta,	{ *Abelia triflora.* { *Buddleia crispa.*	
Chil,	*Pinus longifolia.*	Known to Europeans as "Scotch fir."
* Chitra,	{ *Sapindacea.* { *Staphylea emodi.*	Not uncommon.
Choda,	*Pyrus baccata.*	Common; fruit eaten.
Chuchra,	*Butea frondosa.*	Stunted and scarce.
Chumiari,	*Cerasus puddum.*	
Dadru,	*Rhamnus virgatus.*	
Damun,	*Grewia oppositifolia.*	Fibrous bark used for ropes.
Daruni,	*Punica granatum.*	
Diar,	*Cedrus deodara.*	Scarce in Hazara.
Doda,	*Pyrus Kumaonensis.*	
Drawi,	*Cedrela serrata.*	

† Barungi appears also to be the name of the *Q. ilex*, which occurs from Spain to the W. Himalaya.

Hill Name.	Botanical Name.	Remarks.
Gurgura or Gunger,	*Sageretia.*	Common at low elevations.
Gurunda,	*Prinsepia utilis.*	Not uncommon.
Kahû,	*Olea Europea.*	A very slow growing tree ; abundant.
Kâi,	*Ulmus campestris.*	
Kalakât,	*Prunus padus.*	The railing of the Abbottabad road is made of this timber.
Kalanchi,	*Desmodium.*	The bark used as a paper stuff in Rawal Pindi jail. Very common.
Kamela,	*Rottlera tinctoria.*	Abundant in low situations.
Kandar,	*Cornus macrophylla.*	
Kandiara,	*Carduus.*	
Kangur,	*Pistacia integerrima.*	In demand for furniture.
Kanti,	*Indigofera heterantha.*	
Khair,	*Acacia catechu.*	In low valleys.
Kiamil,	*Odina wodier.*	Very rare.
* Kolar,	*Bauhinia variegata.*	Common ; planted.
* Kuke,	*Flacourtia sapida.*	
Kuti-lal,	*Daphne oleoides.*	Very abundant in Hazara.
Lûn,	*Cotoneaster bacillaris.*	Abundant.
Paludar,	*Picea webbiana.*	Common.
Pan,	*Rhus cotinus.*	Frequent ; bark used for tanning.
* Patharman,	*Callicarpa.*	
Phalja,	*Populus ciliata.*	
* Phulwai,	*Cæsalpinia sepiaria.*	
Pipul,	*Ficus religiosa.*	Planted near temples.
Pishor,	*Fothergilla involucrata.*	
* Râl,	*Mimosa rubicaulis.*	
Rinj,	*Quercus incana.*	Much of the fuel and charcoal is made of this oak.
Saki,	*Euonymus fimbriata.*	Wood hard and useful.
Sanatta,	*Dodonæa Burmanniana.*	
Shishum,	*Dalbergia sissoo.*	The most valuable hard wood in the Punjab.
Shrol,	*Alnus.*	
Sofaida,	*Populus alba.*	A handsome tree near houses ; wood not esteemed.
Sûm,	*Fraxinus.*	The large species ; wood much prized.
* Sumlu,	*Berberis lycium.*	Not found west of Hazara.
Tawi,	*Grislea tomentosa.*	Red petals used in dyeing.
Tetri,	*Rhus Buckiamela.*	
Timbur,	*Xanthoxylon hostile.*	
Trikadna,	*Acer cultratus.*	Tree prized for shade, but not for its timber.
Tûn,	*Cedrela toona.*	Very scarce near Murree.
Tût,	*Morus lævigata.*	Attains a large size ; wood excellent.

* Names marked with an asterisk are entered upon the authority of Dr. J. L. Stewart.

Rules for the Conservancy of Trees and Brushwood in the Rawal Pindi District.

1. In the mountainous and hilly portion of the Rawal Pindi district, all trees and shrubs of spontaneous growth are hereby declared to be the property of Government. They are available as far as they are really required by the villagers for domestic or agricultural purposes, but with this exception may not be cut, or appropriated by any person, without the permission of the civil authorities. This rule, however, is to be liberally construed as regards the comfort and convenience of the villagers.

2. Upon receipt of an application for timber trees the district authorities are entitled to determine the quarter in which they may be cut, and are to demand a tax. On payment of the tax they are to depute an official to mark, in concert with the applicant, the very trees he is allowed to fell. But no trees are to be selected for this purpose within 300 yards of the main site of a village, or which have been evidently appropriated for shade, or ornament to religious buildings, or for the comfort of the villagers.

3. The tax on fir trees of every description is fixed at one rupee per tree.*

4. On trees of greater value, such as Kangur and Toon, a higher tax may be laid, provided that it do not in any case exceed 5 Rs. for one tree.†

5. Where permission is given to cut brushwood either as firewood, or for lime burning, the tax in the former case will be 2 Rs. per 100 maunds of fuel, and in the latter 1 rupee per 100 maunds of lime. The civil officer is to select the spot at which the cutting may take place, and the cutting is to be effected in such a manner as to leave a length of stump sufficient to ensure a reproduction of the supply.

6. The setting fire to forest grass, or other combustible substances, in a manner calculated to destroy or injure trees, or shrubs, or felled timber, is prohibited; and the owners and occupants of the land will be rendered responsible for such conflagrations occurring within their bounds.

7. This prohibition is not, however, to extend to the burning of grass in open spots with a view to improve pasturage, provided care is taken that the conflagration shall not extend so as to commit the injury described in the foregoing para.

8. The heads of villages, village accountants and watchmen, and the police and revenue establishments, are all bound to aid in carrying out these rules.

9. Of the fund obtained by means of the taxes, the proprietors of the villages in whose area the trees or brushwood are situated will receive one-eighth or 2 annas in each rupee, on the condition of their co-operating with the officers of Government in enforcing the rules. The remainder of the fund is intended to pay for the cost of surveillance and to provide means for reproduction of trees.

10. Any person who shall infringe any of these rules, may be fined at the dis-

* Subsequently increased to Rs. 3 for chir, and Rs. 4 for biar. *See* p. 205.

† Raised to Rs. 10, for a toon tree.

cretion of the civil authorities to any amount not exceeding 100 Rs. for each offence. Such fine may be realized by sale of personal property, and in the event of its non-realization the offender may be imprisoned for a period not exceeding three months, with or without labor.

11. The above rules do not concern the forests on the hilly range from Shaldetta to the Jelam river alone, but all tracts of considerable extent in other parts of the district also, such as the Khairi Moorith mountain, with its surrounding jungle and off shoots, the range commencing on the Indus and coming down beyond Futteh Jang, &c.

J. G. CRACROFT,
Deputy Commissioner.

Rawal Pindi, 24th December, 1856.

There are considerable tracts of waste land, partly hill and partly ravine, not producing lofty trees but yielding a large amount of fuel, on which sissoo might be raised and existing species reproduced. The area of these lands cannot now be stated, but it is considerable and the revenue will increase. As the settlement progresses, the boundaries will be defined, a sufficient portion being assigned to the zemindars and the remainder reserved for Government.* Description of forests in Rawal Pindi.

The principal timber trees are the "chir" and "biar," (*p. excelsa,*) *quercus ilex*, mulberry, toon, and its congener, "drawa," the sissoo and olive, with *acacia modesta*, and a *vitex*. Principal trees.

For several years efforts have been made to preserve the forests, but the demand for public works and private purposes has been very great, and the finest trees have been felled. In the tracts contiguous to Murree, where fires are strictly prohibited, young trees are springing up in great numbers, but in other places, reproduction does not appear to keep pace with expenditure. The consumption of fuel is enormous, and in some places small success has Present state of forest and fuel tracts.

* It would be important to ascertain, if there are any compact and productive tracts not included within village boundaries

attended continuous efforts to grow trees by broad-casting the seed.

Rukhs demarcated as reserves.

The subjoined statement of Rukhs, or waste land separated from village boundaries is given by Major Cracroft, in a report submitted to the Financial Commissioner, in 1862.

Tehsil.	Rukh.	Number of Villages within Rukh boundary.	Area in Acres.	Remarks.
Futteh Jang,	Khairi Moorith,	53	68,302	The measurement is given approximately. The land is all uncultivated.
Rawal Pindi,	{ Topee,	1	297	
	{ Dhannial,	1	1,091	
Goojarkhan,	Pind Kala,	7	766	
Kahoota,	Mallakpur,	1	623	
	Total,	63	71,009	

Rukh Topee.

The Rukh Topee, close to Rawal Pindi, has for three years been carefully preserved and inspected. It is hilly with patches of level ground, and is now covered with indigenous vegetation, springing from the roots of shrubs felled some years ago. This tract was formerly leased for grazing but as the young trees were much injured, the practice has been discontinued. The growth is now satisfactory, and the experiment interesting, shewing that nature unrepressed reproduces rapidly if all cutting and stubbing out the roots is stopped. Roads have been made to open out the Rukh and facilitate supervision. A large number of seedlings of chir, sirris, toon, pulahi and olive, have been raised by broad-casting seed without watering. The toon requires some care and also the chir. It is desirable that Rukhs near other large towns should be treated in a similar manner.

Rawal Pindi establishment.

The establishment consists of 4 Jemadars, 3 Duffadars, and 43 Chuprassis. This seems to be a larger number than is necessary. The cost is defrayed by a fuel tax similar to that of octroi.

The following rates of seignorage are levied:— Seignorage.

No.	Description of timber or fuel.	Rate per tree.		
		RS.	AS.	P.
1	Toon, *cedrela toona*, - - - - - - -	10	...	...
2	Sheeshum, *dalbergia sissoo*, - - - - - -	6	...	...
3	Barungi (oak), *quercus ilex*, - - - - - -	4	...	...
4	Biar, *pinus excelsa*, - - - - - -	4	...	...
5	Kangur,* *pistacia integerrima*, - - - -	3	...	...
6	Tut, (mulberry) *morus*, - - - - - -	3	...	...
7	Darŏh, *cedrela serrata*, - - - - - -	3	...	...
8	Chir, *pinus longifolia*, - - - - - -	3	...	...
9	Simul, *bombax Malabarica*, - - - - - -	1	...	...
10	Palundar, *picea webbiana*, - - - - - -	1	...	...
11	Pulahi, *acacia modesta*, - - - - - -	...	8	...
12	Khair, *acacia catechu*, - - - - - -	...	4	...
13	Kahu (olive), *olea Europea*, - - - - - -	...	4	...
14	Bankahu, *vitex*, - - - - - - -	...	2	...
15	Rinj, *quercus incana*, - - - - - - -	...	2	...
16	Dhamman, *grewia oppositifolia*, - - - - -	...	2	...
17	Pusser or Pishor, *fothergilla involucrata*, - -	...	2	...
18	Birmi, *taxus baccata*, - - - - - - -	...	2	...

Rate at which Timber and Fuel are sold in the city of Rawal Pindi.

Sirris,	.. .. ..	1 foot 4 inches cubic per rupee.	
Kangar,	.. .. ..	Ditto ditto ditto.	
Khair,	.. .. ..	Ditto ditto ditto.	
Ban Kahu,	.. ..	1½ foot square per rupee.	
Diar,	.. .. ..	Ditto ditto ditto.	
Pulahi,	.. .. ..	1 foot 2½ inches cubic per rupee.	
Fuel,	Unsplit wood,	8 maunds per rupee.	
	Split ditto,	4 ditto ditto.	

No other description of timber is sold in the Rawal Pindi market.

J. E. Cracroft,
Deputy Commissioner.

The information given below regarding the receipts Forest Revenue.

* The Kangur is of the same value as toon—the rate might be raised. The vitex and yew are also underrated.—R. C.

and expenditure of the forest revenue for the years 1860-61 and 1861-62, is furnished by Major Cracroft.

RECEIPTS.									EXPENDITURE.								
In 1860-61.			In 1861-62.			Increase.			In 1860-61.			In 1861-62.			Increase.		
RS.	A.	P.	RS.	A.	P.	RS.	A.	P.	RS.	A.	P.	RS.	A.	P.	RS.	A.	P.
3,436	3	0	5,864	4	11	2,428	1	11	695	1	1	1,985	3	0	1,299	1	11

NOTE.—The increase in receipts is due to enhancement of rates, and in expenditure to increase of establishments.

Work to be done.

The Deputy Commissioner defines the work in prospect thus—" 1st, to demarcate all rukhs, or preserves, for fuel and timber; 2nd, to distribute the establishments so as to ensure the careful preservation of the rukhs; 3rd, to provide for the reproduction of trees and fuel, by closing tracts of country where fuel is exhausted, and by broad-casting seed; 4th, to persevere in, and extend the area of experiments in Rukh Topee, and preserves elsewhere." The chief points to be remembered are, the selection of a tract where young trees are springing up, showing the capabilities of the soil and its fitness for growing wood, and then the careful protection of the young trees from grazing of every kind.

Major Cracroft.

Major Cracroft has a long acquaintance with the district, and deserves great credit for his continued exertions, which have been highly useful. If a forest officer should be appointed to the Jelam Division, the cordial co-operation of the Deputy Commissioner will be valuable, and must be attended with good results.

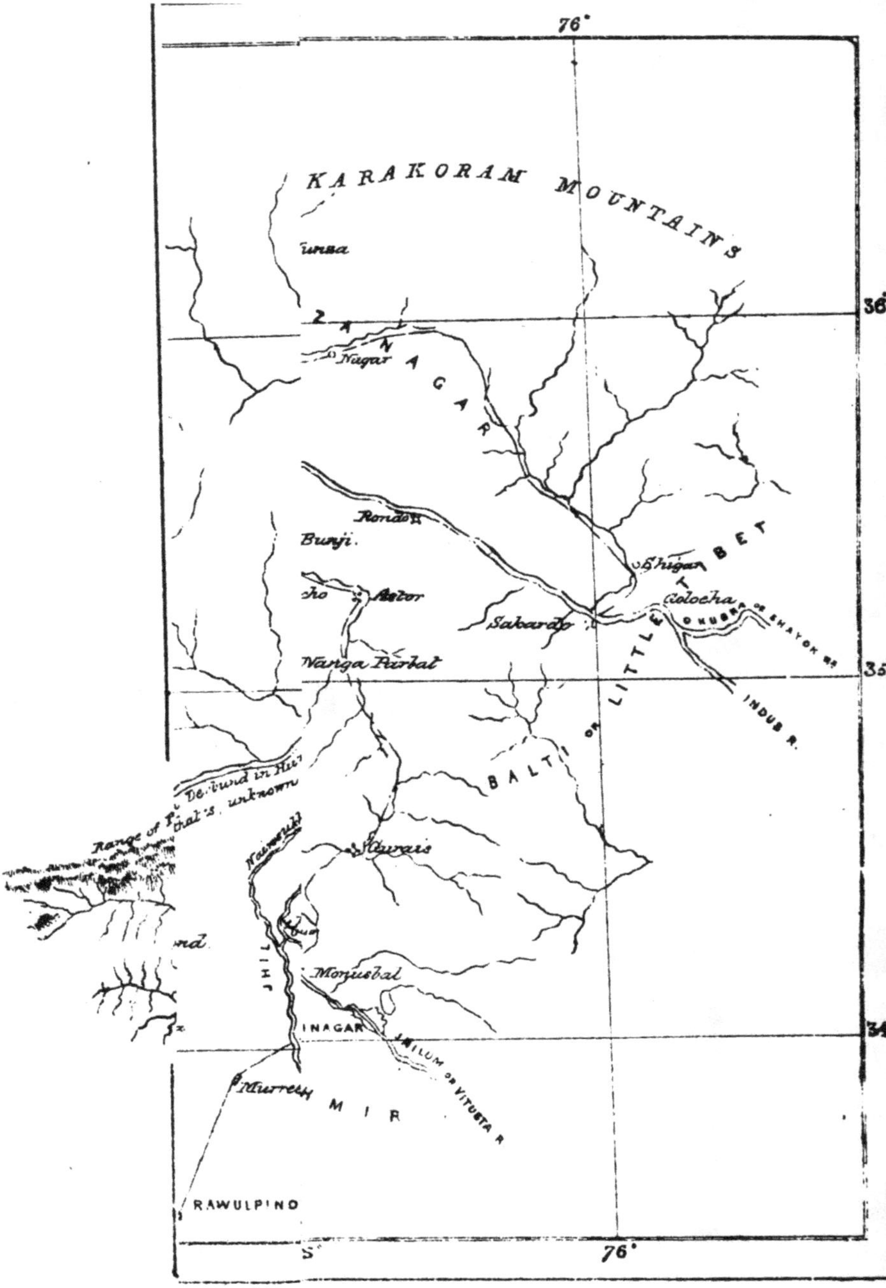

76°
KARAKORAM MOUNTAINS
36°
Nagar
Rondo
Bunji
Astor
Nanga Parbat
Shigar
Golocha
Sabardo
35°
BALTI OR LITTLE TIBET
INDUS R.
Gurais
Monusbal
34°
JHILUM OR VITUSTA R
RAWULPINDI
76°

MEMORANDUM

ON THE

TIMBER PROCURABLE FROM THE INDUS, SWAT, AND KABUL RIVERS.

DURING my visit to the Trans-Indus territory, I saw considerable stores of deodar and other timber at Attock* and Peshawar, and having an opportunity of conferring with the native merchants, as well as with several officers of the Public Works Department, I collected all the information obtainable regarding the state and prospects of this new and interesting trade, so important both in its commercial and political bearing. I here notice the supply procurable from each of these rivers separately, embodying the replies given by Engineer officers,† who have used the wood in the construction of Public Works at Attock and Peshawur.

Sketch map. The accompanying sketch map shows so far as known the localities whence timber is procured beyond our boundary, and the depôts for sale within our territory.

Indus river. There is no record of the timber supplies of the upper Indus, the forests of which are beyond our control or even inspection, but some facts may be gleaned from a Report on the River, by Lieut. Wood, Indian Navy, published in Burnes' Kabul,‡ p. 304; though

* Generally hauled up on the Khairabad side of the river.

† Major Sandilands, Capt. Pollard, Lieut. Browne, R. E., and Mr. Nugent, Assistant Engineer.

‡ Re-printed from *Jour. As. Soc., Beng.*, x, p. 518.

as regards timber it treats solely of boat building materials and fuel for steamers.

Valley once wooded. The valley of the Indus appears to have been famous for its timber from the days of Alexander to within twenty-two years of the present date. Forests of sissoo existed on either side of the river and on the numerous islands from Torbela to Attock, but "these were wastefully felled during the rule of the Sikhs, and the remaining trees adorning its banks were swept away by the terrible flood of 1841."* (Major J. Abbott, in *Jour. As. Soc., Beng.*, xvii., 231). "Indeed the most striking effect of the cataclysm (*Cunningham's Ladak*, p. 135,) is the entire absence of trees in the valley of the Shayok, while the lateral valley of Nubra was full of trees upwards of a hundred years old."

Fall of river. From the junction of the Gilgit river to Attock, the course of the Indus is south-west; the distance is about 300 miles, and the fall of the river 3,500 feet, or 11·6 feet per mile.† This part of the course is little known, but even at Ohind, fifteen miles above Attock, where the river debouches on the Chuch plain, Cunningham (*Ladak*, p. 89,) found the current more rapid than that of any other river of the Punjab. From Derbund‡ in Hazara, to Acho at the bottom of Astor valley, *i.e.*, for 160 miles, the course of the Indus is quite unknown to Europeans. (Capt. Montgomerie, G. T. S., in *Jour. As. Soc., Beng.*, 1861).

Native traders. Few natives of the plains proceed beyond Umb, the only persons who can do so with safety are the Shaikzadas of Ziyarat. They bring down deodar logs from

* Inundation of the Indus, taken from the lips of an eye witness, A. D. 1842, *Jour. As. Soc.*, xvii, 280.

† Capt. Henderson makes the mean fall from Nubra valley to Attock, 18⅜ feet, and 21⅜ feet from Attock to Kalabagh. *Jour. As. Soc., Beng.*, xxviii. 207.

‡ Derbund is an appropriate name—the door is shut.

the forests in the independent states upon the upper Indus. The sanctity with which popular superstition invests them as the descendants of a notable saint, is the safeguard of their lives and property among the wild Kohistanis from whom in the first instance they get the wood, and in their passage through the independent Pathan settlements lying between Derbund and the forests.

The timber is floated in single logs as far as Derbund, where it is stopped and a toll of eight annas per log is levied. This presses unequally, as the value of the logs varies much. Major Adams has tried to persuade the chief of Umb to charge a light *ad valorem* duty. Merchants from Attock and elsewhere, with boatmen of Jehangera come up here to make purchases, and remove the wood in rafts. Derbund.

The chief of Umb (a minor) has possessions on both banks of the Indus. He is a feudatory of the British Government, but the police and fiscal arrangements are entirely in his own hands. It is his interest to encourage the wood trade as he obtains *mahsul* at a fixed rate; the Kardar raised the transit duty, but it was reduced two years ago to the former rate. This chief possesses great influence in the upper Indus, and is entitled to toll, but when this has been paid, there should be no detention of the wood; his dues should be well defined and limited. Chief of Umb.

The independent Pathans of Kabbul and Kyab, opposite Torbela, also began to levy an impost on all timber that came within their reach, but this has been stopped by Major Adams. They receive payment for any assistance rendered in floating rafts or launching stranded logs. Independent Pathans.

Until three or four years ago, very little wood came down the Indus. The wants of the Sind Incipient trade capable of extension.

Railway Company first created a market, but the cessation of the demand has dulled the trade, which is capable of great extension. The supply is irregular and depends upon the wants of the hill people, who send large quantities of timber to Derbund when it suits them.

Quality of Indus timber.

According to the native dealers and Attock carpenters, the Abba Sein* deodar is the best in quality, being more resinous and durable than the wood brought down the other rivers. Many logs were tested in 1856 by Major Robertson and Capt. Henderson; an abstract of the experiments was published in the papers prepared for the use of the Thomason College, No. II, Strength of Materials, Appendix 2.

Swat river and valley.

The course of this river is imperfectly laid down in our latest maps, the valley through which it flows, though so near our frontier, being almost a *terra incognita*; a description of it will be found in the *Jour. As. Soc. Beng.* 1862, p. 227, by Capt. Raverty, based upon the narrative of an intelligent native of Kandahar, who states that the lower ranges are destitute of trees, but covered with grass. The higher hills on either side are clothed with forests, consisting chiefly of the edible pine and wild olive. The plane also flourishes in cultivated tracts. At the extreme head of the valley near Sardzaey, where there is a pass leading into Kashkar, "there are immense numbers of trees both along the river banks, and on the mountains on either side to their very summits." I am informed, by Dr. Bellew, that the dues for large pines are four annas seignorage to the Khan, and four annas for felling and launching.

Principal trees.
Cedrus deodara.
Pinus gerardiana.
Platanus Orientalis.
Olea Europea.

Papa Mea.

The timber trade on this river appears to be nearly monopolized by Papa Mea, head of the Ka-

* Abba Sein, *i. e.* Father river, or main river of the Indus.

kakhel Sayads, described by Major Sandilands of the Peshawur road, as " a fair dealing old man, somewhat stubborn and difficult to manage, but frank and independent." He sells at his own price, rarely at less, fulfils his agreement, and seldom supplies bad material. He lives on his own jaghir, called Walli, near Nowshera, where there is an expense yard. His people go where they choose up the three rivers, and the perils of eternal punishment attend those who injure them in any way. Papa Mea therefore, is the principal man with whom extensive dealings may be carried on. He has a large woodyard at the village of Hashtnagar, near the confluence of the Swat and Kabul rivers, and in British territory. This depôt often contains 5,000 logs of various sizes, and he may be said to command the market in its present limited state. I believe that considerable quantities of deodar may be obtained from the Swat valley, if Papa Mea's terms are agreed to, and intimation is given to him six months before.

Scantling.

The great proportion of logs brought down the Swat and Indus rivers are of very short lengths. This arises partly from the local difficulties of transport from the forests to the rivers, and partly from the singular fact, that the natives formerly valued logs, not according to length, but according to thickness, and they are slow in apprehending our object in desiring long scantling.

Lawlessness of Swatis.

The following circumstance illustrates the lawlessness of the Swati Afghans. A trader of Peshawur lately felled in the hills above Swat two thousand deodars, which were thrown into the river to be floated down to Peshawur. When the trader entered the Swat territory, the Swatis would not allow the rafts to proceed. The trader complained to the Akhund, who expostulated with them. The people of lower Swat gave up all the timber they had not made use of, but the inhabitants of upper Swat did not, and the logs may now be seen in hundreds on the river's banks.* (*Jour. As. Soc., Bengal.* 1862.)

Kabul river.

The vegetation of the valley of the Kabul river was first described by the late Mr. Griffith, who traversed it on his journey to and from Afghanistan. In his Private Journal† and Itinerary Notes, the most characteristic plants observed by him are enumerated. He writes, that the lower ranges of the Sofaid Koh, (white mountain,) which bounds the valley on the south, are black with firs in some places (p. 414,) and that the course of the Kabul river is rapid, flowing between singularly rounded ranges (p. 422). Timber is cut in considerable quantities and is floated down in spring to Kabul (p. 390). From Kabul to Jellalabad the river is often fordable, but only useful for irrigation; below this it affords the means of safe and speedy descent. Towards the lower end of the valley, in the direction of the Khyber pass, no

* Dr. Bellew has supplied me with the following additional information:—

"Formerly most of the timber came from the hills of Paltan, Palas, Chilas, and Taldardial, all in the Kohistan. Of late, however, this trade has been stopped by order of the Akhund, who decreed that it was better to abstain from a trade that led to quarrelling amongst the faithful whilst infidels alone benefitted. The circumstances mentioned above led to the Akhund denouncing the trade which is now suspended at least in the hills of Swat. At present, the only timber coming down the Swat river is felled at Tal Patrak, a district of Bajawar, under the control of Ghazan Khan of Dir. The river at the foot of the hills is called Malizai Sind, and appears to be either the Panjkora river or a branch of it. It joins the Swat river at Arang Barang, and the united streams are called Sandai. The timber is collected in the Malizai and marked by the traders, who come down on the rafted timber as far as Mian Banda. Below this, the Likandai rapids occur, and the logs must be floated singly. A few miles lower is the ghât of Abazai, where the timber is again rafted and floated to Charsadda, Prang, and Babarra, between which contiguous ghâts is a timber depôt, supplying Nowshera, Akora, and Attock. Timber can only be floated in the summer months. The usual scantling is 20 feet × 10 × 6 inches. The traders take guns, pistols, &c., as douceurs for Ghazan Khan and Akhunzada. With care and encouragement the trade may be increased, but the rapids at Likandai are an obstacle to the safe passage of large timber."

† Griffith's Posthumous Papers. Calcutta, 1847.

forest whatever is visible, the arborescent vegetation being confined to solitary or scattered trees.

The distance between Jellalabad and Peshawur by the river route is about 90 miles. The current is usually about seven miles an hour. This journey is performed in from twelve to fifteen hours, on a raft of twenty-five skins impelled by two large oars. Accidents rarely happen in May, June, and July, when the water is of sufficient depth to cover the rocks, which are dangerous at other seasons. Half way is the large village of Lalpura, on the left bank, where the chief of the Mamund tribe resides. Below are several whirlpools and dangerous places—of these the Shutr gurdun (camel's neck) is particularly dreaded. Tolls are levied on rafts at the village of Michni. River route from Kabul.

A few miles below Jellalabad, the Kabul river is joined by a broad stream of considerable volume, which drains the Kuner valley and is likewise practicable for rafts. By this tributary the best wood comes down to Peshawur. Mr. Griffith, who visited Pushut, the chief town, gives some account of this narrow valley (*Itinerary Notes*, p. 433); "the mountains are well wooded at a certain height, and in greater quantities" than in the valley of the Kabul river; "very different, however, from Himalayan forests, dotted in parts rather than uniformly clothed with forests." The distribution of the trees is as follows:—the baloot (*quercus ilex*) ranges from the bed of the river to an elevation of 2,000 feet above it, or 4,500 feet above the sea. Towards its upper limit, it is mixed with "zaitoon" (*olea Europea,*) which soon supplants the baloot, forming the chief part, if not the entire forest, as far as the lower limit of the deodar, Kuner* tributary.

* The Kaure of Elphinstone. MacGregor calls it Kashkote river, and mentions that grain, iron, &c., are brought down to Jelalabad on rafts of inflated hides. *Jour. As. Soc. Bengal. 1842.*

6,500 feet above the sea. "Between this and the summits of the ridges, which attain a height of about 10,000 feet, the deodar reigns supreme, vast in abundance and in size. These forests are available for the timber supply of Jellalabad and Peshawur." Griffith regrets that "in consequence of the lawless character of the inhabitants there were no means of access to the beautiful forests visible in several directions." At great personal hazard,* he acquired much valuable information, but it is to be regretted that he was not spared to edit his manuscripts. It would appear that large pine forests lie along the Olipore branch of the Kuner river, which comes from the western portion of Kaffiristan, and falls into the Kuner river at Chighar Serai. Below the pines *baloot* woods occur.

Flora of Afghanistan. From the absence of rain during summer, and the great heat, the vegetation is that of a hot dry country. "On the southern slopes of the Hindu Kush, the great elevation of the chain produces more humidity than elsewhere in Afghanistan, and there is therefore a forest belt, which extends from 5,000 to 10,000 feet. These forests are entirely confined to the mountains which rise out of the valley of Jellalabad, and do not extend further west than the 69th degree of longitude, elsewhere the country is extremely barren, and almost destitute of tree vegetation. The trees are chiefly oaks and pines. There is also a pine forest on the northern slope of the Sofaid Koh range, which bounds the valley of the Kabul river on the south, it being lofty and snowclad almost throughout the year. The pines are *pinus excelsa* and *gerardiana*,

* Mr. Griffith, accompanied the army which marched in 1838-39 from Sind, through Quetta and Kandahar to Ghazni and Kabul. From Kabul he crossed the chain of the Hindu Kush to Bamian and Singhan, and spent some time in the Kuner valley. His collections, though formed under circumstances of great difficulty, are very good, amounting probably to about 1,000 species, many of which are deposited in the Royal Herbarium at Kew.

abies smithiana, and *cedrus deodara*; of these the deodar appears to be the most abundant. In the temperate zone, *juniperus excelsa* is of occasional occurrence. The oak of these forests is *quercus ilex*, a species which extends from the south of Europe as far as Kunawar. With the oak, species of *æsculus*, *olea*, *myrtus*, and *amygdalus* occur."*

Naguman Ghât, near Peshawur.

For some years past all the timber required for the city and cantonment of Peshawur has been brought down the Kabul and Kuner rivers. The timbers are ready squared, often split with wedges, and roughly dressed with an adze, but never sawn, and without special agreement the size does not exceed 24 feet × 5 × 8 inches. Up to 1858, larger scantling was not procurable save by accident. Major Sandilands in visiting the ghât on one occasion, observed a log of unusual dimensions, and inquired if such could be obtained. The native merchant said he was going to Kabul for wood, and would endeavour to procure large timber. He brought down several logs 28 and 30 feet long × 15 × 10 inches. Subsequently some thousand fine logs have been brought down. There is always great delay in procuring such timbers, and sometimes two years have elapsed before they have reached Attock.†

* Hooker and Thomson's Introduction to Flora Indica, p. 255.

† Dr. Bellew states—"that timber floated down the Kabul river is felled on the Karr Kacha, an offshoot of the Kuner mountain, between Jelalabad and Kabul. Nakhtar, the generic name of pines among the Afghans, of which there are several kinds, is the only wood cut. The mountaineers fell, mark, and convey the timber to the stream below. They then float the timber down in rafts to the Naguman ghât, where they sell the wood to the agents of the Peshawur merchants. There are agents for the purchase of timber at the ghâts of Michni, Matta Dauzai, and Khizana. The timber is felled at all seasons, but can only be floated down from the middle of June to the middle of September, when the streams are swollen by the melted snows. Most of the timber brought down is of small size, but a few logs are 2 feet in diameter and 80 feet long. The supply is very uncertain. No Peshawur men can visit the timber districts. Their agents at the several ghâts agree with the timber cutters of the Kohistan as to the quantity and dimensions of the timber they are to bring down the

Native traders.

Major Sandilands and his assistants have generally dealt with Hindu merchants. They incur dangers and difficulties to which Mahomedans would not be subject and usually disappoint in the tardiness of delivery. They dare not ascend the rivers themselves and employ Pathans, who often treat them badly. A Pathan, Azuf Shah, has offered to procure timber of any scantling within four months, and to give security for punctuality. Large timber is not now required on the Peshawur road, and an opportunity of giving him a trial has not occurred. Papa Mea's tribe are privileged to ascend the rivers, but their trading operations are confined to the Swat and Indus rivers. Both these rivers are practicable for rafts, and if a stimulus be given to this incipient timber trade by the extension of railways and public works, a permanent traffic may be established.

Qualities of the timber on the different rivers.

According to native carpenters the Indus or Abba Sein timber is the best, being more resinous. The next is the Swat timber, which is very good and free from knots. The Kabul river wood often appears to be immature. It splits well, has few knots, but is considered more brittle than the other sorts; some beams have broken straight across and very suddenly. The timber, however, being scarce and expensive has not been subjected to many experiments. Mr. Browne, Excutive Engineer, Kohat, states that the deodar received from the Kashgar hills, by the Kuner tributary, is beautifully grown, without knots and splints, equal to the Jelam wood, while he agrees

next year. Of late years the timber trade on this river has greatly increased. The timber is used in the city and cantonments of Peshawur, and also in boat building. The number of boats built on the Naguman is much greater during the last few years. They are built entirely of Nakhtar wood, and carry merchandize (chiefly wool) as far as Karachi. The chief impediments to the further increase of the trade are the disturbed state of politics at Kabul, uncontrolable delays, and the faithlessness of the contractors."

with Major Sandilands, that the wood from Jellalabad is not so fine in quality.

The Indus timber is generally sold at from 4 to 6 annas per cubic foot. For logs of extra length, 7 to 8 annas is occasionally charged. The average length of the logs is from nine to twelve feet; a few range up to eighteen feet. Prices of timber. Indus.

The Swat river timber was formerly 5 annas: the present arrangement with Papa Mea is 6 annas 3 pie per cubic foot of picked timber. The logs are short, and usually very thick. Swat.

Kabul timber is procurable of any length, according to demand, and varies in price from 5 annas to 1 rupee per cubic foot. The Public Works Department is the principal consumer, as natives do not require long timbers. Traders make sure of the price they are to receive for wood before going up for it. Kabul.

The scantlings which have hitherto arrived are— Scantling of Kabul timber.

1st sort,	50′	× 18″	× 18″	only one log.
2nd „	43′	× 18″	× 18″	4 or 5 logs.
3rd „	36′	× 18″	× 16″	20 or 30 logs.
4th „	30′	× 16″	× 15″	many.
5th „	28′	× 16″	× 14″	„
6th „	24′	× 15″	× 11″	„
7th „	24′ to 28′	× 12″	× 9″	„
8th „	24′ to 28′	× 10″	× 7″	„

Almost the only means of becoming acquainted with the vegetation of the forests round Peshawur, is to study the twigs and branches brought for sale as firewood, or as pads for camels. To explore the woods without a guard is dangerous and against regulation. Mr. Griffith was attacked when botanizing in the neighbourhood, and his faithful servant Abdul lost two fingers (*vide* p. 17). Deodar and chir are brought to Peshawur by the Kabul river, and mulberry, babul, and sissoo are found in the plain; walnut and ash are also obtainable, but only to a Flora of Peshawur.

small extent. Dr. J. L. Stewart, endeavoured to identify the woods used for fuel by means of the bark and the Pushto names, and has published a valuable account of the Flora of the Peshawur valley; of which the following is an abstract:—

Firewood of Peshawur.

"The uncultivated parts of the Peshawur district, are barren in the extreme, there being no forest, and shrubby vegetation is only seen towards the base of the surrounding hills, where small streams occur. This consists of *acacia modesta, olea europæa, dodonæa burmanniana,* and *reptonia buxifolia,* which grow abundantly as one ascends the hills, while in the dry and barren low ground, the most conspicuous shrubs are *zizyphus jujuba, adhatoda vasica, capparis aphylla, salvadora, vitex negundo* and *tecoma undulata.** All timber of any size is afforded either by the cultivated trees of the valley, such as the mulberry and sissoo, or by the timber rafts brought down the Swat and Kabul rivers, which consist of deodar and other pines. The firewood supply for the cantonment is furnished by the above named shrubs, and large quantities of oak (*quercus ilex*) are brought from the Khyber. It appears not unlikely that, ere many years elapse, the supply of firewood for Peshawur at reasonable rates will be difficult or impossible."† Firewood is sold at Peshawur at about 4 maunds, and charcoal at 2 maunds per rupee.

Waziristan.

The value of the timber of the hills of Waziristan to *us* is very small; if we except the limited supply of firewood afforded by the shrubby vegetation of the outer zone, which is similar to that along the frontier, few of the indigenous shrubs are used and these only in the construction of agricultural implements,

* Less frequently observed are *celastrus parviflora, celtis, pistacia integerrima, sageretia, grewia oppositifolia.*

† *Jour. As. Soc., Bengal,* 1863, p. 225.

and the roofs of small buildings, &c. The oaks ot the inner hills are so distant from the plains that their timber is not in request for building purposes; while the labour of conveying pine timbers from Pir Gal would be very great.

There is no portion of the Trans-border territory so convenient for the supply of timber as that adjacent to the sources of the Bara river, whose numerous tributaries flow from the southern spurs of the Sufeid Koh mountains between Koorum and the Khyber. I learn from Major Lumsden that this elevated region held by the Afreedee and Orukzie tribes and known as Teera Maidan, has the summit and slopes of its ridges clad with deodar and pine forests, while walnut, plane, horse chesnut, apple, apricot, and other trees are also found below. The intestine feuds of the tribes inhabiting Teera Maidan, have hitherto debarred the development of the resources of these forests, from which short timbers could be floated in the season of flood down the Bara stream to Peshawur. Bara River.

The valley of the Koorum river, which rises near Huryoob, beyond the ridge of the Solimani mountains, is little known, but is said to contain fine forests. These are mentioned in Elphinstone's Kabul and Bellew's Political Mission to Afghanistan, p. 137. They were also seen by Dr. Stewart in the Waziri expedition. Lieutenant Browne, Executive Engineer, Kohat, has suggested that timber should be procured from this source in the same way as Major Sandilands has obtained it from Swat.* The political and Koorum river.

* Major P. Lumsden, supplies the following information. There is no reason why timber from Huryoob, Chumkunnie and Koorum itself should not be floated down the Koorum river to Bunnoo, though there are portions of the stream, where except in floods assistance to long timber would be required, owing to its tortuous course. The valley of Koorum and its adjacent tributaries being held in jaghire by Afghan Sirdars, who are poor, arrangements could doubtless be made to cut and float the timber down to our territory; from Thul Billandkhel it must be sent either by land to Kohat or down the stream to Bunnoo.

economic advantages would be great, but the Koorum is a small river even at its mouth, and it is doubtful if pine logs can be floated down from the hills.

Kachi forest. The Kachi sissu forest, of spontaneous growth, extends over 14 or 15 miles on low alluvial land upon the left bank of the Indus, between the villages of Bukkri and Futtykhan, and more sparingly for 15 miles lower down, or altogether 30 miles from Kalabagh. It was mentioned to me by various officers at Mooltan, and it seems very desirable that it should be well conserved, the wood being highly prized for boat building on the Indus, and for railway carriages, &c. From the increase of population and of cattle, the trees are represented as suffering damage, and and the forest is said to be gradually diminishing and in danger of extinction. There are few trees in India which so much deserve attention as *Dalbergia sissoo*, the "talo" of the Punjab, considering its rapid growth, the durability of the timber, and its usefulness for many purposes; the wood is universally employed when procurable by Europeans and natives where strength is required. Great efforts have been made to introduce this tree, and where there is depth of subsoil (as in this forest) it grows to a large size.

Sissu and olive forest. There is a large forest of sissu and olive about ten miles from Kohat, on the Hangu and Meranzai road, which might yield a considerable supply of timber, though not of large size. This, and the Kachi forest* in Bunnoo, are the only sources from whence any great supply of sissu can be obtained in the Punjab. The olive wood (*zaitoon*) is remarkably heavy, sinking in water, the grain is close and the timber useful in engineering works.

* A small establishment for guarding this forest was sanctioned by Government of India in 1862.

Boat building materials.

There are five kinds of boats used between Attock and the sea; those best known are the "zoruk" of the upper Indus, the "dunda" which plies from Mithankote to the sea, and the "dugga" which is specially suited from its strong build to the navigation of the rapids between Attock and Kalabagh. The better kinds of wood used in their construction (sissu and large babul,) are procured with difficulty, and various species of timber are generally seen in one boat, such as sissu, babul, deodar, chir, bahn, and karil. Malabar teak is much prized in the lower Indus and fetches a large price.

The ordinary ferry boats are constructed by the sides and bottom being prepared separately and brought together to be secured by knees or crooked pieces nailed to the bottom and sides. The bottom is made of sissu, the knees of mulberry or olive, and the side planks of deodar. The wedges and trenails are usually made of tut and kahû. Ropes for rafts and boats are prepared either from hemp (*cannabis Indica*), sirki (*saccharum spontaneum*), *typha latifolia*, "dib," or other reeds, common on the river bank. Munj (*saccharum munja*), is also largely employed by the native boatmen.

The great boat building localities of the Punjab are Pind Dadun Khan, Wazirabad, and Jelam, but there is a marked increase on the Indus, not only at Attock, but at Nowshera, Hashtnagar, Mokhud and Kalabagh. The "duggas," after dropping down to Sind, are sold, as the cost of towing up against the stream would exceed the value of the boat.

PUSHTO NAMES OF TIMBER TREES AND SHRUBS.

Pushto	Botanical	Pushto	Botanical
Adai pashtawar,	*Abelia triflora.*	Khar wula, (*i. e.*, big willow,)	*Salix.*
Aghzakai,	*Prosopis spicigera,*	Khīrcha īndzar,	*Grewia betulæfolia.*
Anār,	*Punica granatum.*	Khiroba,	*Cotoneaster rotundifolia.*
Badar,	*Taxus baccata.*	Khowun or khowund,	*Olea Europea.*
Bahān,	*Populus Euphratica.*	Khwa,	*Tamarix dioica.*
Bajūr,	*Picea webbiana.*	Khwaga wula (*i. e.*, sweet willow),	*Salix dioica.*
Bandūkai,	*Ephedra.*	Kirra.	*Capparis aphylla.*
Berra,	*Zizyphus jujuba.*	Kuraskai,	*Berberis lycium.*
Buja,		Laghunai,	*Daphne* ,,
Dzīga wuna,		Lor,	*Ehretia aspera.*
Cherai,	*Quercus.*	Linandza,	*Pinus excelsa.*
Khārpata cherai,	,, *ilex.*	Mandata,	*Amygdalus persica.*
Ghwara cherai,	,,	Mānra,	*Pyrus malus.*
Sper cherai (*i. e.*, white oak),	,, *incana.*	Mārchob,	*Staphylea emodi.*
Chinar,	*Platanus orientalis.*	Marghwalwa,	*Viburnum cotinifolium.*
Ghujbai,	*Alnus.*	Marwandai,	*Vitex negundo.*
Ghuraskai,	*Dodonea burmanniana.*	Mumanrai,	*Sageretia.*
Ghurghushtai,	*Amygdalus persica.*	Mzarai,	*Chamærops ritchiana.*
Ghwa,	*Tamarix orientalis.*	Nashtar,	{ *Pinus longifolia.* *Cedrus deodara.*
Ghwartja,*		Nawukai,	*Jasminum.*
Ghwardza,*		Palosa,	*Acacia modesta.*
Gira,	*Alnus.*	Parwata,	*Hedera.*
Gulab ghuri,	*Rosa brunonis.*	Pasta wuna (Perai),	*Grewia oppositifolia.*
Gurgura,	*Reptonia buxifolia.*	Plewan,	*Salvadora persica.*
Hagai,	*Fraxinus buxifolia,*	Regdāwan,	*Tecoma undulata.*
Hanja,	*Acacia farnesiana.*	Sanjata,	*Eleagnus orientalis.*
Indzar,	*Ficus carica.*	Sarap,	*Taxus baccata.*
Jar langai,	*Lonicera quinquelocularis.*	Sarawān	*Rhus integerrima.*
Karkanra,	*Zizyphus nummularia.*	Sarlashtai,	*Spiræa lindleyana.*
Karkanrber,	,, *vulgaris.*		
Kaskai,	*Indigofera heterantha.*		
Kbarra or khbara,	*Capparis spinosa.*		
Khamasar,			

* These seem to be different pronounciations of the same name. Dr. Stewart notes the former as *Edwardsia mollis*, and the latter as *Cratægus oxyacantha*.

Shakai,	*Urtica hypoleuca.*	Taghö,	*Celtis.*
Shamshād,	*Buxus sempervirens.*	Torjaga,	*Pavia indica.*
Shawa,	*Dalbergia sissoo.*	Tritch gandera,	*Calotropis gigantea.*
Shne (green),	*Pistacia terebinthus.*	Tsanda-wuna,	
Speda (*i. e.*, sofaida),	*Populus alba.*	Waghz,	*Juglans regia.*
Spera wuna,	*Buddleia crispa.*	Wara wuna (small tree),	*Ribes.*
Spilecha,	*Fothergilla involucrata.*	Warmandai,	*Vitex.*
		Wula,	*Salix.*
Sur aghzai (red thorn),	*Celastrus parviflora.*	Wurak,	*Rhamnus virgatus.*
		Wurāskai,	*Dodonea burmanniana.*

For the spelling of the Pushto names, I am indebted to Rev. I. Loewenthal, and for the identification of the botanical names, to Dr. J. L. Stewart's Memoranda on the Peshawur Valley. *Jour. As. Soc., Beng., 1863.* A short list of plants found in Kafiristan with Pushto names is given by Griffith, (*It. Notes, pp.* 441-2,) but it contains numerous typographic *errata.* Some remarks on the soil, climate, and horticulture at Peshawur, by General Burnitt, are recorded in *Jour. Ag.-Hort. Soc. Ind.* viii. 41.

Fruits of Afghanistan.

Afghanistan is rich in fruits, and although the people are acquainted with grafting, the remarkable perfection which several of the finer fruits have reached is certainly more due to climate than to skilful treatment. Fruits are more important in Afghanistan than in other countries, in which they are not generally considered as necessaries of life. Several kinds contribute very largely to the sustenance of the people. "Few things," says Griffith, "can be more striking to a person accustomed to India than the display of fruit in the markets of Kabul, and even after the whole army of the Indus had been encamped for some weeks, they still continued remarkably cheap." The list includes—(vide *Griffith's Itin. Notes, p.* 355.)

Apricots (*zard-alu*), 2 or 3 vars.	Pomegranates (*anár*), 2 kinds.
Peaches (*shaft-alu*).	Grapes (*ungoor*), several.
Nectarines,	Musk-melons (*kharbúza*).
Plums (*alu bokhara*), several, including damson,	Sarda melons (*kharbúza, sarda*).
Bullaces (*alucha*).	Water-melons (*tarbúza*).
Cherries (*alu walu*).	Mulberries (*tut*).
Apples (*seu*), several.	Walnuts (*char mughz*).
Pears (*naspatti*), several.	Figs (*anjir*).
Quinces (*bihé*).	

Of these, the most important articles of general consumption in the country are apricots, plums, grapes, melons, and mulberries. The thick-skinned grape, the seedless pomegranate, walnuts, sarda melons, apples and figs are exported; the first in large quantities.

Many forms of preserved fruit are sold in the bazars, and a great variety were contributed from Peshawur to the Punjab Exhibition (1864). Some are prepared by drying, especially the apricot, (kubani,) fig, white mulberry, and kismiss grapes, these are sold to a considerable extent.

The Sarda melon is finely flavoured, and in great demand; being generally damaged by camel carriage, it is brought down the Kabul river on rafts, and sold at about 4 annas each. This melon is in perfection (Oct., Nov.), when frost touches the plants.

Vines are very extensively cultivated in the suburban gardens of Kandahar, and produce no less than nineteen kinds of grapes. In two or three of the largest vineyards there are wine presses, but the quantity of liquor produced is limited. It is red, and is prepared from grapes of the same colour, which are known by the terms of "rocha-i-surkh," "sahibi surkh," "lal-i-sufaid," "lal-i surkh," &c. Fruits of Kandahar.

The Hindu population consume large quantities of a fiery spirit distilled from dried grapes, called "kishmish-i-sufaid," and "kishmish-i-surkh," and they are secretly helped in this by many of the Mussulman inhabitants of the city. The Khátin grapes produce the well known Manakka raisins met with in India. The "sahibi surkh," and "sahibi ablak" produce sun-dried raisins, called, from their being void of seeds, "kishmish-i-bedána." These are very small, of a light green colour and very sweet taste. They are largely exported, and consumed at home in immense quantities. The "rocha-i-surkh," and "rocha-i-sufaid," as also "toran," are grapes of an inferior kind, and are mostly consumed by the poor. The "Hasaine" and Shaikh Khalli grapes are of great size, of pale green colour, and delicate flavour. They are gathered before they have quite ripened, and packed in drums of poplar wood between layers of cotton, are exported to Hindustan in vast quantities, and even find their way to Calcutta. The Vines.

Note.—The information regarding the fruits of Kandahar is condensed from *Bellew's Mission to Afghanistan*, p. 287. The vines are planted in trenches, and the vineries are well enclosed.

"Acta" grape is also of large size, but its flavour is inferior. It produces, however, excellent raisins, called "kishmish-i-daghi," or "abjosh," which resemble the best bloom raisins met with in the English market; they are prepared by dipping the fresh and ripe branches for a moment or two into a boiling solution of quick-lime and potash, previous to drying in the shade. There are other varieties which are either altogether consumed in the fresh state, or are largely exported to Hindustan.

Apricot. The gardens around Kandahar produce many other fruits, such as the apricot, plum, peach, cherry, apple, pear, quince, &c. Of the apricot (*zardalu*), eleven varieties are found in the Kandahar district. The "kaisi,"* "charmaghz," and "charbaghi," are the most esteemed. They are largely consumed fresh, and also preserved for exportation to Hindustan by drying in the sun. But previous to this process the fruit is sliced open, its stone removed and split, and the kernel replaced in the fleshy part of the fruit. In this form the apricot is called "khubani." The variety named "pas ras," is as its name implies, the last to ripen. There are two kinds, large and small. These, with other varieties named "surkhcha," "sufaidcha," "plan," "shams," and "shakarpara," though generally consumed in the fresh state are also dried, but the stone is not removed, these are called "taifi." They are very acid, being generally dried before quite ripe: they are chiefly used as a relish, and as a component of some kinds of sherbet. Gold and silversmiths use a hot decoction of this fruit for

* An excellent smooth skinned apricot, produced from grafts. The native name "alu" indicates a pomaceous fruit. The Afghans understand little of their culture, and rarely prune the trees. In Kaghan, apricots are seen in heavy clusters weighing down the branches.

the purpose of cleaning and giving bright lustre to their metals.

Of the peach (*shaft-alu*) there are only two kinds at Kandahar. The one called bábri, is an inferior fruit of small size and acrid flavour, but that known as tirmah, is large and luscious much superior to any I ever met with elsewhere. **Peach.**

Of the quince (*bihi*) there are three kinds, viz., the "shakar," or sweet quince; the "tursh," or sour quince; and the "miána," or quince of medium quality. The first is generally consumed fresh, and is often carried about the person on account of its agreeable perfume. The other kinds are candied, made into jams, or cut into slices and dried for future use as an adjunct to other dishes. The seeds of all are demulcent and are added to sherbets. Both the fruit and the seed are exported. **Quince.**

Of the pomegranate (*anar*) there are six or seven varieties. Those grown at Panjwai are the finest, and most esteemed; they are of great size, the pips of blood-red colour, very juicy, of excellent flavour, and perfectly sweet, without any of the tartness belonging to other kinds of this fruit. They are justly celebrated throughout the country, and large quantities are carried to the Kabul market. The fruit rind of all the varieties is an article of export, as well as of home consumption for the use of tanners and dyers. The root bark is a common remedy for diarrhœa, and is also used as a vermifuge. **Pomegranate.**

Of the fig (*anjir*), which generally grows wild, there are two varieties; one bears a black fruit, called "makkai," the other a white, "sada." The fruit of both kinds is small and sweet. The former are strung on thin cords and exported, the latter are consumed at home. **Fig.**

Mulberry. Of the mulberry (*tut*), which also is indigenous, there are nine or ten varieties. Some of them are preserved in the dried state and eaten with almonds and raisins, or with walnuts and parched maize, or lentils. In the northern parts of Afghanistan the mulberry tree is very abundant, and the people use its fruit as a substitute for corn flour. The bread made from the flour of dried mulberries is said to be sweet, wholesome, and fattening.

Cheapness and variety of fruit. The abundance and consequent cheapness of fruits is quite astonishing. The natives indulge in them often to excess, and suffer in consequence, especially the poor, who for several weeks of the summer season know no other food. The variety and low price of the fruits in Kandahar is noted by every traveller, and especially by Forster (Journey from Bengal to England, 1808.) Irwin (Memoir on the Soil, Climate, Produce and Husbandry of Afghanistan.) *Jour. As. Soc. Bengal*, 1839,) and Griffith (Report on Subjects connected with Afghanistan.) *Jour. As. Soc. Bengal*, 1841.

FUEL SUPPLY IN THE PUNJAB.

THE winter season being unfavourable for visiting the forests of the inner Himalaya, and the question of fuel for steam boat and railway purposes in the Multan division being important, I proceeded in January, 1862, to Gugaira and Multan, passing through several of the fuel reserves, which fringe the Lahore and Multan road, and thence to Muzaffirghur, traversing the sandy tract between the Chenab and the Indus. In travelling south, the wastes become more covered with jungle, the population and cultivation less. I had an opportunity of conferring with the District Officers,* the Senior Naval Officer, Indian Navy, the Superintendent Indus Steam Flotilla, and several of the Staff of the Punjab Railway Company. Captain Hampton, Superintendent of Navigation was absent on duty. From all of these officers I sought information, and received approximate estimates of their departmental requirements. It will be seen from the accompanying summary how great is the demand for fuel for various purposes, but chiefly for locomotive consumption and the supply of fuel to steamers.

Consumption at Multan.

Fuel required at Multan, 1862.

	Maunds.
Indus Steam Flotilla, ...	200,000
Her Majesty's Government Steamers,	110,624
Railway Workshops, ...	60,000
" Bricks, ...	60,000
Commissariat, ...	20,000
Executive Engineer, ...	20,000
	470,624

= 230,000 cubic feet, or 4,600 loads at 50 c. ft. the load.

Supply for railway.

The locomotive consumption had not then commenced, and as there is now only a small portion of railway open, it is difficult to calculate the annual amount of fuel required, but it is evident that without careful management, difficulty will ere long arise in procuring the adequate supply for public purposes, and perhaps inconvenience may ensue to the neighbouring population. It is necessary, therefore, that certain tracts of jungle available should be reserved, demarcated, and put under regulation. It would also be important to ascertain the qualities of the different kinds of wood, and to take care that no

* Commissioner of Multan, Deputy Commissioners Multan, Gugaira and Muzaffirghur.

waste of material occurs in working and using the fuel. The provinces of the Punjab and Sind are more sparingly provided with tree vegetation than other parts of the Indian Empire, and conservancy is therefore more requisite. In the latter province, a forest department has been organised for some years which fulfils the desired object, and yields a considerable revenue to the State.

Rukhs or fuel reserves.

At Lahore, the great demand for wood and grass led to the reservation of a larger area of Rukh land, and some attention was given to the question at an early period of our administration. In Multan, the selection of Rukhs took place with reference to the position of fuel stations on the rivers; the demand for locomotives is now commencing and the pressure will be greater in the south than in the north, because both railway and steamers have to be supplied.

Area of rukhs in Multan division.

The result of my inquiries in the Multan Division shows that tracts of scattered jungle exist in the different sub-divisions as below:—

	Total area in acres.	Reserved tracts—acres.
Gugaira, - - - - - -	12,71,832	26,000
Multan, - - - - - -	20,00,000	77,000
Muzaffirghur, - - - - -	9,00,000	92,000
Comprising altogether, -		1,95,000

which it is proposed to set apart as "*fuel preserves*;" and these it may be well to place under a system analogous to that now in force in Sind, the vegetation and requirements of the two provinces being remarkably similar.

Mr. Edgeworth's views.

In 1851, when the question of steam fuel on the upper Indus and Punjab first attracted attention,

Mr. Edgeworth, then Commissioner of Multan, an accomplished botanist, recorded his views in a letter to the Board of Administration, of which the following is a summary:—"On the banks of the Sutlej in Gugaira, Capt. Marsden reports a sufficiency of fuel to last twenty years at the rate of 22,000 maunds a year. In the Multan district fuel is abundant, and a large proportion of it tamarisk, I should say there is an inexhaustible supply, as the reproduction would equal the consumption. The native agent at Bhawulpore reports that the territories of the Nuwab cannot supply any continued demand."

Mr. Edgeworth suggested that "it would be worth while to form plantations of babul and tamarisk in some of the abundant waste land along the rivers at suitable places for the steamers. The tamarisk grows readily either from seeds or cuttings, the babul very readily from seed, and scarcely any expense would be incurred after the original planting. A single watchman at each plantation or reserve would be sufficient. These reserves should be so arranged as to present a succession for copsing through a course of eight years, which would allow a sufficient time for the wood to attain a size suitable for fuel." These views were submitted to Dr. Stocks, forest ranger in Sind, who entirely concurred as to early planting of babul and tamarisk on the waste land along the rivers. Proposal to plant babul and tamarisk.

"The Sind forests were made by the Sind Ameers for hunting purposes, and the mode they took to ensure the growth of a jungle was well suited for the ends proposed. They enclosed by stakes or walls, large tracts of ground, and let the natural jungle come up unrepressed, carefully taking care that no goats nor camels (most destructive animals Dr. Stocks' views.

to young trees) got admittance, or indeed any living being as far as they could prevent it. The annual inundations of the river, and the babul seeds contained in the soil from the dung of domestic animals, and the perfect and unrepressed growth of whatever should come up, produced in the course of a very few years, a thick and impenetrable jungle, which by degrees rose into the name and dignity of a forest. Not that the Sind forests resemble forests in the rest of India, they are but skeletons lining the river bank, and presenting only clumps of trees in the interior, the whole connected by low jungle or bare wastes. Should it be wished to begin the formation of new forests in Sind, there are excellent localities, and the same facilities as in the Ameer's times; as perhaps similar circumstances and localities exist on the Punjab rivers, I may describe them."

Land suitable for planting.

"Capricious though the Indus is, deserting one year a channel which it had formed the last, and washing away a bank only just made, still there are certain localities presenting features of greater stability, and which can be pretty well depended upon as likely to continue along low level spots, common on both banks, these have at first nourished only tamarisk, but in which afterwards sprung up trees of the babul and poplar. High freshes of the river, on a high inundation, cover partially spots of the land. Nothing is required to form a forest here but to protect the jungle from the grazing of camels and goats, and the inroads of the charcoal burner. This requires co-operation of the neighbouring village authorities, combined with the presence of a Government keeper, or a fence and keeper. A great deal will depend upon local circumstances, upon the distance or nearness of villages, and upon the help obtained from the subordinate Civil authorities. But probably, as suggested by Mr. Edgeworth, a single person would be sufficient at each preserve; one person, however, should never have a beat of more than a mile in all directions, or he will not attend to the outlying parts of his duty. Babul seeds might be saved in favourable localities, to scatter over places where they would not spring up naturally. The chief points to be insisted on, are to choose a place where a jungle already springing up shows the capabilities of the soil and its natural aptitude for the development of wood, and then carefully to protect the young trees from grazing of all descriptions."

Growth of jungle on river banks.

" In Sind, where, as a general rule, there is absolutely no rain, this is the only way of encouraging the growth of trees. In some parts of the Punjab, however, the presence of regular rain would modify the above remarks; in such parts forest may be made from seedlings or cuttings in places removed from immediate inundation, and yet in spots whence wood could be collected for steamer fuel. In Sind, all growth of wood and of natural jungle, as well as all the operations of agriculture, are dependent on the river, and must be limited to its banks or to the banks of its branches. And hence it is that advantage must rather be taken of the state of the river banks as they at present exist than by forming any large reserves of picked or chosen woods on more elevated and stable ground above the river bank. So that the cutting of wood for steamers is more a thinning of jungle which has come up in free and unrepressed growth, than a regular and systematic cutting down of portions of a planted reserve, regulated by calculations of growth and expenditure."

Colonel Hamilton's opinion.

Colonel Hamilton, Commissioner of Multan (1862), considered that the supply of fuel near the city would be exhausted in a few years, but that an almost inexhaustible supply can be obtained from the *bar*, at an enhanced rate; while Capt. Tighe, Deputy Commissioner, Muzaffirghur, informed me that there is much jungle in the tract subject to the overflow of the Indus and Chenab, and that favourable sites for planting exist near these rivers, some of which I had an opportunity of inspecting.

System of supply to steamers.

The steamers are supplied by native fuel agents, who superintend the cutting and stacking of firewood at equidistant points on the river bank; they engage labourers and measure the fuel, which must be always ready for use. Their pay below Multan is Rs. 20 a month, and the fuel stations are six in number, viz.

Fuel stations.

Multan,	Bakri,
Khangur,	Jibbi,
Sultan ki shah,	Mittenkote.

Steamers proceeding from Multan to Jelam, or from Mittenkote to Kalabagh, receive fuel on application to district officers, and pay the same rate as charged by the fuel agents, at present Rs. 15 for 100 maunds, or 4 tons, *i. e.*, 1 ton = Rs. 3-7. The quantity prepared for these occasional trips is usually in excess of the consumption from fear of a deficient stock, but below Multan the system is now well understood, and no complaints are made. In Sind, the wood stations are under the forest ranger and all the steamers obtain fuel from his stock.

Measurement.

The measurement of fuel is preferable to weighing, which is a tedious process still adopted in some places. It has been ascertained that 100 maunds of the wood supplied forms a pile 15 feet square and 3 feet high. The duty of the fuel agent is simply to measure the stack of wood by a fifteen feet rod. The billets are required to be not less than 8 inches in circumference and of uniform length.

Seignorage or Royalty.

At Multan, a charge of four annas per boat load, and two annas per camel load, has been recently sanctioned; this is reasonable, considering the enhanced demand for wood.

The jungle on the banks of the Indus and Chenab chiefly consists of the following trees:—*Acacia Arabica, prosopis spicigera, populus euphratica, salvadora oleoides*, and *tamarix orientalis*.

1. Babul (*Acacia Arabica.*) This tree produces excellent timber, adapted for many useful purposes, and its value as in Sind will daily be more recognized. The supply is not very large, and the wood being in demand for agricultural implements and boat building, the growth should be extended. Dr. Henderson has successfully raised plantations of babul at Shapur. His method is given below.* In the Sind forests

* I have tried to raise *kikkur* trees by simply scattering the seed in the jungle. Most of the seeds germinated after the first shower, but few survived the first week of hot dry weather. I next tried scratching the surface with a native plough, but again failed. I then tried sowing, exactly like wheat, but rain falling before the seeds germinated, the ground caked afterwards, as hard as a stone, and scarcely a single seed ever germinated. At last I hit on a method which having succeeded at Shahpoor, one of the most arid districts in the Punjab, is likely to be more successful elsewhere.

The directions to be followed are very simple, and with ordinary rains will almost certainly ensure success.

1. Low ground should be chosen where water remains for a few days after rain; or wherever grass grows well.

2. Plough the ground thoroughly as if for a grain crop, as soon after the 1st July as possible; if it can be done before the end of June, so much the better.

3. Collect fresh seed in June, thoroughly free it from the pods, and scatter it on the ploughed surface at the rate of 8-10 seers at least to each beegah, and double that amount if seed is abundant. Thick sowing makes the young trees shoot up rapidly and straight, and it is much easier to thin them afterwards than to fill up blanks. I may mention that seed does not keep well through

some of the babul logs have produced as many as four sleepers. For steam fuel the wood is excellent.

2. Jhand *(prosopis spicigera)*. This is one of the characteristic trees of the Punjab, yielding a larger amount of firewood at Lahore and Multan than any other. The heart wood is strong, tough, and dark coloured; it is sometimes used for boat building and weaver's shuttles. In Sind it is called "kundi."

3. Bahn (*populus euphratica.*) The Euphrates poplar, called "sofaida" on the Sutlej bank, is common in clumps, but does not grow large and is generally crooked. It flowers in February, and throws up root-shoots with great rapidity. The wood is objected to for steam fuel, owing to the great emission of sparks, which endanger the awning of the boat.

4. Pelu (*salvadora oleoides.*) This tree is very abundant, fringing the sandy tract as the Jow (*tamarix dioica*) does the river. It is often called Jal, and yields an inferior fuel.

5. Tamarisk (*tamarix orientalis.*) Is abundant in the saline tracts, and yields a great part of the fuel of Sind and Southern Punjab. It is easily propagated

the cold weather; a weevil attacks it; and unless collected the moment it is ripe the goats leave very little to collect.

4. The seed must be left on the surface, and not covered up, and the first heavy rain will make it germinate.

5. The plantation must be thoroughly fenced with thorns to keep out goats and sheep for two seasons at least; after that if the seed have germinated well, it will probably form such a thicket that no animal can penetrate it. Then it is time to thin out one-half of the trees, after which a fine crop of grass will grow under the shade of the remainder. To shelter the plantation from frost strips of *joar* may be sown at intervals from east to west, and allowed to stand till all chance of frost is past, but neither *joar* nor anything else should be grown amongst the trees. During the first winter many of the stems will die down if frost is severe, but the first shower in spring will cause the root to sprout again.

Dr. Henderson mentions that *kikkur* seed sown in July, 1862, and treated as above directed without irrigation or watering has produced trees from 12 to 18 feet high, and 8 inches circumference at one foot from the ground, and that some sown at the same time and freely irrigated has produced trees 25 feet high and 12 to 18 inches in circumference at 2 feet from the ground.

by cuttings and is quickly reproduced from old roots. The wood burns fast but gives out great heat. Mr. Fenner, forest ranger, in Sind, considers "a tamarisk jungle of ten years growth admirably adapted for fuel purposes; the wood contains a good deal of resinous matter, which makes it the more valuable. It is easily felled, and usually procurable within reasonable distance from the wooding stations. All that seems necessary, therefore, for future supply is that these tamarisk jungles be conserved in eligible localities and not sacrificed entirely for the benefit of cultivation." (Report 1862-3, para. 14).

FUEL SUPPLY FOR THE PUNJAB RAILWAYS.

No. 80, dated 29th January, 1863.

Resolution—By the Hon'ble the Lieut. Governor, Punjab, Revenue Dept.

Read a memo., dated 13th instant, by the Financial Commissioner, on the best mode of dealing with the Rukhs of the Lahore and Umritsur Districts.

Resolution.—With reference to the following memorandum, the Hon'ble the Lieutenant Governor is pleased to resolve that it shall be stipulated in Deeds of Sale of all waste or uncultivated lands in the Umritsur and Lahore Districts, that all timber standing thereon, together with roots, shall, in the first instance, be offered to the Railway Company for purchase.

Secondly, that the Commissioners of Umritsur and Lahore submit without delay descriptive list of the Rukhs referred to in paragraph 7, of Mr. McLeod's memorandum, in order that it may be notified to the public on what terms offers for their purchase will be admitted.

Thirdly, that it be notified in the Gazette that Mr. Birnie Browne is appointed Superintendent of Grass and Wood Preserves in the Punjab, on a salary of Rs 500 per mensem, with travelling allowance at the rate of eight annas a mile for all distances exceeding ten miles from his head quarters.

His duties will be defined hereafter.

Fourthly, that an extract of paragraph 9 of the memorandum be sent to the Military Department for consideration and orders.

No. 18, dated 13th January, 1863.

From D. F. McLeod, Esq., Finl. Commr., to Secy. to Govt. of Punjab.

I have the honour to submit, for the consideration and orders of Government, a memorandum embodying the results of a meeting of Officers assembled this day at the Office of His Honour the Lieutenant Governor for considering the best mode of dealing with the Rukhs of the Lahore and Umritsur District.

Memo.—By D. F. McLeod, Esq., Financial Commissioner of Punjab.

As there are many applicants for grants of waste land in the Government Rukhs of the Lahore District more particularly, while the permission to dispose of these lands has been hitherto withheld, as it was believed that the wants of the Railways in the matter of fuel could not be readily met unless a portion of these were reserved from sale, and it was uncertain how many of them might be required for furnishing continuously the required supply, a consultation was this day held by order of His Honour the Lieutenant Governor for the purpose of coming to a decision on the matter, at which were present, besides the Secretary to Government and Financial Commissioner, Captain Hall, Assistant Commissioner of Lahore, Mr. Forsyth, Commissioner of the Division, and Major Warrand, Consulting Engineer for the Railway.

It appeared that the consumption of fuel by the Railway Engineers for the 60 miles comprised within the Lahore District at an average of about a maund per mile would amount, supposing three trains to travel either way daily, to about 1,20,000 maunds yearly, while the estimated amount of timber standing on the 11 Rukhs already set apart for the Railway is about 2,00,000 maunds only, being sufficient for little more than 1½ years' supply, supposing the above rate of expenditure to be attained. It has been heretofore calculated that ten years are required, and are sufficient for the renewal of the timber, if the roots be not molested, so that to maintain a continuous supply about six or seven times the area already reserved on this account would be necessary.

3. The entire amount of timber standing on the available Rukhs of the Lahore District, is estimated to be about 20,00,000 maunds, so that if the above mode of supplying fuel should be resorted to, nearly the whole of them would be required, and seeing that owing to the natural fertility of the soil in the greater portion of their area, they require water only to render them exceedingly productive, and the whole or nearly the whole of them will ere long be capable of irrigation from the main channel and various branches of the Baree Doab Canal, the sacrifice to both Government and the people involved in such a reservation would be very great. These lands are yearly increasing in value owing to the above consideration. Offers are already made with great eagerness for many of them, as much as Rs. 20 per acre, or even more being offered in some cases, and there can be no doubt that all

will gladly be taken up ere long if thrown open to public competition. Accordingly, it was the general opinion of the Officers present, that the advantage to be obtained by the reservation of these Rukhs for the supply of fuel would be altogether incommensurate with the sacrifice involved.

4. It appeared to them at the same time that such a measure is not necessary for the object in view. For while the timber above ground standing on the Rukhs is estimated at 20,00,000 maunds it was stated by Captain Hall that, owing to the large dimensions of the under ground portion of the trees compared with that above ground, actual experiment had shown that if they were entirely rooted out, the above quantity would be more than double, which would afford a sufficient supply of fuel for the Railway for 20 or 30 years. If therefore on these Rukhs being disposed of, it were stipulated with the purchasers that as the area was reclaimed all the standing timber, including roots should be sold to the Railway, there would be no grounds for apprehending a deficiency of fuel for some years to come at all events.

5. In addition to this, there are vast areas of waste lands, covered similarly with brushwood, existing further down the line of Railway in the Googaira and Mooltan Districts, as well as across the Ravee, in the pergunnahs of Sharrakpoor and Kamalia, whence the timber could, if necessary, be floated down the river to any point required. And it was further suggested that if special arrangements for growing fuel should hereafter be found necessary rather than reserve valuable lands of large extent unirrigated on this account, it would be more expedient to form a strip of forest of timber trees or brushwood along the several branches of the Canal, deriving moisture from its presence, or at all events to reduce the extent of land to be reserved by selecting suitable spots where the land could be partially irrigated, so that greater quantity and superior quality of timber could be grown.

6. For these reasons, it was determined to be inexpedient to reserve generally either the Rukhs of the Lahore District or those of Umritsur,—which are analogous in character and circumstances, though fewer in number, smaller in area, and situated in tracts better cultivated generally than those of the Lahore up-lands, and the conclusion was arrived at that such portion only should be explicitly reserved in the first instance, as would probably be required by Government for making grants to deserving individuals, given in lieu of lands taken up for public purposes or for other desirable objects, for which requirement it was suggested that the Rukhs which have recently lapsed from the death of Rajah Tej Singh would perhaps be suitable and sufficient.

7. The remaining Rukhs it was considered should not be regarded as generally exempt from sale. But at the same time it was fully admitted that they by no means fall properly within the category of "waste lands," in the sense intended by the Government Resolution. They were reserved by the Government which preceded us for special purposes, having in some instances been actually formed out of cultivated lands in which deserted wells are still existent. They would long since have been brought more or less under cultivation had this been permitted. Their

position in the vicinity of the Governmental and commercial capitals, respectively, of the Punjab, and in tracts about to be largely irrigated gives them great importance. And it is as yet uncertain what requirements connected with the public service may from time to time arise which may be most advantageously made by appropriating portions of them. On these grounds they must clearly be regarded as quite exceptional, and it was proposed, therefore, and is now recommended that it be announced that applications for grants in them will be received, but that as heretofore none will be complied with until explicitly sanctioned by Government on special report in each case,—a discretion being reserved by Government in respect to these lands, both as to determining those which shall be sold or reserved, and prescribing the mode in which the sale shall be effected.

8. To assist Government in forming a correct judgment on these and other points connected with these Rukhs, it was felt to be most desirable that a special Officer should be nominated to the charge of them primarily, and possibly of those also of Googaira and Mooltan, and the Pergunnahs on the right bank of the Ravee. Some measure of this kind was verbally urged by Dr. Cleghorn, at an early period of his stay in this Province, in view of the great and increasing importance of these forests of timber and brushwood, and the impossibility of properly husbanding their resources, or turning them to the best account without some such special arrangements; while the expense attendant thereon, amounting probably to about Rs. 7,000 or Rs. 8,000 per annum, would be readily met out of the proceeds of the Rukhs themselves, which are already very considerable, and will certainly become progressively larger. It was suggested that Mr. Birnie Browne, whose services in connection with the Irrigation Department of Baree Doab Canal will shortly be dispensed with, is a gentleman peculiarly qualified for such a post.

9. The question of Rukh lands reserved for the supply of grass to the horses of the Cavalry and Artillery at Meean Meer also came incidentally under consideration. These are of very large extent, probably not less than five or six acres per horse, and comprise some of the very finest lands in this Doab, capable of the fullest irrigation from the new canal. On the first issue, therefore, of rules for the sale of waste lands, the Commissioner of Lahore was directed to put himself in communication with the Military Authorities, with a view, if possible, to a reduction of the area thus reserved. As yet, no such reduction has been assented to by them, partly because it was thought probable that the number of horses requiring fodder at Meean Meer might be increased; but the officers present were of opinion that Government should renew its efforts in a more decided form to have such reduction effected as may be possible. The Rukhs were made over when the number of Government horses at Meean Meer were, it is believed, more numerous than at present, and when the lands were incapable of irrigation unless by sinking wells; whereas now, the Mounted Force permanently allotted to Meean Meer is of limited strength, and irrigation can at any time be supplied to the lands in question, to such extent as may be required, rendering the supply of grass consequently both more certain and more abundant.

No. 113, dated 27th May, 1863.

Endorsed by Foreign Dept. with G. G.

Forwarded to the Public Works Department with the Governor General for an opinion, as the case involves question affecting the supply of Railway fuel.

No. 1013, dated 11th June, 1863.

Office Memo.—Major G. Chesney, Under Secy., for Secy to Govt. of India, P. W. Dept., with G. G., to Secy. to Govt. of India, Foreign Dept., with G. G.

With reference to docket No. 113, dated 27th ultimo, from the Foreign Department, forwarding copy of a Resolution by the Hon'ble the Lieutenant Governor of the Punjab, regarding the management of Grass and Wood Preserves in those Provinces, for the expression of an opinion thereon in connection with the requirements of the Railway, the undersigned begs to communicate the following remarks.

2. There appears in the first place to be a want of definite information as to the requirements of the Punjab Railway in the matter of fuel, and all doubt on the subject should, it is thought, be removed before these reserves of wood are finally disposed of.

3. The Punjab Government might therefore be desired to cause the question of fuel supply for the Railway to be thoroughly taken up and considered, having reference to the whole line from Delhi to Mooltan. The necessary supply per mile per train should first be estimated, then the approximate position of the fuel stations should be settled, and the annual demand at each ascertained. From this the area of land for the supply of each station could be fixed. It must also be considered up to what distance transport of wood fuel by rail is likely to be possible, having reference to the first cost of the wood and the charge for transport; and then some idea may be formed as to the extent to which wood can be brought up from the better wooded districts near Mooltan, where cultivation is sparse and wood cheap, to the neighbourhood of Lahore, where land is much required for cultivation and wood is scarce. An estimate may, on such considerations, be formed of the area that will be required to grow the wood that should be provided at each locality, and on this the Punjab Government should fix the area to be reserved from existing Rukhs, and will be able to judge how much land should be planted to maintain a proper supply, if no spontaneous growth exists, or no present artificial preserves are available.

4. It calls for remark that the question may now advantageously be settled as to what agency is to provide this supply of wood; should the Government undertake it, or the Railway Company? Probably the Punjab Forest Department, when it is organized, should be charged with the duty.

5. It is plain that before it can be said that the sale of the Rukhs will be *profitable*, it must be known that the Government will not eventually have to make up, in the shape of the payment of guaranteed interest on Railway Capital, for the cost of wood enhanced by the clearance of the existing reserves. The present

receipt of a few thousand rupees by the sale of these waste lands, and the consequent increase of land revenue, will possibly not compensate for the loss that will arise from enhanced working expenses owing to high priced fuel. On such points, it is dangerous to make assumption without due consideration.

6. Again, if it be thought the best plan to give up the existing Rukhs, and to plant fresh wood for the supply of the Railways, it must be remembered that such new plantations will not come into proper bearing for eight or ten years, and that meantime a supply from existing sources should, under any circumstances, be kept in hand. It is believed that the Rukhs only exist in the Punjab Proper. Between the Sutlej and Jumna, some special arrangements will be necessary, and so also for the line through the Doab.

7. The questions involved in the provision of a cheap and constant supply of fuel in these Provinces, where coal is almost certainly never to be got, and the existing quantity of land planted with wood is not great, are on the whole of a nature that will call for very careful consideration, and they cannot be too soon taken up.

Note by DRS. D. BRANDIS *and* H. CLEGHORN, *on the subject of Grass and Wood Preserves of the Punjab.*

With reference to recent correspondence on the Government Rukhs of the Punjab, we think it necessary to draw attention to the following points.

2. After reviewing in a preliminary way, the probable contents and annual yield of the intramontane forests, as far as existing data enable us to do so, we have come to the conclusion that unless the price paid for Deodar timber by the Railway Company, the Public Works Department, and the general public, rise considerably, the management of these hill forests on *conservancy principles* is not likely to yield a large (if any) net revenue.

3. In favourable years there may be a surplus of receipts over working charges, cost of conservancy, and quota of establishment, but upon the whole we do not expect (without cutting more timber than conservancy principles warrant) that the receipts will exceed the total charges.

4. A larger net revenue might indeed be obtained by limiting *strict conservancy* management to a small number of well defined tracts, conveniently situated for the removal of timber, and well stocked with trees. The remaining forests being worked merely with a view to obtain the greatest possible amount of timber at the present time.

5. This concentration of forest conservancy operations is a point worthy the consideration of Government. It may be urged that, under proper management, all forests, including those less advantageously situated, ought to give a good supply of timber, and consequently a surplus revenue, but this is a fallacy which must be guarded against.

6. In the first years of forest conservancy, it is only the best tracts which yield

a surplus revenue, and before the rate of timber production on a certain area has been ascertained, it may be necessary to limit the cuttings to a low figure to make sure that timber is not removed in excess of the annual rate of production.

7. It is, indeed, possible to work the hill forests profitably for a short time in a revenue point of view, if the agency system merely be carried on over the whole extent, but this is not conservancy, and the forests would be annihilated in a few years.

8. The conclusion at which we arrive, after a careful consideration of the data before us, is, that the hill forests are not likely to be more than self-supporting, and occasionally from physical obstructions, uncertainty of floods, &c., the outlay may exceed the proceeds. We look therefore to the forests in the outer hills and plains of the Punjab for the yield of a regular surplus revenue.

9. In the intramontane forests, the trunk of the tree only is removed, the tops and branches very rarely bear the cost of transport, and thinnings below a considerable size are valueless.

10. In the forests upon the slopes of the outer ranges this is not the case, and in the plains all loppings and thinnings are valuable, while the sale of grass yields a considerable income.

11. Independently of the grave question of fuel supply for Railways and Steamers, a sufficient area of the best Rukhs (grass and wood preserves) should be reserved, and permanently placed under the Forest Department for the production of timber, fire-wood, charcoal, &c. This will yield a steady surplus revenue, which may from time to time be required to make improvements in the other forests.

12. If the Rukhs in the Lahore, Umritsur, and other districts, be capable of irrigation, they should not, on this account, be given up to cultivation, but a suitable area of compact shape, and having good soil, should be appropriated for the growth of timber trees.* Sissoo, Babul, Siriss, and Jhand, grow well in the Punjab on lands liable to be submerged, or with a little irrigation, and other useful trees will doubtless be found to succeed.

13. The admission of these premises does not imply the necessity of reserving all the Rukh lands. The expediency of concentrating forest conservancy to a comparatively limited area, holds good in the plains as well as in the hills. The more favourable the soil, situation and other circumstances, the larger will be the production of timber and of forest revenue on a given area. According to the measure of our success in improving the management and increasing the productiveness of the Rukhs, we will be able to follow the suggestion of Mr. Macleod, Financial Commissioner, in his memorandum of the 13th January, 1863, in reducing the area of the reserved tracts.

14. However, the selection of the Rukh tracts to be reserved should be made by the Conservator of Forests, and until that Officer has indicated the tracts which he considers necessary for the welfare of the country, and the requirements of the Forest Department, no Rukh land should be sold or otherwise disposed of.

* *Dalbergia Sissoo, Acacia Arabica, Acacia Sirissa, Prosopis Spicigera.*

Until the selection is made, we think that the management of all the Rukh lands, whether ultimately reserved or not, should rest with the Forest Department.

15. One source of revenue from these lands is the sale of grass or grazing dues. By resolution of Government in the Financial Department (dated 11th February, 1863,) this item of sayer was excluded from Forest Revenue. This may be regarded as an objection to the transfer of the whole of the Rukh lands to the Forest Department, but the above resolution may perhaps admit of reconsideration. We are of opinion that it would be highly inexpedient to exclude the amount realized by sale of grass on lands under the control of the Forest Department, which appears to be a legitimate item of forest revenue, and is so considered in Sindh and elsewhere.

16. The question of the comparative advantage and disadvantage of the occupation of land by forests or by grain, is one upon which there is much difference of opinion, but it is generally admitted that an extension of the forests would tend to preserve a little moisture in the exceedingly dry climate of the Punjab. The heavier falls of dew where forests are, and the retention of moisture tend to ameliorate the climate and to fertilise the soil.

SIMLA,
19th August, 1863.

D. BRANDIS,
H. CLEGHORN.

Extract from a letter from Offg. Secretary to Government of India, P. W. Department, to Secretary to Government of Punjab, P. W. Department, No. 5102, dated 7th December, 1863.

Para. 2. Respecting the management of the Rukh lands, I am desired to say that it would appear expedient, in the first instance, to make them over to the Forest Department. The selection of the lands not to be retained can be made subsequently.

Extract from a resolution from the Government of India, P. W. Department, No. 1053—1053A, dated 5th March, 1864.

Para. 1. On a reconsideration of the above papers, the Governor General in Council is of opinion that the orders given in Public Works Department Letter, No. 5102, dated 7th December, 1863, were issued under a misapprehension, and is now pleased to direct that the management of Rukhs in the Punjab shall be entirely withdrawn from the Forest Department, and remain as heretofore in charge of the Revenue officers.

Para. 3. This determination as to the executive management of the Rukhs, which should be altogether in the hands of the District Revenue officers, need not in any way interfere with the employment of the forest conservator for the purpose of inspecting these tracts, and advising as to their management, should such advice or inspection be thought desirable by the Punjab Government.

Note.—While these sheets are passing through the press, I have read a clear and full report of the fuel resources for the supply of the Punjab Railway, by Dr. I. L. Stewart, Officiating Conservator of Forests, Punjab.

TO MAKE CHARCOAL.

THE best sized wood for this purpose is of the form understood as billets. An ordinary kiln for smelting measures 18 feet in diameter, and requires about 25,000 billets, cut as nearly as possible of the same length. Procure a pole about 25 feet long and 6 to 8 inches thick, straight and of uniform thickness. Provide yourself with four forked sticks of the shape of *Fig.* 1. Erect the pole perpendicularly on the spot where the kiln is to be made and place the four forked sticks round it, arranging pieces of wood from fork to fork and across, to make a hollow space in the centre of the kiln, of about 18 square inches, as in *Fig.* 2, for containing combustible matter. Provide the person stacking the billets with a yard measure, and with one end of the measure against the pole, let him sit at the other end and place the billets in an almost perpendicular position against the cross pieces, and as close together as possible, each cooly stacking right and left to join his neighbour's work on either side. Thus he goes on stacking until he has come to the end of his measure; all having done the same, a perfect circle will be the result. After having filled up with

Fig. 1.

Fig. 2.

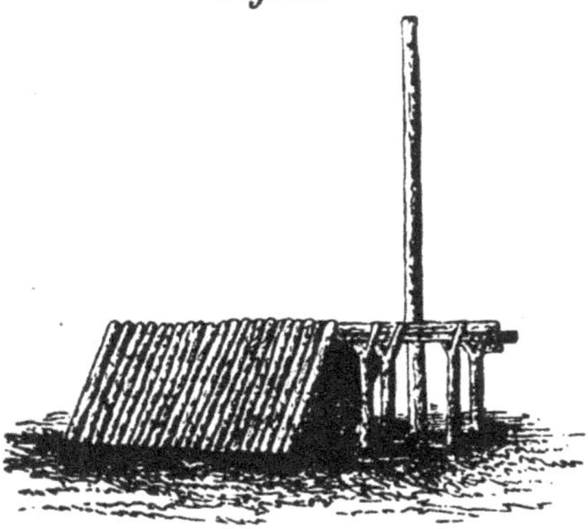

brushwood or old charcoal all interstices there may be from crooked or large billets, each cooly pulls out his measure to another yard in length and proceeds as before. Having done this the third time, the kiln will measure 18 feet in diameter. The coolies then mount the first layer of billets and commence stacking from the pole, until they come to the end of the second layer, making an allowance for the curve, and so on a third and fourth layer, until the kiln is completed, as shown in *Fig.* 3. Cover in the whole kiln with turf, 3 to 5 inches thick, turning the grass side inwards, commencing from the bottom; after which throw a small quantity of loose earth over the turf, beating it down with the back of a spade; if turf is not procurable, put a compact layer of earth over leaves and brushwood, moistened with water.

Fig. 3.

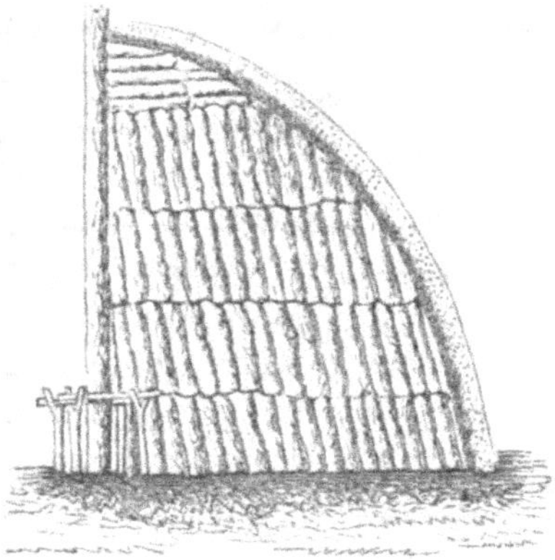

Section of one-half of the kiln.

Fig. 4.

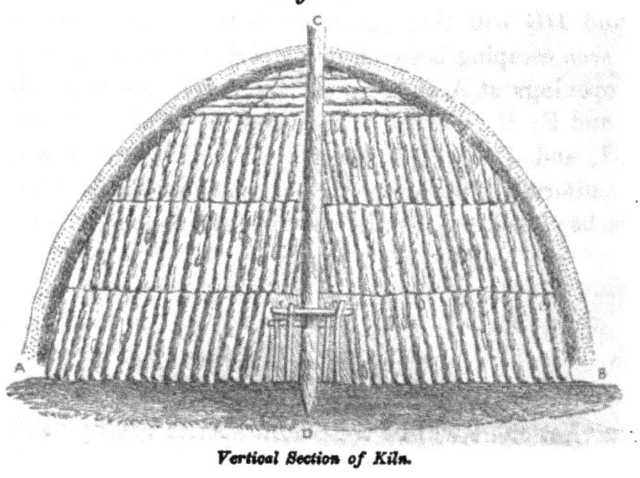

Vertical Section of Kiln.

After the whole kiln has been covered in, let one or two men ascend and pull out the pole, leaving an empty space from top to bottom. From the top, drop in a ladle full of ignited charcoal, and immediately this is done, open out one turf at the bottom of the kiln, say at A. This will cause a draught of air in the direction of ADC, *Fig.* 4, and in a few minutes, dense smoke will be seen ascending at C, and vapour condensing on the coating, after which flames will burst forth. Let this continue for 5 or 10 minutes, till it is clear that the billets in the centre of the kiln are on fire, when a man must be sent up with a large turf to close the opening at C, over which he should sprinkle earth to keep in all flame, and secure uniform combustion in all parts of the kiln. *From this moment no flame must be allowed to escape from any part of the kiln.* When the opening at C has been closed, one at B should be made. The billets in the direction of DA and DB will then ignite faster than any other, and when smoke is seen escaping between every turf in the direction of AC and BC the openings at A and B must be closed and fresh ones made, say at E and F; these will be closed in their turn and others made at G, H, I, and J, *Fig.* 5. Shortly after this, smoke will be seen to issue uniformly from every crevice, when all air holes at the bottom must be closed. After the charring is complete, the whole kiln

Fig. 5.

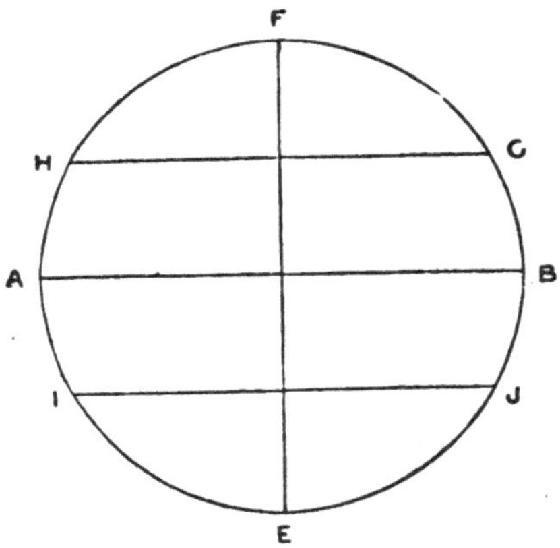

Horizontal Section of Kiln.

Fig. 6.

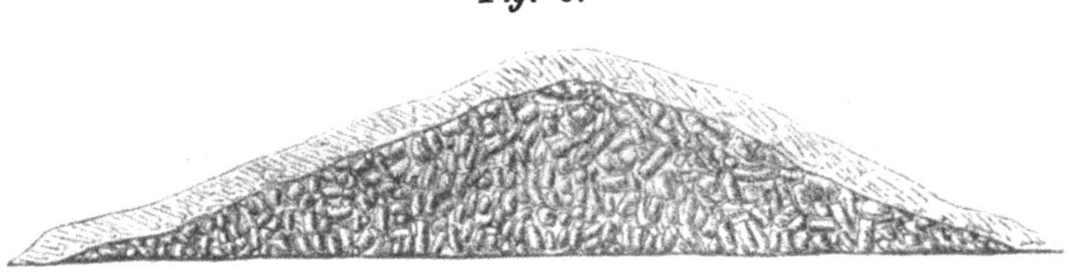

will fall in at the end of 2 or 3 days, according to size, and assume something of the shape in *Fig.* 6.

Earth must then be thrown on with shovels to *extinguish all smoke*, and at the end of 36 hours, the charcoal may be raked out. A few buckets of water should be in readiness, if required to put out the sparks of fire which may remain.

Great care must be taken to stop every fissure in the casing, and if from bad management the heap settles, and the casing falls in at any part, the cavity must be filled up with green wood kept ready for the purpose, and the covering replaced. As soon as the dense smoke ceases, and the wood burns with a light transparent smoke, the whole must be closed in and watched, lest any fissures appear.

In burning in pits, vent-holes are made in the sides, and the covering of sods being of smaller extent, is easily formed and the wood is more conveniently packed, as shown in *Fig.* 7; the logs in the middle of the lower course should be dry with a few chips and refuse charcoal from former kilns among them.

Fig. 7.

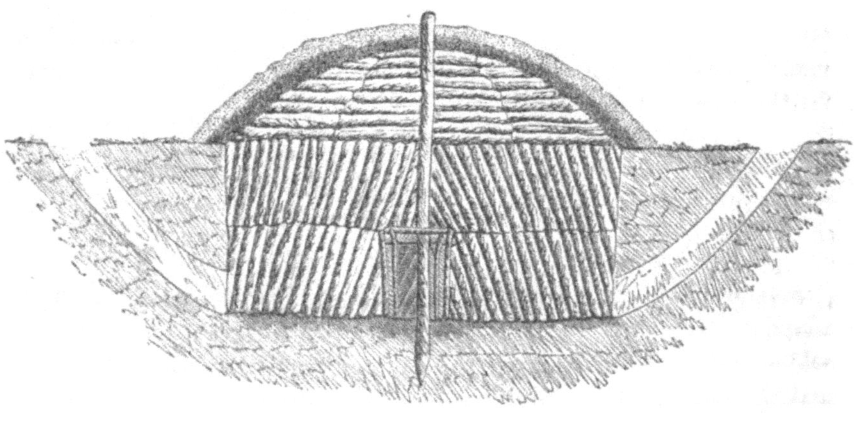

Section of a Charcoal Pit.

Sometimes, it may be convenient to form a kiln by digging out the side of a hill, (*Fig.* 8), but in all cases the system is the same. If the process is properly conducted, the bulk of charred wood is not greatly reduced.

Fig. 8.

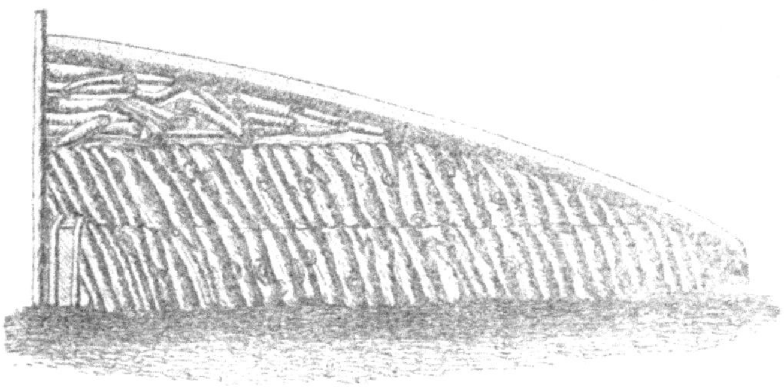

In climates, where vegetation is rapid, it is not necessary to cut down trees for charcoal, but merely to lop off lower branches; refuse wood should be used in the manufacture, and dry wood is superior to wet, as it splits more easily and saves labor. On dry forest land, a crop of wood sufficient for charcoal can be obtained every fifth or sixth year, and on marshy land, every third or fourth year.

Some woods are better suited for the purpose than others. Hard woods, with a close grain, make the best charcoal; in England, oak, elm, beech, and ash, are generally used. The following abound in many parts of India, and amongst others have been found suitable for the manufacture :—

Sál, *Vatica robusta*,
Sissoo, *Dalbergia sissoo*,
Kikar, *Acacia arabica*,
Kheir, *Acacia catechu*,
Teak, *Tectona grandis*,
Nim, *Azadirachta indica*,
Sandun, *Oojeinia dalbergioides*,
Lohira, *Tecoma undulata*,
Box, *Buxus sempervirens*,
Oak, *Quercus incana*.

Soft woods with an open grain and quick growth are not so well adapted for making furnace charcoal: white and resinous woods are seldom used. The comparative value of Indian hard woods in charcoal-making is an interesting subject of inquiry, and careful experiments to determine the best sorts of timber for special purposes are required: the proportionate produce from 1000 parts of several kinds is given by Brande, as follows :—

Ebony, - - -	300	Box, - - -	202
Satin wood, - -	207	Fir, - - -	181

The Beypore Iron Company, I believe, find the loppings and thinnings of the teak plantations in Malabar specially adapted for smelting purposes, and in a short time the prunings of sissoo, &c., in the canal plantations of the Punjab and North West Provinces may be equally valuable. The utilising of thinnings and of refuse timber is urged upon all forest officers.

The economic preparation of charcoal at the different hill stations is most important, and the best mode of initiating it, is to collect the charcoal burners and to give them practical instruction by firing a small kiln in their presence. The out-turn of slow charring is so much larger than that obtained by their rude process in open pits that they will generally be found ready to adopt the principle of a closed kiln. In several experiments in the Himalaya, where the common hoary oak *(Quercus incana)* was used, one-third more in bulk was obtained than by the common method, and the charcoal was in larger pieces, heavier, and well charred. Wicker baskets, being elastic, do not break the charcoal and are generally used for transport.

H. CLEGHORN,

Conservator of Forests.

INDEX.

A

B

C

D

E

G

H

I

J

N

O

P

S

CPSIA information can be obtained
at www.ICGtesting.com
Printed in the USA
LVHW040024180422
716440LV00005B/457

9 783752 594669